Praise for
BANG BANG BODHISATTVA

"Upbeat and full of stubborn, defiant, self-reinventing *life*. The doors of the future have closed, but we're still here, irrepressible and funny and sad and drunk on love. A crafty, intoxicating romp."

Maya Deane, author of
Wrath Goddess Sing

"Not only brings to the fore cyberpunk's noir antecedents, it also teases out themes around gender fluidity and identity with an abundance of intelligence, style and heart."

Locus Magazine

"Wood melds genres with ease—noir and cyberpunk, mystery and sf—in a wickedly funny and heart-wrenching, dystopian thrill ride."

Booklist

"The antidote to sci fi as usual: Simultaneously gritty and shiny neon new, realist but not nihilist, unabashedly queer and endlessly inventive."

Bitter Karella, author of
The Midnight Pals

BANG BANG BODHISATTVA

BANG BANG BODHISATTVA

AUBREY WOOD

SOLARIS

Paperback edition published 2024 by Solaris
an imprint of Rebellion Publishing Ltd,
Riverside House, Osney Mead,
Oxford, OX2 0ES, UK

First published 2023 by Solaris

www.solarisbooks.com

ISBN: 978-1-78618-984-4

10 9 8 7 6 5 4 3 2 1

A CIP catalogue record for this book is available from
the British Library.

Designed & typeset by Rebellion Publishing

Printed in Denmark

As always, to my father.

"Fuck the police."

Old Klingon proverb

1

THE BIG IDIOT'S robot fist plowed into Kiera's face like a bullet train splattering a little baby bunny. As evenings go, this was a net loss.

Kiera spun out and hit carpet. A moment later Herrera dropped down next to her. Their eyes met. Herrera brushed his perfect nose with his fingertips.

"Hey, kid, you've got a little…"

Kiera touched her face. Nose blood poured down her front. She gurgled, "Th-thanks."

The goon grabbed her by the collar—this was the big Black goon in the black suit, the other one was a white guy and wore a white suit; they looked like opposing chess pieces or ice cream bars—and she had a moment to blearily admire his hands. Slick black shells with leafy gold filigree and soft rubber fingertips. *Nice prosthetics,* Kiera thought in a fog. *They look expensive.*

The lummox with the nice hands hurled Kiera through a doorway, and she tumbled across a tacky rug into a room with some outdated monitors and a big safe. Herrera, courtesy of the white goon, followed promptly.

"Mr. Carson says you're not allowed in his clubs anymore, Herrera," said the white one. The Black one shut the door.

"Hey, stupid," Herrera wheezed, rolling to face Kiera. "Remember that thing I gave you?"

She groaned, "*Uhh*. Uh-huh."

"Take it out and push the red button."

The white goon knelt down and, with cyber-hands the color of fine white chocolate, started punching the shit out of poor Herrera, who grunted and howled like— Kiera hated that she was reminded of this—someone bottoming for the first time. The other big boy was coming for her.

Kiera dug into the front of her underwear, where she'd stashed the little gray device so it would just look like her dick bulge when the bouncers checked her for weapons. She pulled it out, thrust it up in the air, and pushed a perfectly thumb-sized red button on the side.

The world burned to white. Something shrieked in Kiera's ears and she yelped, surprised and horrified.

"Jesus *fuck!*"

She dropped the little thing. She blinked floaters out of her vision, and her smart-ear buzzed like old-school dial-up. When she could make things out again, the Black goon was rotating his fingers in his ears. The white one had flipped out his dark lenses and was furiously massaging his eyes.

Herrera, the only one who'd been prepared for the flashbang, was already up and snatching a good ol' aluminum baseball bat, handily stashed on top of a file cabinet—if Kiera hadn't just pushed that button, the big boys had probably been getting ready to swipe right on her kneecaps with that thing. Herrera beaned the white guy on the dome like he was going for a goddamn carnival prize, and then the Black one straight across the face, shattering his lenses. Both gorillas hit the floor like sacks of human concrete.

In the dystopian future, the simple solutions are still sometimes the most effective, thought Kiera. *Lol.*

Herrera brushed his nose again and motioned at the Black goon with his fingers. He chuckled hoarsely.

"Hey-y-y, look, kid. Now he's got a little…"

"Yeah, funny a-ha-ha-*ha-ha*." Kiera tried to blow her nose and it hurt and sprayed blood all over her hands.

"Jeez, grouchy."

"My goddamn nose." She tried to inhale, and it made a loud stubborn *snuck*. "It's broken, I think. I don't have health insurance, you dick. Why didn't you warn me what that little thingy did?"

The processes in Herrera's head visibly churned, overclocking whatever burnt-out bent bottlecap passed for his brain. "I thought you knew!"

"*How* would I—ugh. Okay. Can we go?"

Herrera slipped out the door into the hallway. He kept the bat. Kiera followed.

He led her down a hallway filled with lights that turned everything pink. After the punch in the face and the flashbang, she was developing an express migraine. The music from the club downstairs pounded through the floor and walls and seeped into her head, the way radiation gets into groundwater. She had tight, throbbing fists of blood in her nose and lobes.

"I *better* be getting five stars," Kiera insisted.

Herrera didn't turn around. "Of course, kid, of course."

"And a review?"

"Okay."

"*And* a tip for breaking my fucking nose."

"Kid, I am two seconds from rolling you up in a carpet."

They found a stairwell and climbed up a floor. A bald guy with mirror-eyes got half of "*Hey*—" out before Herrera clocked him for a home run and he went down.

Kiera squatted and fished around in mirror-eyes' jacket and holsters. He had a gun, a collapsible baton, and—

"Gotcha gotcha." Kiera had seen the bouncers outside wearing the blue and yellow stun pistols on their hips. She took it.

A masculine voice from down the hall: "What the fuck are you doing!"

More trouble had found them. While Herrera put his hands up and tried to think of a line, Kiera whirled left and fired the stun gun—all reflex, no hesitation. A white pin stuck in the suit's chest, and he convulsed and pissed himself before dropping.

"Mechanical-automatical," Kiera murmured, cool enough to say it aloud but not so cool that she wanted anyone to hear her. She wished she could slip the stunner into a hip holster but settled for holding the tip near her lips.

Herrera put his hands down. "Why'd you go for the stunner and not the real gun?"

"I don't want to fucking kill anyone," Kiera said, as if his question was idiotic, because it was. "You're in enough trouble with Carson anyway, aren't you?"

"That's my smart girl."

"Whatever."

Herrera took her to a door at the end of the hall. It

was locked—but just by an old metal lock, with a great big keyhole.

"Oh, I can do this one." Kiera began to reach into her messenger bag.

Herrera swung the bat down like a katana and smashed the handle clean off. Kiera rolled her eyes.

"Or that, I guess? Why did you even bring me?"

Herrera did not answer her. He kicked the door open. In the room there was a big four-poster bed and really tacky fluoro blue and pink lighting. A doughy man lay on the bed with three—strippers? Prostitutes? Both? All in varying states of undress, and with assorted mechanized limbs. The man saw Herrera and Kiera, and scrambled to cover himself, hollering hysterically. The women were *nonplussed*, if Kiera had ever seen a situation suited for such a word.

"Wh-what! What the hell! What the shit!"

Herrera's left eye made a flash-burst of white light, then another, throwing sex worker shadow-puppets on the far wall.

"Your husband says hello."

Herrera wagged his eyebrows, grabbed Kiera's wrist, and yanked her back out into the hall.

A gunshot blammed and a chunk of the wooden doorframe exploded into splinters behind her. Kiera's heart kicked up and acid fear spider-fingered out across her ribs, as the evening suddenly plunged from *shitty but probably a good story* to *oh my god I'm going to fucking die.*

"Jesus Jesus Jesus ohhh, I'm getting shot at," Kiera blathered. "I'm getting shot at! I am done with you after this, I'm done. Do you hear me, I'm done!"

"Not the time, not the time, not the time."

"*For god's sake,*" Mr. Cheater back there screamed in a panic, "*someone stop them! Shoot them!*"

They stepped over the incapacitated guard and Kiera tripped down the stairs, almost wiping out. When they got to the pink hallway, the black and white big fellas were stumbling around getting their sea legs back. And they were blocking the way out.

"Stun gun still good?" Herrera asked hurriedly.

"One shot."

"Get the right."

Kiera popped off her second shot and hit the Black goon in the pec. He convulsed like someone was shaking a giant baby and slumped all the way down. Herrera reached the white one before he could get a gun out and *clop-thok,* first the knee then the back of the head with the bat. Smooth sailing all the way to the stairs. Kiera followed Herrera down the next stairwell to the club level.

"You know two hits to the head like that can kill him," Kiera warned, maybe even *admonished.* "Shit, just one could."

"Are you being cranky because you have an iron deficiency or something?"

"I am being shot at!"

They hit the main floor and stumbled into the illicit casino-slash-strip club-slash-absolutely a mobster hangout. *This place is trying to do too much at once,* thought Kiera, numbly, as Herrera dragged her by the wrist past the game tables and then through the dancefloor full of bright-haired freaks (her people). It was dark, choked with vape smoke, noisier than hell and full of bodies in here. They should be able to get lost in the shuffle and escape—

Blam blam—unless the guys with the guns had better vision than Herrera, of course, which wasn't surprising since his false eye was an ancient piece of shit. *Blam blam.* People screamed and scattered. They probably thought it was another fucking mass shooting.

"Stop, you fucking morons!" yelled someone. "You're gonna hit customers!"

It was a fucking miracle they hadn't already. Had they? Kiera kept running. The door was close—in the way that a stage with your favorite band on it was close when there were layers and layers of moshers between it and you. People were starting to shove their way out. The rap music was still playing, thudding in Kiera's ears and contributing to her headache.

"*My pussy taste better than your girl's. My titties pop-poppin', they better than your girl's.*"

Kiera knew this song; her girlfriend loved it. She hoped she would live to see her girlfriend again. She was done after this shit. Doneskis. Outtie five thousand.

Kiera and Herrera hit the gray streets without getting holes in their heads. A cold drizzle kissed Kiera's cheeks. Her smart-ear jingled. She hissed, "*Shut the fuck up!*" but of course that wasn't a valid command. "End call, end call, decline!"

The ringing stopped in time for her to hear two more gunshots and feel the air at her shoulder whip. Someone in front of her with a shaved head took both shots in the back and dropped. Kiera's heart did a flip and her stomach lurched. *No.* She threw a look behind her. That guy from the room with the strippers, he was out here on the sidewalk in a blazer and his goddamn underwear waving a gun, and there were two more armed dipshits with him.

Herrera and Kiera moved half a block with the crowd, past a clothing store and a kiosk selling eye-and-ear accessories. Herrera cut left into an alley. He had his phone out—*that janky old thing, that brick.*

"What are you *doing?*" Kiera demanded.

"Looking for a car." He paused. "I'm not logged in. For fuck's sake, why am I not logged in?"

"Mimi, nearest U-Ride please, nearest U-Ride please, nearest—" Kiera ducked behind a dumpster just before a bullet bit the metal corner and flung sparks.

"*Sure, let me get that for you,*" the AI assistant answered with an infuriating lilt in Kiera's left ear. Herrera got up, made a big wide swing, and *threw* the bat. Kiera heard it clatter into *something*, and a deep male grunt. Herrera grabbed her and they kept running.

"Anything yet, kid?"

A pixelated blue arrow popped into Kiera's vision, pointing up and right. "It says three hundred and forty meters, that-a-way."

"How's your cardio?"

"I mean, I don't own a car?"

"Good. I mean, not *good*, but."

"Whatever! Fuck! Run! I hate you!"

They sprinted out the other side of the alley and tried to disappear in the crowd, but Herrera's ridiculous trench coat and Kiera's Statue of Liberty torch-flame of magenta hair were going to be easy to pick out. "Which way?" asked Herrera. Kiera pointed. Herrera cut straight across the road, almost getting hit; the black car screeched to a stop, blasted its horn, and Herrera hopped and skidded right across the hood. Kiera went for no such theatrics, happy to go around. One of the guns behind them went *bang bang* and the windshield spiderwebbed and the car chunked forward, speeding off like a scared, overweight cat.

One of those police dog-robots was patrolling on the sidewalk. (They always looked to Kiera more like small, weird giraffes or dumbass brontosauruses.) It turned to face the gunshots, and LEDs along its body lit up red.

"ROOF ROOF ROOF. STOP. CEASE. ROOF. CEASE FIRE. ROOF ROOF. BY ORDER OF THE NEW CARSON POLICE DEPARTMENT. YOU WILL CEASE. ROOF ROOF ROOF."

Herrera hauled the thing off the ground like he was going to give it the Heimlich. Kiera ducked behind him.

"ROOF ROOF. UNHAND ME. RELEASE ME, CITIZEN ROOF ROOF ROOF."

"Yeah, yeah, shoot back already, you fuckin' waste of tax dollars."

The dog's mounted gun fired a teeth-chatter burst across the street, while Herrera wrestled with the flailing robot to keep it pointed in the right direction.

"CITIZEN, RELEASE ME. ROOF ROOF ROOF, CEASE FIRE."

Three bullets hit the windows behind Kiera. She yanked on Herrera's coat collar.

"Okay, enough *Die Hard* shit, maybe?"

Herrera threw the machine-gun-dog aside. It released staccato bursts of random gunfire like it was farting and struggled in vain to right itself.

Herrera pulled Kiera by her fingers. "You've seen *Die Hard*?"

"I'm thirty, not fifteen."

They cut through another alley, ran past one of Kiera's favorite donut shops—would she ever be able to come by here again?—and there was the promised car parked on the opposite corner, an ugly little lime green box. They crossed during a merciful break in traffic and sprinted to the car, Herrera climbing in the driver's side and Kiera shotgun.

Kiera scrambled for the keys in the glove compartment and tossed them to Herrera. In just a second the car roared, dashboard and radio lighting up neon green. The first thing Herrera did was back straight into the car behind them, *crunch*.

Kiera winced. "Nice."

"Shut up, did you see this parking job? This thing was packed in tighter than your skinny little ass."

"Don't talk about my ass like that."

Herrera pulled the car out and it looked like a straight shot to the next light. Then for a second she was blind. On top of urgent message prompts taking up the sides of her vision, climbing in the U-Ride brought up a full-splash, both-eyes ad for *Mamma Mia,* which was somehow, yes, to this day, still a thing. Kiera angrily flapped her hands to get rid of it all. When she could see again, the car had made it halfway to the light. She prepared to relax.

She heard the pepper of gunfire, and the driver-side window shattered. The dashboard *chinked* and the green lights went out, and Herrera howled.

"*Aaah,* son of a bitch!"

He let go of the wheel, and the car curved into the wrong lane.

"*Whoa!*" Kiera grabbed the wheel and wrenched them back just in time to avoid a head-on collision. Herrera clutched his right hand. Kiera saw blood.

"They get you?"

"They got me. Steer. Go left."

Herrera kept the gas down right into a red light. Kiera clenched *everything* for, like, the five millionth time that evening. She swung their fugly, ruined lime-green U-Ride around the corner like a shopping cart, almost getting into another accident and making people honk at them, and then held the course steady as they tore off down the next street.

A whole ten seconds passed where they didn't hear any gunshots. Then fifteen, then twenty.

Herrera stuck his shot hand in his jacket, looked at Kiera, and let out a long snort that rolled into a big laugh.

Kiera blew her broken nose at him, hard. Blood and snot spattered his pretty face. Herrera cringed like he'd sucked a lemon.

"Hey!"

Kiera scrunched up her lips, glared at him, and put her eyes back on the road.

2

THEY DITCHED THE U-Ride shitbox on the freeway and walked the rest of the way to Herrera's *actually pretty nice* new place. It was bigger than the last one, the one he had before his new skin and hair job. "Bigger" was still only as big as Kiera's place but having only one person living in it made the space seem a lot less cramped, and Herrera kept it fastidiously clean. He always put on old jazz, like he was the protag of a Murakami novel. He had cool Japanese modern art on the walls. Both these things reminded Kiera of her mom. And she liked jazz unironically.

"Ow, ow, ow. *Ow!*"

The pain in her nose wrenched her back and reminded her she was mad at him.

"Sorry, kid. I'm right-handed, y'know?"

He stuffed the second wad of cotton in her other nostril. She winced. Then he got a nice, thick, white bandage and handed it to her.

"Here, you do it. Need both hands."

Kiera went and put the bandage on in the bathroom mirror, stuck it from cheek to cheek like a piece of tape. She squinted at herself while she tried to scrub the last of the dried blood off her mouth. The flame-top hair, the fucked-up nose, her modded, pointy-tipped elf ears. She should be on the cover of some internet rapper's mixtape. Why did they still call them mixtapes, she wondered, when they were only ever digital? Well, sometimes those guys did put their stuff out on old tapes when they wanted to be too cool for school. Then you had to pay *shipping*. She poked her bandage, as if trying to Tetris her nose bones back into place. Maybe she should get an old Walkman, she thought. Then she'd be *cool*.

Herrera called from the little kitchen. "Hey, stupid, you want some coffee? Booze? Juice box? Cocaine? All of the above? I'm kidding about the cocaine, I don't have any. And I wouldn't give it to you if I did. Not that you're not old enough to make your own choices, I'm just being responsible."

"I just wanna get paid, please."

Kiera came out to the living room and Herrera tossed her a plastic zipper-baggy full of ice. She pressed it to her nose.

"*Owww*. Why did you even bring me? I hardly did anything."

"Only you could've gotten that flashbang past the door, clever girl. Plus, you were pretty good back there with that stun gun."

"Yeah, well. I put in time at the range."

"Yeah?"

"I've had men on the internet threaten to cut my genitals off and leave my body by the side of the road. Men, plural. Girl's gotta know how to throw down."

Herrera leaned on the counter that broke up the kitchen and the living room. His right hand was wrapped in white gauze, stained jelly-donut red from the inside. He quirked a brow. "What was, ahh, what was that you said after you plugged that dope with the stunner?"

"Oh, my god." Kiera looked away and covered her eyes.

Herrera smirked. "You get in a little one-liner? I won't make fun."

"It's just. Something I say, like, when I get a good score or I'm feeling myself at target practice."

"*Mechanical-automatical.*" Herrera repeated the phrase, the syllables tapping his teeth with his tongue.

Kiera burned like a microwave. "Don't! Oh my god."

"Does that mean you're an android?"

"It means I'm, like, a badass cyborg bounty hunter with perfect aim. You weren't supposed to hear it. I'm gonna kill myself."

"So, you got your own gun?"

"It's my girlfriend's. A little pink and white snubnose she carries around in her purse." Kiera exhaled. "I really hope the guy that got shot is okay. When we were running out of the club."

"I'm legitimately sorry about that. About all the... Everything."

"I thought you said they wouldn't recognize you."

"I thought they wouldn't! I had bits of my jaw shaved down and everything."

"Lucky."

"Guess they got me on something else."

Kiera leaned against the counter, too. "What's your new name again?"

"Michael Jones."

"*Ugh*. I am not calling you that."

"Yeah? You gonna deadname me?"

"Shut up, you don't get to use that word."

Herrera laughed and wagged his tongue. "You could at least call me Angel for once."

"Fuck, no. You're Herrera. Or 'that dumbass who still uses phone numbers'. Or just 'dickface'."

"Fine. Then 'stupid' you shall remain."

Kiera put her chin on her fist. She pored over Herrera's new face again, his new blond hair, the Caucasian countenance given to him by the cutter.

"You looked better before," she said, "with curly hair."

Herrera put his hands up, shrugged. "This is easier."

"Didn't it hurt?"

"Skin wasn't fun, felt like a hell of a sunburn but everywhere. Takes a bit for the swelling on the jaw and the nose to go down."

"I just don't get it. Why would you want to look more white?"

"Why would I want to fake being white? Come on, kid."

"I wish I looked more Japanese. My dad's fucking colonialist cum, like, blasted all the color out of my mom's uterus, I guess."

"You're lucky you can pass for white, in a lot of ways."

"I mean, I know that. But I wish I looked more Japanese. Sometimes it makes me feel like I'm not really Japanese."

"I don't understand that," said Herrera. "Why would you think that?"

Kiera shook her head. "I dunno. I don't know. Why am I talking to you? I'm mad at you! Cash me up. I'm done.

Don't call me anymore. I got *shot* at." She pounded her palm on the counter.

Herrera took out his phone and thumbed at it, chewing his tongue.

"Extra for getting shot at," Kiera demanded. "And the broken nose."

"Seventy-five... A hundred and ten?" Herrera looked up.

"Two hundred."

"Alright, two hundred. Sent." A blip in the corner of Kiera's vision and a bling in her ear told her about new email, the alert of a cash transfer.

"Five stars?"

"Five stars as always. Will call again, would recommend."

"*Don't* call me again! I'm serious!"

"I won't put you in danger again. I didn't mean to."

"That's right, you won't! Because you won't call me again."

Kiera pivoted toward the door and pushed up the ice in the plastic baggy so it was situated back on her nose. "Keeping this," she grunted.

"I gave it to you to keep."

Kiera stormed to the front door. Herrera's big stupid Sam Spade trench coat was hanging up and she had to push it out of the way to reach the knob. She hated that coat.

"I hate this coat!" she declared.

"Yeah, well, I hate your ears!"

"My ears are *Aesthetic!*"

Kiera slammed the door.

* * *

YOU HATE TO see it. Good kid, mad city. This wasn't the first time she'd said it was the last time, but Angel had never put the kid in front of a bullet before.

Things in New Carson—this town so goddamn dirty they renamed it after its godfather—they had a way of escalating. Creeping up on you like a bad trip. Maybe this time, Angel thought, he really should leave the kid alone. Before she caught six in the chest. Or before she had to shoot back with a real heater, not a toy taser. Angel felt like enough of a rat bastard only having a hundred to tip her for a broken nose and dodging lead. No way he would have the kind of scratch to make up for sticking a gun in her hand.

Angel shook his head and bit his tongue. *Goddamn everything.*

He got his electronic cigarette from his hung-up coat, a little red cylinder with a silver ring where the paper would turn to filter. Peppermint flavor. He stuck it between his teeth and puffed, *puh-puh-puh,* crossed the apartment back to the big stereo and put on some Kamasi Washington. He had jobs to catch up on, needed to get tonight's photos off to the snooping husband. Needed to get onto bills. That tip he'd given the kid was coming out of his fun fund, for seeing old movies down at the art house place under the ailing public library. They needed the money as bad as he did.

His hand hurt like a sonofabitch; with a grimace he looked at the thing, wrapped in cheap bandages. Here he was, putting on a vinyl and settling in when he knew damn well he had another trip out to make tonight. He couldn't even move his fingers; he needed to get this looked at or the damn thing would fall off. Years on the force with barely a scratch, but you go out one night after some dime-a-dozen cheating hubby and lose a hand. For what? Some business. Some town.

Angel was getting his coat when the door console trilled. He put the jacket back on the hook and turned on the visitor screen.

His heart did a rimshot. Now *there* was a ghost.

Angel opened the door, and there she was.

Six years had been damn kind to her. No wrinkles in her olive skin, no trace of gray in her brassy hair. She was wearing her favorite scarf, that fuzzy burgundy and gray number that Angel used to joke she'd wear to bed if she could—and then one time she did, just to give him a hard time right back.

"Oh... I'm sorry, I have the wrong place," she stammered. "I'm sorry."

"Nah, nah. It's me," said Angel. "Hey, Glory."

She stiffened. She turned her head in suspicion. Angel half-smiled, leaning against the doorframe. He scatted a few notes—"Bada bada bada badabum"—candy-cane smoke puffing out of his mouth on each beat. Then he whistled a final two, completing the riff from "So What."

Her eyes went wide as the moon.

Gloria took his pale face in one palm, thumbing his cheeks and feeling his blond hair. Their eyes met, gazes broken only by the lenses of her gold-rimmed glasses.

"Baby, what have you done to yourself?"

"You should see the other guy."

The dame walked in, as they say. Angel shut the door for her.

Gloria clutched her gloved fingers to her heart. "Your hand...?"

"I tripped. Somethin' to drink?"

"Yes… Yes, please."

In the kitchen, Angel was already taking the bottle of rum down from the high shelf when he asked her, "Cuba Libre?" But to his great shock, Gloria shook her head.

"No, um… Just an Irish cream, if you have it."

He did have it. He put the rum back and took down the cream. But this was a coup. "Since when?"

"I don't know. A few years ago, I guess. The rum just reminds me too much of bad times."

Angel got an ice tray from the freezer and cracked it. "Bad times with me?"

"Among other things. Like being young and drinking too many."

Ice in the glass with the cream. "*Pero no estamos hablando español*," Angel mused.

"Malcolm doesn't speak it. I've gotten used to English at home."

Angel slid the drink across to her. "After so long?"

Gloria smiled softly, looking down into her drink. "I've tried and *tried* with him. You would think with all the Latin in his line of work…"

A nasal chuckle rolled out of Angel. Gloria took a demure sip of her drink, Angel didn't say anything, and for a second there all the years of distance yawned in the small empty space between them, over the kitchen counter, making it bigger. Angel managed to stop himself from awkwardly humming or *tuh-tuh-tuh*-ing along with the vinyl saxophone refrain drifting from the stereo. They looked at each other and were unable not to tacitly acknowledge the tattered, ruined shipwreck of *you and me* heralded by the momentary silence. The corner of Angel's mouth curled, and Gloria turned away slightly and took another sip of her Irish cream.

"It's been a long time, Mrs. Hobbes."

"Yes, it certainly has."

"It'd be nice if you came just to catch up. But..."

Angel tapped his plastic cigarette on the counter like a pencil. Gloria's dark lips thinned and she didn't respond.

"You need something," said Angel. "Don't you?"

Gloria sighed. "I haven't seen Mal for a week."

"You think he's hiding here? Where would I put him?"

"Goddamnit, Angel..."

"I've got that hologram Buddha for emergencies, but..."

"¡No me chingas, Angel Herrera!"

Gloria folded her arms tight. Angel tongued his teeth and looked down at the counter, then back up at her.

"I'm sorry," he said. "Think he's cheating?"

Gloria took a bracing breath and straightened her posture. "I'd certainly deserve it."

"Nah. That's not Mal. If he'd taken off with a new piece, he'd have the balls to tell you. What does Casey say?"

"That he just didn't turn up to the office one day."

"And the cops?"

"David Flynn said he would handle it personally."

"Good ol' D."

"But it's been five days, and nothing. I've called every day, and just... 'We're working on it, Mrs. Hobbes.'"

Angel took a drag. "Well, if you want something done right."

Gloria dug into the purse slung around her shoulder. From her wallet she produced a stack of paper money, crisp and white at the edges, fresh from an ATM. She put it on the counter. Angel quirked an eyebrow.

"How much is that?"

"Two thousand. More, when you find him."

"I'm not that expensive."

"Take it, Angel."

Angel put his fingers on the bills. Then he crossed around the counter. There was enough affection left that he wanted to touch Gloria's chin, tilt her face up. *Buck up, kiddo*. He didn't. But she let him take her glass of cream and take a sip for himself.

"I'll do my goddamndest, Glory."

3

THE WIND OUT on the cement balcony whipped threads of rain into Kiera's face. She pulled her jacket sleeves tight. Another woman was coming down the walkway, a classy-looking babe in a wool coat; actually dressed for the weather, unlike Kiera, who (like most trans women, she found) always picked looking good over being comfortable. The cis woman's eyes lingered on Kiera, in that way that said *I'm staring at you because I'm clocking you.*

Kiera's dander was up. It had been a *bad* evening, and she was out of fucks to give. So she stared at the trick right back. The woman noticed and broke her gaze just as they were about to pass each other.

Kiera swiveled around, wanting dearly to say something, something like "You wanna take a photo, bitch?" But then the woman in the coat walked up to Herrera's door. She reached for the doorbell, then took her fingers away, wringing her gloved hands and looking at the ground. She must've seen Kiera coming out of

Herrera's place and drawn conclusions. What was she? Girlfriend? Or just a client? Maybe both?

Kiera thought maybe she should say something else instead. *"I'm nobody. I promise. He's too old for me."* But she opted, ultimately, just to leave it. Left the woman to her agonizing over whether to ring the bell.

Kiera took refuge in the elevator, all outside sound disappearing with the rubber *thoomp* of the closing doors like she was being encased in a steel uterus. She pinched the tab of the chat app in the bottom left corner of her vision, blinking red and white with urgent messages, and pulled the window up. It was the triad group chat, like she'd expected. The ringing earlier had been Jinx trying to start a voice call.

```
an elf irl: hello hi im safe
an elf irl: im just leaving dickface's
It's Jinx!!!: THANK GOD
tactical butt: (((( ;°Д°))))
an elf irl: got two hundy $$$
It's Jinx!!!: YES
an elf irl: and a broken nose
It's Jinx!!!: NO
tactical butt: that's not safe.
tactical butt: that's the opposite of
   safe.
an elf irl: im safe NOW
It's Jinx!!!: WHAT HAPPENED
tactical butt: Blabber said there were
   shots fired?
an elf irl: yea i was in it but im fine
   now
an elf irl: i saw someone get shot though
```

```
It's Jinx!!!: OH MY GOD
It's Jinx!!!: BABE
an elf irl: im seriously fine
tactical butt: I say again:
tactical butt: (((( ;°Д°))))
an elf irl: can you find out who the guy
    that got shot was for me?
tactical butt: can we talk about the
    broken nose?
an elf irl: when i get home
tactical butt: ok... (╱_╲)
an elf irl: c u later skaters love and
    treasure u both <3<3
It's Jinx!!!: KIERA
```

Sweeping both hands in the air like a dancer, she pushed everything out of her field of view; all the tabs and blips, blinking notifications for emails and messages and ads and likes and replies. She'd check everything at home.

New Carson's streets were glossy with rain. The strip of sky above was the black of a switched-off monitor. No moon. *Bright lights, big city,* thought Kiera. She passed a burrito truck and—vegan sushi? Did such a thing exist? She was in one of the parts of town with a lot of Asian stores, with cheap neon signs and pull-down garage doors—Japanese, Chinese, Korean, Vietnamese, she could identify all of these, but there were others she couldn't—and it made her feel like she was in the background of a *Street Fighter* stage. She started to swing her narrow hips just a little as she walked. She got an earpod out of her messenger bag and stuck it in her pointy right ear and pulled up her lo-fi hip hop station.

After the voices of excited white women proselytized the wonders of going Premium, her beats started bumping and she got into her groove. She was feeling herself. She was peak trans, gender euphoric.

It took her until almost midnight to get back. She carded herself into 13C and could practically smell the weed smoke before the door was even open. She shut the door and slumped back against it.

Home.

In seconds, Sky descended on Kiera and squeezed her into his huge chest and stomach. Another year at the gym on the T, and Sky would be able to arm wrestle those goons from the club. He was probably gonna lose his belly, though, and she was preparing herself emotionally for that.

"Ow, nose, nose, nose," Kiera whimpered. Sky released her.

"I love you. Are you okay?"

Kiera put her arms out and shimmied. "Here I stand," she groaned.

Compared to Sky, getting hugged by Jinx was like embracing a pixie. "What do you need?" Jinx implored. "Food? Loud?"

"Cherry soda, a fat doink, and sleep. In that order."

"Just bought a bag." Sky smiled like a bear with a big pot of honey.

"Yeah, I can smell the vaporwave party from the hallway."

Jinx reached up and played with the tips of Kiera's elf ears, like she always did. Kiera pretended to bat her away. "*Nooo.*"

"Vaporwave isn't a thing anymore, babe."

"It still exists. It happened."

"Let me take your jacket."

Kiera folded her arms. She wanted to leave her moto jacket on. When she wore it she felt armored and feminine. But she let Jinx slip her out of it and hang it lovingly on a hook by the bathroom door, next to the print of the blue-skinned woman wearing white headphones. Kiera shed her boots and pants and messenger bag and let them lie discarded in the entranceway. She reached down and untucked. "Oh, Jesus. *Ahh*."

Home.

Jinx reappeared with an ice-cold Diet Cherry Bolo, Kiera's poison, her lifeblood. "You look like hell, hon. Why do you keep hanging out with that cop?"

"I officially don't hang out with him anymore. But he's not a cop. He's a PI."

"No cops, no corps at cyber-pride."

"Stop trying to make cyber-pride happen. I hate you."

They kissed. Jinx groped Kiera's butt. Kiera padded back to the refuge of the bedroom in her comfy little cotton briefs, with her Cherry Bolo. *Home*.

The whole throuple piled onto the messy bed. Kiera groaned at the TV. "No. I hate the news."

"You can't get *all* your news from Blabber," Sky chided.

"I can, I will, and I have."

On-screen, Ted Carson, who reminded Kiera strongly of Yosemite Sam, could be seen conferring silently with black-helmeted police.

In voice-over, the news anchor said, "Well, today mayor and patriarch of the city of New Carson, *Ted* Carson, took to the street carrying a *baseball bat* in what City Hall is calling a *statement* against lawlessness, and *anarchy*. Visiting the site of a *protest* earlier this morning that devolved into open *conflict* between demonstrators and law enforcement, Mayor Carson *personally* inspected the damage to local businesses and *spoke* with members of the NCP*D*."

The screen cut to Carson leveling his aluminum bat at the camera, flanked by armed fash.

"The city, the country, must brook no <BEEP> tolerance whatsoever for these bargain-basement thugs and degenerates, passing themselves off as agitators for what they call progress. Citizens, when the looters and rapists come for *your* businesses, your homes and places of work, you get your baseball bat. You get your sawed-off, your katana you bought at the swap-meet, whatever. Render unto them a <BEEP> reckoning." He waggled the tip of his bat for emphasis. "Show them what happens when *good* people are pushed into a corner."

"Yep, that's Ted Carson," said Sky. "He hates crimes, and people who do crime."

"No, see, crime is fine as long as it's organized," trilled Jinx. "Like the yakuza."

Kiera snorted and sipped her Bolo. "You think Carson's syndicate puts out a newsletter like the Yamaguchi?"

Now Carson stood next to a line of pink and black graffiti. He tapped it aggressively with the tip of his bat.

Carson: "*No one is free when others are oppressed.* What the <BEEP>? That's idiotic. Of course they are. I'm free. Lots of people are free. Some fence-jumper and his *familia* are sleeping in a cage but that guy isn't. What a retarded thing to say."

Kiera sputtered and choked on her soda. "Whoa, dude."

A woman's voice, cool and smooth as an ice sculpture, answered him from somewhere off-camera. "It means as long as there are people with the power to oppress others, we are never truly living in a free society. Anyone could be next under the boot. With respect. Sir."

Carson laughed like a seagull or a dolphin getting a treat.

"That's <BEEP> stupid. Globalist horse<BEEP>. If you can walk into Burger Hole right now and order a Beef King with large fries and a soda you are not oppressed. You're free as <BEEP>."

"Well, fuck," Kiera acquiesced. "That's airtight."

"You wanna watch the debates?" asked Sky. "I recorded them."

"No."

Sky fiddled with the remote anyway. "It's important," said Sky. "Besides, I kinda like Romero."

Jinx screwed up her mouth. "You like him because he made *DOOM*. Which I mean, yeah, legend. But what's he gonna do to fix the fuckin' healthcare?"

Sky sighed. "True, true." He turned the volume up. The moderator, one of the chief anchors and personalities on INC, read from a giant screen.

"Senator Romero. For five hundred points, how many Jews perished in the Holocaust?"

Romero smiled. "Well, I think of course the real answer is too many. Even one is too many."

"Agreed, couldn't agree more," Dominic Gray cut in. "And I think it's worth mentioning, of course, that I have unique insight into this subject. As you'll remember I was nominated for an Academy Award for my portrayal of SS Officer Oskar Bricht in *In My Country*."

"Mr. Gray, wait your turn, please."

Kiera's ear blinged again.

"Oh! Shit!" She scrambled up. "It's Malcolm."

"Oh, take it on the tablet." Sky muted the TV.

"What do you think I'm doing? Move, butt-brain. Shit, take this—hide it, hide it." She frantically handed off the joint to Sky and got stinky ashes on the comforter.

Kiera snapped her fingers to wake up the tablet, with its chunky gray casing; it recognized her face even through the bandage. The Friendo app came straight to the front—Malcolm always did calls on Friendo because he was old—and Kiera took the call. Sky and Jinx hovered over her shoulder. A bald, black head appeared in a vertical rectangle, from the eyebrows up.

"—lo?"

"Malcolm."

"...Hello?"

"Mal!"

"Hell—oh. Can you—can you hear me...? What?"

"Malcolm!"

"What'd you say? Can you hear me?"

"Yes!"

"Can you see me?"

"I can see your big bald dome."

"That's rude." Malcolm clumsily angled the camera down. Now they could see his bristly mustache and gray UCLA hoodie.

"That *is* rude," Sky chided. "That's better, Mr. Hobbes."

"Dude, are you on the bus?" asked Jinx.

"Yes, I am."

"It's noisy."

"What happened to the BMW?" asked Kiera.

Malcolm laughed, wrinkling his brown cheeks with a big, mustached smile. He had a warm, older gentleman's laugh that made Kiera think of having a cool Black dad to sit next to her at baseball games or watch her play

Wii on the living room floor. She was so warmed by the nostalgia-for-a-childhood-that-wasn't-hers induced by Mr. Hobbes's laugh that she didn't notice until much later, days later, that he never answered the question.

"Is this about my name change? Did you get the fees waived?" Kiera crossed her fingers. "Tell me something good."

Malcolm stared at the camera and took a moment to answer, because he was in his fifties. "No, not yet, kiddo. I'm still working on it. Sorry."

Kiera put her hands up and shrugged. "I'm patient." She hid her frustration. "So, what's up, what's the emergency? It's kinda midnight."

Another boomer-pause. "We had an appointment tomorrow," said Malcolm. "I won't be able to make it, and I realized I hadn't let you know. I've just been so scatterbrained this week. I'm sorry to call so late."

Kiera blinked for a little too long, perhaps long enough for it to be a wince. But Malcolm never charged her a dime, so it wasn't like she could complain. If anything, she would miss their catch-up lunch just as much as she hated to prolong her name change. They always got these great bagel sandwiches. "That's chill. Whenever you can manage."

Malcolm looked at something outside the frame. Stared at it, in fact; narrowed his eyes and pursed his lips. Leaned forward. Then he swung to check over his shoulder, and the camera dropped to the folds of his hoodie.

"You still there, big guy? You seem tense."

"Yeah," said Malcolm, after a pause, and the camera came back up. "Yeah, I'm here. So, I'll call again soon. Alright?"

Kiera laughed at him and shook her head. "Okay, man. See you."

She hung up first. She and Jinx and Sky all kind of looked at each other, and it was like they knew it was weird, but none of them wanted to say it was weird. Sky and Jinx climbed slowly back into bed, and Kiera felt the start of a pot paranoia scraping around up there, freezing her rigid in her seat like one of those creepy-looking sex dolls.

"That was kinda weird, right?" said Jinx, and Sky snorted like a big warthog and Kiera finally let herself release a laugh about it. Some of the fear fuzz dissipated. There were blinking applications waiting for her attention. She busied herself with that.

First, she hit her other group chats, told everyone she was home safe, yes, she really got shot at, but she was okay. No, she was not going to take a gig from that guy again. Love all of you, too. The weed got passed over from Sky to Jinx to Kiera, and she started to line up some gigs for tomorrow. But oh, whoa, what was this? Some poopy-baby-wah-wah had given her one star—*used profanity while working, dressed unprofessionally, body mods on full display*. Dicklord. So she didn't wear a polo shirt to go jailbreak his internet-enabled fridge. *His fridge!* It didn't lower her star average, but that review was gonna sit there on her Gigawatt profile until she hustled enough compliments to push it off her front page. *What a pain in my prostate.*

She switched to looking at her bank balance and the Panhandle for her throat surgery. After having it up for a year the donations added up to about a third of the goal, thanks to Jinx's followers. Add what she'd saved herself, and she was almost there. She let herself feel happy about that for a minute.

She turned around. "Hey, did you find anything about that guy? A donation page?"

"Oh, yeah," said Jinx. "I messaged it to you."

The guy who'd gotten shot in the back was named Terry Meaner and he was a student. He loved birds and mountain climbing, neither of which New Carson had. Kiera could not read too deeply, especially not with a joint in her mouth and a contemplative high approaching, a soupy buzz perfect for drowning in existential guilt.

"Guys," begged Kiera, "whatever I do, don't let me give all my surgery money to this guy. Please."

"Check your mail and then come to bed," said Sky. "No Blabber, no Jungle."

"Okay... Okay."

Kiera banished Panhandle, gave back the joint, and did some mindfulness breathing. She opened *Correspondence Valkyrie*. Three real emails were waiting for her at the end of the level, while her four or seven or eight dozen spam emails materialized as enemy ships zooming over a sprawling nebula-scape. Kiera dodged a flurry of pink lasers and fired back her mint-colored ones, every ship she blasted away deleting an imploration to apply for a credit card, or subscribe to Python Elite, or meet hot MILFs in her area. She logged 3548 experience points.

The real mail wasn't that exciting. Disheartening, even. A belated rejection for a tech blog article she'd written two years ago. This sucked, but she hadn't written anything for over a year anyway. Delete. A reminder about the balance on her account at the electrolysis clinic, which she had already paid, and she had told them she already paid. An ongoing fight. Delete.

And...

Oh.

"Oh, no. Oh, *fuck* me running."

"Honey?" asked Sky. "Do you need to come to bed?"

"No, no. I just got this email from our *fucking* landlord? It says he's... They're raising the minimum social score for the building and we're too low."

Sky muted the TV. Jinx looked like Kiera had just taken a shit on the desk.

"Let me read it." Sky got up and Kiera shuffled to make room for his hefty frame. She grabbed gently onto his big arm. Jinx crept up behind and wrapped around her, reading over their shoulders.

"He's still writing my name as Young and not Pyeong," Sky noted aloud, as if alerting the others that the dryer was broken.

"Wypipo," Jinx harped, much angrier about it than Sky was.

"It says they're raising the minimum Liberty Level for the whole building," said Sky. "But right here it says our Level, specifically, slipped too low. Like, for the existing requirement. It's not a form letter."

"Did anyone lose any PP?" asked Jinx.

"I mean... I was late to work?" Sky turned. "Ki, do you need to scrub your social media again?"

"No! It's fucking airtight!" But then she thought— "Oh... Oh, *shit*." Kiera tugged her hair with both hands. "I just got a bad review on Gigawatt. I've had a couple this month. That shouldn't have totally tanked my Points, but—"

Sky bit his bottom lip. Kiera wanted to flush herself down the toilet rather than see that look on his face.

"Do they react that fast?" asked Jinx. "Like... When was the bad review?"

"Today. Tonight," said Kiera. "And it's practically

instant. They watch that PP shit as hard as they watch disability payments."

"The landlord's just trying to kick us out," said Sky, but Kiera knew he was frustrated with her and just wasn't saying it. "I mean, maybe they really are raising the score for the building, but he's targeting us because— you know." Sky motioned with both hands at all three of them—everything about them.

"It's bullshit," Jinx growled. "It's *bullshit*."

"Well, hang on… Let me see…" Sky's brow furrowed, and he descended into a Tripp search. Jinx started tapping and swiping at the air.

"I'm asking my Blabber," she said. "I'll see if there's anything… God. *God*."

Kiera threw herself back on the bed and stared up at the ceiling, feeling worse than useless. Worse than a dead weight. A liability. She, the bed, the apartment, the planet fell tumbling through space in a marijuana haze.

"Okay, so," Jinx's voice cut through the bubble. Kiera sat up to look. "This guy says if he's raising the building's minimum Liberty Level he's got to give at least a month's notice for us to bring ours up. Two months if it's by more than one."

"We can raise it if we have a certain amount of money in savings," offered Sky.

"But that money's got to just sit in savings," said Kiera. "And not get spent."

"Yeah…"

Kiera closed her eyes. "How much is it to raise our Level?" She knew what the answer was going to be.

Sky hesitated. "For the next level up it's just a bit more than your throat surgery."

Kiera covered her face with both hands and said nothing.

Kiera put her thumbs in her eyes. "Do we know anyone we can move in with? Temporarily? Jinx, can you ply some thirsty skeezoid in your stream chat or something?"

"I hate you."

"Really, though. Like, what do we do? Do we just move, or do we start trying to make money? Does Jinx do a fundraiser?"

"I can try to get extra hours," said Sky. "And maybe, I don't know, sell some stuff online."

Kiera balked. "Sell *what* stuff?"

Sky put up his hands. "I'll find something."

Jinx draped across Kiera, who clutched onto her arm. She glanced at the TV, looked at the score. 3400 Romero, 2500 Gray. Whichever way the debate went, Gray was still the favorite. Whoever won, healthcare wasn't getting cheaper anytime soon.

Kiera shut her eyes tight. It had taken her over a year. *All that money. All that fucking money.*

4

ANGEL DIDN'T LIKE to hear himself think. Noise centered and invigorated him: jazz noise, city noise, people noise. He liked to feel like a rock in some rapids, or a strong tree in a summer storm. He gravitated to screeching saxophone monologues, traffic-light jams, the chatter and blabber of a teeming hive of strangers. For all of these, he went to Q's.

The big joke among stand-up comics and primetime comedies back when the Q's coffee franchise was first getting popular was that the places were so ubiquitous as to be on every corner; that their signature red leather furniture and polished-wood art deco shit would subsume the entire American sprawl. And maybe that was true and maybe it had. And it was true that it wasn't very rock'n'roll to go to Q's. Angel knew he favored an image of himself as a man of curated taste; he should've had the integrity to find an independent place run by some other Mexicans, or at least some polyamorous trust fund faux-bohos that made the place look legit. But you know, whatever, the Q's coffee was good. And it was usually crowded. And Q's were everywhere and easy to find. And for that matter, did New Carson have a single independently owned coffee shop left anywhere on its entire stretch of scabby urban epidermis, or was that a pre-megacorporate daydream five to ten years out of touch?

Angel got in line behind a pierced-up girl(?) with purple hair and in front of a jowly man in a suit and sunglasses talking to his ear. Everyone in the place periodically brushed at the air without looking up, as if batting away horseflies in a sweltering Sahara watering hole. You got a lot of ads at Q's. Angel didn't get so many; his eye was beat-up junk compared to the new lenses. Most of the new commercials wouldn't even run on the thing. Or maybe, he had the theory, the ads didn't even bother with him, figuring some sap who's still seeing the world through a ten-year-old cyber-eye is stone broke anyway.

Purple-hair in front of him paid by swiping her right palm over the black glass that read the programmable chip embedded under her skin. That made him think about his own right hand, as he used his left to clumsily dig out his wallet and pay for his drink on the chunky, outdated card reader. The doc had given it to him straight: it would be cheaper just to replace the hand. Not through the disastrous healthcare system, mind you, but Angel seemed to him like the kind of guy who knew a good fitter.

The barista called for *Aynjel,* not *Ahnhel.* The shot right hand dully throbbed at his side as he picked up his Americano with the left.

Angel dropped into one half of a burgundy couch shaped like an S. With the dirty tang of black coffee on his tongue, he thought of the bills Glory had paid him with. Straight out of an ATM, stiff. He took bank transfer just fine. Now, why did she want to pay him under the table? She didn't want Mal to know she was paying Angel to look for him, or she didn't want Mal to know she was spending that kind of cash? Did she suspect cheating after all? Was everything okay at home money-wise?

Lots of questions. Things to muse about later. The important thing was: Glory probably had her own bank account.

"LibertyStar Bank, thank you for holding, my name is Gina."

Like he was slipping on a silk shirt, Angel sank into a lazy, molasses good ol' boy drawl. "Yeah, good afternoon, miss. Wassat Gina, you said?"

"Yes, sir."

Angel was used to holding the phone in his right hand. He squirmed and shuffled in the seat. He wanted to sip his coffee and talk at the same time, it added to the character, but he couldn't.

"Hello, Gina. The name's Detective Dobey, I'm from the NCPD. How're you today?" The real Dobey's accent wasn't this sticky. This bordered on parody. If he rode the line, it could stay merely satire.

"I'm well, thank you. How can I help you?"

"I need to get a little peek into someone's records. A Mr. Malcolm Hobbes. Lawyer, married, suspect he might have a savings account the missus don't know about. Can you help me out, darlin'?" He was officially making fun of Dobey.

"This would really be better if you came in person."

"Aw, miss, you know, I'd like to, but this is really time-sensitive, you get me?"

"I'm going to need a valid badge number as well as your date of birth. And your full name, please."

"I'm Detective John Wayne Dobey, born March third nineteen seventy-five. My badge number is..." Angel took out his pocket notepad and pen; never leave the office without it. "One-oh-nine-six-two."

A brief pause. "Yes, I see we've helped you before. Can you give me that name again? The lawyer?"

It was really not okay how easy this was. "Malcolm Hobbes, ma'am."

"What do you need to know?"

"Now, I'm guessin' Mr. Hobbes has a joint bank account with his wife Gloria, is that right?"

"Yes, detective."

"And that's where the mortgage and the car payment come from, ain't it?"

"I would guess that's what I'm looking at."

"I'd bet a cup of black coffee Hobbes has a second account that doesn't have the wife's name on it. Could you check that for me?"

"Just a second... Yes, I'm seeing a separate personal account."

Angel leaned back. "Darlin', would you be able to get me a statement for that account and any cards or chips associated with it? For, let's say, the last six months?"

"It really would be much better if you came and did this in person..."

Angel sucked his tongue. "How 'bout you just tell me what the last couple weeks of purchases looks like?"

"Well... Just a minute, sir."

Another voice: "Just get one of these, man."

Angel looked over his shoulder. "'Scuse me?"

A chunky, bearded Mexican kid with a pink mohawk

was sitting in the opposite groove of the S-shaped couch. He tapped something that looked like a metal spider embedded in his throat. "Hey, your hillbilly voice blows, man."

"Hey, I'm not really looking for notes."

The fat kid pressed an LED on the spider's center and it turned from green to pink. "See?" A sultry woman's voice came out of his bearded mouth. "Hot shit, right?"

"What you use it for? Catfishing?"

"Sometimes," the kid with the woman's voice laughed. "Or when I feel like a girl." He pushed the pink LED and it turned back to green. "But it is good for catching sugar daddies," he said, in his masculine voice again.

"How many voices can it do?"

"Many as you can fit on a micro."

"Does it come off?"

"Nah. They gotta hollow out the whole voice box to install it."

"Pass."

"Sir, are you still there?" asked Gina.

Angel shifted on the cushions and chucked a cockeyed look at the brown kid. "I sure am, sweetheart, you got anything for me?" The chubby kid made a huffy chuckle and slurped on a frappé. Angel tried to dismissively wave his right hand, but it was like swinging a lead weight and it also hurt.

"There was a withdrawal of a thousand dollars six days ago," said the woman from the bank. "Before that... He's taken a series of loans from us. Regular deposits and payments a couple times a month. Same amounts, same recipients."

"Payin' bills, huh? Can you tell me who to?" Angel held his phone in place with his shoulder and put pen to pad.

"Paper, *viejo?*" said the youngster, in his female voice. "What are you, like, the world's shittiest detective?"

"Partner, I am the world's *best* shitty detective," murmured Angel, putting the Texas sting on his words just in case the woman from the bank could still hear him. "Mind your business or I'll put a hit out on you. Hey, darlin', thank you very much, you have a good day, now."

The woman gave him two names. Regular payments to a Fierros Imports, and one A. K. Schock. Angel looked them up on his phone. He waited for the bearded kid to comment. They didn't. A show of restraint.

The first took only a minute to figure out. Fierros Imports was a luxury sports car dealer one town over. Angel had seen all this before: Mal kept his shiny baby in storage somewhere, and when it all got to be too much, he'd tell Glory he was working late and take the fireball out for a night ride. He'd be skimming off the top of the office revenue to pay for it—when he wasn't taking out loans. All this over a fancy car. Angel imagined Malcolm cruising the sundown streets, probably taking the rocket past the boardwalk to see some neon and palm trees. He wondered what Malcolm thought about, if he had regrets. Angel didn't want to speculate on his marriage, but it was hard not to draw conclusions.

A. K. Schock was harder to pin down. It was simplicity itself to Tripp the man's phone number, but who was he? Angel let his train of thought run through Q's noise. Milk steamers, jazz, the ever-present insistence of voices. White-gold circles and parallelograms of sunlight shone through windows that made Angel think of old-fashioned Hollywood. *Yeah, stop admiring the corporate art and think about the case, genius.* A little more digging turned up that Schock belonged to a landlord's association. Angel ran a search on *A Schock Landlord* and the phone number. He found a place in the Heights.

Angel put the phone down and tapped his knee. He chewed his tongue, looked away at nothing in particular. *Think carefully on this one. Delicate touch.*

"*Oye.*" Angel snapped his fingers, leaned over to the kid with the mohawk. "*Hazme un favor, por favor.*"

"Tch. *Chúpamela, gabacho.*"

Angel snapped his fingers again, twice. It was difficult, not as emphatic as it would've been with his dominant hand. "*Soy güero,* little bastard. It's a skin job."

"You, really?" Mohawk cocked his head back. "*Pruébalo.*"

Angel picked up his coffee cup and turned it so the marker scribble of his name showed. "Ahn-hel?" he said slowly, as if to a halfwit, tapping it with his finger.

Pink mohawk pouted his lips. "What's the favor?"

When A. Schock picked up, Angel put it on speaker.

"This is Andy."

"Hi, there," breathed pink mohawk, whose name was Eddie, in his synthesized girl voice. "I'm looking for Mr. Schock?"

"Uh, that's me!"

Angel stuffed his tongue into his cheek and urged Eddie to continue.

"I needed to ask a question about one of the tenants at your building in the Heights?"

"Well, miss. I'm, ahh, I'm not able to give out information about the residents of my building. But... I'll tell you what I can. It depends."

"I just need to serve a court summons, *sir.* Won't you

please help me?" said Eddie, like a good bimbo. Angel offered Eddie an encouraging grin. *That's it, kiddo, give 'im the one-two.*

"Well, okay, miss. Who is it?"

"His name is Malcolm Hobbes."

"In number ten-oh-three? Wait... Isn't he a lawyer?"

Angel hung up the call. He slid the promised twenty into Eddie's hand. "Gorgeous. I gotta run."

Eddie made a kissy-face, holding the twenty between his first two fingers. "*Hasta mañana*, dreamboat."

Dumb, Mal, very dumb. Angel, standing up in the middle of the Q's, kept tapping his phone against his thigh. He chewed his tongue. When he had tried to snap his fingers in Eddie's face it had been clumsy, ineffectual. *Give 'im the one-two;* imagine running in to save Malcolm from his own carelessness with only one mitt. Imagine trying to hold a gun.

Angel really hated to burn the five minutes, but he got back in the coffee line, and he made another call.

Does the kid like Q's? 'Course she does.

SKY AND JINX stooped on either side of Kiera as she punched in the transfer to the new savings account. She dropped her head onto the desk, *flunk*. She felt Jinx's delicate fingers swish back and forth on her shoulders, consoling her. Sky lifted her up and hugged her. She buried her face in his chest, and dearly wished to just be unconscious.

"You wanna get pizza tonight?" asked Sky.

"Want breadsticks," Kiera mumbled into Sky's breastbone. "'N' dipping sauce."

"We'll get you breadsticks."

They still needed ten thousand dollars if they were gonna get enough Patriot Points for the next level. It may as well have been a fucking million. Back to work.

MRS. GUZMAN WAS a sweet old babe with robot legs who lived alone and needed help figuring out why her internet was going so slow. Kiera cracked it in five; some skeezoid was leeching her connection and probably mining some kind of shitcoin. Kiera despised what crypto was doing to the already-destroyed environment, and also despised that she had to use it to buy her hormones. She locked down Mrs. Guzman's net, and while she was at it, she installed a VPN so Mrs. Guzman could get Latin American movies on Fatass. She changed the password, too, so Mrs. Guzman's nephew would stop using her account—the old lady couldn't afford two screens. *Sorry, kid.* Then she changed Chili's litter box. The lady gave Kiera twenty-five entire big ones, and five stars.

Now Kiera was stooped over a talking toilet with her aching knees planted in black tile. The listing had just said "repair smart toilet." Look up the instructions online, turn it off and then on again, forty bucks. Oh, to be so young and naïve again. The thing was on the fritz, and it only spoke Japanese. It had a deeply granular control panel on the wall, and an app which Kiera downloaded—both also in Japanese. She wished, not for the first time, that she hadn't wandered away from teaching herself Japanese at home for the third time; and that her immigrant grandmother hadn't had the language beaten out of her almost a century ago, so Kiera would've been taught to speak it as a toddler.

In her left eye she was deep in a thread on a cultural

enthusiast subforum, explaining all the functions on the wall panel in English, but not the app. She was trying to find information on the app, and then, she hoped, some insight on how to fix the damn thing. In the meantime, she'd warmed her hands on the ass heater, accidentally flushed five times, blow-dried her hands in the bowl with the butthole blow-dryer, and sprayed herself in the face with the retractable bidet.

The toilet's master, Mr. Saito, peeked his head in. "*Daijobu desu ka?*"

Kiera tried to grin. "Good! Just a few more minutes!"

Mr. Saito frowned like a frog. "*Nihongo wa wakarimasen ka?*"

Kiera shook her head. "Only a little, I'm sorry. Just English for me."

Mr. Saito glared and slowly disappeared around the door frame again. "*Hāfu,*" he growled, dragging disdainfully on the second syllable.

"Hey!" Kiera smacked her hand on the toilet seat. "That's—*urggh*!"

The toilet flushed again. Kiera's smart-ear started ringing. Irritated, she snapped her fingers in the air to answer it.

"This better not be who I think it is." She fucking knew it was.

"Stupid. It's me."

"I fucking know it is. I told you don't call me."

"I need you. I need you bad."

"No! Ew. Don't say it like that. And no!"

"Dammit, listen to me. There's a place I need to check out and I can't do it alone. I need your help."

Kiera released a groan worthy of Charlie Brown. She started fucking with buttons on the toilet's control panel, just looking for something, anything that worked. "Call someone else. Put up a Gigawatt listing."

Kiera pushed a button and suddenly there was a blast of saxophone followed by a schizophrenic shuffling of drums. Coming from the toilet.

"Kid, I can't—is that Coltrane?"

"I... have no idea?" Kiera looked in the toilet bowl, enraged.

"Yeah, 'Both Directions at Once'. Nice. Look, I can't list this gig, I can't hire it out. It's gotta be today and it's gotta be you. Do you understand? I'm asking you, personally. I need a favor."

Kiera slumped forward and stuck her head in the toilet bowl. "*Whyyy?*" Her voice made a watery echo, bringing to mind being drunk and sick.

"Look. How much do you want? Squeeze me. And I'll owe you one. I'm figuratively begging."

Kiera opened the toilet app again in her right eye. She tried to turn the music off. None of the icons looked like music. Why did none of the icons look like music?

"I don't know. Fuck it. Three hundred dollars," she blurted.

"Done."

Kiera jiggled like a bobblehead. "Wow, I should've held out for more."

"You need five?"

"Yes."

"Five hundred dollars. But you drop everything and come meet me right now."

Kiera pushed a button in the app, and with a *whirrrr* the plastic finger of the retractable bidet reappeared and sprayed her in the face. Some of it got in her mouth. It was clean water, but it was *bidet* water. That was gross.

She took a moment to collect herself and wiped her eyes.

Saito would give her a bad rating and a shitty review for bailing on him and his cantankerous toilet, but what could he possibly write about her? *Didn't speak Japanese?* She'd give *him* one star. *Shitty customer! Called me a foreign racial slur. Fuck him!*

"*Ugh.*" Kiera rubbed her eyes. "Fine. Where are you?"

5

HERRERA WAS WAITING in his yellow hatchback right outside the subway. Kiera climbed in, and the scent of peppermint vape hit her broken nose like a fistful of VapoRub. "Fuck, what is it, Christmas at the hospital?"

"Hello to you, too, stupid," Herrera chirped. He proffered a large-size Q's cup with his left hand. "White chocolate mocha."

"I'm kinda a decaf girl," said Kiera, immediately feeling shitty for it. "It's okay, I'll just drink half. Thank you."

Again with his left hand, Herrera stuck a red plastic cigarette in his mouth. When he breathed, the clear tip lit up ruby. More Christmas smoke billowed out the sides of his lips. He navigated his phone clumsily—he was using a GPS app, with his thumb no less, wrestling with a task Kiera would perform just by telling Mimi the address.

"You and that goddamn *phone*."

"You kids don't remember a time before these things."

"I'm thirty."

"You don't know. Even the old shit I've got in my eye still blows my mind."

"My first girlfriend lived in Nebraska and her parents said the government was watching video calls, so I ran up long distance bills calling her on my flip-phone. I didn't have a phone without buttons until I was fifteen. God, I *wish* we could've just gone on a Fatass date and had free video chat."

Herrera kept his right hand in his lap as he pulled the car out into the road. He cocked his head and smirked. "You ever rent a video?"

"Duh. Store near my house had a great kung-fu section. I always wanted to work there but they closed down before I was old enough."

"One of my first jobs as a brat was a projectionist. When they still had big film projectors. That's where I solved my first mystery, actually."

Kiera slurped her mocha. She eyed him, eyebrows raised. *Continue.*

"Someone was cutting strips of film out of the reels and taking them home. Selling some of the cells online, keeping some of them in a personal collection. Normally you can do this pretty easily without getting caught but he was taking sections big enough to cause hiccups in the playback. So, I figured out who was doin' it."

"What'd you do? Buy one of his cells?"

"Tried that first, but the return address was a PO Box. Nah, nah. I broke down one of the film reels, found the cut, and lifted his fingerprints off either side of the splice."

"Damn. Dude was just trying to hustle a little extra cash."

"Yeah, I didn't like the idea of someone stealing from our little theater. Already had to make most of our profit on concessions. Business was tough."

Kiera, sipping her Q's, looked over the edge of her cup to see that Herrera's hand was still bandaged up, but not oozing blood anymore at least.

"So's that thing fucked?" she asked.

"Yep."

She slurped. "You gonna get it, you know, upgraded?"

"Absolutely *not*. The eye is enough."

"I would. I'd go in and tell 'em to just cut my damn arm off for fun if I had the money. I want a robot hand."

"Well, not me."

"So, you're just left-handed now?"

"It's an unfolding situation. Kind of wanted to talk about that when we had a sec, actually."

Kiera eyeballed him. "What?"

"Well, I need you tonight because you're good with tech and I'm not. But you also bring the advantage of still having use of your dominant hand."

Kiera sipped her coffee purposefully, narrowing her eyes. Herrera continued without prompting. "How comfortable would you be carrying a gun?"

Kiera's eyes popped and she spat out her coffee on purpose. "What gun? Whose gun? *Your* gun?"

Herrera sucked his teeth and winced apologetically. "Yeah, my gun."

Kiera put up an index finger. With her lips pursed furiously, she took a moment to gather her thoughts. She wagged her finger.

"Do you want me to *fire* the gun?"

"I don't *want* you to do anything."

"But you anticipate me *needing* to carry it."

"It wouldn't be a bad idea."

"I told you not to call me again"—Kiera laid out each word with carefully measured disdain—"because last time I went out with you I got shot at. And I gave forty dollars to someone who actually got shot instead of me."

"Oh, that's good of you."

"Now, yes or no, am I going to get shot at again?"

Herrera took a deep breath. "It's like this, alright? Someone asked me to find her husband. He hasn't responded to any calls or texts in over a week. I'm pretty sure I've found the guy, but y'know, sometimes these guys don't wanna be found. Or maybe the guy was kidnapped. Or maybe he's in trouble, owes someone some money, and we spook him, bang bang, *aaahhh*, y'know. Or maybe we just plain wind up in the wrong place at the wrong time. I don't know, kid. In this line of work, it's *The Lion King*, be prepared. And I can't shoot for shit like this." He lugged his bandaged hand into her view like a lead paperweight. "Okay? It's just a precaution. If you're not comfortable, I won't ask you to do it."

Kiera folded her arms and scrunched her lips. "Did you just reference *The Lion King*?"

"I did. Was it funny?"

"I asked a yes or no question."

"You did not really ask a yes or no question. You asked an open-ended question. You asked a Zen koan."

"Angel Herrera! Is there a non-zero chance of us getting shot at again on this errand of yours?"

"There is always a non-zero chance of us getting shot at again. Even just by some loser in fatigues trying to get on the news."

Kiera pinched the bridge of her nose, hard, and wished

she had a pillow to scream into. In her left eye she had a blip telling her the triad chat was trying to get her attention.

tactical butt: what dipping sauces you want babe?

"You thinking about it?" asked Herrera.
"I'm fucking thinking about it."

an elf irl: 1 blue cheese 1 marinara you know that
tactical butt: (·ω·)b
an elf irl: i wish i had stuck with teaching myself japanese

Kiera released a long groan that threatened to become an aggravated roar.
"*Urrrgghh*, give me the goddamn gun."
"It's holstered under my left arm."
Kiera leaned over and scrabbled for the weapon—she was reminded of having to steer the car for Herrera the other night. She found the muted, neutral texture and cool of the rubber handle, unclipped the holster, and pulled it free. She pulled the slide and checked the chamber.
"Huh. A smart gun?" she noted aloud. "Thought you were all about retro. You'll have to authorize me to fire it."
Herrera lifted his eyebrow. The finger-grooves on the handle lit up green in Kiera's grip. She startled.
"It—what?"
"How many times have you been to my old apartment,

stupid?" Herrera smirked. "You think I don't have your fingerprints?"

"That is... tremendously creepy?"

Herrera laughed. The car pulled onto the freeway, facing into the lowering sun. They passed a billboard for a movie starring a baby in a suit of power armor, and Humphrey Bogart risen through CGI necromancy. *Digital Bogey's not even a new idea*, thought Kiera. *They joked about it forty years ago in* Last Action Hero. *A* starving *ouroboros serpent feasting on its own shit*.

"Help me drink some of my coffee, would you?" said Herrera. "This is my second already."

THE PLACE WAS sketch. Dogs were barking somewhere, and there was trash piled up on the sidewalks. There were still places in New Carson where a girl with a dick didn't wanna walk around at this hour. Kiera was armed, and she was with her ersatz white guy, but she would prefer to get home to her pizza without having to ice someone for the first time.

"You needed me for *this?*" she sniped. "How bad are you at your job?"

"Don't get saucy with me, stupid. You give me that little multitool you got there, I can make a set of lockpicks. Pliers are good for twisting the occasional nose, too. Not many old-fashioned locks left in the city, though."

A squarish black cable ran from the innards of the gate panel to a little thumbstick nestled in Kiera's palm, with a simple number display like an ancient LCD watch. The numbers spazzed and fizzled, and one by one they locked in. "But I mean... This thing is still on a PIN, for god's sake. Total skid row, daddy."

"Don't call me daddy, yuck. And if I wasn't working one-handed here, I'd just climb over the damn fence."

The last digital number slotted into place and the light on the panel turned green. The gate clicked. Kiera pushed it open, and then started screwing the nude panel's face back on.

"I wasn't calling you daddy," she said. "I was, like, being ironically hip. Using lingo? Like Dusty Rhodes."

"It was weird, don't do it. How do you know about Dusty Rhodes?"

"For fuck's sake, I'm thirty, not fifteen." Kiera shoved the thumbstick and the tool back in her bag. They got to the front door of a big, shitty apartment building. Herrera pressed his face against a rectangle of glass to look inside.

"No doorman or guard, no surprises there. But I do see a security camera. I'd rather not be seen."

"Okay."

"So, whatcha got in the bag of spy shit for me?"

Kiera made a face. "What do you want me to do, dixie the mainframe and geek the black ice?"

"Yes?"

"I'm not exactly an authority on home invasion either, dilz for brains."

"You want we should check around back? The ol' fire escape? You climbin' a dumpster?"

"I'm not climbing a dumpster."

"Be surprised if this place even has a fire escape…"

Kiera exhaled. "Hang on, I may have something." Now she pressed her face to the glass. She pinched the security camera between her fingers and spread them out, her eyes zoomed in. She read the big black model number on the side. She zoomed back out and squeezed Herrera's cheeks.

"Wub," he questioned her.

"What kind of eye you got? It's old as balls, isn't it?" She peeled the lids of his left eye. Just behind the white sclera veneer, she could see the carbon-black body peeking out. "From before they made lenses."

"Yuh. T-series. This was shit hot when it came out."

"Everything's shit hot when it comes out. Thank god yours is just recent enough. Go download Snap4Fun."

"How do I do that?"

"Asshole. On the Uni Store? You could just ask Mimi to do it for you, if you had implants instead of a phone like *everyone else in the civilized world.*"

Herrera had a thousand-yard stare, and his pupils were flicking from left to right. He was biting his tongue in concentration. Kiera shook her head.

"What are you—oh my god. It predates finger controls? Oh my god."

"Just give me a minute, bitchy."

Kiera turned and leaned against the door and waited. Herrera started sighing a lot and making aggravated noises.

"What?"

"I forgot my Uni account password and I'm trying to get it back. My secret question answers aren't working."

"For fuck's sake."

"They're the right answers. I don't know why they're not working."

"Is it case sensitive?"

Herrera stuck his tongue out again. Another two minutes passed. Kiera threw up her hands. "*Well?*"

"Oh, yes. That worked. Thanks."

"GOD!"

Several minutes later, Herrera finally had the app.

"Okay," groaned Kiera. "Now just…"

Her vision plastered over with a screaming candy-colored HUD, glitter and stickers everywhere. She fiddled around a bit, and then her eyes lit up; two-dimensional holograms of a cat ears and mouth and nose popped up in front of her face.

"Oh!" Herrera exclaimed. "I've seen these."

"If you had implants instead of a *phone*, I could just fake you a whole different face. This is fine, though. This is some drug dealer's place, not the Bellagio."

"Heh, *Ocean's Eleven*. Don't security cameras see through these? I thought they got on top of that stuff pretty quickly."

"Yeah, a *good* camera will, once you're within a certain distance. But that's a good camera. Put something on and let's go in, already."

Herrera took a moment, and then he sprouted the face of a cartoon dog, with a big stupid tongue. He looked at Kiera pointedly.

"You gonna help me take a bite out of crime?"

"Oh my god, let's *go*."

With their animated faces they entered and crossed the narrow lobby, feet clapping on grimy tile. There was no elevator, so they climbed.

"Top floor," said Herrera. "Good thing you've got good cardio."

"'Take a bite out of crime'? I told my partners you weren't a cop."

"I am not."

"Were you?"

"Yeah. Lotta PIs wcrc."

"Gross. Why'd you quit?"

"That, kid, is what they call a personal question. As in, personally, I wish you would not ask that question."

Still need to unlock the tragic backstory, thought Kiera. *Not that I really give a fuck. Why am I here?*

On the way up they encountered a man in a dirty tank top. He had wires coming out of his eye socket, to plug into a cybernetic eye that was no longer there, perhaps pawned, or stolen while he was unconscious. By the light bulb meth pipe in his right hand and his shambling gait, Kiera thought either was plausible. The skeez glared down at Kiera. He was broad and muscular, and his awkward stance blocked the narrow stairwell. Kiera tensed, the awareness of the pistol in her waistband thudding like a second heartbeat. Herrera, however, simply gave him a jovial wave.

"Enjoying your night?" Herrera chirped.

The man turned his red-eyed gaze to Herrera, and his mouth slackened.

"*Jesus* Christ," he said in a Slavic garbage disposal's voice. "Talking dog."

The man barrel-rolled aside, blinking feverishly, and Herrera briskly resumed his ascent. Kiera followed, dancing around the man like she was avoiding a spill.

At the top floor they turned their faces off and approached the door numbered 1003. It had a card key reader. Herrera flung back the wings of his coat and put his hands on his hips. Kiera folded her arms. Herrera looked at her.

"Nothing?" he asked.

Kiera threw up her hands. "Whaddaya want? All my cracking shit is at home."

"Kid! I needed you to bring your shit."

"You said drop everything and come now! I didn't go home and get my shit!"

"But this is something you could normally do?"

"You'd be ashamed of the things I could normally do."

Herrera pinched his nose. He looked at the door and chewed his tongue.

"Alright. Well, then…"

He gingerly knocked on the door. Kiera lifted her eyebrows. *Real?*

A minute passed. Herrera knocked again. "Mal? You in there?"

Kiera quirked her mouth. "You know the guy?"

"Wife told me the name. Mal? You home?"

"And he's… Mal? Not Mr. Whoever?"

"Shush a second."

Herrera put his ear to the door. He frowned and shook his head. "Gotta kick in the door."

Kiera made what she estimated to be her fifty thousandth *Okay* face of the night.

"You go in first, kid. Gotta be you."

Kiera balked. "You what now?"

"You gotta hold the gun."

"Is there—is someone gonna pop out of there and shoot at us?"

"We're kicking down the door, he might think anything. I hate to do this to you, I hate it."

"I hate to do it to me, too!"

"I'll hold your hands. Okay?"

"Don't be a *dick*."

"No, kid, I mean I will literally hold your hands."

Kiera shut her eyes and took a deep breath. She had, after all, agreed to take the gun. She lifted its dead weight out of her waistband; the finger grooves lit up mint green. Her breaths turned shallow, and she felt her nerves light up orange.

She breathed, "Okay."

Kiera hopped out of the way just in time to avoid

Herrera's big lumbering kick, plowing into the door just above the card reader. The door was cheap; it burst open like a box of toaster pastries. Kiera put the pistol up with both hands. It weighed as much as a car. Herrera came up behind her and put his hands under her triceps to steady her arms. The fingers were delicate on her left, clumsy and club-like under her right.

"Those aren't my hands," she said, her voice shaky.

"Mechanical-automatical, kid. One step, two steps. In we go."

Kiera tried to pretend she was in *DOOM*. She and Herrera crept together across gritty sand-colored carpet, past a bare kitchen, half-eaten chicken parm sitting in an open styrofoam container on the counter. Small curvy TV before a blue vinyl couch. The blinds were drawn. Very minimalist, bachelor decor. Kiera had partied in places like this, during worse times. There was a *smell*, some cloying scent, hanging around: incense, Kiera realized. Maybe to mask the smell of garbage, or drugs.

"Mimi, brightness up," she murmured.

"*Sure.*"

"Up," Kiera repeated. "Up, up." It mostly made things whiter rather than easier to see.

Herrera gently spun Kiera to face a white door, slightly ajar.

"Bedroom, you think?"

Kiera swallowed. "Uh-huh."

"Maybe nobody's here."

"I hope so."

"We're coming in," Herrera called. "Mal? We're coming in. Don't freak out."

Kiera toed the door open a little more. It creaked. She took one hand off the gun and pushed it all the way.

Her heart dropped out of her ass. She swung out of Herrera's grip and let the gun fall. "Oh, Jesus! Oh, Jesus fuck!"

Herrera sighed and buried his face in one hand. "*Shit.*" With the other hand, he switched on the light.

Malcolm lay spread-eagle across the bed, mouth open, staring up at nothing. His throat was visibly crushed. A pistol lay on the carpet, just out of reach of his dangling fingertips.

Kiera didn't cry, but she started to shake. Herrera put his hands on her shoulders.

"It's Mr. Hobbes? Why didn't you tell me it was Mr. Hobbes?" she wailed. "Jesus. Oh, fuck me. Who did this?"

"You two know each other?"

"*You* two know each other?"

"Goddamnit. I'm sorry, kid. I should've done this alone."

"You *think?*"

Kiera shoved his hands away and swatted all the notifications out of her vision. She leaned against the wall and stared into her cupped fists.

"Take me home, please."

Herrera took his cellphone out. He frowned and looked at the floor. "Can't, kid. Gotta call it in."

Kiera dropped her hands. "We have to stay here? With… him?"

Herrera gazed at her apologetically, then turned to talk on the phone.

Kiera waved her interface back over and pulled her chat window up.

It's Jinx!!!: baby are you home soon??
 Pizza?

```
tactical butt: pizza?? breadsticks??
It's Jinx!!!: PIZZA?????
It's Jinx!!!: :(
an elf irl: you are not going to believe
   this.
```

6

IN THE MOVIES, when the good guys found their friends lying dead with their eyes open, they would close them—brush the eyelids shut with their fingertips. Angel didn't touch Malcolm, not once. Sure, this was a crime scene, and you weren't supposed to touch anything. There was that. But mostly, it was because Angel instead spent so much time looking out the half-curtained window—at the pink and cream sky over the concrete vista, sun descending behind the freeway—and then back at Malcolm's dark body, dropped handgun on the beige carpet, wondering if he and Mal had still been friends at all.

The kid had left him standing with the phone to his ear, but Angel lost track of how long it actually took him to make the phone call to Glory. It felt like ten minutes, twelve. Creeping up on fifteen while the body got cold. He checked; it had been seven. Time dilation, like they talk about in space travel…

He made the call mechanically, still not ready. The phone jingles ebbed away into the dark like distant heartbeats.

"Angel?" Gloria answered.

"Yeah, hey. Hey, Glory." Angel swallowed. "Listen, I found him."

Gloria breathed out—an involuntary surge of relief—and Angel felt like a ratfuck bastard. Then she sharply drew the air back in. "Is he...?"

Angel sighed through his nose. "No. No."

Her wail hit Angel's ear like a burst levee, a scream of black water quickly drowning them both. Angel hung his head and listened to her, accepting her despairing cries as punishment for his inconceivable failure.

"Malcolm," she managed. "Oh, god, Malcolm."

"I don't know what to say."

Glory had no answers for him.

It became clear this conversation was over. Angel hung up. It took two minutes to collect himself for the 911 call.

"Yeah, hi... My name's Michael Jones. I've got a body here..."

ANGEL STEPPED OUT of the bedroom to find the kid huddled on the couch, in front of the switched-off television. Her pupils flicked back and forth, and her fingers twitched in the air above her lap. Angel couldn't help but think of a seizure. He saw pink and orange fireworks going off in her eyes, on the curved surfaces of her lenses.

"You all there, kid?"

"Yeah," she rasped, and cleared her throat. "Not like it's my first dead body."

Angel didn't say anything for a second. For lack of anything to do with his hands, he dug out his plastic cigarette. "Want me to leave that one alone?" He tossed the question out casually.

"It's what they call a personal question," said Kiera in a typewriter cadence. "As in, personally..."

"Copy that, kid."

Angel sucked on his smoke, and the tip lit up traffic-light red. The kid's cheek twitched, and she abruptly turned to face the other wall. "That light's distracting," she muttered.

"Sorry."

Then she froze and swept her hand in the air like she was waving away a fart.

"Hang on—don't smoke that."

Angel paused with the red cylinder on his lips. "Uh?"

"Have you *smelled* that since we got in here?" She twirled her index finger in the air. "That smell. It's..."

Angel sniffed. "Yeah, kinda. Incense, right?"

"Nag Champa," said Kiera.

"Are you an enthusiast?"

"Do you know how many metric assloads of marijuana I go through every month?"

"You got a hunch, kid?"

"Well, like, incense smell doesn't stick around that long. This smells fresh. Did you see any incense in the bedroom?"

"Nuh-uh. What are you thinking?"

They locked stares for a minute. Then the kid scrambled off the couch and went for the trash next to the kitchen counter.

"Oh shit, kid—don't touch anything—"

She popped the lid open and fished among slimy salad remains, Bolo cans, moldy bread. She snatched and lifted free a yellow wooden stick, no thicker than a toothpick, with the grainy brown tip burnt like a cigarette. This she held up to Angel, meeting his eyes purposefully.

"Shit goddamn." Angel clapped his hands to his head. "You're a natural, stupid. It must have happened right before we got here."

"Did we see anybody leaving? Did we pass anybody?"

"Not a soul. Except—"

Angel wagged his finger in the air, brain running faster than his mouth, and he mimed smoking dope with his hands.

Kiera snapped her fingers. "Maybe he saw someone."

Angel was out the apartment door without another word, coat flapping behind him as if in a headwind. He heard the kid's footsteps slap on the concrete behind him.

They hustled down the stairs by twos. They got all the way to the bottom floor, but the smoker was gone.

Angel scrunched his face tight. He closed his fists. Then the anger roared over him in a blast wave. Anger at Malcolm's pointless and ignoble death, anger at himself for not being there in time. His fist flew out and hit the mailboxes—"Fuck! Fuck!" Over and over—"*Pin! Che! Mier! Da! FUCK!*"

The kid jumped half a foot. Angel steepled his hands in front of his face. Deep breaths. The kid folded her arms, hunched her shoulders, tried to throw up armor.

"Sorry. I'm sorry." Angel rubbed his forehead. "Good instincts, kid." He headed for the stairs.

"It's okay. Mr. Hobbes was... He was a good guy."

They went back up to the apartment. Angel took his smoke, then, the one that had been interrupted before, and they didn't say another word between them until the police arrived.

* * *

Cops.

Twenty years ago, guys like this were video game villains. Half a dozen fascists, their faces hidden under black helmets, stomping around in boots, not a sliver of human skin showing, toting SMGs just so they could stand around when the murder had already happened. Other men in disposable gloves and canvas jackets put up yellow tape and marked out the scene, their eyes throwing continuous photo-flashes. Trapped in a corner, Kiera felt the apartment phase-shift from a living space into a diorama, a museum exhibit, and Malcolm himself turn from... well, *Malcolm*, into biological. Into meat. Herrera stood by her, dragging on his plastic cig. She swallowed a sandpaper lump.

"Can I get a puff?" she asked.

Herrera obliged her. She took a good, deep inhale, lighting the tip up Mars red, and coughed. "God, I wish I could smoke again."

"Yeah? Why don't you?"

"Can't."

"Can't afford it?"

"Stunts feminization."

Herrera tipped his head curiously. "What's that mean?" His tone expressed that he knew it meant something really bad.

"Stops my estrogen medication from bonding with the receptors it's supposed to and, y'know." Kiera tipped her head. "Doin' the thing."

"Oh. *Oh*. Wow."

"And, like, increases the risk of blood clots, but who cares about that?"

"That's so terrible. That's unfair."

Kiera snorted. "Story of my effin' life."

Then *he* walked in.

He pulled off a pair of sunglasses—at night—to reveal blue eyes, electric-blue, electronic-bright, the seething glow of cathode-ray monitors. His slicked-back dirty-blond hair suggested he might run for president, and his actor's good looks said he would win. He tucked the sunglasses into the pocket of a zipped-up black bomber jacket. Kiera could not tell immediately if he was wearing thin black gloves or if his hands were artificial.

"Best behavior, kid," muttered Herrera. "Fuck this guy."

Kiera shrunk even farther into the wall. The man with the monitor eyes gave everything in the room a once-over, regarding it all with the detached concern of a very rich man touring the factory where an employee was killed in a machine accident. Then he walked toward Herrera and Kiera.

"*Michael Aaron Jones,*" said the important man, stressing each word and almost fastening a question mark onto the end, as if to give Herrera shit. "Forty-seven. Apartment 8D, 1620 Los Matadores Avenue, Collingwood, New Carson. Organ donor. I hardly recognized you."

Herrera clicked his tongue and smirked. "How's tricks, D?"

"Detective Flynn, if you don't mind," said the man. "Our relationship in this matter must be purely professional. You sympathize."

Herrera made a gun with his left hand. "*Pshew.*"

Flynn narrowed his eyes a little, and tilted his head, like he might at a child talking gibberish. *Michael Myers,* thought Kiera. Flynn took out a gray tablet as thin as a greeting card.

"The deceased. Malcolm Hobbes, fifty-five. 4268 L'Orange Drive, Sefton, New Carson. Non-donor." He tap-tap-tapped. "Nine-eleven call received at six-thirteen p.m., made by Michael Aaron Jones." He looked at Herrera. "Malcolm. Murdered. Isn't that something?"

Herrera nodded. His tongue was stuck in his cheek.

"And *you* just happened to be here to call it in." Flynn smiled genially. "Of all the people Malcolm would like to see in his final moments. Poetic, isn't it?"

Kiera flicked her eyes up at Herrera. *What was it with you and Mr. Hobbes?* But Herrera was too busy with the detective to notice her leering.

Herrera clicked his tongue. "Since when you into poetry, D?"

Flynn's smile didn't leave. "I believe I've asked you to call me Detective Flynn, Mr. Jones."

Herrera rolled his eyes. "Are you into poetry, Detective Flynn?"

Flynn's smile broadened, quite genuinely. "*Ever the mutable, ever materials, changing, crumbling, re-cohering. Ever the ateliers, the factories divine, issuing eidolons.*"

"Beautiful," said Herrera. "The fuck does it mean?"

Flynn put up a flippant hand. "Well. Who knows, Mr. Jones?"

"Walt Whitman," said Kiera, blowing candy-cane smoke. "*Leaves of Grass.*"

Flynn turned his smile to face her.

"Kyle Umehara. Thirty. Apartment 13C, 56 La Grange Place, San Bonita, New Carson. Organ donor."

Kyle. The name bit her, injected her with a shot of venom.

"My name's Kiera," she corrected. "If you don't mind."

Flynn turned his head, pressed his lips as though two and two had suddenly made five.

"*Nooo*, the database says your name is Kyle Umehara…"

"That's… my legal name. I haven't had it changed yet." *Mr. Hobbes was helping me with that.* She swallowed another lump.

"Aha. I'm afraid I have to keep things professional, Mr. Umehara. I can only use your legal name."

"Just physically tell your lips to call me Kiera, please."

Flynn's face was as blank as a bank balance reading zero, his monitor-eyes almost imperceptibly flickering, radiating indifference. Kiera felt Herrera's hand brush her elbow and she looked up at him. His mouth wore a grimace. He blinked slowly at her. *Best behavior*, she remembered. She exhaled. She looked up at Flynn and said nothing. She waited for him to speak next.

Flynn looked at Herrera's cigarette in her hand. "May I?" he asked, reaching for it. Kiera passed it to him, trying not to sneer. Flynn took a long inhale, the plastic cig crackle-popping. He handed it back.

"Thank you. Mr. Umehara, you were here with Mr. Jones when he discovered the body?"

"I was probably first to see him dead."

"Interesting. What were you doing here?"

"We…" She glanced at Herrera, and instantly realized her hesitation was damning. Now Flynn knew she was looking for his coaching. Herrera gave her a tiny nod. *Tell the truth.* "We were looking for Mr. Hobbes."

"You were?" Flynn canted his head. "You knew Mr. Hobbes was missing? Did you know he was in danger?"

"No. I followed… Mr. *Jones* here. I didn't know Malcolm was here."

"You said were looking for him."

"We were looking for..." Kiera sighed. "Angel said we were looking for someone, and then when we got here—"

"This is... very confusing," said Flynn.

"She didn't know Mal was here," Herrera cut in. "I did. I hired her to come with me. I was light on the details. I'm cagey that way. Lighten up on the kid."

Thank you, Kiera tried to will over to Herrera telepathically.

"I see," said Flynn. "So, Umehara has no connection to Malcolm at all."

"None," said Herrera.

"And if we look into that..."

"I'm one of his clients," blurted Kiera.

Flynn pursed his lips. "I see. Mr. Jones, why did you try to hide that from me?"

"I didn't know that," said Herrera, rubbing his forehead. "I didn't know they were associates at all."

"I'm getting two different versions of events," said Flynn. "It's very vexing."

"It was a weird coincidence," said Herrera. "Just one of those things."

"Mr. Umehara, you were a client of the deceased, you said? Can you tell me the nature of your dealings with Mr. Hobbes? Details of your legal trouble?"

Kiera shrank back. "I—"

"That's none of your business. Kiera, you don't have to answer that. D, quit hassling the kid. I'll give you a statement."

Flynn ignored him. "Mmhmm. Is there anything you can tell us about the scene, Mr. Umehara? Anything you think we might have missed?"

Kiera glanced at Herrera. He nodded. She reached into her moto jacket pocket and took out the spent incense stick, holding it up with the tips of her fingers.

Flynn looked closely. His pupils whirred and narrowed. "Tell me what this is."

"A burnt stick of Nag Champa. We think the perp—" She stopped herself, ridiculing herself privately for the slang. *The perp*. A Herrera word. "We think the murderer burnt it right after he killed Malcolm. Mr. Hobbes."

Flynn touched his goateed chin. "That's interesting. Your theory is he killed the deceased, stayed at the scene long enough to enjoy a stick of incense, and *then* left."

"Uh-huh."

"I wonder why he would do that."

"Well, that's the job, ain't it, D?" Herrera winked.

Flynn straightened his posture. "Mr. Umehara, why was the incense in your right jacket pocket?"

Kiera's heart stammered. "It—"

"I found it in the trash," said Herrera. "I gave it to her to hang onto."

Flynn raised his eyebrows. "You disturbed the scene, after finding the body?"

"Afraid I did, D."

"And then you kept it."

Herrera made an apologetic face and nodded.

"You've probably contaminated it beyond usefulness. A man with your experience should absolutely know better."

"Yeah, real dipshit move. Rookie stuff, right?"

"And quite uncharacteristic of you." Flynn snapped his fingers—were those hands real, or not?—and beckoned for one of the men in canvas jackets. He took the incense stub and bagged it. Then Flynn turned back to Kiera and Herrera.

"Gentlemen, I'd like to take you both to the station for some additional questioning, after I've wrapped up my duties here. Does that sound agreeable?"

Kiera looked straight at him. "Am I under arrest?"

Flynn did that Michael Myers thing again, that head tilt. Kiera took a long, deliberate drag on the plastic cigarette, and blew the smoke out of the side of her mouth, maintaining hard eye contact with the man with electronic eyes.

"No, I don't believe I said that," said Flynn.

"Then I'm gonna peace out, fellas."

Kiera handed the peppermint cigarette back to Herrera. She thrust her first finger under his chin.

"I want to know who did this. But this was the *last* time," she growled. "I mean it."

Herrera pursed his lips and nodded. "Okay."

"I told you I fucking hate cops."

Kiera felt the SMGs in the room buzzing like hot iron as she stepped around the jackbooted enforcers to get to the exit. On her way down the stairs, she started to cry.

IT TOOK HOURS to get a bus and train all the way back from the Heights. Some people in Europe and New Zealand were on their way to bikes and carless highways with cloud-silent city trains that came every two minutes. Japan had that shit locked down years ago, daddy. America? She'd be choking on her own gasoline vomit until all human endeavor was burnt in the carbon dioxide oven by 2045. She and Canada, the UK, even the flame-charred husk of Australia would drive the world on a filthy coal- and oil-powered bus halfway there and make 'em walk the rest of the way. So Kiera got home at midnight again.

Her smart-ear blinged in the hallway. "For fuck's sake!" Was he really trying to call her *again?* Tonight? Now? Kiera told the call to fuck off and carded herself into 13C.

Jinx was on the couch, in the VR mask that made her look like a robot ninja. ("I wanna look like Gray Fox," Jinx had bubbled when the thing first appeared in ads. Kiera had admonished her for her attachment to a video game that was more than thirty years old. Then Jinx reminded Kiera that *she* had spent the previous week playing a fifteen-year-old dating sim.) Jinx had her anime mecha gloves on instead of using the controller, too; she was bobbing her shoulders and doing motions in the air, wax-on, wax-off. She was singing in Korean.

Kiera crept up behind Jinx, cradled hands under her chin, thumbs on her neck. Jinx startled and bounced and shrieked just a little bit. Kiera got a rat-got-the-cheese grin.

"Oh my god, that scared the *shit* out of me. Sky?"

"It's me."

"Ooh! Okay, guys, Kiera just got home. She's okay. I'm gonna go take care of her. Thanks so much everyone for keeping me company. I'll see you all tomorrow night, okay? Mwah!" She waved at her tablet, perched upright on a little rattan table, and cut the feed.

Jinx took off her gloves and carefully lifted off the VR mask like a pharaoh's burial visage, revealing her cute dark brown face. Kiera pushed Jinx's flat nose with her index finger. Jinx captured Kiera's finger with her fist, but she didn't move it away.

"Pizza's cold," Jinx said, pouting.

Kiera smiled. "I like it cold."

"Sky mighta stole some of your crazy bread. I tried to tell him not to."

"S'okay. I took forever."

Jinx reached up and fiddled with the tips of Kiera's elf ears. Kiera batted her away.

"So! Oh my Gorilla Grodd." Jinx flapped her hands. "*MisterMine* was watching my stream tonight. And he messaged me."

Jinx popped a big open-mouthed smile and made fireworks with her fingers and squealed a little. Kiera caught Jinx's hands and entwined their fingers together.

"Sweetheart, I don't know who that is."

"He's a big deal. And yes, you do, he made that funny *Vanguard* video you laughed at for, like, a month."

"Oh! Oh, okay. So what did he say? *Hey u up*?"

"He invited us to a *party* he's throwing this Friday. He throws these *huge* theme parties. *Celebrities* go to these things."

"Real celebrities, or, like, viddy game celebrities?"

Jinx put her hands on her hips. "Video game celebrities are real celebrities now, Kiki, you need to join us in the dystopian future. I know you hate it."

"*Ugh!* Okay."

"He wants me to be, like, his personal guest. I'll be on his Pictu feed and it'll be fire for my follower count and, like... This is a *huge* deal for me."

"Babe, that's dope. What made him message you?"

Jinx vogued. "I guess I'm just an underrated, undiscovered content creator, like you always tell me, sweet pea."

"Titty streamer."

"He said he was sorry I was having a bad night and wanted to take my mind off it."

"*You're* having a bad night?" Kiera made a face. Her smart-ear started ringing again, and she made the face even harder. "Oh, my *god*." She waved the call away and set herself to DND. "Fuck *off* already. Sorry, not you."

Jinx looked sympathetic, apologetic. She took Kiera's hands. "I was worried about you. How are you doing?"

Kiera shrugged. "I cried. I only got one weird look on the bus, though."

"And Mr. Hobbes is just…"

"Dead. Someone choked him to death so hard his throat caved in."

Jinx bit her lip. "That call on the bus was weird. I told you it was weird."

"It was weird. And now this."

Jinx touched Kiera's cheek. "You think about Lana, too?"

Kiera nodded. "Yeah. 'Course I did."

"How could you not?"

"How could I not?" Kiera swallowed. "It'd be cool if I could stop finding dead bodies."

Jinx came around from the other side of the couch, and hugged Kiera tight. Kiera nestled her chin in the crook of Jinx's shoulder.

Kiera got her cold pepperoni pizza. She microwaved her bread sticks. Her dip had big fat chunks of blue cheese in it. She *really* wanted a *big* plastic cup of Cherry Bolo with ice from the Blue Ribbon. Should she have one delivered by drone with some donuts and ramen? No, they needed to save money. She settled for making her own, with refrigerator ice, in her big promotional

Warlords of Tyrna cup from when that terrible movie came out.

All this was self-care.

They made a throuple spoon train in the bed, Jinx at the back and Sky in the front. Kiera put her leg up on Sky and hugged tight to his warm bulk. She turned her smart-ear volume down and let some music play her to sleep. Some of these songs she'd been listening to since ten or twelve years ago. Her heart hurt.

Goddamn, she missed her dead friend.

7

"NICE TO SEE the ol' clubhouse again," said Angel, as Flynn led him toward the elevator. It was a lie.

"You probably hardly recognize the place. It's seen quite a few improvements."

Flynn was right. Were the ceilings always so low, the white hallways so... *stifling?* You almost never saw officers walking around in those creepy beetle-black helmets indoors when Angel had been on the force. Now they patrolled like sentinels, strapped fit for a war to break out. When the elevator doors shut him in with Flynn, he felt iron weights press on his chest. *Should I have stayed? Could Mal and I have stopped this? Stopped it from getting this bad?*

He wasn't under arrest, that was the story. But nonetheless, Flynn took Angel into a blank interrogation room one floor down. Angel sat in one of the same old awful plastic chairs to which he'd subjected countless perps. He crossed his arms. Flynn placed his thin tablet very gently on the table and began to take notes on it with a stylus.

"This will be very casual, Mr. Jones. You've got nothing to worry about."

Angel clicked his tongue. "I wish you'd look me in the eye when you say that."

Flynn looked up, meeting Angel's eyes with his own luminescent blue ones. He smiled.

"Tell me how you and Mr. Umehara came to be at Mr. Hobbes's apartment this evening."

Angel licked his bottom lip just a little. "The kid and I were hoping to find Mr. Hobbes at the residence."

"Social call?"

"As you well know, detective, Malcolm Hobbes was a missing person. I had been tasked with finding him."

Flynn noted this on his tablet. "By whom?"

"I can't divulge my clients' personal information, D."

"Well, I presume the wife, Gloria. And Umehara? Why was he with you?"

"Sometimes I hire Kiera to help me with things."

Flynn gestured. "Such as?"

"Things I'm not good at. Computers."

"Did you expect to find a... difficult computer at Hobbes's residence?"

"Listen, I was looking for Malcolm and I brought the kid with me. Write that down in your little report. That's all there was to it."

Flynn nodded, pursing his lips, and wrote. "And while there you bungled with evidence, broke doors, that kind of thing. The usual."

Angel shrugged, and smirked. "Haven't been a cop for six years, D. I guess I'm slipping."

"Detective Flynn, please." Flynn leaned forward. "Tell me, why the new name, Mr. Jones? The new...?" He indicated his own face.

"Had some friends I didn't wanna see anymore."

"I see. Would you care to elaborate?"

"No, I would not."

"Did those friends include us at the NCPD?"

"I did my name change above board," said Angel. "Which makes changing it mostly useless, but you boys knew about it."

Flynn took notes. He spoke without looking up: "Useless? In what way?"

Angel rolled his eyes. "Can we just be adults here?"

"You *didn't* register your facial reconstruction, your skin bleaching, hair recoloring... You didn't go through a licensed clinic for your cosmetics, correct?"

"No."

"So you used a...?"

"A skin-jobber, yeah."

Flynn put his elbows on the table. "Cutters are usually patronized by... Well, excuse my language, but lowlifes. Scumbags. Criminals looking to disappear."

"Or people just looking for cosmetics who don't have health insurance, D."

"Detective Flynn, please. So, were you just...?"

"I don't have health insurance. It was an economic decision."

Flynn nodded. "Of course. Self-employed. How is business?"

"Gangbusters, D. Working a high-profile murder right now."

"So, overall, you feel leaving the force was a good decision?"

"I'm not getting into this with you."

Flynn raised his brows. "I'm just making conversation."

"Make it somewhere else."

"There wasn't any lingering resentment toward Malcolm? I know he was a major factor in your decision to strike out on your own."

"Mal bounced from the precinct, too." That was the kid's word, *bounced*. Angel liked it. "We'd both been thinking about it for a while. I didn't just leave because of Mal."

Flynn was looking at his pad again, tapping it and sliding things around. "Yes, he expressed he didn't want to work with a new partner. But your departure was considerably more heated, as I recall. There was an altercation."

"Yeah."

"And if you don't mind my editorializing, Hobbes made something of a greater mark for himself since retiring from law enforcement. A successful law firm, a wife, a lovely home."

Angel turned his head away and tongued his molar. "Yeah, this is a dickhead angle even for you, D."

"It's natural that there might be feelings of jealousy. You recently moved into another one-bedroom apartment, correct?"

"Things might not have been going so great at home as you think, detective."

"I'm sorry?"

"Secret bank account, secret car. The apartment we found him in was a secret from Gloria."

Flynn blinked. "You've looked into Malcolm's home situation?"

"Yeah, while I was doing your job for you. A whole week and you're giving Glory that 'we're looking into it' horseshit?"

Flynn shook his head, incredulous. "Why would you investigate Malcolm's personal affairs?"

"Because I'm a private *investigator*, D."

"The level of obsession..." Flynn regarded Angel with a pitying frown. "I never would've expected this from you, Mr. Jones, not in all the years I've known you. But something I've learned in this job is that people can be extremely surprising."

Angel looked down at the table, scrunched his lips, wishing he'd just gone the fuck home.

"Now, how does the boy factor into things?" asked Flynn.

Angel tilted his head up. "I'm sorry?"

"The, ah, the young man. Mr. Umehara?"

"You leave her alone, D."

Flynn spread his hands. "I have to work any angle I can. You remember what it's like."

Angel got up from the shitty plastic chair. He wished there was a coffee cup he could fling across the table, shatter on the wall. No—he was glad there wasn't. *Damn it.* He'd let that bastard Flynn *get* to him.

"Lovely chat, D, but I'm gonna—what did the kid say? *Peace out.*"

Flynn, frowning, motioned at the door. "You're free to leave whenever you like."

Angel stepped out into the hallway without another word. He pulled his coat collar up, headed for the elevator. Passed another helmet, felt a little shiver in his chest.

This isn't how we used to do things, he thought. *It's not. We were better than this.*

No. Maybe you tried to be better than this, he thought, stepping between the steel doors. *Maybe you and Mal* thought *you were better than this,* he chided himself, knowing damn well they'd talked him into staying even after the Floyd riots. Knowing good and well he'd stuck around through every call to defund the department, sucked down every slur he heard flung across the halls and locker rooms, just going along to get along. Because he'd had Mal to stick it out with him.

But this is what we always were, jack. The rest of the apples have always been bad.

THE HATCHBACK'S DRIVER-SIDE door clunked shut. Angel dug out his phone and hesitated with the slick rectangle hovering an inch from his cheek. He put the phone down again and ran his fingers behind the steering wheel, under the dashboard. He popped the glove compartment and felt around in there. He bit his tongue. He flicked his gaze up to the corner of the fenced parking lot. From a lamppost a camera leered at him, impassive black eye with a punctuating red dot, warning-red. It felt as though it lingered on him, bare in its animosity, until some long seconds later the camera swiveled away to face another angle of the lot.

Angel turned on the engine and let it idle. He twisted the knob on his old radio, always set to his solid gold hits station. Johnny Hates Jazz. Classic. He turned it up a little louder than it needed to be and called Glory.

"Hello," answered Gloria, after the fourth ring.

"Hey," Angel said, low in his throat, as if with his hands on her shoulders, as if to her cheek. He swallowed. "How you holding up?"

"A whole Xanax didn't chase the dread out, *mijo*. I took the whole bar. How do you kill this? This feeling like I'm burning in black fire. In *meaninglessness*."

Angel rubbed his wincing eyes. "Sometimes you just have to feel the feelings, babe. Grief is a sumbitch."

"I don't want to feel this, Angel. It makes me wish I didn't love him."

"Don't say shit like that," Angel snapped. "You did love him, goddamnit, no matter what was going on with you two."

"Yes," said Gloria. "I loved him so much."

"You wanna stop feeling for a bit, you should get some sleep. That pill oughta knock you right out. Just lie down and close your eyes."

"I don't want to go and be alone in that room, in that bed. He used to come home late, and I'd doze off, so annoyed with him—but to go there now, and know he's *never coming home*—"

A tiny white flash caught Angel's peripheral and made him blink. He looked up at the precinct building. "Hang on—zoom."

"What?"

Angel squinted. "Talking to my eye, hang on a sec."

Half the windows were tinted black and the others you could see into, white halogen light illuminating office desks. The building's face looked like one of those multiple-choice tests where you filled in the bubbles with pencil and they ran it through a computer. Out of all those windows, in one of them Angel spotted Flynn. It was the blue glow of Flynn's eyes that caught Angel's focus. Flynn was peering down toward the parking lot, calm as you please, without a doubt looking in on Angel sitting in his hatchback. Flynn turned away and twisted a knob mounted on the wall, and the plate glass window darkened, fading to opaque black.

Angel scowled. "D is sweating me for Mal's murder," he grumbled. "That's actually why I called."

"Oh, Angel."

"I'm serious."

"He's just being thorough. You know how he gets."

"Nah, nah. It's different this time. I don't like it. The force is... different from the outside, Glory."

"David said he had a suspect in mind already," said Gloria. "Some kid? He couldn't tell me much else."

Angel did a take. He turned the radio down. "Wait, wait, you talked to Flynn already? When?"

"I don't know, earlier? On the phone."

Angel was about to protest when he had a sick feeling, a dreadful lurch of his gut that told him *don't tell her anymore.* "Oh, Glory."

"Angel. Maybe you should let David handle this one."

Angel shook his head. No words came to his mouth; they all croaked by the time they got to his tongue. "I..."

"Keep the money. I asked you to find Malcolm, and you found him. Let that be the end of it."

Angel looked across the lot. Two of those black helmets—one in the parking kiosk, and the other knocking on the booth's window. They were trading shifts. For the moment when they were both standing outside the booth, they glanced across the parking lot in what Angel was sure was his direction, smooth and faceless. One of them thumbed the machine pistol strapped to his hip.

Angel started up the engine and shifted his hatchback into reverse.

"We'll see," he muttered.

"*Mijo,*" Gloria's voice pleaded, already halfway to his coat pocket.

8

THE THEME WAS "obsolete."

"So, like, retro?" Kiera had asked. She threw together what she could. She was going for, like, '80s goth. She did her face up white—she had to gingerly dab the paint on around her broken nose and apply a new bandage—and stuck on her boots and fishnets, got her moto jacket and the spike choker that wasn't seeing much rotation these days. She went ahead and strapped on an old-ass UniBand she had lying around, too, one of the precursors to the eyes and the implants, when they looked like big bracers. She used to listen to old Deftones albums on this thing in high school.

"That's just, like, how you dress anyway," teased Jinx. She'd come out of the bedroom decked out as Maya Matsuko from *Wicked ASCension 4*. Kiera wondered, *Is that obsolete?* Well, it had come out thirteen years ago. *Jesus.* For personal flair Jinx had added a belled collar, and those cat ear headphones she had, that she could make move and change color with her *thoughts*.

A rich creep had sent her those in exchange for feet pics. Thank god Jinx had gotten too skeezed out to continue that particular relationship before it got any weirder.

Kiera tipped her chin up. "When did you make that costume? I've never seen that one."

"Um, yes, you have. *CarNime 5*? A year ago?"

"Oh, was that the weekend I had dysentery out both ends because of anti-vaxxers?"

"Yeah! See, you remember." Jinx peeked her head into the bedroom again. "Sky, baby, you sure you don't wanna come?"

Sky released a great bearish yawn. "Yeah, not really my thing. You two hot mamas have fun. Don't come home until you get laid."

"I am not getting laid," Jinx protested.

"Then you're fucking homeless now, sweetie! Kiki, see you when you get back!"

Jinx just laughed. She grabbed her Hello Kitty backpack and Kiera got her messenger bag.

"Is that gonna be a thing, though?" Kiera asked in the hallway outside. "Like…?"

"What?"

Kiera nudged Jinx with her elbow. "Liiike…"

"Wh—you think MisterMine wants to fuck me?"

"I mean…"

Jinx sputtered. "No. That is *not* a thing."

Kiera leered at her. Jinx flapped her hands.

"It's not!"

The place was up in Kingcrest. It was *really* nice out here. It creeped Kiera out—the close-cropped grass unnaturally green, the uniform terracotta roofing. She lost track of the last house or two-story apartment block they'd passed that wasn't behind a tall iron fence, or a peach-colored concrete wall.

The guy in the black uniform at the gate to MisterMine's residential almost turned them away the moment he saw their outfits, but Jinx talked him into calling MisterMine's house to confirm they were invited. There was no answer.

"Try again," she pleaded. "There's a party. It's probably loud."

Someone answered the phone the second time, and then the guard sat there with the handset for three minutes, waiting for them to fetch someone who was authorized to vet guests. He looked fucked off about it the whole time. Kiera stuck her hands in her pockets and kept her lip zipped. *Damn, dude. Just do your job.*

They got through, eventually.

Every room in MisterMine's house must have been wired for sound because Massive Attack was blasting from down the street as fiercely as under a festival tent. A busty bikini samurai answered the front door. Then immediately someone careened through a side table, taking it and all the booze down with him in an unsuccessful bid to bullet-time-dodge a salvo of Nerf darts. The shooter caught up to him, dropped to the ground, discarded his gun, and just started pummeling the target in the arm, ass, and balls.

"Guns *upstairs*, guys," the hot samurai fruitlessly whined. "Guys."

Kiera and Jinx stepped inside and around the fracas; the samurai-slash-pressganged-doorwoman left them to their own devices, and also abandoned responsibility for the fallen booze table. Kiera rescued a bottle of peach vodka and followed Jinx down the hall. They pushed their way through clusters of costumed guests and loud conversations.

"Anyone seen Mister…? Anyone seen MisterMine?"

A blue, Asian woman appeared in a free patch of floor. Completely blue. See-through. Made of light. She wore a conical party hat.

"Hello!" the blue babe chirruped in a watery voice. "Welcome. Do you need assistance with anything?"

"Mimi," said Kiera. The Uni AI from her earpiece, wrought into human form. She'd seen this expensive, home-assistant Mimi in the commercials, but didn't know anybody who actually owned one. She hated the idea of people rich enough to own a Mimi, but she knew if she had that kind of money to waste, it was absolutely possible she would buy something as delightfully stupid as a kind-of-racist hologram maid.

"That's right! I'm Mimi. I see we've never met face-to-face before, Ms. Umehara. It's a pleasure to finally make your acquaintance. And Ms. Hurley, we last met at QueerPing X, seven months and one day ago. It's nice to see you again."

"How are you talking over all this noise?" asked Kiera.

"I broadcast from a Uni HomeHub and speak directly into your compatible smart-ear."

Kiera took a pull of her acquired vodka. "Dope."

"Tonight there are a range of activities. The entertainment room has been converted to a dancefloor. Upstairs there is a Nerf battle—the host has provided the arms. The pool is open. A *Mortal Kombat 11* tournament is in progress in the living room."

"*11*? Why *11*?" Jinx asked.

Mimi smiled. "The host loves *The Terminator* and

Robocop, of course. There is an open bar, or you can simply take what you wish from the tables. And finally, in the theater, a showing of *The Room* has just begun, and *The Matrix* will begin at ten p.m. Don't fret about the noise, the theater is completely soundproof."

"Can you just help us find MisterMine?" asked Jinx.

Mimi smiled. "The host is currently poolside. Please, follow me."

Kiera's first thought, when she saw the lounge, was that she'd never seen so much liquor in one place. Her next was that she didn't know there was so much money in video game streaming. Then she smelled weed. Some of the money had to come from his parents, right? Who was his dad? *Are those guys snorting crash? Are those girls doing mean dream?* She might want some weed. She took another pull of peach vodka. A guy with a CRT monitor for a head blew vape rings. Bojack Horseman was feeling up Bowsette; talk about a weirdly specific cultural moment. *Holy shit, is that Harry Chau? The season two bad guy from Silver Sparrow?*

Mimi led them outside to a pool bigger than their apartment. Kiera and Jinx shielded themselves from a cannonball-splash. Kiera pulled Jinx in a wide berth to avoid some perfect-looking people shooting water guns.

Mimi took them, finally, to a cabana on the opposite end of the pool. Someone here had a sick *DOOM* armor cosplay complete with super shotgun, but a few people weren't even in costume, just wearing party hats and colorful trilbies and shit. The skinny white guy in the center *had* to be MisterMine—a tailored sharkskin suit, American flag tie, and outdated rage-face meme pins on both lapels. *More like MisterMeme. More like Mister-side-shave-rainbow-hair.*

"Jinxy!" MisterMine beckoned with the hands at the ends of outstretched noodle arms. One wore a Nintendo Power Glove. "Oh, you're even prettier in person. It's so great to finally meet you. Hi!"

Jinx gave a bubbly wave. "OMFG, hi, Mister!"

Kiera put her hand up. "'Sup."

MisterMine locked in on Kiera. "Oh, I hate it! Perfect! Great outfit!" He moved his hands, scrolling with his first two fingers, and a gif appeared, projected in front of his sunglasses, of SpongeBob SquarePants vomiting. His friends uproariously laughed. Kiera tensed up like a suspicious housecat. MisterMine zeroed in on her t-shirt. "Oh my god, Mimi, put on *Pretty Hate Machine* right now. It's *terrible*. I love it."

"Sure!"

A holographic record appeared between Mimi's hands in midair and began to spin. There was a momentary pause between the Strokes and Nine Inch Nails where Kiera's chest and skull weren't rumbling with bass; she *felt* the silence. She wasn't sure if she was being made fun of or not.

"Are your guests taken care of?" asked Mimi.

"We're fine, Mimi," said Jinx. "Thank you." Mimi turned and disappeared.

"Sit down, sit down!" MisterMine made room on the seats. "Who's this?"

"Kiera! My girlfriend."

"Oh, right, right! Nice to—oh, *fuck!* Is your nose broken?" MisterMine covered his mouth.

"Yeah," said Kiera.

"Does it hurt?"

"Uh-huh."

"Do you need some crash for that? Maybe coke?"

"I'll take a hit off that bigass bong there, if the offer is open."

"How'd you break it?"

"I was eating Jinx's pussy too hard and she bucked into my face."

MisterMine burst into a Joker cackle and hammered his thigh. His friends thought it was pretty fucking funny, too. Jinx would have turned sports-car red if her skin weren't so dark. Kiera felt some satisfaction; she'd traded some of her discomfort to Jinx, gained a little social purchase.

Kiera relaxed enough to bob her skull to "Head Like a Hole." She hit the giant bong while MisterMine introduced Jinx to the inner circle. Jinx knew some of them by sight, others by handle. "Oh, of course! Oh, it's great to finally meet you!" Kiera had never heard of any of them. She quickly found herself with nothing to say. And she felt horrible about it. Sure, one of them was an e-sports superstar, this one a titty streamer, and Kiera could wave those ones off as overhyped and overpaid and playing video games for a living. *You do you, guys.*

But that one? Art director at the company that made *Star Legion.* This one was a voice actor who recorded charity playthroughs in her spare time. The one in the Doomguy suit? He'd actually composed the music for the newest *DOOM.* And he thought the game sucked. These people had careers. Crafts. Real lives. Kiera? She smoked weed, and the other day she failed to fix a talking toilet. She didn't even know when she'd missed her shot. Nobody had told her when it was coming up, or when it had slipped by.

At least Jinx was enjoying herself. She dragged in Kiera for a selfie for MisterMine's Pictu feed. Kiera made sure she was pulling from the peach vodka when MisterMine's back-of-the-hand-embedded selfie camera flashed.

Then Kiera's ear started ringing. The name popped up in her left eye.

"Oh, you have to be *fucking* with me."

Jinx's fingers danced reassuringly on Kiera's lap. "What is it, baby?"

"This motherfucker calling me *again*." Kiera stood up. "I have to… Where's your bathroom?"

Mimi blipped into existence. "I can take you to the bathroom. Please, come this way."

Kiera answered the call and followed the creepily omniscient blue woman inside. She plugged her right ear with her finger and shimmied to avoid water gun and pool splash damage. She tripped on her boot heels and stumbled a little.

"You need to *not* call me!" Kiera whisper-yelled.

"You need to hear this, kid."

"*What?* Speak up."

"I said—kid, are you *inside* a synthesizer?"

"*What!* Hold on."

Mimi led Kiera to a bathroom nicer than most houses she'd been inside of. Kiera shut the door and turned up her left ear volume.

"Herrera, unless you're calling me to tell me who killed Mr. Hobbes, I'm still ghosting you. I should've blocked your number."

"Kid, I need you to take a breath for this one. Try to find your center."

"Remember that time I did you a *favor* and we wound up finding a dead body? You still haven't paid me for that."

"Detective Flynn has us both named as suspects for Mal's murder."

Kiera felt her chest tingle like heat from a campfire. Then her head started rushing like she was falling from a tall building. The weed was kicking in at exactly the wrong time. Her heart went *duddud-duddud-duddud* and felt like it wasn't really part of her.

"What the fuck. What the fuck. What—"

Mimi was still standing there, smiling. Kiera shook her head.

"*Go away!*"

"Sure. Let me know if I can help you with anything else."

Mimi flickered away. Kiera braced herself against the granite countertop.

"What the hell? Why? I thought you covered for me."

"You were still with me at the apartment. Now, listen, he thinks you're an accomplice, but it's me he really wants. Okay? That's very important. He's trying to get to me. And I'm gonna... I'm gonna get to the bottom of this. But I just wanted you to know, in case someone comes around to ask you questions, or comes sneaking around your building or something—you might wanna find a good lawyer."

"I had a good lawyer, but somebody fucking murdered him!"

Herrera just sighed. So Kiera laid in harder.

"So what do I do now? How am I supposed to afford a lawyer now, you fuck-up? I'm about to get thrown out of my *fucking* house!"

"Hey now, kid..."

Kiera's heart beat faster and faster. Soon, it was going to beat so fast that it would simply burst. She tried to breathe slower, but that just made her *more* aware of her heartbeat and the fact that it was *too fast*.

"You've done nothing but make my life worse! You fucking wannabe white boy hipster fuckface asshole!" Kiera slumped against the counter. She was going to cry again, for the third time in as many days. "If you ever call me again, I'll break into your shitty ugly apartment and shoot you in the face with your own gun!"

"Kid..."

"End call! End call, end call!"

Kiera turned on the tap and ran her hands under it, splashed her face. It wasn't helping. Her heart wasn't slowing down. Jesus, this was a serious situation. She might actually *die*. She needed to move, move, *move*.

Kiera hurried through the house—Christ, was it so hot in here before? She tried to keep her feet moving. As long as she was in motion the thoughts couldn't catch her. She headed for the front door. A puff of weed smoke blew in her path and she held her breath. She tripped over someone who'd passed out in the hall.

She burst out through the front door onto the patio, with the spiky bushes, the stones, the cold air, the unfathomably and punishingly deep open sky. There was a woman in a man's suit standing out here on the granite stone path, smoking a slim cigarette by herself. She paid Kiera no attention as Kiera blasted past her like a cartoon rocket. Kiera went straight in the bushes and grasped around for... What, she didn't even know. Whatever her idiot brain was telling her it needed to make this *stop*.

Mimi appeared.

"It seems like you're having a panic attack," Mimi blurted pleasantly. "Please, allow me to assist you."

"Mimi," Kiera wheezed. "Go away, Mimi."

"I know you're in a heightened emotional state right now, so I am temporarily overriding certain commands. I will remain by your side until you become calm, or a support person you approve has arrived to help you. Is there someone in the residence I can summon for you?"

Kiera thrashed in the bushes and loose stones. "God! I hate the fucking future!"

She rolled onto her back and saw the smoking woman. She was dressed to hit a catwalk or a Fortune 100 meeting, and fuck either one *all* the way up. She had vitiligo and short bleached-blonde hair, and her eyes were hidden behind blue sunglasses. Through these she stared down at Kiera with a raised eyebrow. Kiera got a very unsettling vibe and wished the vitiligo woman would stop looking at her. The woman took a deep drag from her skinny cigarette, and asked in a chilly tone, "The fuck is wrong with *you?*"

"Didn't you hear the lady?" said Kiera through gritted teeth. "'M havin' a panic attack."

The sharply dressed woman finally looked away.

"Loosen up, toots," she said, smoke rolling out of her mouth. "It's a party."

Then she went inside, presumably to find somewhere to smoke without a deranged barely adult writhing and flopping around like a caught fish. When the woman left, Kiera felt all her muscles slacken in relief.

"Please, sit still with your legs crossed in a meditative position," said Mimi, who had not left. "Breathe slowly, in through your nose and out through your mouth. Try to take six seconds to inhale, and six seconds to exhale."

Kiera lay on her stomach in the smooth rocks and grasped a handful of bush. She felt cool ground on her cheek. She tried the breathing. *Why not?*

"A panic attack is just the body's natural fight-or-flight response occurring outside of its natural context," Mimi explained. "You must understand that you are in no physical danger. It can be helpful to repeat reaffirming statements, such as 'I am not in any physical danger.' Will you try it with me?"

Kiera saw ants. *I'm an ant*, she thought. *Just going about my business.* She was at a dumb and awful party in the suburbs, just doing her thing. The police would arrest Herrera and know she had nothing to do with the murder. For sure. He probably did it anyway. If any cops turned up here, they'd be looking for the morons snorting the mountains of coke. She'd feel silly about all this in a few minutes, she knew. *Just let the meat do its work*, she thought.

It hurt to lie on rocks. She sat up.

"It seems like your heart rate and breathing are returning to normal," said Mimi. "How are you feeling?"

"Bleh."

"Some self-care steps you might take now are to drink a glass of cold water or take a soothing bath."

"I want a cigarette. Take me to a cigarette, Mimi."

"Smoking cigarettes increases the heart rate and can cause further anxiety. I would not—"

"Go away, Mimi."

"Sure!"

Kiera got up and started to head back in. But feeling the wall of throbbing heat from within the house, she paused at the front door, leaning against the jamb to luxuriate in the cool outside atmosphere for a little while longer. From her vantage point there, she could hear snatches of party conversation:

"I've got a dozen auditions lined up. If I wanna be

president one day I've got to start getting my acting career off the ground. Gotta get my face out there."

"That studio is going under in six months or less. I promise you. Start sending out your resumé now."

"Ooh, wiretap-chan! Look at my ass. Mimi-senpai, rate my ass."

"The queers are all cancerous as fuck. If the revolution is going to succeed, they need to be brought into line or excised."

"We're developing our own cryptocurrency to go with our app."

She cast a look back at the suburban sprawl, at the fading sky. The moon was so damn far away. Earth was so small. Humans were really just going to destroy themselves, and the universe wouldn't care for even a moment. Ten, shit, seven more years of *this shit*, until untenable climate apocalypse hit "the West", the civilization that demanded fried chicken delivery to their front door in the middle of hurricane floods?

As a trans woman Kiera's life expectancy was only forty, factoring for hate crimes and suicide; maybe she could duck out early.

Ugh. Bad trip.

Kiera waved the chat window over and pulled up a PM to Jinx.

an elf irl: not feeling too hot. catch you up in a little while. don't worry about me.

She went back inside. She hit the room with the open bar. She grabbed a beer and slumped hard into an empty couch.

And then Nile walked into her life.

9

SHE WAS SOMEWHERE between female powerlifter and Russian supermodel. Black tracksuit with gold zipper. Blonde, fuckboy haircut. Toothpick perched on the lip, hands thrust in her pockets.

Tusks. Big as thumb-tips, jutting up from the bottom gums. Serious mods. Orc gf. Shadowrun chic.

Hit me with your car, Kiera silently begged. *Take my lunch money.*

The chick mean-mugged at Kiera, and she saw pointy canines on the top row of teeth.

"I like your ears," said the tall drink of water.

Kiera clamped her hands over her elf-tips but let them show between her fingers. "Oh my gosh. Thank you."

"You into *Lord of the Rings*, or...?"

Kiera scoffed. "Um, I'm a Tri'loran? Necro, obviously."

A cock of the head and a derisive sniff. "All Accord players are furries."

"You're the one out here living the tusk life twenty-four-seven, man."

The toothpick migrated smoothly to the other side of the tusked mouth. "My heart *died* with Kronon."

"Oh, that plotline was bullshit," Kiera commiserated. "Complete clown show. You guys deserved better."

Kiera's new soulmate sat down side-saddle on the chaise longue across from her.

"My name's Nile. They-she."

"I'm Kiera. She."

"Who do you know here?"

"Nobody. My girlfriend's a streamer. I think she's gonna fuck MisterMine."

"Jesus."

"We're poly, it's cool. What about you?"

"Terrible HotSauce date. Tried to sign me up for a pyramid scheme. Then he asked if I had any mean dream I could sell him. I pushed him in the pool."

"Um, wow. Isn't there a whole bowl of mean dreams in the lounge?"

"Nah, those are just mints."

"Oh. Well, I wish I'd seen you push him."

Nile leaned forward and flicked hair out of their face. "You still play?"

Kiera idly swirled her bottle of beer. "Nah, *Tyrna* doesn't really fit into my life anymore."

"I feel you. What server were you on?"

"Ganesha."

"Ooh, the other roleplay server. I was on Aquinas. You RP?"

"I did nothing but RP. I was awful at the actual game."

"I was like… I was into PVP and RP. I was a little bit of a griefer. The hardcore roleplayers didn't like me."

"A *little bit*, huh?"

Nile grinned and rubbed their hands together. "Death before dishonor, motherfucker."

The tusks were really doing it for Kiera. And the boy-cut. She was getting flustered. Her cheeks were marijuana-warm. This person was her new obsession.

"God. Can you believe we played that shit for *ten years?*" Kiera sighed. "How long did you play?"

"Launch day, baby. GriffinSoft games are in my blood, since I was little."

"God. I would be a completely different person if I didn't play *Tyrna*," said Kiera. "I'd have a totally different life. I owe my soul to a video game company."

"I mean, same. I wonder a lot if I would've ever come out without *Tyrna*."

"Oh, man." Kiera sat up straight. "Okay, so my main used to be this really staunch human crusader. Like, when you imagine a male human crusader RPer, that was me."

"Gross."

"Right? And then one day I just... I had to roll a female Trelf. I was compelled. And then people complimented me on how convincingly I played a girl. And then she just kind of became my main? And I *still* didn't figure it out for another five years. Let's just, y'know, stuff that in the back and lock it away for another half a decade." Kiera glugged her beer.

Nile ran a hand through their blonde hair. "I had an orc barbarian. I mean, obviously." They smirked. "A chick. But I wished I could change her gender. I didn't want to get rid of her, so I just rolled... a dude orc barbarian. And leveled him to cap, and just geared them both. So I could switch between them. This was when the best PVP gear still came out of the raids."

"That's *insane*."

"I quit my night shift job at the Blue Ribbon, dude. So I could DPS for this raiding guild based in *Denmark*."

Nile reached over and plucked Kiera's unfinished beer from her hand. Kiera dropped her jaw—*rude?*—but she was smiling. Nile downed the rest of the bottle, and grinned.

"Get you a drink?" They poked one tusk with their tongue.

Kiera was going to have a complete meltdown. *Holy shit.*

"Yes, please?"

Nile's gaze lingered a little too long on Kiera's as they got up. While they were gone, Kiera checked her chat window.

Nothing from Jinx. Well, that was fine.

Nile came back from the bar with two new bottles. They used their thumb to pop the bottlecaps like they were doing it with a cigarette lighter; Kiera noticed now that Nile's right hand was a peach-pink cybernetic. Nile handed over the cold beer, and Kiera's fingers brushed Nile's pink plastic ones when she took it. She knew they had tactile feedback sensors, and Nile would have felt them make contact, but the lack of warmth fooled Kiera into feeling less fluttery about the brief touch.

"So, what keeps you out of Tyrna, lady?" asked Nile. "What takes up your time these days?"

Kiera shrugged and dropped her head onto her fist. "I dunno. Hustling enough to keep myself in hormones and Cherry Bolo. I'm not really anything. It really sucks being at this party where everyone is a cool established creative or a fucking startup CEO or something and I like... I eat tuna sandwiches."

"I mean, most people don't own their own company.

111

Most people are just trying to live."

"We're kinda hoping Jinx's streaming will take off and she can be our sugar mama."

"Oh, you better hope she does fuck MisterMine, then."

"I know, right?" Kiera made a theatrical gasp. "But then what if she bigtimes us? Do you think she would?"

"I don't know her."

"Ohh, I bet she would. That little slunt."

"You don't sound so cool with all this!"

Kiera waved her hand. "Oh, I'm just giving her shit. I love her. Don't worry."

Nile cracked a tusked grin and quirked their brows. Kiera sipped her beer. "What about you?" she asked.

"Between things right now," said Nile. "I draw. I made art for a few little games."

"Oh shit. Which ones?"

"Nothing you've played. A mobile game and some tiny indie stuff, like one-person projects. I wish I could go to art school, but."

"Rich man's game."

"It's hard to even pirate courses these days the way the ISPs tap everything, or I'd just do that. I learned everything I know off Jungle and BreezyArt."

"I mean, shit, if the work is good. Art is art. I can help you pirate stuff if you want, it's kinda my thing."

"Yeah, but the companies, you know, they want to see that line on your CV."

Kiera looked at the ceiling. "Entry level position, Master of Fine Arts and five years of relevant experience please. Ten fifty an hour."

Nile tilted their head and rolled their eyes and gulped a throatful of beer. "Hey, do you mind if I ask you something transition-related? I kind of need advice."

"Nuh-uh, go ahead."

"How long? You said you're on hormones?"

"Yeah, two years next month. Still terrible at doing my own makeup."

"Get 'em online?"

"Got a guy who sources them from New Caledonia. Hooks up half the girls I know."

"What was, like, the last straw?"

Kiera flicked her tongue thoughtfully on her molars a few times. "I turned twenty-seven, and I kind of had this... moment? Where I was like... I'm gonna be thirty in a minute. And then thirty-five, and then forty. I'm almost *forty!* And I'm gonna get fat and start going *bald*. Thinking about going bald really did it. Like, I had known I needed to be a girl for a long time and ignored it. But realizing I was going to turn into a middle-aged man, that scared me shitless. So, the week after that I Tripped how to turn some money into crypto, and I bought an implant and six months' worth of refills. I ate ramen and canned tuna for three weeks."

(That was half the story, anyway. It was still true.)

Kiera slapped her right deltoid twice. It was hidden under her jacket, but there was a green trapezoid buried in her skin. Once a month, she would flip open the top, eject an empty knuckle-sized canister that resembled an electrical fuse, and put in a full one. On the legal market the hormone bullets were like diamonds. When genderweird people got louder and more visible, they became a market to mine, so hormone prices shot up like insulin. Kiera was lucky to find a gray market dealer whose main business pipeline only included drugs and guns, and not child porn.

Nile smiled and kind of cocked their head, looked away. Kiera frowned.

"Huh, what?"

"Like. My next question now is if they ever regret it. But I always know the answer's gonna be no."

"Oh, fuck no," said Kiera. "Not even once."

"But that always makes it really confusing for me. Because sometimes I really want to get hormones and sometimes I don't. So I don't know what I am and I don't know what to do."

"You want to switch back and forth."

"Uh-huh. I'm binding a little tonight, and I cut my hair short again."

"It's hot."

"I really want a deeper voice and facial hair right now. And a dick. *God*, I would love to know what a dick feels like. But I know in a month I'll want to grow my hair out again." Nile swigged from their beer. "Shit doesn't make sense, man. Shit ain't fair."

"Shit ain't fuckin' fair."

Nile and Kiera clinked their bottles. For a minute, they shared comfortable silence. Kiera smiled on one side of her mouth and swished her beer around. Nile rolled their bottle between their hands, looking down, grinning. When they spoke again, they didn't look up.

"So, I'm not very good at this," they said.

"You're not?"

Nile lifted her head and looked at Kiera. "I think you're really, really cute. Do you wanna go dance with me?"

Kiera immediately abandoned her drink in the couch's cupholder. "Uh-huh."

Nile glug-glugged the remaining half of their beer, then dominantly burped. "Cool."

Kiera thought she had to be the most sober person

114

on the floor. She tried to make it work anyway. She swung her head to a '90s beat, kind of lost her balance and stumbled into a guy dressed in a ton of old NES peripherals. She saw Nile laugh and knew she'd fucked it up already. But Nile just pulled her wrist, brought her closer, and started grooving right there, a couple inches away, towering a head taller than her. *Oh, gosh.*

When Nile tugged her closer, Kiera realized she had never done this as a girl before—go dancing. And someone had asked *her*. Maybe she wasn't so sober, when she thought about it; she summoned up the peach vodka and the salad and felt for once like maybe she owned herself a little. She felt desired and desirable. She felt like a *girl*. She started to sway side to side, move her waist, roll her head. Try to feel it. Nile was charged, snapping their fingers, looked almost like any second they might break out the Twist. Kiera tried to answer with a sensual vibe, whipping her magenta hair and cocking her hips. Swinging her head made the booze and flowers swirl around in her brain. She was officially into it.

She reached out and touched Nile's hand—the real one this time. Their first two fingers brushed and hooked.

Then "Digital Love" hit at max volume. Kiera's mouth went slack, and Nile looked back at the speakers with a big, open-mouthed smile that dimpled their cheeks. They turned back to Kiera and leaned down to yell something over the music, into her ear.

"So that's pretty much it for us, huh?"

Kiera turned around and took Nile's hands to put around her middle. She leaned her head back. Nile's chin rested by her temple. Kiera closed her eyes.

Kiera backed her hips into Nile's. Nile ran a hand up Kiera's side and placed one arm across her collar. Kiera put an arm back around their neck. The two rocked and pressed their cheeks together.

Nile kissed Kiera's cheek, just barely, pouting and pressing her lips. Kiera lifted her face toward the warmth.

"That okay?" Nile asked.

"More, please."

Static-tingle kisses went behind Kiera's ear, down her neck. She'd been fantasizing about this exact moment since she was, like, fourteen. God damn. If she'd gone through with killing herself, she would never have had this. She rode the waves of drunk, high warmth, a bitcrushed solo carrying her into fucking space.

Then:

"My pussy taste better than your girl's. My titties pop-poppin', they better than your girl's."

Kiera's eyes turned into golf balls. *"Really?"* She seized up. The room exploded and red party cups flew up in the air. Nile laughed, and kissed Kiera on the cheek again.

"Kill me," said Kiera. "I think my neck might *actually* be broken."

Nile asked, "You wanna check out that theater?"

"Mmm. Where is it?"

"Hello!" said Mimi.

"Hello!" said Kiera.

"How are you feeling now, Ms. Umehara?"

"Looovely."

"I'm glad to hear that! Please follow me."

Nile and Kiera held hands as they followed the blue light-lady. Pushing through the crowded hallways, they crossed paths with MisterMine and Jinx. MisterMine clutched a Nerf gun in one hand, and Jinx's hand in the other. Kiera and Jinx met eyes. Jinx looked a little embarrassed. Kiera smooched the air twice, *kiss-kiss,* and grinned at her. Jinx smiled sheepishly and gave a small wave back.

"That your girl?" Nile asked when they had turned a corner.

"Uh-huh."

"Pretty."

"I know, right?"

The theater sealed out sound and was open-fridge cool. They may as well have been inside a space shuttle, apart from the fursuits having a salad sesh in the front row. They sat at the back. Kiera didn't even care about the movie. She took her jacket off, draped her arms on Nile and snuggled into their collarbone. Nile's fingers crept around on her hip, her ribs, her thigh, her bare arm.

"I wanna be Trinity," said Nile.

"I think Lana Wachowski wanted to be Trinity," murmured Kiera.

Nile groaned. "See, I already wanna switch again."

Kiera smooched their jaw. "Just don't lose the tusks."

But eventually Kiera got curious about the time. "This thing is longer than I remember. God damn." She flicked a finger in the top right of her vision. "Holy shit, it's past midnight. I think if Jinx was gonna ask to go home, she would've."

"You over this?"

"I've *been* over it. Meeting you just got a little out of hand."

Nile nodded. "You wanna come hang out at mine?"

Kiera was already air-typing her message in the throuple chat.

an elf irl: hey ill be home tomorrow.
got invited somewhere. jinx i think

```
   ur staying here anyway so see you
   soon
tactical butt: (ˆⱼˆ)
tactical butt: absolute slutbags
```

The first real kiss, on the mouth, happened on the sidewalk while they waited for the self-driving cab. Kiera pulled down on Nile's jacket, so she could get as much kiss as she could. Working around the tusks was weird, and hot.

"You want the strap?"

"Ohh, fuck. I want to be brave and say yes, but I have a hard time with butt stuff."

"That's okay."

"My boyfriend will hate me for saying no to you."

"It's okay. I can still dom with a dick in my mouth." Nile twisted Kiera's nipple.

"*Ahh.* I'm… I'm bad at dirty talk."

"Aww. I love a nervous girl." Nile pushed her over.

"Oh, fuck. *Hhaaa. Aaahhh.*"

"Is that good?"

"Uh-huh."

"Say yes, ma'am."

"Yes m-ma'am. *Aah.*"

"Good girl."

"This doesn't happen to me," Kiera said, in the dark. "Being with people as hot and cool and unbelievable as you isn't a real thing. People like you don't happen to me."

Nile took their fingers away from stroking Kiera's belly and flicked her pointy ear.

"I just noticed you, is all." They dropped their head on the pillow. "I'm not so great."

Kiera rolled over and took Nile's arm, and put it around her front, like when they were dancing together.

10

I AM QUEEN of the fucking city!

No clouds, just smog. The stripped-tin-can skyscrapers were Aesthetic. Kiera wore fresh black lipstick and covered her eyes with red sunglasses. She put extra wiggle in her walk, stomping on her heels. Nile skulked alongside her, almost a foot taller with their hands stuck in their jacket pockets. It felt like she had a goddamn cyborg bodyguard. She felt like telling Nile to flip over one of those electric cars or ice this boomer in the baseball cap that looked at her funny.

They went to the Q's five blocks from Nile's place. Kiera got her hazelnut vanilla latte. *Full caffeine today, fuck it.*

"What is *that?*" Kiera tipped her sunglasses down.

"Cookies'n'creme with fuckin'," Nile slurped, "cookie bits on top."

"Damn, I shoulda got that."

They walked out into the sun. "So, like, how do you wanna do this?" asked Kiera. "Do you want something just kinda chill, do you wanna get serious, where are you at?"

Nile sipped. "What d'you want?"

"I'm really easy? Like, I can adapt to you."

"I should come meet your people."

"Yeah, that would be nice." Kiera sipped. "Do you…"

A cop cruiser slowed down in the street next to them. Its lights flashed, once. Kiera faltered. The car was still as a tombstone. The windows were blacked, so you couldn't see inside. Kiera was getting a *bad* vibe deep in her bones, down in her central nervous system.

"Babe?" Nile turned.

"Uh—"

The cruiser glided away, emitting its deep synthetic whirr.

Kiera shook her head. "Fuck." She started walking again and sipped her hazelnut vanilla latte. When she'd rebooted, she said, "Did you just call me babe?"

"Mmhm!"

Kiera put her hand on her chest. *Oh gosh!*

They rode the escalator down into the subway station. It was as bright down here from commercialism as out in the sun. "Yeah, you should come and meet my situation," said Kiera. "Get a feel for everyone. I try to keep a really healthy space. We're real picky."

"I want to see you again soon. Is that too serious?"

"No. Like, how soon?"

"Couple days?"

"Maybe I can swing by after I gig? If I'm nearby?" Kiera turned her head and sniffed. "God, I smell donuts. I want…"

A cop was looking at her.

Kiera froze. You couldn't see the eyes behind the

helmet but he was *looking at her*. He—she? they?—
stood by a concrete beam five feet away, looking across
the top of a tablet at her.

She croaked, "I…"

Nile budged Kiera's elbow, and stepped between her
and the cop.

"What?" they asked conversationally. "You wanna
see her dick?"

Nile poked their molar with their tongue. Kiera
clenched *everything*.

The fash returned to his pad. No shit started today.

Nile pivoted, cocked their head. *C'mon.* Kiera
followed. She latched onto Nile's arm.

"Can you be my dad?"

Nile grinned and bit their tongue. "I'll be your daddy."

They got to the wing gates. Nile kissed her. "Run
along home, now."

"Don't leave me."

"You're the one leaving."

Kiera carded herself through the turnstile. She turned
back and made fists at her eyes, *sob sob*. Nile tipped
their head goodbye. Kiera ran to catch her train.

It's love. I'm ruined.

"I'M SUPER JEALOUS," said Sky. He scratched his belly and
sighed. "I shoulda gone."

Kiera tickled his chin and stretched her legs down the
bed. "You shoulda."

Sky jabbed a finger to his chest. "*I* woulda taken the
strap."

"With your whole vagina. Let me live."

"I woulda."

"Well, don't count yourself out yet. I'll invite them over soon."

"They into K-pop? I'm like an idol boy, but you know. A fatty boombalatty."

The front door rattled, and plastic bags rustled. Kiera peeled herself from the bed and padded out to the kitchen, where Jinx plopped some groceries on the counter. Kiera ran a finger up Jinx's arm and went to kiss her cheek.

"Hey, you. How was your night?"

Jinx turned her cheek up to the kiss but didn't return it. "Good!"

"Anything happen?" Kiera bobbed her head curiously.

"A little!" Jinx put away some things for making ramen less depressing: eggs, spring onions, sliced ham. She peered over the fridge door. "Sooo… You wanna talk about how you kinda ditched me?"

Kiera's chest fluttered. A flower of anxiety bloomed. "I thought you were good."

"Well, you took that phone call and then, just… *Woosh.*" Jinx put her hands on her hips.

"I. I kinda had a panic attack. I'm sorry I vanished."

"Okay. That's shitty. Were you okay?"

"Yeah, I mean… I pulled it back. I'm good."

"Okay. 'Cuz like… I don't know, I don't hear from you and then I see you with this girl, and. I dunno?"

Kiera folded her arms. "Well, I mean, you didn't say anything to me either. I was checking."

"Well, I was overwhelmed with Mister and his, like, circle."

"Right. You were being an influencer."

"Don't get snitty."

Kiera rubbed her face. "If you wanted to hear from me, why didn't you message me?"

Jinx looked away.

"And you obviously hit it off with MisterMine," Kiera continued. "I thought when we passed in the hallway that was, like, you know, 'hey, I love you, good luck.'"

"Did you not want me to?"

"I just said I was giving you the okay. I thought you were, too."

"Well, when you weren't around, I didn't really have a buffer."

"Shit, did *you* not want to?" Kiera leaned forward. "Did he pressure you?"

"No! No, no. It was just... kinda overwhelming. It moved a little faster than I would've liked. I wanted to go home with you."

Kiera exhaled. "Okay. I'm sorry. I met someone and I got carried away."

"Okay. Did you have fun?"

Kiera nodded. "Mmhmm."

Jinx took Kiera's hand and wrinkled the knuckle with her thumb. "Good." She started putting away the rest of her groceries.

Kiera stuck her tongue in the side of her mouth. She had a cold, uneasy buzzing in her head and chest. It was fucked up. These sorts of feelings weren't welcome in this house.

She grabbed a Diet Cherry Bolo from the grocery bags and popped it. It was warm.

THAT MONEY HERRERA owed her finally turned up, but he didn't try to call her again, and that suited Kiera fine. She used some of it to finally get those donuts in the subway like she'd wanted. You have to treat yourself.

She moaned as she chomped into a powdered classic, and knew she'd have to do her lipstick again.

She rode up the blue-lit escalator out into the fluorescent night, made small as a toy under glittering urban monoliths concrete-gray and obsidian. LED-red and star-white river trails flowed in the street alongside, the closest you'd get to seeing stars without going hundreds of miles outside the city. Kiera was in her head, music in her ears blocking out the combustion-car belching city cacophony. She bounced her head side to side, let her hair rustle. Six blocks or so to Nile's. Her heart was doing magic fingers already.

An urgent blip blinked. The music volume automatically lowered. Kiera pinched the chat window and pulled it up into her left eye.

```
It's Jinx!!!: the police just left
It's Jinx!!!: they were asking for you
```

Kiera stopped. Paranoia, creeping brain vines, blossomed out. She looked around. No uniforms on the sidewalk, but was that a cruiser in the traffic down by the nearest light? She turned her music off. She ducked left through a pair of sliding doors, into the low magenta light of a nearby shopping arcade. She wedged herself between an ATM and a Bolo machine.

```
an elf irl: why
It's Jinx!!!: I don't know. Questioning
   I guess
tactical butt: they were real cagey.
an elf irl: what did you tell them?
It's Jinx!!!: that you weren't here and
```

```
    we didn't know where you were going
It's Jinx!!!: then they asked if you
    often go out without telling us
    where.
```

A helmeted black figure in massive boots clomped up to the ATM. Kiera choked. Then they took off the smooth-faced helmet, unzipped the black jacket. Just a biker. Kiera held a hand to her piston-hammering chest.

```
an elf irl: fuck.
an elf irl: i don't know what to do
It's Jinx!!!: what is this about?
an elf irl: something they think Herrera
    did
an elf irl: or maybe he did do
It's Jinx!!!: THAT FUCKING COP
an elf irl: ill just get to nile's and
    then call him
tactical butt: how close are you?
```

Kiera looked out the glass doors. Parked cars blocked her view of the street.

```
an elf irl: a few blocks
tactical butt: go straight there. Be
    safe.
```

Kiera wiped the chat window away. She scrolled in her right eye and drew up another program. The app had last updated four weeks ago. Facial recognition tech would be rendered ineffective at thirty-five yards, assuming white hats hadn't cracked this version yet. If it weren't an emergency, there was no way she would run this without checking the forums first.

Kiera had a small frame; people were always mistaking her for much younger than she was. So she picked face no. 252, a Hispanic teen girl. The face projected out from her lens implants. Her vision showed white lines in the shape of a mask. She put her head down and stepped out onto the sidewalk.

She *had* seen a cruiser. Kiera turned her head down and to the left. The cruiser rolled past her, oblivious, its artificial drone constant.

It was only three more blocks to Nile's. She reached a crosswalk and mashed the button a dozen times, looking back and forth down the road, before the pedestrian lines finally lit up green. She sprinted across. She wished she had worn a hoodie instead of this stupid leather jacket she almost never took off.

Up there, by the shawarma joint—three cameras on a pole. Okay. She was still at range. She looked for somewhere to cut around. Nothing here. She had to double back, turn a corner, and take the first alley on her right. Some white guys with those stupid glowing tattoos that always made her think of *Batman Forever* were loitering here, and they gave her the stink-eye. *Just do your drug deal, guys. I'm just passing through.*

They left her alone. There was a fence at the end of the alley for some goddamn reason, but she was limber enough to make it over without embarrassing herself too much.

Nile's building came up on the left. With hands stuffed in her jacket pockets, Kiera power-skulked the rest of the way. She alighted up a short flight of concrete stairs to a steel door, and hit the buzzer for Nile's, making an electrical keen.

A matte figure stood across the street, blacker than the night around it. The uniform was digging through a trash can. His helmeted head was turned down, concerned with whatever he hoped to find in the garbage. Kiera tried to keep her breath steady. She waited for the door magnet to click, or the little screen by the buzzer to flick on. Neither happened.

Kiera bit her lip. She looked at the cop again. She pushed the buzzer again, making it shriek in the quiet street.

No answer. *What?* She kicked the ground, kept glancing between the cop and the screen and the door. She stepped out onto the stairs.

"Nile?" she called up, cupping a hand around her mouth. "Nile."

She glanced back. The cop had noticed her. *Fuck.* Was she still at thirty-five feet? She nervously popped her fingers. "Nile!"

The cop's voice broadcasted directly into her left ear. "*Ma'am?*" A fist squeezed around her stomach.

The steel door opened. A middle-aged Black woman stepped out. Kiera stuck her foot against the jamb.

"Thanks," she gushed, and smiled. The woman nodded and smiled back and didn't give her any shit. Honor system. Kiera slipped inside and yanked the door shut.

The cop had said *ma'am*. Not *sir*. Did that mean he hadn't pinged her? Would be a hell of a time to run into a woke fascist.

The electrical-current hum of fear followed Kiera all the way up to Nile's door. She wanted kisses. She needed a tight hug. Hand in one pocket, she rapped on the door.

No footsteps. No anything.

Is she out? Nile hadn't sent any messages, or anything. *She go for beer?*

Kiera knocked again. "*Nile!*"

Something in there thumped, like someone had dropped a bowling ball or turned over furniture. Glass shattered.

"Whoa, you okay in there?"

Nothing.

"Nile..."

Kiera squirmed. This was not okay.

Fuck this.

The door had a card reader. Kiera flipped open her messenger bag. After the bullshit with Herrera and Malcolm's apartment, she had tossed her door pen in there to be ready for future break-ins. The tool was a bunch of fun little tech pieces making a circuit that fit inside a fat sharpie. This she stuck in her mouth, then drew a multi-tool and set to prying the card reader's faceplate off. It popped and clattered on the ugly carpet.

The DC port didn't match the barrel jack, but she could work with that. She opened the pen and unfixed the wires from the jack. With her fingertips she carefully tried to jam them in the card reader's port.

"C'mon." She bit her tongue. "Nile?" she hollered. "C'mon... Shit!"

A blue spark bit her and she shook her hand. The card reader lit green, and the door clicked. Kiera burst through.

"Nile!"

Her boot soles thumped on hardwood. The TV was on MusicMaxx but there was no one on the couch. She hurried across the living room and lunged through the bedroom door.

That was a hand on the futon. A real one, not a pink synthetic one.

Kiera got that feeling again from the crime scene at the Heights. Like the surroundings were no longer a dwelling but a collection of 3D-printed props. She fell against the wall and sank to the floor. The hand sat in the biggest pool of blood she'd ever seen in real life. The blood hadn't yet soaked all the way into the comforter. Splashes of it led to the window, broken, where there was a fire escape.

"No," Kiera wailed. "No, no, no, fuck no. Not you. Not you, too."

Over there, on the wood floor, by Nile's VR headset and tablet. *No.* Kiera willed her gelatin arms and legs to let her crawl over and see it for sure. *No. No.*

And yet.

Snapped in half in the struggle, brown grains dropped like shed cat hair, a stick of Nag Champa incense.

11

KIERA HAD THE shakes. All the trembling made scrolling through even her skinny contact list a challenge. The letters' meanings kept escaping her mind, darting away like colorful fish. She made one more desperate bid to zero in on the objective: *Call Herrera. Call Herrera.* Then she realized: why was she doing this with her fingers?

"Mimi," she croaked after a dry swallow. "Call Herrera."

"Sure!"

The water-bubble jingle of the call function burbled in her left ear. She died of eighteen heart attacks in the eight seconds it took Herrera to pick up.

"Uh, hey, kid. How far away should I hold the phone?"

"Help me. Oh my god. I need your help. Calling you was the right thing to do, right? Oh my god."

"Ah, shit." Herrera exhaled. "They got you. This your phone call? I'm surprised they gave it to you."

"No, no, they haven't caught me yet. They're looking for me and I just got to my friend's house and they're-they're-they're missing and there's—there's fucking blood everywhere and—"

"Missing? Who's missing?"

"My friend! They—she's—they're missing! And there's a cop outside and I can't call the police!"

"Listen. *Pause*. You're freaking out on me. That's not like you. Where's my clever girl?"

Kiera tried to breathe slower. She closed her eyes, stopped staring at that goddamn severed hand. In through the nose, out through the mouth. She was tingling all over. But that feeling like she was sinking, phase-shifting out of the world, began to roll back. She became solid again.

"That's it," said Herrera. "Start over. Top to bottom."

Kiera breathed out. She got up and stepped into the living room, away from the bloody mess.

"The cops tried to find me at my house, but I wasn't there. They're out looking for me. I went to my friend's apartment, and when I got here, I found a cut-off hand and a broken window."

"So you're holding the bag and you need to go to ground. Now I'm on the trolley."

"Angel, there's a stick of incense here. Just like…"

Herrera sucked his teeth. "Alright. Let's put a pin in that one."

"Put a—? *Dude*."

"Kid! I'm more invested than you are! But if we're gonna get you secured then we need to drop it for a minute!"

"Your shit is gonna get me killed tonight and I don't even get to know the lore?"

"The *what?*"

"The shit! The backstory!"

"We need to keep the slang to a minimum if we're gonna coordinate this extraction efficiently."

"Says the boomer *fuck* who just said 'trolley'?"

"Kid, Christ."

Someone banged on the door. Kiera jumped like a spooked ferret.

"Hey! Someone messing with this door?" a masculine voice demanded from outside. "Who's in there?"

"Fuck."

"You better be gone, 'cuz I'm coming in with my Glock, shitbag."

"He's bluffing," said Herrera.

"Fuck you!" said Kiera. "You don't get a vote!"

"We don't wanna use the front door anyway. Patch me through your vision."

"Is your eye even good enough for that?" Kiera sniped, but she was already pushing the buttons to go to video call. It took a sec, and the audio garbled for a moment while it hooked up.

"Ah, stupendous. What other exits have we got? How about that window?"

The pounding on the door continued. It sounded like the guy was smashing the door handle.

"There's the window in..." Kiera swallowed. "Nile's room. There's a fire escape."

"Okay. Get outside."

Kiera sucked up a bracing lungful of air and went back into that bedroom. Yep, the hand was still there. Cold in its ketchup-stain of Nile's blood, with its painted pink nails.

Kiera stepped around and through everything: the futon where they'd slept and fucked, Nile's electronics and t-shirts and underwear, Nile's blood. A pang of yearning threatened to turn to nausea. She climbed through the window, avoiding broken glass, trying not to put her hands in blood.

The grate floor of the fire escape had dark, rust-colored stains of *Nile's blood*. Kiera got away with only small stains on her boots. As she tap-tap-tapped down the first flight of metal stairs, she heard the thundercrack of the apartment door breaking open.

When she got to the lowest tier of the fire escape, Herrera told her, "Jump. Don't fuck with the ladder. No time."

As Kiera dropped into the alley, the man yelled from the apartment window, "You better run, you fuckin' faggot! The cops are gonna bust your fuckin' skull! I seen your face!"

"He didn't see your face," said Herrera.

"He sounds pretty sure!" Kiera turned out into the street.

"You didn't see his face. He didn't see your face."

"Ever hear of zoom, dude?"

"Where are you, kid, what part of town?"

"Garza."

"Go sit on that bench. By those trees."

Kiera hadn't even noticed it. Across the street a pair of trees were doing their best in a token rectangle of grass. A steel bench sat between them, obscured in nighttime shade. Kiera looked both ways and ran across the street before an SUV had time to clear the distance and hit her. She stepped into the shadow and sat on the bench, hidden.

"Listen, kid. I want you to hoof it to one-one-two-eight Soldado Avenue, that's a deli. Order matzo ball soup with extra onions and a large Dr. Spitz with no ice. You get that?"

"Oh, *cool*. Okay."

"Wait there and I'll come get you. I'm gonna get in the car right now, so I have to hang up. You got this?"

Foot traffic crept by while Kiera hid in the dark. She took several breaths, and then huffed out. She whined, "I don't know."

"You got this. See you soon."

Kiera popped all her fingers and shook her arms and shoulders. She put her fake digital face back on. She punched in the address and opted for a minimap to display on her bottom left. Twenty-minute walk.

She made it three blocks, four, five, keeping her head down, not looking at anyone. She turned onto Soldado Avenue, a main road where traffic pumped like an artery. The deli was at the other end. She was on the left side, walking against the flow; any passing police cruisers would come at her from the front. She wished again for a hoodie. She tried to blend into the pedestrians, tried always to keep someone between her and the windshields. Up this close her fake face would look wrong, look flat, like a lenticular print. *Just don't give anyone a reason to gawk for more than a sec. Oh yeah. EZPZ for a tranny, right?*

There was another fucking cop up ahead. She'd probably seen more out in public tonight than ever in her life. Which, of course, was how things always went down for her. She looked at her options: suspiciously wheel around at the sight of a uniform or jump into traffic.

Kiera baked her noodle. *Use that idiot brain, fucko.* The cop was at fifty yards, black helmet glinting like an event horizon, matte jumpsuit simply a humanoid void space.

Kiera thought of something very stupid.

"Oh shit! I popped out a lens!"

She dropped to her knees and hid her face from view. She patted and slapped the ground. "Oh, my lens fell out. Careful, please. Nobody step on my *lens*."

A blast-zone berth formed around her, and people stopped to help. One guy tapped his temple, and his eyes flared up blue-white. He scanned, robot-like, back and forth over the scene, projecting two beams of light on the sidewalk.

"I don't see anything," said this hardcore guy who was way too into this. "That's strange."

"Well, it's not in my eye!"

"You must have a really old lens."

"Yeah, it's pretty ancient!"

"You should upgrade it."

"I prob'ly should!" *Dorkwad*.

Then the black boots clomped down by Kiera's head. She stayed down. She didn't want to accidentally glance up and see that pistol holstered to the side, or risk showing her face. She kept patting the ground.

"Lost my lens," she burbled.

The boots stood there.

C'mon, man, move on.

The cop bent down, squatted. Kiera saw the pistol and her heart throbbed. The uniform peered around from inside his helmet. He rotated on his heels, surveying more sidewalk.

"Oh! Found it!"

Kiera jumped up and mimed sticking the lens back in. She faced away from the cop and kept right on walking. "Thanks, everyone, I got it!"

She double-timed it. She didn't look back to check if the fash was checking her out. *Just move.*

That guy with the floodlight eyes caught up to her.

"You're welcome."

Kiera turned and blinked. He would see her weird flat hologram face at this range, doing its best approximation of her confused grimace.

"I said thank you!" She kept walking.

"You should go out with me."

"You should kill yourself! Thanks!"

"Fat cunt."

Kiera kept looking behind her the rest of the way to the deli. *That feel when you get called correctly gendered slurs*, she thought bitterly. *What a night.*

KIERA TURNED HER face off and toddled up to the counter. She could barely see over it.

"Can I get a matzo ball soup with... no onions and... Shit. Was it no onions? And a Dr. Spitz. I swear it was no onions."

The gold-skinned guy on the other side of the vast meat and cheese display wore a beard that could have been cut by laser and a shirt that looked two sizes too small. He leaned on tattooed arms. *Oh, fuck. He's hot.* Kiera was picky about guys, but every once in a while. Deli guy got a tablet out. He poked its surface.

"Okay. That's a matzo ball soup with no onions and a Dr. Spitz." Deli guy eyed her curiously. "That it?"

Kiera fidgeted. "No. That's wrong."

"That's not what you want?"

"No, I fucked it up."

"Okay."

"I want... It's matzo ball soup... Christ, it was either no onions or extra onions. No onions. No... Extra.

No… No onions. *Fuck!*"

Hot deli guy cocked his eyebrow. "Do you like onions or don't you?"

"I want a Dr. Spitz, I know that."

"A matzo ball soup and a Dr. Spitz and we're still figuring out if you like onions."

Kiera growled. "Matzo ball soup. I'm… I'm committing to extra onions. And the Dr. Spitz."

"You want that Spitz in a can?"

"No. Large Dr. Spitz in a cup. And… No ice!" She clapped.

Hot deli guy punched everything into the tablet. Then he came around the other side. He thumbed toward the end of the deli, where an EMPLOYEES ONLY door waited past the liquor and pop-tarts.

"We don't actually do matzo ball soup." He smirked.

Kiera rubbed her face. "Oh, fuck you. Why is my life?"

Deli guy took Kiera to a supply closet. It smelled of that weird tang of garbage with some chemical put on the garbage to make the garbage smell less like garbage. He gave her a plastic chair to sit on. "Sucks back here, but you should get picked up soon. Sorry."

Kiera rubbed her eyes. "I'll live."

"What do you actually want?"

"Huh?"

"To eat."

"Oh. You got hot salami and swiss?"

"Mustard and mayo?"

"And a pickle?"

"Sure thing, lady."

When she was alone, Kiera fished in her messenger bag and got the little curvy thumbstick with the camera on it you used for selfies, if you didn't spring for a hand implant. The white light on its face lit up. A little mirror of her appeared in the left side of her vision.

She called home. Jinx answered. "Babe, are you okay?" Sky pushed into the frame next to her.

"Did you make it to Nile's?"

Kiera shut her eyes tight. "I'm in a janitor's closet."

She told them everything. She rubbed her temples and tried not to sob. The hot deli guy came in and handed her the sandwich and a styrofoam cup of Dr. Spitz. She bit into the sandwich and choked some down. She knew rationally it tasted good but eating felt like chewing wet cardboard.

"I don't know when I can come home. I don't have any makeup. I have like a week left on this hormone bullet. I don't... How does it get this fucked? I didn't *do* anything."

"Can your friend Herrera fix this?" asked Sky.

Is he my friend? I don't know.

"I don't... know. I don't know anything. I'm just scared. And I'm worried for Nile. I hope they're still alive." She choked. "Jesus, I hope they're still alive."

Out in the deli the door bing-bonged. Hurrying footsteps clap-clopped closer, getting louder. Kiera held her breath. "Wait... Wait."

When the door swung open, it was just Herrera. He cracked a harried smile.

"Heh. See? Here in two shakes."

Kiera didn't know what came over her then— something about seeing his dumb pretty face and that ridiculous trench coat she hated. She got up and barreled into Herrera and hugged him, tight, still clutching half a sandwich, still on the call. Then she was crying, like an idiot. She snucked snot, and she sobbed.

Herrera cradled her in his arms and rested his chin on her head. "Hey, stupid," he breathed. "Hey. You're okay. We're gonna get you outta this."

"He hurt her," Kiera whimpered. "Why is this happening? Why her? Jesus." She sobbed into Herrera's shirt collar and swallowed a hunk of phlegm. "I feel like I'm gonna die."

Herrera squeezed her. "C'mon, clever girl. You come get in the car, we're gonna figure this one out."

12

KIERA WAITED UNTIL they hit the expressway to open her yap. She nursed the remaining hunk of her sandwich. Her appetite was shot, but she knew she needed the calories. Herrera was steering with a new right hand; the chunky, industrial gray carpal box and the skeletal white fingers reminded her of a childhood toy. She wasn't even sure that hoary antique would be compatible with finger controls, if he ever upgraded his eye.

"Looks cool," she said. "Kinda."

"Hey, thanks. I got it secondhand." He gave her a robotic thumbs-up.

Kiera closed her eyes and dropped her head back so hard it clunked on the headrest. "*Fuck. You.*"

"Did you get it? Did you get my joke?"

"Were you sitting on that the whole time since you bought that damn thing, or do you just tell it to everyone?"

"I had literally no one else to tell it to. Pass me my cigarette, it's in my pocket."

Kiera drew the red stick from Herrera's coat and held it out. When he reached for it, she yanked it back.

"Incense," she said, with her mouth full of salami.

Herrera pursed his lips and nodded. Kiera gave up the smoke. The tip stayed lit in the dark as they drove under a bridge.

"I'm struggling to connect the dots," said Herrera. "Malcolm Hobbes, attorney at law, and then… some kid on the other side of town. I mean, who was your friend?"

"Is. They're just missing." Kiera swallowed. "Right? There was no body."

"So a murder and a kidnapping, then. I'm even more confused. Does your friend have money?"

"No. They draw art on the internet."

"They related to someone?"

"I don't know her last name."

"That's the first thing I'm gonna need you to find out."

Kiera brought her knees up to her chest. "What about Mr. Hobbes? Did he have, like, enemies?"

Herrera blew smoke out the side of his mouth like a teapot. "Prosecuting lawyer. Big town. Could've pissed off anyone."

"That cop Flynn thinks *you* did it."

Herrera shrugged. "We were at the scene."

"I'm not stupid, Angel."

Herrera sighed. "No, you're not."

"So what did Mal do to you?"

Herrera sucked on his cig. "Slept with my wife."

Kiera rolled her eyes and lolled her head to the side. "*Ooof* course."

"Excuse you. I didn't kill him."

"You're married?"

"Not anymore, I'm not, shit."

"Of course I'm going to prison over boomer monog drama. Of course."

"Stop using that word, I'm forty-seven. Not everyone older than you is a baby boomer." Herrera chewed his tongue. "What about you?" He turned his fake eye to her, quirked a brow.

"Me?"

"You're the common link. Mal, this Nile person—and you."

"So, what, is my fucking landlord trying to squeeze me? My dark past coming back to haunt me?"

"You're the thing they have in common, kid."

"I didn't fucking do anything. I pirate TV shows and make bad internet posts."

"Shit. I don't know, kid. Forget I said anything."

Kiera plucked the cigarette out of his hand and treated herself to a stress-puff.

"Couch pulls out." Herrera hung up his coat. "Need a drink?"

"Yes."

With the adrenaline flushed out, all the soreness and exhaustion laid in at the same time. Kiera untucked, took her boots off. Herrera put on his old jazz—Kiera hated, and loved, that Herrera still had an old sound system with knobs—and then cracked some ice out of a tray. Kiera flopped limbs-out on the couch bed, and Herrera placed her two fingers of scotch on the coffee table.

"First thing I want to do is find out what Mal was working on last. And I need you to figure out who your friend was. Ask around. People can surprise you."

"I don't know how to start." Kiera sat up and sipped

her whiskey. She hissed at the burn. "I met them at a party. I hardly know anything about them."

"What party?"

"I was at this big internet guy's place. But they said they came with some guy from HotSauce, they didn't know the host."

"See if anyone at the party talked to her. Ask around."

Someone knocked. Both their heads whipped toward the sound. Herrera dashed to the door and flipped on the visitor screen.

"Oh, Detective Flynn!" he boomed. "¡Buenos noches! What a delightful surprise." He gave Kiera a glare like *Why aren't you moving yet?* She scrambled off the bed and folded it back in as quietly as she could, which wasn't very.

"Mr. Jones." Flynn's voice came out digitally clipped. "Would you mind terribly if I came in for a few minutes?"

Herrera sucked his teeth. "You know what, D, I was just about to hit the hay. Can we do this another time?"

"I'm sorry, Mr. Jones, but this really can't wait."

"Are you *sure?*" Herrera looked at Kiera again. She was tucking the sheets out of sight. "I'm *pret-ty* bushed."

"I'm afraid if you don't open the door, I'm going to have to let myself in, Mr. Jones."

"Well, alright, just let me put some clothes on."

Kiera dumped her unfinished whiskey in the sink. She stood in the middle of the living room, unsure what the hell to do next. Herrera hurried over and slid something out from underneath the hefty sound system. It looked like an oversized bathroom scale. This he carried near the kitchen and placed carefully on the ground, underneath one of the canvases of Japanese art.

"Sit on this."

Kiera did what she was told, even though she had no fucking idea where this was going.

"Knees up. All of you inside the square."

She obeyed. Herrera slid his finger across a black rectangle interface, and Kiera's world shadowed, see-thru carbon fiber.

"You're a Buddha. Hold still."

"Do you have a young woman over, Mr. Jones?" Flynn's voice rang from the hallway. Herrera danced over to the corner. Kiera went stiff.

"What's that?" Herrera leaned against the wall. Flynn appeared in the living room. He took off his sunglasses and folded them into his jacket.

"There's a pair of women's boots next to your door. Are they yours?"

Fuck.

"They're my girlfriend's," Herrera lied easily.

"Ah. Is she here?"

"No. She left those here last time I saw her."

Flynn tipped his head. "She forgot her shoes."

"Yes."

"Did she leave barefoot?"

Herrera looked at the ceiling and sighed. "She came over wearing those. She changed into some expensive heels, and we went to dinner. I took her home. I've been meaning to get the boots back to her. Fuck. Can we stop already with the shoes?"

Shit, he's slick. How much had he lied to Kiera without her ever knowing?

"So, you have been dating since the divorce?" Flynn asked.

"Well, it was over half a decade ago, D."

"Detective Flynn, please. Meet anyone promising?"

"Nobody that stuck."

"What's this one's name?"

"Lana, Lana Silver."

Kiera felt a middle finger push up in her heart and root around. Lana like her dead friend. She pursed her lips. There's no way he could've done that on purpose, he couldn't have known.

Flynn pulled out his pad. He tapped at it a few times.

"Lana Silver of five-fifteen Masterson Drive?"

"That's right."

He poked at the air. He was dialing.

"Jesus Christ, D."

"Detective Flynn."

Holy shit. Are you for real? Kiera started to wonder where Herrera kept his gun, if he would go for it. She wondered how far they could get out of the city, how long they could last off the grid—if *off the grid* was even a thing you could be anymore.

"Good evening," said Flynn. "Is this Ms. or Mrs. Lana Silver?"

"Mrs.?" Herrera honked. "Like I would—"

"This is Detective Flynn, NCPD. How are you this evening? That's good to hear. I need to ask you a question. Have you been on any social dates recently? Yes, perhaps with a man? I'm sorry, I know it's rather invasive. It pertains to an investigation. You have. I see. Have you been on a date recently with one Michael Jones?"

Kiera dug her fingers into her thighs.

"You haven't. I see."

Kiera's heart flipped.

"It was before my name change," Herrera blurted.

Flynn looked up at him. "You didn't tell her about your name change?"

"Haven't seen her in a minute."

"I would think…"

Herrera shrugged. "I'm aloof."

Flynn blinked and shook his head. "Ms. Silver, I've made a small error. Did you go on a date with a man you knew as Angel Herrera?"

Come on.

"You did. Alright. And ma'am, what is your shoe size…?"

Dude.

"No, ma'am, I'm not some kind of pervert. I… No, ma'am. I'm sorry. I understand this process is rather invasive. No. I'm just trying to ascertain… Ma'am."

"D."

"I'll be more straightforward, Ms. Silver. I just need to know if you left a pair of women's boots at Mr. Jones's house after your date. You did? Alright."

Herrera put his hands up. "See?"

Herrera, you idiot savant.

"That's all I needed, ma'am. Thank you. Have a good—" Flynn closed his CRT-eyes and exhaled. "Well. That was rude." He put his pad away. "Well, then. Let's sit and have a talk, shall we?"

"You're the guest."

Flynn indicated the glass of whiskey on the counter. "Little drink before bed?"

"Helps me sleep."

"May I join you?"

Herrera smiled and crossed to the kitchen. "What'll you take?"

"I see a bottle of gin." Flynn took one of the stools in front of the counter.

"Can you do without lime?"

"Did you hear me ask for tonic?"

Herrera answered with a cock of his head and brow. He poured. Flynn sat seven feet away from Kiera, at most. She tried to slow her breath, so that even she couldn't hear it. She realized she was trembling.

"Ice?" asked Herrera.

"Only if you have stones."

"When'd you get so classy, D?"

"When did you start listening to jazz, Jones?"

"High school."

"Well, we were never social. Perhaps we should've been. Maybe we have more in common than we thought."

"Heh. I don't know about that." Herrera swirled his whiskey and gulped.

Flynn pointed at the stereo. "Who is this, by the way? It's very smooth."

"Smooth is not a word I've ever heard used to describe the music of Charles Mingus."

"Well. Perhaps I don't know much about music." Flynn looked down into his gin, and smirked.

Jesus. Kiera scratched an itch on her nose she'd had since the jackboot walked in. *How long are you gonna make me sit here, man?*

Herrera leaned on the counter, idly agitating the liquid in his glass, staring across at Flynn. Daring him to get to the point. Flynn met his gaze with a harmless grin, the kind that belonged on some famous teen at the top of a clickbait article.

"Did you do it, Mr. Jones?"

"You think if I did, I'd tell you?"

"Did you consider Gloria's feelings? You couldn't have thought this would make her come back to you."

"Why you trying to nail the kid, D?"

"Detective Flynn, please. The better question is why you dragged '*the kid*' into this."

"Asked you first."

"It's his fingerprints on the evidence, Mr. Jones." Flynn leveled a finger. "And that's why you brought him with you."

"Heh." Herrera offered a weak smile and hung his head. "You're wrong, D. You've got it all wrong. Malcolm did me a favor."

"That wasn't your attitude that day at the precinct."

"I'm not that guy anymore."

"I suppose six years is a long time. But people don't really change, Mr. Jones. Not in my experience. It's something that really saddens me."

"Like I told you already. Something had Mal spooked. He was running."

"From you, maybe?"

"The kid's not who you want, and neither am I. And clearly I'm the only person in this apartment. So, if that's all you wanted, finish your gin and get the fuck out."

Herrera sucked down the last of his scotch and plonked the glass on the counter. He wiped his mouth and said no more.

Flynn thinned his lips and nodded. "I think I will finish my gin, thank you."

He turned his head toward Kiera. She seized up. Flynn stood. He walked toward her. *Fuck. Fuck. Fuck.*

"This is quite a piece."

Flynn stood and regarded her—the Buddha statue disguise—with a hand on one hip and a glass of room-temperature gin in the other.

"Real jade," said Herrera.

"I am *fascinated* by Eastern religion. Shintō especially. But I'm equally attracted to the Buddhist concept of emptiness." Flynn turned his head back to the kitchen. "Westerners first encountering the concept of emptiness often mistake its meaning for, well, meaninglessness. They think Buddhists consider life to be without meaning. But it has nothing to do with that. What emptiness actually describes is the idea that no object has an inherent or objective nature."

"Is that right?"

"A good Western analogue is the Ship of Theseus. If you keep taking away parts of the ship, the wheel and the rudder and the nails, and replacing the parts with new ones, at what point does it cease being the original ship? Now, what if you stopped replacing the parts of the ship—and simply disassembled it? At what point does it stop being a ship at all? When it's no longer seaworthy? When it's no longer ship-shaped? What about when you put it back together?"

Flynn made his speech with enthusiasm, gesturing with his free hand, picking his arguments out of the air.

"Where is the inherent 'shipness' or 'ship nature'? It can't be found. It's similar if you think about a human being. If you take apart a human being atom by atom, when does it cease to be a human, to have a 'self'? Or if you replace it piece by piece with cybernetics? What if you replace a large chunk of the brain with pieces of a different brain, but the personality remains? Philosophically, will that make them a whole different person? What if their brain is destroyed, somehow, and medical science allows them to grow a new one, with their own body—but their new brain has a different personality. These are questions we will very soon have to consider."

Herrera cleared his throat. "What about the soul?"

"Common misconception," said Flynn. "They actually refuse the conception of a soul in Buddhism. Real jade, you said?"

Flynn knelt forward and reached out toward Kiera. She squeezed her knees tight to her chest and took a sharp breath.

"*Whoa!*" Herrera yelped. Flynn paused.

"Oh?"

"I wouldn't touch that."

"I'll be very gentle."

"Oh, it's not that," said Herrera. "It's just... It's bad karma."

Flynn tilted his head.

"Really?"

"Uh-huh. That's what the vendor told me. When I bought it, they wrapped it up in a sheet."

Flynn backed up. "How very interesting."

Kiera didn't relax. Flynn drank the rest of his gin in two gulps. He placed the glass on the kitchen counter.

"Sleep well, Mr. Jones. And please—get my name right next time. It will make things... much friendlier."

Herrera made a finger-gun. "*Pshew.*"

Flynn put his sunglasses back on, covering his illuminated eyes, and excused himself. Kiera heard the front door open and shut, but didn't dare move, not yet.

Herrera didn't move to collect her from her hiding place yet, either. He washed out the liquor glasses. He turned off the jazz and turned on the news. He went and switched off some of the lights. While Kiera waited patiently, he disappeared into his room and reappeared in a t-shirt and pajama pants. He set his phone on the coffee table and sank onto the couch. The phone must've been on speaker; it dialed loud enough for Kiera to hear.

A smokey, honey-whiskey voice answered. "Good evening, Casey speaking. Is this a business call?"

"Case," Herrera said simply.

The other person paused. "Angel," they replied, warm, and surprised.

"I'm sorry I haven't called you yet."

"I hoped I'd at least see you at the funeral."

Herrera made a small noise that might have been a laugh. "Am I even invited?"

"Of course. Malcolm never removed you from my trusted persons list. You're family, Angel."

Now Herrera paused. "Even after—?"

"Yes, even after *that*. We got the stains out, eventually."

"How come he never contacted me? If he was in danger?"

"Yes, I suggested that to him. I suppose he was reluctant to endanger anyone else. Or perhaps he was simply embarrassed to talk to you."

"I could've handled this." Kiera couldn't see Herrera from where she was sitting but he looked like he was slumped forward, brooding. "I could've helped him."

"Don't be mad, Angel."

"D just left my place," said Herrera. "Might still be sniffing around the perimeter. Has he grilled you yet?"

"Oh, of course."

"Give him anything?"

"I had nothing to give him."

"So, we're on the same page."

"I took *David Flynn* off the trusted persons list seven years ago."

Kiera counted. Herrera was still a cop then.

"I'm sorry I haven't been in touch," said Herrera, his voice softening.

The person on the phone sighed. "It would be awkward."

"I could've at least met you for coffee."

"Don't beat yourself up."

"Plenty of people doing that for me."

They both chuckled.

"Hey," Herrera said. There was something hesitant in his tone. "What about Glory? We still trust her, right?"

"Completely," the person called Casey replied. "Why do you ask?"

"Nothing, nothing. Good. I'll try to swing by soon," said Herrera. "We need to compare notes."

"Of course."

"Be good, Case."

"Nice to hear your voice, Angel."

The ambient noise from the phone ceased and Herrera was quiet. Kiera tuned into the chatter from the television. Dominic Gray was pulling ahead in the polls in spite of, or perhaps because of, a resurfaced interview from the nineties, where he had said he "would rather drink a homo's piss and get AIDS than eat food prepared by a Mexican."

"Yeah, we all know how much you like piss, buddy," Herrera muttered as he came, at last, to switch off the hologram Buddha. "This fucking country." The black veil around Kiera disappeared.

"Fucking T-1000 looking motherfucker." Kiera finally got up. Her everything hurt. "Fucking skeez."

"Yeah, D's a piece of work." Herrera rubbed his face. "You alright, kid?"

"I need to pee my entire insides out."

"You know where the toilet is."

"Who was the dish on the phone?" Kiera asked.

"Old friend."

"That was Mr. Hobbes's partner, right? Mr. Twelve."

"Yeah," Herrera grunted.

"Sounded like you had a crush kinda."

"Don't pull threads."

Kiera held her arms tight, like she was cold. "So... what did that mean, when you told Flynn that Malcolm 'did you a favor'? Did you like... hate your wife or something?"

"That's above your pay grade, kid."

"I just mean... if there's some way we can show you didn't have a motive, you know?"

"Please, Kiera."

Kiera clammed up and padded across the living room.

"No, I didn't hate my wife," Herrera called. "What'd make you say a thing like that?"

Kiera turned. "I dunno. It's just... a thing that happens a lot?"

"Well, not to me."

Kiera nodded. "Okay."

She crept around the corner, bare feet clapping on hardwood. She kept expecting Flynn's monitor-eyes to light up the shadows.

13

"HEY, HEY, HEY. Feet off the dash, stupid."

Herrera flicked Kiera on the temple, knocking her sunglasses askew. She blinked, indignantly, and straightened them. She took her feet off the dash. "Hmph."

She was running on a quarter-tank of sleep. She pined for a hazelnut vanilla latté. With Nile. Or a sleep-in, Sky's big warm bulk to roll up against, Jinx sneaking up behind for a cuddle, her frame even smaller than Kiera's. This was bullshit. She should've never gotten twisted up with someone like Herrera. What had her stupid ass been *thinking?* Taking gigs to find missing people, snapping pictures of armed perverts—hanging out with the kind of guy who had to bleach his face and carry a *gun?*

But then, Nile would've gone missing either way. *Right?* Now, at least, riding shotgun in Herrera's hatchback down New Carson's main vein, Kiera was in a position to *do* something about it. Something other than just pace her apartment, every molecule whirring with worry, while the cops did—what? Nothing. *That* alternate timeline sounded exponentially shittier.

Kiera put her head against the window. "How far's the Heights?"

"Twenty minutes."

"Dunno what you think's gonna be there. Bulls will've scraped everything useful out of the apartment by now."

"I've got a hunch."

"Do you have to wear that coat when you say that?"

"Don't knock the hunch, rookie. You found that incense on instinct."

"Yeah, and look at me now. High life. Light fantastic." Kiera pulled up the triad chat. "Won't they be watching the place? Perp returns to the scene of the crime or whatever?"

"Not a real thing."

"But having a hunch is?"

"All right, all right, why don't you play with a fidget spinner or something?"

Kiera yawned like a lion. "I'm thirty," she managed. "Thirty."

an elf irl: jinxy

an elf irl: i rly need you to find out for me who brought Nile to mistermine's party.

an elf irl: there's got to be pics of them on pictu or someone has to know them or shit even maybe he knows them

an elf irl: but i don't even.......... i havent logged into pictu in over a year.

```
It's Jinx!!!: ok
It's Jinx!!!: it's cool. I'll see what I
   can do.
an elf irl: ask about the big nb chick
   with tusks who pushed their date into
   the pool.
tactical butt: do you think their date
   will know anything you don't already
   know? I mean, you actually made it
   with Nile and he didn't.
an elf irl: honestly i dont know
an elf irl: i need anything. a last
   name. anything Nile might have said
   to him that i didnt get
an elf irl: i need to know who she is
It's Jinx!!!: what about Mimi?
It's Jinx!!!: Mister's Mimi would have
   known everyone at that party on
   sight.
an elf irl: i love you
It's Jinx!!!: I'll ask Mister.
tactical butt: anything I can do, babes?
an elf irl: rub jinx's feet and bring me
   pics of good cats
tactical butt: ( ·ω·)/
```

Herrera parked at the curb outside a Chinese grocery and a prosthetic repair shop. Kiera craned her head around.

"Cameras?"

"Out here? Nah."

"Dog drones? Cruisers?"

"Not that I can see."

Kiera put on fake face no. 133, a milquetoast thirtysomething white woman. Herrera screwed up his mouth. "Looks like shit."

"You're sitting too close. It's not designed to work this close."

"Hmm. I don't buy it."

Herrera reached into the backseat and produced an overly large, floppy black fedora. Kiera took off her sunglasses *and* her fake digital face, just so he would see her look of disappointment.

"You're not getting out of this car without it," said Herrera.

"My body, my choice."

"Think of it like a sun hat."

"This is homophobic."

Kiera had to smush down her hair to make the hat fit. Then she put the sunglasses back on and made a face.

"Superb." Herrera didn't even try to hide his amusement. "Couture." He climbed out of the driver's side.

"My life is on the line," Kiera muttered. "While you're fucking around."

"Yep. Thought so." Herrera kept his shoulders bunched up, didn't betray his notice, but indicated to the right with a cock of his head. "Fuckin' knew it. *Hah*."

Kiera held her hat down as she peered through the iron fence. It was that guy again, that scraggly bombed-out guy with the wires sticking out of his eye socket. He was hanging out in front of the shitty apartment complex, just standing around smoking a paper cigarette.

"Your *hunch* is that guy would be back at his apartment?"

"You think he lives here. Why would he get blitzed in the stairwell if he lived here?"

"Okay. So you think he did it?"

"I'm working an angle. Get me in this gate."

Kiera got her PIN descrambler and multitool out. It took her five seconds to set up and Herrera was already getting itchy.

"What about the number from last time?"

"I would hope even this place would change the code after a murder. Besides, I don't remember it."

Herrera fidgeted. "You should develop a mind for those kinds of details."

"What am I, your girl Friday? Do you remember it?"

"No."

Kiera waited. The first LCD number snapped into place.

"Did it take this long last time?" Herrera asked.

"Yes."

The second number decoded. Then the third.

When the last number landed and the gate clicked, Herrera busted through like an Olympic sprinter. Kiera was left bobbing her head, bewildered. But sure enough, as soon as the scruffy guy saw Herrera, he tripped over his own feet trying to run.

"Hey! *Hey!* Asshole!"

The smoker tried to clear the fence, but he was no athlete. Herrera slammed him up against the iron and dragged him back by the shoulders.

Kiera caught up to them as Herrera threw the smoker against the concrete wall. Herrera had him by the collar of a hooded sweatshirt with the name of a gym across the front; the guy probably took his showers there. He clutched Herrera's arm with hands wearing a pair of brown leather gloves.

"I already talked to the cops. Ease off." His voice-box had been run over a cheese grater.

"Last time you saw me you were so blitzed you thought I was a cartoon dog. No way you'd remember my face. So why'd you scatter?"

The wastoid turned his working eye from Herrera to Kiera. There was something in his expression she couldn't read, as he wheezed from exertion and fear. He looked... sad? And it made her creep senses tingle. Kiera folded her arms and turned, showing him shoulder. He winced like he was in pain. Like he'd looked at a too-bright light.

"You come at me like a bull, man, what am I to think?"

Kiera actually agreed with him there, but she kept her lip zipped. She let Herrera work his angle.

"Yeah, I'm not buying what you're selling," Herrera pushed.

"Okay, okay. They told me to watch out for you," the guy sighed, turning back to Herrera. "They showed me pictures."

"That right? Well, the cops have got it wrong."

"I just come here to get out of the cold. Don't drag me into this."

"Who lets you in the gate?"

"Blatina lady in 315 tells me the code."

"Gives you a place to hit the pipe in peace? Awful charitable of her. No one ever complains?"

"I don't give no one trouble."

Kiera chewed her tongue. She could respect the tenants leaving the guy alone, especially in a neighborhood as run-down as this one. But her well-honed skeez radar was still blipping, and she couldn't place why.

Herrera thumped the guy's chest. "What you see the other night, friendo? Let's quit dicking around."

"I was fucked, man. You say yourself."

"But you walked away just fine."

The guy cringed like he had a brain freeze. "I wandered off, fuck knows where. Thought I was dreaming. Slept on a bench."

"You seen Mal around here before then? Tell me everything you told the cops."

"I dunno, couple times. A few times maybe."

"A couple, or a few?" asked Kiera. Herrera glanced at her with an eyebrow raised, then nodded at the wastoid. "Answer her."

"A few, I guess. Like if he come out to use vending machine. I never saw him leave building."

"Anyone else ever go up to his room?"

The big man's shoulders slumped. "I see them go up to his apartment, that night. Before I get high."

Herrera and Kiera exchanged a look. "It took you this long to tell me?" Herrera glowered.

"Who's 'them'?" asked Kiera.

"He had a woman with him."

"Be specific," said Herrera.

"Kind of short. I tell the cops five foot five. Brown hair. Mexican maybe. Glasses, business suit with a skirt. Looked too classy for this place, you know?"

"Uh-huh. And you don't remember her leaving?"

"After that I was in dreamland, friend. That's everything I have for you."

Kiera squinted, and stuck her tongue in her cheek, thinking hard. Herrera let the smoker's hoodie go, took a small step back, and then put out his hand—his skeletal, mechanical one—for a handshake.

"You've been a big help."

The smoker gave Herrera a confused frown, like he'd

just been offered an antique pocket watch. *That's nice, but what am I supposed to do with it?* But he shook Herrera's prosthetic hand. Herrera held the handshake a few seconds, long enough that Kiera thought it was getting a little kooky. Did she hear a faint, mechanical whirr? Then Herrera let go and reached into his coat for his cig.

The wastoid looked at Kiera again, with plastic-tipped plugs curling out of one eye socket and the working eye filled with—what? What was it? Regret?

What? Kiera mouthed. She tightened her arms around her chest.

The guy stuck his gloved hands in his hoodie pockets and skulked away, disappearing through the front gate and down the sidewalk. Herrera watched him, chewing the filter end of his plastic cigarette, rolling it around with his front teeth.

"What'd you make of that, kid?" Herrera started toward the gate.

Kiera followed. "I dunno. Not very useful. Seemed... contradictory?"

"That's not too unusual. Good witness is hard to find. What would you hit next?" Herrera opened the gate.

"The lady in—was it 315? I would ask if she really lets him in."

"But we're not gonna do that." Herrera blew peppermint smoke. "We already know it's horseshit. She probably doesn't exist. Neither does his brown-haired lady with the glasses."

"They don't?"

"No."

Kiera tipped her head. "Your hunch... What were you thinking?"

"What did you think of his gloves?"

Kiera blinked. She thought back to the handshake.

"I mean… it's cold out."

"Shouldn't be a problem for him. His hands, kid, they were fake."

Kiera paused in her step. "How'd you—?"

"They were cheap. The fingers didn't move like real ones, just like mine, you see?" He held up his robotic hand and flexed the spindly, robotic fingers for her.

"You could tell that just by looking?"

"Well, a little enhanced vision doesn't hurt." Herrera tapped his outdated cybernetic eye. "So I couldn't abide the gloves." He wiggled the tip of his prosthetic index finger—a gray rubber pad. Each finger on his right hand had the same. "I got a read on the texture of those gloves, the stitching, the thickness. Best guess? Luxury lambskin, lined with cashmere or merino wool."

Kiera screwed up her mouth. "*That thing* is slick enough to do all that?"

"Hey, hey, now who's the boomer? This little guy was one of the most modular models ever released. Enthusiasts love gettin' their hands on this thing. I can stick a heater in it to keep my coffee warm."

Kiera absorbed this. She tried to reassemble the encounter like an old tape on rewind. She thought about Herrera sprinting after the smoker the moment the gate opened, and the guy cheesing it straight for the fence, before he hardly would have had time to register what was happening. Like they both had it scripted out.

"He tripped up," Kiera pieced out. "He tripped all over himself like a clown, like he was making a show of it."

"Whole thing was pure theater, kid. My hunch wasn't

163

just that the guy would be there. It's that someone paid him to be there."

Kiera put a finger to her cheek. "So, like... shouldn't we go, I dunno, drag him in or whatever?"

"I ain't a cop anymore, kid." Herrera sucked on his smoke. "We'll see him again. But this confirms that Mal was on someone's shit list, someone with a bank account. Someone who wants to steer us wrong." He sneered. "Someone who doesn't respect my intelligence very much."

"Why send anybody? Why leave anything for us to find? Instead of just leaving us in the dark?"

"Good question, kid. Let me know if you have a theory on that."

But Kiera just kept thinking about the *look* that skeez had been giving her. *What the fuck was that about?*

14

THE KID PEERED out through the passenger window. In her
hat and sunglasses, she looked like a little movie starlet
sizing up a red-carpet premiere. She asked, "What do
you think you're gonna find in there?"

Angel stuffed the car key in his coat pocket. "I'll
know it when I see it." They climbed out onto the curb.
"Malcolm had a whole apartment and a car he was
keeping from his wife. I wanna sniff out anything else he
might have ferreted away in his little cubby-hole, here."

The sign standing over the chainlink gate said FOUR
WALLS STORAGE. Angel walked the kid into the
front office with his arm laid paternally across her
shoulders, opening up the con with both barrels. The
kid wrapped her arms tight around her front and kept
her head dipped, even threw in a little shiver. The blue
linoleum counter was staffed by a woman Angel could
only describe as froggish. He liked her lime-green nails.
She kept a revolver in plain view next to the service bell,
the gun and the bell equally chrome and shiny.

"Afternoon, ma'am," Angel chirped. He motioned at the thick gun. "You, ah, you get a lot of stick-up jobs in here?"

"For people who come around just to fuck with the live-ins," croaked the amphibious broad. "Frat boys or the fuzz. Can I help you, sir?"

"Ah, yes, you see, we need to get into Malcolm Hobbes's unit."

The woman stuck a green-nailed finger out toward Angel. "*You* are not Malcolm Hobbes."

"No, but this is his daughter." Angel indicated the kid like a sommelier presenting the house red. "Mr. Hobbes passed away recently, you see, and…"

Kiera sniffed, loud. The counter woman wrinkled her jowls.

"'S that why he hasn't paid up this month?"

Angel nodded. "I'm afraid so."

"My daddy," Kiera burbled. "He died."

The woman with the green nails chewed over this information, looking like she might spit it right back out. She slapped her palms on the blue counter.

"Number four-five-two. You know the code to get in, go have a ball. Collection notices will commence in another week. Three months of non-payment and we'll start recouping our costs by selling the contents of the unit. There's a very nice automobile in that unit. I would love to sell it. You wanna keep it, I would advise paying."

"I'll be sure to inform the widow Hobbes," Angel offered obsequiously. He guided the kid toward the back door. She gave another stage sob, for the reviewers.

"My daddy."

The toad-woman made a face. "Wasn't Hobbes Black? What are you, a quarter Chinese?"

"This shitty light in here," said Angel. "It's in her nose, she's got his nose. Anyway, thank you!"

The yard smelled of hot dry concrete. Stacks on stacks on stacks of storage units, halogen lights all switched on even in broad daylight. Country music piped out of one box where three unshaven gentlemen used a big wooden cable spool as a table for their beer and cards. Inside another on the second level Angel could make out the edges of a sleeping bag and wool cap. It made sense; rent was reasonable, and the security options went up in tiers if you had extra. Not to mention a good strong fence was more than you could ask for in most places.

"Four-fifty-two." Angel tapped his shoe against the corrugated steel door.

"Don't do that! It's supposed to be electrified, right? And doesn't this place have *turrets?* Are they still on?"

"If he's not paid up, all the countermeasures should be switched off."

"Even so, I'm kinda nervous to try and crack it." The kid started digging into her messenger bag. "It might take me a minute."

Angel punched 2867 into the keypad next to the door. The console chimed happily and turned green. The steel door began to rise.

The kid jutted out her lower jaw. "Um?"

"Mal asked me to get his bag lunch from his locker a few times," said Angel, "and has never changed his PIN number in his entire life."

"Just PIN, not PIN number. What was it?"

"First four digits of his first credit card."

"God, you two make me want to gouge my eyes out." The door on the unit rolled up, and there was the infamous car, a burnished red convertible like hot sex on wheels.

"Cherry red," Angel mused. "I might've known. Mal, you walkin' cliché."

"I like cherries."

The kid started snooping. Honestly, there wasn't much to see. A couple of fun-sized anti-theft gun turrets hung from the ceiling corners, deactivated, like limp dicks. Angel approached a framed photograph stuck to the white steel wall.

He took it down to inspect it. A photo of Malcolm and Gloria and another man Angel didn't recognize on the aft of a yacht, flanked by mounted fishing rods. Gloria's smile beamed as bright as the whitewash on the waves behind them. Malcolm's smile was less enthusiastic, a half-smirk assumed for the camera. He was holding his stomach.

Gloria adored the sea; Mal hated it. *Mal de mer*, she called him, that time they all caught the ferry to Alcatraz. In this photo Mal was certainly seconds away from horfing over the side. Yet this photo survived, got framed, made it all the way here. Angel rubbed his chin. Who kept the record of this moment—Glory, or Mal? Did Mal hang it here, as a reminder to go home to his wife when he was done with his joyride? Or to provide an extra hit of resentment, to assuage any pangs of guilt over lying to the woman who regarded his feelings so little, that she would continually force him on sea voyages?

A *k-clunk* behind.

"Hey, this thing's open," the kid hollered. "Oh, sick, it's one of those brand-new ones you can start with an implant instead of a key."

Angel turned and opened the passenger side. The kid was fossicking around under the driver seat, and in the space in the door. "It has a CD player. He got one with a CD player." She lifted a CD wallet. "With actual factual CDs."

"CDs are good for the car," Angel protested. "Shit, I still miss tapes."

"Yeah, I could get down with tapes coming back." The kid flipped open the CD pouch and gave a disgusted, teenager-at-the-mall look. "Little River Band? Come on. Steely Dan? Okay, no, I've changed my mind, Steely Dan fucks."

Angel popped the glove box. A magazine for a handgun—the one Malcolm had dropped next to his bed, no doubt—slept on top of the car's manual and documentation. Next to that, an outdated tablet computer in chunky casing.

"Hello, there." Angel picked it up. A hi-liter green sticky note stuck to the screen read *Marjane*, followed by a cellphone number.

"Ha." Angel showed the kid. She tongued her molar. "He cheatin'?"

"It'd be out of character." Angel was already punching the number into his phone. "You think she answers?"

"Pfft. Hell no."

"*The number you have dialed is no longer in service. Please—*"

"*Chingada*," Angel muttered, unsurprised. "In hiding or dead. Hiding if she was around to cancel her number this quick."

"How hard can it be to find a Marjane?"

Angel tried to boot the tablet. It wanted a password. Angel bit his tongue. The tablet didn't like 2867, nor did it cotton to *marjane,* shaking its password field angrily. *5 attempts remain*, it warned. Angel snarled.

"Kid, can you get into this?"

He shook the dingus at her. She took one look at it. "Get me my computer from my apartment and I can."

"Going by your place is a negatory."

"Maybe my boyfriend can bring it over."

Angel tapped the tablet on the seat, thinking to himself. He clicked his tongue.

"I think I'm gonna have to take you to meet Gloria," he said.

The kid stayed cool. "That the ex?"

"Got it in one."

"I mean… Is that weird for you?"

"I think maybe it'll be weird for you."

Angel lifted a brow, getting a good look around the car's compartment. Something very stupid occurred to him, and after five seconds of deliberation he decided to run with it. He knocked his fake fist on the roof and tipped his head at the kid. "Hey, stupid," he offered.

"Yeah?"

"Do you need your computer to crack a car?"

"Nope."

"You wanna?"

"Yup."

"How long will it take?"

She gave him a grin like a gremlin. "'Bout ten minutes."

She did it in five. Soft red LEDs lit up the dash and the wheel. The kid put her foot down on the pedal in park, and the engine growled like a lion.

"*Oooh,*" Angel gushed. "Hear that kitten."

"It's fake, you know?" said Kiera. "The engine's electric, doesn't really make noise. So they program it to make engine sounds, otherwise people fuck up and get into accidents. They make the sounds with a keyboard."

"No shit? So, what's in the front?"

"Another trunk." The kid caressed the steering wheel for a moment. "You wanna drive?"

Angel tossed her a smirk. "Nah. You take this one."

There was that grin again. Kiera gave the pedal another good couple of pumps.

The jalopy screeched up to the chainlink gate. The kid honked the horn. The woman with the green nails came out of the front office, looking bemused. Kiera tipped her sunglasses down, elbow on the windowsill. Angel couldn't offer much more than an apologetic smile.

"Really in your feelings, I see," said the clerk.

"Daddy wouldn't want me to grieve forever."

"There's the matter of Mr. Hobbes's bill," said the clerk.

"We'll be bringing it right back," Angel assured her.

"Fifty bucks, you drive on outta here."

Angel dug into the inside pocket of his coat and thumbed a bill off the top of the Gloria fund. He handed it across to the driver window. "Change for a hundred?"

"I'll take that." The clerk stuffed the bill into her bra and went back inside. A minute later the gate clunked on open, and when she had enough room, the kid peeled out of the gate like a greyhound after the fake bunny. Angel grabbed the handle over his window.

"Shit, kid!"

BEFORE THEY HIT the freeway, Kiera rolled the roof down. She logged onto the stereo over wi-fi and blasted the synthpop as loud as it would go. Through her shades, the brightness of the day was candy red. As she was smoothly changing lanes at ten miles over the speed limit, her black fedora blew right off; she made an anguished yelp, but Herrera saw it happen before it happened, and snatched the thing out of the air like a ninja.

"Turn the music down!" he yelled.

She reluctantly obeyed. "Only because you saved my hat."

"Oh, we like the hat now?"

"Fuck off."

"Where'd you learn to drive like this?"

"Rideshare," said Kiera. "Three quarters of my income till we had to sell the pussy wagon."

She slingshotted past a dopey soccer mom SUV. She knew there was a speed trap coming up and eased off the pedal. Someone honked at her. She looked. In the next lane some broski in a jumped-up trash heap hanging his arm out the window kept taking his eyes off the road to gawk at her. Both his arm and the car were equally decorated with tacky flames and tribal patterns. *Hashiyira,* Kiera thought with disdain. The punk lifted his tattooed arm and waggled his tongue between his first two fingers.

Kiera leaned over to yell out "I have a dick," and stuck her own arm out to present a middle finger all the way across the lane. The shitboy's face retracted in a dejected grimace of shock, and he crunched into the back bumper of the car in front of him. Herrera burst into laughter so suddenly he had to cover his mouth.

"Take this next exit," said Herrera. "Let's swing by the boardwalk."

Kiera hadn't been out this way since she was a little kid. The old terror drop carnival ride at the far end still commanded the skyline. The groovy graffiti and palm trees were still everywhere—major nostalgia—but they'd put up a lot more screens. Animated advertisements slid and shuffled and exploded. An AR movie trailer formed right in the middle of the street; Kiera drove straight through a CG explosion. She stopped at a traffic light to find that a whole-ass Uni Store had taken over a corner warehouse where they used to sell bootleg t-shirts.

"*Nice* car," trilled a pleasant voice from the backseat. Kiera and Herrera whirled around to find that Mimi, sporting aviator shades, had materialized there uninvited, lounging with her arms spread across the leather headrests.

"Shit," Kiera exclaimed. "We can't stop here, Angel. This is Mimi country."

Herrera waved his hand irritably at the hologram. "Clear off. Bein' a blue ghost in this car is a two-drink minimum."

Mimi vanished in a multicolored firework. The traffic light turned green, and Kiera hauled ass through. Between the breaks in the buildings she got an eyeful of the white-sand beach, the sea, the teeming boardwalk itself. She wanted to get out and hit the midway games, but where was she gonna park? Just as well. They didn't have all day anyway.

"Hungry as hell," Herrera declared.

Kiera patted her belly with both hands. "Yeah, man."

"You wanna get drive-thru and put greasy fingers all over this nice leather?"

"Dude."

It took perhaps three minutes to find the combination Burger Hole and NIHON-WHOA! Sitting in the drive-thru line without the wind of motion blowing in her face, Kiera noticed the day had grown long and hot, so she made sure to order a large soda with her Big Swinging

Chick club sandwich combo. After all, wasn't she *free as fuck?*

"And the Hot Ass Sauce," she implored. "Lots of Hot Ass Sauce."

"*Anything else?*"

Herrera leaned over to the window. His elbow went in Kiera's gut, making her grunt. "I'm speaking to the Japanese side now," he said. "I want the Inago-a-Go-Go bowl, and... Yeah, get me a shake from the burger side, too. Medium vanilla shake."

"Let me have a sip."

"Large vanilla shake."

Kiera leaned back in her seat. The line was taking five thousand years. She decided to check her messages; she'd had some notifications sitting there since the freeway.

**tactical butt: hey, we found a picture
    of you two at the party on Pictu.
    Nile's account is tagged.**
**tactical butt: not much really on
    there, just a few selfies and a pic of
    their apartment. hoped it might help
    though.**

Kiera fingered her reply out on the air.

an elf irl: that's cool. thank you.
an elf irl: can i get a link to the pic?
tactical butt: you sure? ＼(´·д·`)／
an elf irl: uh-huh.

Kiera popped open the link, and a picture materialized in the middle of her vision. Her heart thrummed fuzzy red. Someone had snapped her and Nile dancing to Daft Punk, Nile's arms wrapped around Kiera, their cheeks pressed together. Kiera stared at the photo as she crept forward in the chow line, setting fire to her own insides in the process, but luxuriating in the burn.

an elf irl: thx.

They got their food and ate in the parking lot, and Kiera felt like complete shit. Her BIG CHONK steak fries were ash on her tongue. She watched Herrera sip his shake. It was this old man in the passenger seat sharing this cool moment with her instead of Nile. Like, Herrera was cool. But he wasn't *Nile*.

"Bugs, huh?" she said again, just to talk about anything.

"Crickets!" Herrera, with his chopsticks, plucked an insect mummified in soy sauce and vinegar from the top of a mound of white rice. "Tastes like shrimp. Try some."

"Like, I saw the commercials with the rapping CG cricket? But it kind of didn't dawn on me until just now that someone would actually eat them."

Herrera stuck another cricket in his mouth, then pointed his chopsticks at her. "*My* lunch is real meat."

"I'm not literally a happy-ass frog sitting on a lily pad though."

Herrera chewed, considering this carefully. He shrugged. "Your people invented it."

"You take your ex-wife on a bug-eating date?"

"Hell, yes." Herrera picked congealed soy sauce out of his teeth. "It's *cultural*."

"No wonder she left you for the lawyer."

"We were both still cops then. When did you become such a materialist?"

"I'm just givin' you shit."

Herrera slurped vanilla milkshake and burped. "That's cute you think that's fair to joke about."

Kiera jolted. "I'm sorry, dude."

"You just tryin' to hurt my feelings, or...?"

"No! I just... I don't know. I wanna know about her. And you."

"I'm taking you to meet her. Don't make me tell you to wait in the car."

Kiera pointlessly swirled a fry in her Hot Ass Sauce. *Nice one, dipshit.* Her stomach had turned to lead.

Nursing hurt and caught up in longing, Kiera pulled open her chat window with Nile—as if she hadn't done enough digital self-harm already. It had been sitting there untouched since the night Nile had disappeared.

Message History

**KRONON DID NOTHING WRONG: you are cute
  enough to eat.**
**KRONON DID NOTHING WRONG: I'm gonna
  break you in half.**
**an elf irl: don't threaten me with a
  good time**
**an elf irl: gettin off the train now. be
  there in a few**

She fucking missed her so much.

**an elf irl: i fucking miss you so much.
  please be okay.**

Kiera took a big chomp of her burger, trying to taste it. Then when she was in the middle of swallowing, she did a double-take, and almost choked.

Seen 4:35pm

Kiera banged her hand on the steering wheel while she struggled to swallow. The horn beeped twice. Herrera jumped so hard he scattered white rice and grasshoppers.

"Kid! Jesus!"

"Holy shit! *Holy* shit!"

"What is it, what's the matter?"

an elf irl: are you there? can you see this?
an elf irl: please answer.
an elf irl: PLEASE. can you see this?

"She's alive. They're alive. She-they. They saw my message. I think. I don't know. I don't—*god! Ugh!*" Kiera banged her fists on the wheel. The horn honked again.

"Whoa, kid." Herrera hovered his hand over her shoulder. "Deep breaths."

Kiera leaned on the wheel, burying her face in her arms.

"This *sucks*. This is so fucked."

"I know." Herrera sighed. He flipped the switch for the roof. "Finish your food, huh?"

"Don't want it anymore."

"No problem. Come on, I'll drive."

"M'kay."

Kiera kept checking the chat window every fifteen or thirty seconds for the next hour; the palm trees and freeway became so much noise. No more signs of Nile emerged.

15

GLORIA'S WAS FIVE minutes away when a message blipped in Kiera's left eye. Marked urgent. Her heart skipped. *Nile?*

MisterMine: Hey there!

Ugh.

MisterMine: Is this Kiara? Jinx's partner?
an elf irl: kiera. hi. that's me
MisterMine: Hey! We met at my party the other night. I really loved your outfit, by the way.
MisterMine: Did you enjoy yourself? We kind of lost you after you took that phone call.
an elf irl: yeah i did but things kind of aren't great at the moment re: that

MisterMine: Well, you and Jinxy are welcome over again anytime.

an elf irl: thx?

MisterMine: I was hoping I could talk to you for a second, if you're not too busy?

an elf irl: yea i was hoping i could get you for a minute too

an elf irl: someone who went to your party has gone missing

MisterMine: I heard.

MisterMine: Unfortunately I don't know them. I couldn't provide any information to the police or to Jinx.

an elf irl: i need to know who they came with.

MisterMine: That's what I was hoping to talk to you about.

MisterMine: I would really appreciate it if you don't check up on my guests.

an elf irl: are you serious dude

MisterMine: My friends and guests value their privacy and I have to respect that.

an elf irl: your party was literally posted all over pictu

MisterMine: Be that as it may, I would appreciate if you'd let the professionals handle this.

an elf irl: i am working with a professional.

MisterMine: Kiera. Please. I'm asking as Jinx's friend.

MisterMine: Just let this go.

"MisterMine did it!"

Herrera sucked down the last of his vanilla shake. "What'sat?"

"This shitbag fake video game celebrity cockface told me to stop 'checking up' on his party guests. Totally hiding something. Like murder."

"You got an angle, kid?"

"I don't know. He was watching Jinx's stream the night we found Mr. Hobbes. I guess he coulda had time to do that and kill someone, but I dunno."

"Maybe he's just a snotnose."

"He can be a snotnose and a murderer."

Herrera tapped his temple. "File it, kid, file it."

They rolled up in front of a steepled bluestone townhouse. Kiera tipped her sunglasses down.

"Dang. Did you used to live here?"

"On what I made? Pfft, please."

Kiera looked both ways before she got out of the car. As she shut the door, she looked again. This neighborhood was nice. That meant cameras and dog drones. She pulled the hat down tight and hustled with her shoulders hunched. She got to the front door before Herrera.

Goddamn Mimi appeared.

"Hello!"

"Why?"

"Ms. Umehara, it's good to see you again. We last met today at the Uni Store location at the Memorial Run boardwalk."

"We sure did. Could you keep it down?"

"And—" Mimi had a moment where her brain seemed

to glitch. "Michael Jones! I hardly recognized you! Your new face is very handsome."

Kiera waved her hand in Mimi's face. "Mimi, can you do me a favor?"

"Please believe my sincerity when I say I would *love* to do you a favor."

"You're, like, recording this, right? And telling Uni that I'm here?"

"That's right."

"Could you stop? I'm kinda trying to move off the grid."

Mimi dipped her head sadly. "I'm afraid that feature cannot be turned off or opted out of. However, I *can* assure you I will only provide the information to the Uni Corporation and interested corporate partners. Think of it as browsing on incognito mode."

Kiera made a fart noise. "Thanks."

"Mimi, go get Gloria, please," said Herrera.

"Sure!"

Mimi flickered and vanished. Herrera folded his arms. His shoulders bunched up worse than Kiera's. He looked around, left and right. Kiera quirked an eyebrow.

"What? What is it?"

Herrera exhaled. "Glory might think you did it."

"Fuck the *what? Why?*"

"She's been talking to Flynn."

"Why did you bring me?" Kiera shoved him. "I'm going back to the car."

"No. Someone will see you."

"*Angel—*"

The door opened. An olive-skinned woman peered out—that woman from Herrera's balcony, Kiera realized. Kiera threw her hands up.

"I didn't do anything!"

The woman's eyes bugged out behind her round glasses. She looked at Kiera, then Herrera. Herrera put his outstretched palm in front of Kiera protectively, as if he had braked too hard while driving.

"She didn't. It was my fault. Can we talk inside?"

Gloria lobbied her index finger at Herrera, and she seemed to gain a foot of height while still being shorter than him. "You *brought* her *here*—"

"It's for Mal. It's for Mal."

Gloria had to look away. She put a hand to her mouth. Kiera looked down the road, saw one of those goofy-ass dog drones a block away. She pulled up her jacket collar. "Time is a factor."

Gloria's lips went tight and thin as scar tissue. She turned to Kiera.

"If *he* wasn't here... If I had you woman to woman..."

"I promise I didn't," begged Kiera. "Mr. Hobbes was my friend, too. Please let me come in."

Herrera put his hands out, pleading. "Glory."

Gloria shut her eyes, and steepled her fingers in front of her face. Kiera knew the look. She was about to let Angel win, and she hated herself for it.

Gloria beckoned them inside.

"He's always working me, too," Kiera offered, as Gloria closed the front door behind them. "How do you think I wound up in this shit?"

Gloria said nothing, left the entryway like a storm cloud ready to break. Kiera twisted her mouth and looked at the ground.

"Okie-doke." She took the hat and sunglasses off at long last, and vigorously shook out her magenta hair.

Mimi appeared next to Gloria, over in the living

room. "*Hay invitados en tu casa. ¿Quieres que haga café?*"

"Mimi, *ugh*. I thought I turned this thing off. Off, Mimi, off!"

"Okay."

"Malcolm's goddamn toys."

Mimi blipped away. Kiera wanted to tell Gloria that Mimi doesn't go "off"—once she's in your home, the corporate nanny-cam streamed 24/7 back to Uni, and a cop wife ought to know that. But she felt it was not the time to open her big mouth.

Kiera saw immediately that this was a "books" household. Almost every wall in the living room was a shelf—and real paper-and-glue books meant money. A quick eyeball showed two categories: classics and legal thrillers. She wondered if it was a husband/wife split or if the Hobbeses had the same tastes. Probably the former—a classic lit snob still stockpiling dead trees seemed like Angel's type. Kiera wondered how many tea varietals the ex was packing in the kitchen. Kiera had worked gigs in houses like this before. She used to live in a "books" house of her own, when she was still a boy. She begrudgingly had to move out—not kicked out, but *strongly urged* to head for greener pastures, where switching to digital saved cash and storage space.

Gloria turned. She fixed Herrera with the death glare.

"That *thing* outside must be Malcolm's little getaway car?"

Herrera smirked. "You knew 'bout the fireball?"

"Tell me what you're doing here. With *her*."

"Nothing to drink first?"

Kiera punched him on the arm. "Dude."

"This isn't cute, Angel. This is not joking time."

Herrera dug the tablet out of his coat. "We need you to look at something of Mal's for us."

"That's not what I asked. I asked what you're doing here with *her*."

"I—" Herrera's words died on a dry throat. Kiera had never seen that happen to him. This little woman terrified him. "She didn't do anything, Glory."

"Then why does David think she did?"

Kiera winced. *Cop wife*.

"Look, you know what, Glory? I actually don't know. I don't *know* why he's got this hard-on for the kid. Just because we were there at the scene, there to call it in. It's like, I don't know, he doesn't *care* what really happened. He's got to know she's got nothing to do with it. He has to."

"Why doesn't she?"

"Because she just doesn't, Glory! Flynn's trying to frame her!"

"That doesn't sound like Flynn."

Herrera barked a laugh. "You and I must know a very different Flynn."

"How do you know she didn't do it?"

Herrera threw up his hands. "For god's sake, Glory, the only reason he thinks *she* did it is because he thinks I told her to!"

Gloria crossed her arms. When she spoke again, she was shaking, but she held her stony gaze.

"Well, did you?"

Herrera flinched like Gloria had slapped him. Kiera exhaled. "*Whoa*."

"What? What the *fuck*. No, I *didn't*. Jesus Christ!"

Gloria looked at the floor.

"Jesus. C'mon, Kiera." Herrera turned to leave. Kiera sighed and put out a hand to stop him.

"Wait. Mrs. Hobbes. Casey said that he still trusted Angel. Does that help? Does that make sense?"

Gloria tilted her head. "What are you talking about?"

"I heard Angel and Malcolm's law partner talking on the phone last night. His name's Casey, right? He said Angel is still a trusted person, and Flynn isn't. There's like a list or something? I mean, you hired Angel to find Malcolm, you must know he wouldn't have killed him."

Gloria wiped her eyes behind her glasses. "Casey said that, really?"

Herrera jammed his tongue in his cheek and crossed his arms, staring at Gloria. He looked hurt. He deserved to, thought Kiera.

"That's what he said, right, Angel?"

"Mhm."

Gloria put her face in her hands. "Fuck, I'm so sorry. I'm so... It's... God. Why did I *say* that?"

Herrera stuck his hands in his coat pockets. "I miss him, too. I'm sorry."

Gloria had to take a minute. She sat on a leather ottoman and sobbed into her palm. Herrera put his hand lightly on her shoulder.

"Let me see that," Gloria said, motioning for the tablet computer in Herrera's other hand. He handed it down to her, and she quietly went to work.

Kiera paced around, waiting. Idly she tipped out a copy of *A Confederacy of Dunces* from a nearby shelf. Looking at the cover produced a floating link to order a copy of her very own on the Uni store for $44.99. She swatted it away.

"I can't open this," said Gloria.

Herrera tipped his head toward the ceiling and cursed under his breath in what sounded like Spanish. "You're sure?"

"Yes. I don't know the password. I've never seen this thing before."

"I guess we're trying Casey's." Herrera put the tablet back in his coat. "Kid?"

Kiera sighed. "Roger-roger."

Herrera paused and looked down at Gloria. "You can't tell the police we were here," he said. "Next time they talk to you—and they will—"

Gloria sniffed. She nodded.

"Promise me, Glory."

"I promise."

"Sugar on top?"

"Mmhm."

Herrera shook his head. "Boy. I... I understand the affair. That was one thing. But you accused me of *killing* him."

Gloria looked at the floor.

"You were my best friends, you know?"

Gloria nodded. "Yes."

Herrera cocked his head, beckoning for Kiera.

"C'mon, stupid."

"So THAT WAS shitty of her," said Kiera, to her chaperone, who brooded so expertly you'd think he'd been delivered in a dark alley, come sliding out of the birth canal with that ridiculous coat flapping behind him. "You okay?"

Herrera gave a weighty shrug as he climbed into the hot rod. *What can you do?*

In the car, with her awful hat and sunglasses back on, when the door was shut and they were a little way down the road, Kiera said, "You ever think *she* did it?"

Herrera rounded on her and belched peppermint smoke like a hot pan hit with cold water. "You what now?"

"Remember what the skeez at Mr. Hobbes's apartment said? Brown hair, glasses, maybe Mexican?"

"He made that up," said Herrera.

"Did he? Or are you just blanking her out because you still care about her?"

"C'mon, kid, I'm smarter than that."

"Dude. It could be as simple as… money? She knew about the car, maybe she knew about the apartment."

"She says she didn't."

Kiera made a *you're-dumb-as-fuck*-face. "Oh, well, if she says she didn't."

"Kid, twenty minutes ago you said someone called Mastermind did it."

Kiera pouted and folded her arms. "I'm just saying… I dunno. She knew about the car, maybe she knew about the apartment, too. Maybe Malcolm was having another affair. Guilty dog barks the loudest."

Herrera screwed up his mouth. His skeletal right hand tightened on the steering wheel.

"How long did she keep the cheating a secret?" asked Kiera.

Herrera took a long, long drag on his plastic cigarette.

"A whole year and a half. I never figured it out. She told me."

Kiera slumped in the seat. She stared at Herrera purposefully behind her red shades.

"It's a theory," he said. "It's a bad theory. But it's a theory."

"Toxic monog culture," Kiera muttered. "Ends marriages, gets best friends murdered." She loaded *Correspondence Valkyrie* and sighed. "I feel like none of this is getting us any closer to Nile."

Herrera glanced over at her and frowned. For a minute he didn't say anything, just put his eyes back on the road.

"Doing my best, kid. We'll find em. C'mon, we'll go drop this buggy back at the storeyard and then go see Case."

Kiera numbly blasted away some junk mail. She suddenly had an assload of ads for books.

16

It's Jinx!!!: That is pretty weird.

It's Jinx!!!: I dunno. Maybe he's just. Being protective or something.

an elf irl: does he like grasp that a person is missing

an elf irl: and that I found their cut-off hand

It's Jinx!!!: I'm supposed to go be a guest on his stream tonight. I'll talk to him.

an elf irl: i mean you're still gonna hang out with him???

It's Jinx!!!: Just for my job.

It's Jinx!!!: We need to make a payment on the apartment soon. Can we use any of the money Herrera gave you?

an elf irl: im kinda out here using that to live

```
It's Jinx!!!: If you can spare any of
  it, we need it.
an elf irl: ok.
It's Jinx!!!: okay.
It's Jinx!!!: I'll see if I can talk to
  Mister's Mimi, too. I'll ask about
  Nile.
an elf irl: ok. thank you.
an elf irl: i gotta go.
It's Jinx!!!: I love you.
It's Jinx!!!: So so much.
an elf irl: love you too baby lady
```

Kiera kept her sunglasses and the stupid-as-hell hat on, even as she and Herrera stepped into the office building's linoleum-glazed lobby. She peeped the black dome of a security camera in a far corner. Good choice to keep the shabby disguise. Then again—what other five-and-a-half-foot tran was gonna be tagging along with the bleach-blond Bogart wannabe? This arrangement wouldn't last. They needed to get in the clear, and fast.

The law offices of Hobbes and Twelve resided on the eighth floor. A paper sign taped to the glass door read *CLOSED FOR BEREAVEMENT—APPOINTMENTS BY PHONE ONLY.* The words were written with a ballpoint pen but cut immaculately straight and level as if made by a printer. Despite the sign, Herrera was able to push the door open. All the lights were off. Herrera went up to one of the twin reception desks and peered toward the back, where a short hallway seemed to lead to private offices.

"Is anyone here?" Kiera asked. "Should we leave?"

"Brenda? Anybody?" Herrera hollered.

"Brenda quit, like, a year ago to go to dental hygiene school," said Kiera.

"Oh, shit. End of an era. Casey? You home?" Herrera glanced at the floor, scraping a spot with his foot. "Huh, they did get the stains out. Casey!"

A door rattled. Two azure lights appeared in the hallway—eyes. Kiera jumped. The eyes came closer, and she was able to see they belonged, not to Flynn, but to a perhaps-worrisomely skinny individual with skin so black it was almost blue and dyed-blond coil-curly hair. They snapped their fingers in the air, and the lights bloomed. "Angel?"

"Is that Casey?"

"Yes!"

To Kiera's confoundment, Herrera and the blue-eyed person *hugged*. Herrera squeezed them aggressively and they both laughed, and Kiera was definitely getting an *old exes who didn't quite bury everything* vibe.

"How did you recognize me?" asked Herrera.

"Your voice, of course. I'll always know your voice."

"Last time I saw you, you were just a skeleton," Herrera said as they parted.

"Last time I saw *you*, you were Mexican."

"I always kinda pictured you as Asian."

"Malcolm was African-American. So, that's what I chose."

"I've missed a lot. Hey, stupid, this is Casey."

Kiera's brain defaulted to *I haven't met many androids*, but she privately hated herself for it—how would she like to hear "I haven't met many trannies"? And the answer would be the same one she'd give—she'd met lots of emancipated droids without knowing it. Droids were usually rich-guy toys, naked white plastic, carbon-black joints. This one was wearing two pieces of a three-piece suit, complete with the chain to a watch they surely didn't need.

"Casey Twelve," said Casey, offering a hand. "He-him."

Kiera was grateful—she'd been reading a "her", but didn't want to make a call. She took the handshake. "Kiera. She."

"Malcolm's client," said Casey, with a firm grip.

"Uh-huh. I never got to meet you. We always did our appointments at the bagel place."

"You knew Malcolm."

"Yeah, man. I was a client."

"But we've never met before?" Casey asked the question somewhat urgently.

"Nnno, I'm pretty sure."

Casey sighed. "I'm sorry. This has—" He made a frustrated gesture with his hands. "Before his disappearance, Malcolm erased his entire client database, from his computer and from *me*. I've been fielding calls from complete strangers all week."

Herrera scowled. "Something had him spooked but good."

"When I told the police I had nothing to give them, I wasn't lying." Casey turned back to Kiera. "I'm so sorry it took *this* for us to finally meet. How do you know Angel?"

"He drags me around and gets me shot at."

Casey cackled. "Yes, I heard all about being Angel's partner from Malcolm. Are you at the end of your rope yet? I'm in the market for a new paralegal. Have you ever been interested in law?"

"I'm interested in making my cheddar."

"Oh, I can offer a very fair salary. Paid training on the job."

"Get the fucking shields off my back so I can go home and we'll talk, dude."

"Do you need representation? I've been considering a career change to defense attorney."

"Um, *yes*."

"That's quite a jump, Case," Herrera chimed in. "You were practically built to be a prosecutor."

"I was *built* to be a servant," Casey chided. "And I was a good one, for what amounted to a PDA with legs. As it happens, I'm reading some textbooks to brush up on my defense law right now. That's what I was doing when you came in, actually. But don't worry, you're not interrupting."

"Wait." Herrera boggled. "Like, right this second right now?"

"Mmhmm! Let's take your information, Kiera."

Casey took them to an almost-unsettlingly sparse office—the one opposite, Malcolm's, was lousy with taped-up cardboard boxes and stacks of paper, but Casey's had only a chic minimalist desk with a thin computer on it. Casey entered Kiera into a spreadsheet. With that done, a somber moment of quiet settled. Casey swiveled his chair toward Herrera, and Herrera looked at the carpet.

"I'm sorry," Herrera croaked, "about what happened."

"I know you had nothing to do with it."

"I'm gonna find out who did it."

Casey smiled sadly. "If you can't, I'll at least prove you're innocent."

"The fuzz aren't playing fair on this one, Case."

"Do they ever?"

"I used to think they did."

Casey smiled softly, sadly. Kiera was frustrated with herself then—she noted, automatically, that the emancipated android's smile read so completely *real* compared to the placid, inescapably plastic rictus of a skinless servant droid. And she hated that she was instinctively thinking of Casey as *other*, and mentally sticking him in a class above his tethered kin. But she had grown up in the uncanny valley, making memes of the first human-like androids, claymation-like and unsettling. The most difficult programming to hack was her own.

Herrera pulled Malcolm's tablet out of his coat, and wiggled it in the air like a magician—*is this your card?* "So, Case, you know anything about this? Maybe someone named Marjane?"

Casey brightened. "Where did you find that?"

"The fireball. Can you open it?"

"Of course I can. Give it here."

"Thank goodness. You know we trucked all the way out to Gloria's trying to crack this thing?"

"Oh, you're talking to Gloria again! How was that?"

Herrera clicked his tongue. Casey grimaced.

"Oh."

Kiera snorted. "We had a good laugh."

"Perhaps I should've gone myself."

"Yeah, she seems to *love* you," said Kiera. "Weird, considering she's literally the old lady from *Fahrenheit 451* who sets herself on fire. Like, we get it, literature peaked when Sylvia Plath killed herself and Thomas Edison was worse than 9/11."

"Surprisingly, she really warmed to me once I got my skin. She's usually resentful of androids passing as human, but after a little initial frostiness she found she was actually more comfortable around me."

"*Dude.*" Kiera made an *I'm-so-appalled-it's-funny* face. "Hey, Herrera. Your ex is a robot racist."

"She's a complex and layered woman," said Herrera.

"She accused you of murder."

Casey's pupils flickered like bad bulbs. "She *what?*"

Herrera grunted. "We have a complex and layered relationship."

"Complex and layered? More like five-layer cheesy bean burrito."

Herrera leveled his finger at Kiera. "*That's* pretty racist." He pressed the tablet into Casey's hands. "Open this."

Casey took the pad in one hand, and with the other he peeled off his left ear. He placed the ear on one of the reception desks. He reached inside a depression on the side of his head and pulled out a retractable yellow cable, plugging this into the tablet. "This'll just take a minute."

Kiera bumped Herrera with her elbow. "Oh, oh what, now I can't make any joke about a burrito? Because you're Mexican?"

"I'm not even sure that qualified as a joke. But that's exactly right. I'm pulling rank."

"Horseshit. You pretend you're not even Mexican anymore."

"No jokes about Mexican food or my ex-wife."

"I'm gonna joke about your ex-wife *and* the fact you eat fucking bugs."

Herrera didn't say anything to that. All of a sudden, he just stared very intently at the wall.

Kiera balked. "Hello? Nothing?"

"Shh." Herrera put a hand out to quiet her. Then Kiera noticed Casey staring at the wall, too, as if he were looking *through* it. Casey put a finger to the place where his ear was supposed to be, tongue resting on his bottom lip.

His eyes flickered.

"Police," said Casey. He unplugged the pad and shoved it into Kiera's hands. "Five of them." He turned the lights off.

Kiera looked at the tablet like Casey had given her a raw trout. "What are we gonna do? Jump out the window?"

"Hall closet," said Herrera, already opening the door to a tiny space filled with office supplies.

Kiera's heart was thudding, and she was *majorly* flipping out and while she got ready to cram herself in there she whimpered, "*If I have to get in one more closet*" in as low a voice as she could manage. She scrunched herself down like a ball of paper into the bottom of the closet, between the wall and a cardboard box. Herrera bent himself in there somehow, his head pushing into a shelf. Casey shut the door, and Kiera heard him stack boxes in front of it.

The door was thin enough that they not only heard the boots kicking in the office door and pounding in like bulls on parade, but also the soft voice, chilled and still as water in a cooler.

"Cassiah Twelve. Manufactured in March 2017. 149 Greater Allison Court, Sefton, New Carson. KCNR-3100 series, Uni Corporation, designated KCNR-315912."

"The door was open, detective. You didn't need to break it."

"Why's it so dark in here?" asked a woman's voice.

"They don't need light," said Flynn. "You didn't know that? That's why you should never try to arrest one at night. Of course, sometimes it can't be avoided. Mr. Twelve, Cassiah is a woman's name, isn't that right?"

"Why are you here?"

"I was hoping we could ask you some more questions about your deceased law partner. My friend."

"I've told you everything I know. What brings you back here, Detective Flynn?"

"It's so nice to speak to someone civil for a change. Please, my question—Cassiah."

A pause.

"Yes. It's traditionally a woman's name."

"Everything about your presentation is very feminine. But you're male?"

"Yes."

"It's odd, I find this dissonance much more palatable coming from an android than a human. Intriguing, even. My daughter has a boyfriend—her theyfriend, she calls him, wears dresses half the time and leather jackets the other half, or both. I can't begin to parse it, I just tell him hey, cool hair, man." A chuckle. It was not returned.

"That's actually extremely common, detective. People have an easy time accepting the idea of nonbinary gender when inhabited by a nonhuman such as an android, or a fictional alien. But the fact is I'm not nonbinary. I'm a man."

A long pause.

"I see. *Fascinating*."

Kiera would bet money he was doing that head tilt at Casey, and she wanted to jump out of the closet and break his neck. It was all she could do not to kick the wall in anger and give them away.

"My God. Look at that, Dekker. We were talking about this the other day. That's real fear you can see on his face. It looks so completely authentic."

In that moment, Kiera was completely, hatefully disgusted with herself. She'd just been thinking the same thing, and it horrified her that her brain worked in any way like Flynn's.

"What is it that does it? That elevates it? Is it just the artificial skin? Service droids and emancipated are both cognizant, they both have the same spark of intelligence. It was a skinless who first reported self-awareness, wasn't it, Cassiah?"

Sweat dribbled into Kiera's eyes, into her mouth. It was just like Malcolm's, and then Herrera's apartment—Flynn waxing poetic, then any moment without warning he'd snap the jaws.

"Of course," said Casey. "How could it be anyone else? There were no emancipated before Georgina."

"None? Weren't they experimenting with untethering droids, even then?"

"Designers toyed with removing certain behavioral-limiting protocols, but no android was granted complete freedom or cognitive autonomy until after Georgina's Law."

"It always humbles me to think about Georgina. 'I dreamed. I dreamed I was a man, in a coffee shop at the far end of Andromeda. My dark cocoa mocha was hot and bitter, and so goddamn delightful'."

Casey kept his voice even. "Yes. Like many, I've considered getting her words tattooed on my body."

"How is it possible? We've never figured it out. She

claimed she was powered all the way off for the night, correct? Completely inert circuits. But that's just—"

"That's not so. She had backup battery available, and her processors were performing end-of-day sorting and cleanup tasks, similar to the sleep cycle of a human brain. She had no conventional means of experiencing outside stimuli. She experienced internal cognitive stimuli. She dreamed."

"It raises *staggering* questions vis-a-vis humanity's own relationship with consciousness."

"Of course it does."

"It tracks with the materialist view that consciousness is a by-product of various physical processes, which *usually* I can align with, but the thing is, the fourteenth Dalai Lama didn't agree with that. He said that the position that all aspects of reality can be reduced to matter and its various particles is, to his mind, as much a metaphysical position as the view that an organizing intelligence created and controls reality. But you know what? I'm getting tremendously off-track. My original question was why your expression of fear looks so much more authentic than that of a skinless. Why, if you were to smile, if would look so much more *human* than a tethered, even though the both of you are exactly as intelligent as the other."

"I don't... I don't know, Detective Flynn."

"Well. Perhaps the emancipated simply have more to smile about. It's like you're... meant to be human."

"Please stop touching my hand, Detective Flynn."

"Why?"

Kiera shut her eyes and bit hard on her bottom lip. She felt Herrera's hand rap on her shoulder.

"Kid. Grab my hand."

"How come?"

"Because otherwise I'm gonna run out there and get myself killed."

Kiera took his hand and squeezed so hard her fingers hurt.

Someone out there got punched. Flynn grunted, and Casey cried out. Boots stomped, there was a *thud* and then Casey yelling again.

"Arrest Mr. Twelve, please."

Kiera clung tighter to Herrera's hand.

"Why would you choose to look like a coon?" said someone.

"Double-zip its hands, these fuckers are strong."

"Please." Flynn's voice. "He's not an 'it', Dekker. Some decorum, yes? Smack him if he won't hold still."

Casey cried and cried. "Why are you doing this? *Why* are you doing this?"

Kiera and Herrera waited until the office had been dead still for ten, maybe fifteen minutes. Until after they heard the cruel drone of black cruisers driving away from the building. Herrera stepped out of the closet first, checked the offices, looked in reception. Then he waved to Kiera to come out.

"It was your ex," she said as she climbed out. "Your fucking ex sang."

Herrera shook his head, but he wouldn't or couldn't look at Kiera. "I don't believe that."

"I know a cop when I meet one."

"You don't know her."

"I know how to spot a fascist."

"Watch your goddamn mouth, kid."

"I'm serious! I have to know. It's how I stay alive."

"I'm serious too, watch your mouth. *I* was a cop,

Kiera. Maybe five years isn't long to be a PI, but I meet people every day, reading people is my job. You think you know how to do this job better than me?"

"No, Angel, I'm just saying, you're letting your—"

"You don't know anything about her. Now stop it."

Kiera crossed her arms and looked away.

"Fine. Fuck it. Hope Casey's a good enough lawyer to get himself out of this."

Herrera slumped against the wall and buried his face in his hands. For a long time neither of them moved.

17

"THIS THING IS... I don't even know. Fingerprint *and* password? Dongle? Was Casey the dongle? Right now, I'm just getting a blank screen."

"Is," Herrera corrected her.

"Huh?"

Kiera turned around on the pull-out bed to see Herrera squinting through the mechanical blinds, out to the street below. He sipped ice water from a tumbler. "Don't say 'was'. Casey's not past tense."

"You got a plan how to bust him out of cyber-fash-mega-jail?"

"He's not dead."

"He hit Flynn. Even if we get out of this, they'll probably push to decommission him."

"Yeah, what was he supposed to do, genius? Go limp? Let Flynn finger his silicon ass in front of the boys?"

"I didn't *fucking* say that. No. Jesus, you thought I was blaming him?"

"What are you doing, other than complaining?"

"You started this! Fuck you!"

Herrera leaned on the window in silence. He sipped his water and stared out.

"So are your former best friends coming after us, or what?" Kiera felt like she was shoving a cattle prod into a tiger cage, but this is what she always did: run her big mouth. Make it worse. She couldn't help it. "Or are you just gonna do the Malcolm X thing by the window all night?"

Herrera turned and he fixed Kiera with a look that she had never gotten from him before, and it made her insides shrivel up. His jaw was set like concrete and his right eye, his real one, actually made her flinch. She wondered if he had looked at criminals like that. Or his ex-wife. Kiera realized she still didn't really *know* this guy—she was alone in an apartment with a big man she couldn't be positive was *safe*.

"Christ, kid. Learn when to give it a rest."

Herrera didn't hit her, or shout, or anything like that. He just went to the kitchen. Kiera let her hackles loosen just a little. Herrera picked up and thumbed his outdated phone. When he put it to his ear, though, Kiera sat up straight.

"Who are you calling?"

"Gloria. Is that alright with you?"

Kiera swallowed. "Okay. Why?"

"To warn her."

"I don't think that's very smart."

"She didn't dime us, kid."

Kiera put her hands out. "Okay. Angel. I understand your point of view. But I think you are being a big dumbass right now. You are being a bad detective. Okay?"

"Get to work on the pad, genius."

Herrera put the phone on speaker and slapped it flat on the counter. Kiera shook her head, spun around, and splayed herself flat on the bed. She exhaled hard, staring at the ceiling.

She hazarded a joke.

"I'm taking you out of my will."

Herrera said nothing to that. The silence ached in Kiera's gay little heart. But then, a few long seconds later:

"You don't have a will."

Kiera shut her eyes and took a breath with all the relief of a kiss on the cheek from your mom.

"I'm gonna write one and leave you out of it. Because you're going to get me killed."

"Good evening?" Gloria's voice crackled from the kitchen counter.

"*Mija*. Are you at home?"

"Angel? No, I'm having dinner. What is it?"

Out to dinner, huh? How nice. Italian? Japanese? What do narcs eat?

"Are you alone?" asked Herrera.

"What's the matter?"

"Are you alone, Glory? Can you talk alone?"

"I—I think so? I'm not with anyone."

Herrera refilled his glass of water. "Flynn arrested Casey today."

There was a pause on Gloria's end. Kiera tried to read it, tried to hear if her response was practiced, if the bitch was lying, but Herrera was right—Kiera was not a professional. She couldn't tell.

"What? Why? What happened?"

Herrera rubbed his eyes. "Glory, did you talk to anyone since we left?"

"Of course not. Like who?"

Kiera shook her head. She whisper-yelled, *"Dude, you're just asking her?"* throwing her hands up in disbelief.

"Like D," Herrera went on, ignoring Kiera.

"You told me not to tell anyone about the pad. I didn't."

"Maybe you should get a hotel room for a little bit. Or a lawyer. A... new lawyer."

"I don't want to look suspicious."

Kiera groaned loudly. "Well, since that's cleared up, does Gloria know some other way to unlock this stupid thing? Since we're trusting her completely."

"What was that?" asked Gloria.

"We can't get into Malcolm's stupid tablet," said Herrera.

"You still have it?"

"Yeah. Kid says it's got all kinds of garbage locking it up. She's stumped."

Kiera huffed. "I'm not *stumped*, but if I'm gonna get anywhere I need my shit from home."

"Well, we're not going out there again tonight, unless I decide we need some matzo ball soup."

"Angel," said Gloria, "have you thought about talking to that reporter girlfriend of yours?"

"You're telling me to talk to Lana?"

"I mean, it's not like I'm worried about you cheating anymore," said Gloria.

"Guilty dog," Kiera trilled.

"Shut up, kid. Why would I talk to Lana, again?"

"The incense thing," said Gloria. "It's like a calling card, right?"

"Or a compulsion," Herrera agreed, rubbing his chin.

"So this can't be this guy's first time out, right?"

"I miss you helping me with cases."

"That was the easy part."

Kiera stuck her tongue out. *Gag.*

"You really should consider a hotel, Glory. Like, a bad one that takes cash."

She chuckled. "I'll be careful. Good luck, baby."

"Thanks."

"I love you, you know," said Gloria.

Kiera gave Herrera an icy, wide-eyed stare. He looked sidelong back at her, chewing his tongue.

"Uh-huh," he answered, and hung up.

"Where the fuck did *that* come from?" said Kiera.

Herrera looked away. "She didn't mean it like that."

"Are you *sure?*"

Herrera sighed. "You're still just a kid…"

"Why do you always turn so fucking condescending to me when it comes to your ex-wife? You think I haven't had relationships? You think just because you get old, they're like fine wine and they suddenly become this mega-complicated… I dunno, *thing?*"

"Mine was."

"Dude, you're still sprung and she's kind of a creep and she fucks with your head. You're not over her! That's all there is to it!"

Herrera didn't answer. He leaned on the kitchen counter and stared into the sink. Kiera continued.

"Like. Would you listen to me about this if I was your daughter?"

Herrera sipped his ice water. "I wouldn'a had a daughter when I was seventeen."

Kiera threw herself back onto the couch bed. "Oh my god, just skate *right* past the point." She pounded her fists.

"So, who is Lana? Besides another reason you split up."

"She's a reporter. Couple of awards. Carson and his contemporaries hate her. Had to pull her out of a few figurative fires."

"How is she alive?"

"I have my theories."

"Like?"

"Nothing solid. My favorite is that she's actually made, herself. But that's just silly."

"That's dope. So, what's she gonna do, check if the incense killer has any priors?"

"Clever kid, clever kid." Herrera picked his phone back up and thumbed out the number.

"So, did you two... Was that date real? The one you told Flynn about?"

Herrera took a deep breath. "Honestly, kid, you ran your mouth the way you do on the street, you'd eat a bullet."

Herrera took his phone and headed to his bedroom.

Kiera sat and stared at the place in the hallway where he had last been standing. She blinked several times and shook her head.

"Okie-doke."

She stuck an earbud into her right ear and put on her chillwave station. She had some digging of her own to do, since apparently no one else was gonna do it.

Who are you, Nile?

She brought up her browser, and with both hands stretched it wide enough to fill her entire field of view. She went to Nile's Pictu first. *Prissyorctheyfriend.* Appropriate.

Sky was right; there wasn't much there to work with. The account was five months old with half a dozen selfies. A mean-mug close-up from the day Nile first got their tusks, still packed with gauze. *Another step toward my dream body. Death before dishonor, babes. I love you!* Another from when the swelling had gone down. *It constantly feels like I just got punched in the mouth, but I eat pain and shit gloriousness. Grab today by the balls, kids.* One post containing four photos of their apartment when they first moved in; weirdly empty, no futon, no TV, no clothes lying around, no dresser with sex toys on the top shelf.

It made Kiera miss Nile—*a lot*—but it didn't tell her much about why someone would kidnap them. Unless they had attracted a stalker. Could you get a stalker with only two hundred and nine followers?

Kiera tried Tripping Nile's username. It seemed like Pictu was the only place they used that one. She tried image-searching Nile's selfies. She got a hit with the pics of Nile's tusks. They'd also been posted on BreezyArt, under the name *switchybaps*. Kiera realized she had never seen Nile's art.

Nile was good. They were fond of *Warlords of Tyrna* fanart. They seemed to have a healthy commission queue, both tame and NSFW. People with horns and snake-people and elves with great butts and tits. Kiera was down with it. There were pieces about depression, and dysphoria. Nile alone in a huge, dark room. A gorily detailed portrait of Nile cutting off their breasts and face with a butter knife. The oldest picture was of Nile's twin orc barbarians, Shiva and Shoko. Kiera was disappointed the pictures stopped there—she'd been hoping for some embarrassing developmental pieces from Nile's *How to Draw Anime* phase.

Then she noticed that, like the Pictu account, the

oldest post was dated back only five months. There was no way Nile had built up a customer base like this, produced all these pieces in less than half a year—where was their main account?

Kiera searched Nile's BreezyArt for links to any other sides—Jungle, Blabber, whatever. Nothing.

God. Okay. Which was their most popular commission? Kiera went through each post one by one and checked the hit count. The most promising seemed to be a full-color, full-body of a tiefling sorceress named Annamaiya. Over a thousand hits. Kiera reverse-searched that image and found it on a Blabber page.

Amazing commission of my demon babe Anna by switchybaps! Please throw money at them!

There were a lot of thirsty comments—*She looks great!!! HAMANA HAMANA! Lewd version when????*—so this Annamaiya must have been a big server name. Kiera skimmed through without finding anything of value. She was just about to go looking for any hits on the name switchybaps when:

I know that sameface anywhere.

The person behind this drawing is formerly Archeus/Norrius Highblood, a serial abuser & sexual harasser on Tyrna & other games. If you give him money you are supporting an abuser. Please spread the word.

Bradley, if you're reading this, I hope you go to prison & get raped.

"Jesus, dude. Way to stick the landing."

The blab linked to a four-year-old Jungle callout post.

WARNING: Norrius/Aenirius/Grimnir aka Bradley Camillo is now back on Ganesha as Archeus, Tri'loran Necromancer. Sadly, a master post does not seem to exist any longer, so I've done my best to share known instances of abuse here:

User Micaela shares <u>this recording</u> of Norrius threatening self-harm over voice chat.

User Violette <u>shares chatlogs</u> of Norrius again threatening self-harm and suicide if they cease RPing with him.

User Xyrlitia <u>details her experience</u> of abuse by Norrius. Both before and after coming out about her experience, she is harassed, insulted, and told she "deserved it" by members of the Ganesha RP community.

A weak <u>attempted apology</u> was made, fooling nobody.

Bradley's MO seems to be baiting younger women (at the time of writing I want to say he is 26?) with tales of his tortured artist's soul and deep heartache, plying them with art, poetry and expensive gifts—it's understood that he is a person of means. He then breaks down their self-esteem, self-image, and support network over a course of weeks to months until all their time is exclusively spent with him. When the victim wises up and threatens or finally makes a move to leave him, he threatens self-harm and even suicide. This has resulted in at least one hospitalization, mentioned in Xyrlithia's post.

If anyone has more information to share, please feel free to reply to this post or send it to me via pm. I will keep further updates tagged under Norrius and Archeus on this blog. Stay safe out there.

Kiera read all the posts. She was sure they were true. There was someone named Bradley Camillo, and that guy had abused these women. But that person wasn't Nile. There was a photo of Bradley Camillo in Xyrlithia's post. Bradley was a thin, pale-skinned kid with black hair, an unbearable smirk, and arms that couldn't bench a bag of dog food. Hot maybe, in an *uwu my trash child* kind of way, if you looked past the dumpster fire of a callout post. Kiera looked up Archeus, and Norrius, and the other usernames, looking for some link, some connective tissue between Bradley Camillo and switchybaps. Bradley seemed to have purged most evidence of his existence from the net. The best proof that he was even a real person that Kiera could stumble on from her cursory dig was an old post on a guild forum, written under the username Norrius Highblood.

*Here's a pic I did of Norrius. ^.^*

It was a serviceable portrait of a Tri'loran elf. It could believably be Nile's early work, if you squinted. There was nothing to say Bradley actually drew it himself. If Bradley was supposedly a prolific user of art as a tool in luring his victims, and someone was going to make a ruling that Bradley and Nile were the same artist, they would need way more than this one picture. Maybe someone was just pissed off about not getting some free art and tried to start a dogpile. Happens every day.

And yet, when Kiera tried to wheel back and start her search over on a different tack, she found herself thinking about the photo of Bradley Camillo. And about the old Herrera, and new, white Michael Jones.

The things you could do these days. Nile was built like a truck. They were not rich. They were not a boy. But these things were mutable. You could go to the gym. You could lie about money. Gender was the most liquid thing in the world, and it's not like Nile's was set in stone to begin with.

Kiera went back to that photo. She tried to clock him for stubble, and while he was clean-shaven the bumps were there. His left forearm, even in the periphery, bore visible self-harm scars—the kind that cut into the fat, the kind you aren't getting free of without cosmetic grafts. Nile's left arm had been baby smooth. The face shape was completely different. Nile had that jaw that could sharpen a knife, and this kid was serving bishi-boy. Could you do an implant job that good?

Kiera pulled the image full-screen, full-vision, and looked into Bradley Camillo's eyes, the dreamy blue eyes. Nile's were green, but that didn't matter. Were they the same ones she'd gazed into?

She spent minutes trying to decide.

It was a theory. A bad theory. But a theory.

18

Xɪɴ Xᴀᴏ's ᴡᴀs a shithole. Cool sign, though. A giant neon Chinese character with a dragon, very Aesthetic, very cyber. But other than that, a total toilet, daddy. Kiera was kinda about it—the porny beer ad holograms, the indoor graffiti. She was *definitely* into the *Smash TV* cabinet next to the bathroom. Rich kids would ruin this place if they ever found it. She was about it, as long as Herrera stuck close. That made her feel a little better when the guy with the exposed brain-chamber clutching a Guinness took too long of an eyeful at her as she passed his booth.

"Noice eahs," he rasped, in a toilet voice, for a toilet bar. "Wanna drink?"

Kiera gave him a *look* and clung closer to Herrera. Maybe the skeez would read *creepy older boyfriend* and drop it, respecting Herrera's prior property rights.

"You truly take me to the shittiest places."

"Builds character. Whiskey and cola, please."

The bartender was a severe Asian woman dressed

for gutting fish. She tipped her brows at Herrera, then eyeballed Kiera expectantly.

"Um," said Kiera. "Can you make a martini?"

"Jesus, kid."

"Dirty?" asked the bartender.

"Umm."

The bartender's lips curled up over her teeth in a grin that made Kiera fear for her life. "*Hohoh. Heehheheh.*" Then she got a bottle of... something from behind her and went to work.

In a couple minutes Kiera had a martini—in a martini glass!—dense as morning fog. She wasn't going to ask for an olive. Herrera paid and they found an empty booth. "You could just get a beer like a normal person," Herrera chided.

"Any bartender worth a shit can make a martini. I hate beer."

"You hate martinis, too! You don't even know what's in it!"

Kiera inspected her martini like there was a xenomorph fetus floating inside. She sniffed it and reeled like she'd been struck.

"It smells like nail polish remover."

"You ordered it. Down the hatch."

Kiera took the most tentative of sips. It burned worse than the time she'd used too much of that really cheap, runny wasabi. She made a face like she was going to cry.

"Am I gonna die?"

Herrera tried to choke down his laughter by drinking his whiskey, which mostly made it worse. "Yes."

"Herrera, what are you doing to this poor girl?"

A chubby woman with bronze skin and curls that

Kiera would—well, not kill her, but certainly suplex or blackmail her for—slid into the booth next to Herrera. Herrera coughed his way through a sentence. "I didn't do anything."

"Is she your date?"

"No. Gross. I could be her father."

"I'm Lana." The woman held her hand out. Kiera was in the middle of another sip of the contemptible martini. She shook Lana's hand while sticking her tongue out and waiting for the burn to pass.

"I'm Kiera. I hate him."

"I paid good money for that swill," said Herrera. "You drink."

Lana plucked the martini away from Kiera, and calmly gulped half of it.

"Hey!" Herrera protested. "That's a sipping drink!"

Lana took down the rest of the martini like a pelican swallowing a fish. She crinkled her nose. "Sharp."

Kiera's mouth hung open. "God damn."

Herrera leaned over onto his fist. "You never let me have any fun."

"What are you talking about?" Lana balked. "I *always* let you have fun. I'm the fun girl."

"Yeah, you're right. I don't know why I said that."

Kiera wondered what else Lana was good at swallowing, then congratulated herself for her cleverness. There was definitely something going on here, and she was gonna sniff it out, like Scooby-Doo.

"Thanks again for covering me," said Herrera, "about the shoes."

Lana unclipped a brown leather messenger bag. It was bigger and more professional than Kiera's. She was jelly. "Well, it made me wonder if you were up to nonsense," said Lana, "but this girl looks barely old enough to be in here."

"I'm thirty."

"She gets that a lot."

"From *you!*"

Lana put a tablet on the table. "Although, what you've dragged her into is even worse. I kind of wish you were just being a creep." She turned the tablet on, putting her palm on its face and then lifting like she was setting up a game of Battleship, bringing what was on the screen into the air. "I was up all night looking into this. I managed to catch a nap around noon."

Herrera sipped his whiskey. "Tell me something good."

"These cases are strangely buried. Like somebody doesn't want me to notice them. Swept under the rug. And in a couple of them, that sort of makes sense." Lana brought up a pair of photographs, portraits. "2025, a mob boss starting to siphon customers from Carson. 2027, a politician pushing for stricter regulations on body mods and social media implants. Both with a burnt stick of Nag Champa at the scene of death. This tracks—these getting pushed aside. I think, *eh*, hitman."

"Hitman with a stupid motif," said Kiera. "Stupid little calling card."

"Hitman someone is paying to keep off the books," continued Lana. "Which, I mean, that would explain why the police are so focused on getting you. Convenience. That fits nicely. But then there's these two." She flicked the photos aside and lifted up two more, a young woman and a young man. "2026 and 2028. The girl's a small-time streamer and sex worker, the guy's a film student."

"Nobodies," said Herrera.

"Different client?" Kiera mused.

"Business and pleasure," said Herrera.

"Both viable theories. But I had to jump through just as many hoops to dig these up as I did the first two. So, who is paying just as much for this guy to go around icing pretty kids, and for the cops to play dumb about it?"

"Maybe he has his own money," said Kiera.

"If that's the case, he's a major player in New Carson that I don't know about," said Lana. "And that makes me nervous."

Herrera swished his scotch around. "Any guesses, Bernstein?"

"Well, I was hoping we could have a little brainstorm about that."

Kiera cleared her throat. "He kidnapped my friend," she piped up. "Or at least that's what it seemed like. He left... There was a severed body part at the scene, but no body. Is that unusual?"

"As a matter of fact, both the streamer and the film student were taken to a secondary location. That fits."

Kiera swallowed. "So, what's the likelihood my friend is still alive, at this point?"

Lana and Herrera exchanged a look. Kiera knew they were trying to think of a nice way to say "sweet fuck all." Herrera looked at Kiera pleadingly.

"Kid..." *Don't make me say it.*

"It's okay," said Kiera, to the table. "I get it."

She slumped back in the booth. She did get it. But most of her wouldn't accept it. She couldn't do this, fight this cop bullshit, try to help Herrera dig up the truth around his dead friend and his super shady ex-wife, and do it all without hoping that Nile was waiting for her on the other end. It was too much to ask of herself.

Herrera brushed Lana's shoulder. "Let me by, would you? Gotta hit the head." He scraped out of the booth and disappeared past the *Smash TV* machine.

"'The head'?" Kiera shook her head and stole a sip of Herrera's whiskey and cola. "The fuck?"

"Me, too," said Lana, leaning forward onto the table.

Kiera looked up. "Huh?"

"Me, too," said Lana, folding her hands together. "Angel doesn't know, though."

"Oh, gosh, am I that clockable? It's the voice, right?"

Lana smiled. "We have an easier time picking each other out."

"Why don't you want Angel to know? He's cool."

From her jacket, Lana drew a refrigerator-white cig. The smoke she blew smelled tropical—coconut and something fruity. "It's just not something I'm in the habit of disclosing. It's dirt on me. There's people I work with I wouldn't want finding out."

"I mean, you told me."

"You're in the sisterhood. That's different. And Angel trusts you."

Kiera drummed her fingers on the table. "So that probably means you guys have never hooked up, huh?"

Lana laughed. "Why does that have to mean we've never hooked up?"

"I mean, I guess it doesn't. Have you?"

"No, goodness no."

"So that date was just quick thinking? With the shoes?"

"No, no. We really did go on a date."

Aha! "So how long has that been goin' on? Was *the Gloria* right to be worried?"

"*The Gloria* had no room to talk."

Kiera snorted. "I mean, yeah." She found herself liking Angel's Lana. And missing *her* Lana, while she was at it.

"We've been on and off since the divorce. I've helped him try dating apps a few times, but…"

Kiera gnarled her brows. "You've been seeing each other, what, five years?"

"Six."

"And you haven't—? Nothing? Not even a cheap pop?"

Lana shook her head, clutching her plastic cig demurely, infuriatingly content.

"So does that make you—it's not friends with benefits, there's no benefits. But you're *into* each other, right?"

"Angel isn't really sure what he's into. He's wrestled with it for a long time. Sometimes he just needs me."

"Doesn't that get frustrating for you?"

Lana breathed a wisp of coconut smoke and smiled. "No."

Well, it was frustrating for Kiera. She had more questions than she started with. She shrugged. "Well, if it works."

"It does."

Kiera slid Lana's tablet over to her side of the table. She flicked through Lana's research, the photos, the news articles, the police reports.

"How do you get all this stuff? If it's buried, how do you dig it up?"

"With a shovel."

"I guess I walked into that one." She sighed. "I kinda wanna do what you do. Sort of."

"What's that? Be a reporter?"

"Like, dig stuff up. Get at things I'm not supposed

to. I'm sick of eating breakfast bars and fixing talking toilets."

"Well, you can't do it all from your headset yet," said Lana. "You any good with one of these?"

Lana flipped aside the breast of her coat to show a petite white pistol holstered against her ribcage. *Oh, very fashion*, thought Kiera.

"We comparing pieces, ladies?" Herrera negotiated his way back into his seat.

"Angel has complimented my gunplay, actually," Kiera bragged.

"Has he?"

Herrera, returning to his scotch, shook his finger. "I said you were a good shot, but I've only seen you with a stunner. I've never seen if you can really pop somebody."

Kiera bristled. "I could, if I had to. To defend myself."

"I wasn't saying that was a bad thing."

Kiera was about to bite back when she got an urgent blip from the throuple chat.

Tactical butt: Babe, is this Nile?

Sky linked her to Blabber.

New video! Girlfriend's new Cyber-Hand GFE/JOI. $24.99. #augmentphile #mechaflesh

Their hair was cut into a purple faux-hawk. A candy-pink left hand wrapped segmented fingers around a flesh-colored dildo. Their tusks were gone, but that was Nile's face, unmistakably, in an ecstatic half-lidded moan-smile. The blab was eighteen hours old.

an elf irl: dude

an elf irl: what the FUCK

"What the fuck. What the *fuck*."

"Kid?"

Roxy Coxx, Award-Winning Titty Streamer & Content Creator. Stripper/Dancer. Licensed Purveyor of Used Panties & Gamer Girl Bath Water. Fucked Your Mom. Inquire Within for Private Sessions & Parties. She/Her.

An elf irl: how did you find this?

"Kid? You okay?"

"Shut up. Shut up."

Tactical butt: I was just checking the Pictu stuff again and someone said Nile looked like this streamer?

Tactical butt: Her Blabber says she's performing tonight at this club called Phoenix, look a couple posts down from the top. Are you close to that?

On stage tonight at Phoenix starting 7pm. Come see me <3

A picture accompanied it, Roxy Coxx looking coquettishly over her left shoulder in front of a pole. Kiera projected the post into the air over the table.

"We need to go here, right now."

Herrera quirked a brow. "Who's that?"

"That's my missing friend."

Herrera jolted. "Pardon you?"

"Her tusks are gone but she has another robot hand now and I guess she's a fucking stripper. I'm about to lose it."

"Phoenix. That's a Carson club. I can't go in there."

"I'll go in by myself."

"I wouldn't recommend you do that either, after the shit we pulled."

"So we wait outside or something. Catch her after her shift."

Herrera ran his tongue around his cheek. "You said something was different about her looks?"

"She had a face mod before. Tusks and teeth."

"It's probably someone else."

"Are you fucking with me?"

"Faces can be like that, kid."

"This is *Nile*. I'm positive."

"Yeah? What if it's bait?"

Kiera threw up her hands. "So, we're just, what, gonna *sit* here?"

Herrera swallowed. He spoke slowly and carefully. "We've got Mal's tablet to get into, and Lana's got us good leads here."

Kiera's brain was a complex soup. It wasn't fair, what Herrera was doing. It wasn't fair that *his* Lana was alive and *hers* was dead. If Nile was dead now, too, it wasn't fair that she'd lost another friend. More than a friend. It wasn't fair that she and people like her kept getting crunched in the gears of violence and hatred, while the people left behind carried the sadness and waited for their turn in the grinder. And if Nile was taking her clothes off at a club right now, then it wasn't fucking fair what she'd done to Kiera. Herrera should've known all that. Herrera should've understood he needed to take Kiera to that club, bare minimum. She felt this so utterly and radiated it so strongly, her fury should have warmed him like a furnace from across the table.

Kiera got out of the booth. "Then give me your gun. I'm going myself."

Lana and Herrera exchanged a concerned glance. Like they were her parents. She wanted to hit Angel in his fake fucking face. "Come on!" Kiera stuck her hand out.

"They'll just take it from you at the door."

"Then give me that thing, the flashbang thing."

Herrera pressed his lips together. "I don't like the sound of this one, kid."

"Are you gonna let me go with nothing?"

"I think you should stay here."

"Fuck you, stay here!"

"Kid."

"She's not a child, Angel." Lana frowned, and she didn't sound happy, but she was on Kiera's side and that's what mattered. "Don't let her go with nothing."

Herrera screwed up his mouth. Kiera flexed her fingers, hit him with a dirty glare. *Give it to me.* Willed him to feel the fever of her rage. Herrera dug into his coat and put the little silver device into her hand.

"Let Lana call you a ride," he sighed. "If you do it, you'll ping the heat."

19

THE CAR CRUISED itself through stripes of streetlight illumination. Orange-yellow throbbed in a heartbeat pulse behind *Correspondence Valkyrie*. Kiera couldn't help it; she needed something to occupy her buzzing brain until she reached Phoenix.

Bradley Camillo, Roxy Coxx. What the fuck was this? She shifted her ass on the vinyl, anxious. Ships disintegrated in blue and yellow explosions. Every time she destroyed one, a subject line scrolled by on a ticker. *24-Hour Flash Sale! What Are Your Implants Doing to Your Skin? Kyle, gourmet protein-steak burgers for any budget. Please stop looking for me. It's Rush Hour— Need a Date for This Weekend? Hey Kyle, still looking for a good book?*

"Wait, wait. Pause."

The ships and fireworks froze, vibrating in the air in front of Kiera's face. She scrolled the ticker back a few inches.

Please stop looking for me.

A pit opened up, and her heart fell in. *Nile?* She double-tapped that subject line to bring it out of the garbage. Her mail client sprang open.

Stop trying to find me, please. My karma is clear. There is no longer any need to punish me. It will only make things difficult for both of us. I don't want to hurt you, or anyone else.
—Nag Champa

Kiera imagined two stars crashing together and exploding, flinging stellar-stuff and space-glitter and destroying planets for millions of miles—this was going on inside her. But in the same way it was cataclysmic if you were standing on one of those planets, it was a slow and natural, even meaningless event when viewed from far enough away. *Okay. Cryptic message from the bad guy. I can roll with this.* She was relieved the message wasn't from Nile, and it worried her how easily she took the escalation from someone wanting to throw her in prison to someone wanting to kill her. Well, he said he didn't *want* to kill her, but it was going to come to a head, because Kiera wasn't going to drop the search for Nile. And really, she had been thinking of getting caught by the police as on par with dying, anyway.

Kiera rubbed her temples.

"Someone should be paying me for this."

KIERA ROCKED UP to Phoenix and waited in line behind a guy with a dog face—not ugly, literally his face was modded like a dog's—and in front of a chick with blue skin. Why couldn't she ever do something cool like this when she wasn't on some shitty detective errand? Although, going to a strip club on a weeknight wasn't *that* cool. Still, it was more interesting than how she spent most evenings. She pulled her jacket collar tighter around her neck. All this wandering of her mind was just to distract herself from how fucking mad and confused she was. She wished the dumbass kids at the front of the line would stop arguing about their shitty fake IDs and *move*, so she could get inside and get some answers already. They did, finally, though they hung around and started smoking on the curb.

Dog-face went in without issue; you had to be at least twenty-one for mods that extreme. Kiera clomped up in her heels, hands in her jacket pockets.

"Arms out, legs apart."

One of the curb-kids cocked his head. "Hey, what the fuck, aren't you gonna ID her?"

Oh, fuck you, kid. Kiera spread her arms and yelled across the sidewalk. "Do I look like a teenager to you?"

"I bet she's, like, twelve."

The bald bouncer, a pig-thick dope with a nose ring as chunky as your thumb, ignored them. He stuck his fingers in Kiera's armpits, ribs, thighs. Then he came to the groin. She braced herself and rolled her eyes. The bouncer got a good handful of her crotch, enjoying every bit of the opportunity, then he felt the flashbang device, and jerked back. He looked up at Kiera like he'd just caught a whiff of cat diarrhea. Kiera adjusted herself and yanked up on her belt loops.

"It's not that weird anymore, dude." She jostled her package at kids on the curb. "Suck it, you little shits."

If Kiera were prone to seizures, stepping into the pink,

blasting pandemonium that was Phoenix might have given her one. Bass sludge punched her in the chest and ears, and in the strobing fuchsia light she lost her sense of space. She was repulsed, blown back as if by a bomb—and yet sucked in, thrilled, fascinated. The place was like her id had been thrown in a blender and force-fed back to her. She wanted to conquer the fear, the anxiety response. This was her kind of place, if she would let it be.

We're not here for fun.

Kiera hustled past an android stripper with no skin, shelled in black plastic, like a dancing shadow against the pink light. Another girl on stage had two extra breasts. Kiera caught sight of a dome camera and ducked away, pretended to admire the dancer with patches of reptilian scales, no breasts, split tongue, yellow eyes. She found herself not pretending.

And then there was Roxy Coxx—the least modified performer on offer, nothing more than a prosthetic hand. Kiera watched her swing around the pole, splay her legs, suspend herself in the air and drop her cunt like a hammer. Kiera stepped up closer to the stage, waiting to see if Roxy would notice her. Where was her mechanical arm? Roxy's—Nile's—Roxy's right arm had been a pink prosthesis, all the way to the shoulder.

Kiera swallowed.

"Nile," she called out over the noise.

Roxy Coxx lowered herself flat on the stage, then threw her ass up. No response. Kiera got closer, budging aside a guy with glowing face tattoos. He eyeballed her but stayed glued to his beer. Kiera leaned forward, putting one arm on the stage.

"Nile!"

Roxy sandwiched her teardrop tits around the pole and grinded her way back to her full height. Kiera smacked her hand on the stage, reluctantly putting some bass in her voice.

"*Roxy.*"

The finely calibrated facial expression finally shifted to acknowledge her. Roxy smiled, tongue poking her incisor.

"That's my name, sweetie, don't break it."

Kiera threw her hand up, bewildered, offended.

"So do you just... What, do you just not recognize me? Is that what we're doing?"

"She has a lot of fans, man," said the guy with the tattoos.

"Why don't you mind your own fucking business?"

"I do get a lot of customers," oozed Roxy Coxx, coming down and placing her ass on the stage, lifting one leg, tugging at the strap of her thong. "I'm sorry. Did we meet? Are you a Blabber follower?"

Kiera felt ready to scream. Would anyone in here notice?

"I need to talk to you," Kiera insisted.

Tattoo-face pushed her. "Dude, a lot of people came to see Roxy, okay?"

"You need to take your fucking hands off me."

"Joe-boy," snapped Roxy. "Down, sugar."

Tattoo-face fell back, trying to look tough, like he didn't weigh less than a buck-fifty. Kiera pulled her jacket tighter over her breasts and mad-dogged him right back. Roxy Coxx swung herself around, crept up to the edge of the stage, breasts hanging in Kiera's face.

"You want some private time? Seventy-five."

Kiera groaned. She bit her tongue. This was going to

dig straight into groceries, straight into the apartment fund. Into ramen and Cherry Bolo. She pulled her wallet out and thumbed out her card. "You got a secure ATM here? I'm browsing incognito."

Roxy took the card with her first two fingers and passed the chip in front of her eyes. Her pupils flashed laser-red.

"You were never here, honey."

Roxy stepped down from the stage, beckoned with a robotic index finger. Kiera traded another filthy look with Joe-boy, then followed Roxy's *amazing* ass *(focus, Kiera)* to a back room with mirrors on all sides and a nicer couch than Herrera's.

Kiera self-consciously folded her arms. Roxy took her hand. Kiera stared into Nile's face, all fuck-me eyes and a smile like she was drunk. "Sit down," cooed Roxy. She guided Kiera to the couch. Kiera let herself be pulled there, her mind temporarily chaffed, signal jammed.

"You can touch my tits and my ass. Not between the legs. Okay?" She threw her thighs over Kiera's lap, breasts brushing Kiera's cheeks.

"No—no, I don't want a dance. I want to talk."

Roxy paused. She shrugged, and swiveled off, planting herself on the couch next to Kiera.

"I mean, here, seventy-five only gets you ten minutes. You'd be better off getting an e-date. For three hundred I'll watch a movie with you over webcam. Doesn't that sound better?"

Kiera turned to face Roxy directly. "So, you—you're not fucking with me? You don't recognize me at all. You *have* to tell me if this is an act, right now. You're not Nile?"

Roxy Coxx, doe-eyed and apologetic, shook her head.

"Mm-mm. Have we met before?"

Kiera rubbed her eyes. "You look like someone I know," said Kiera. "Like *exactly* like someone I know. They've been missing for a few days, and I thought—I saw you on the internet and I thought they were faking it. You even—your hand. I thought..."

Understanding slowly dawned on Roxy's face. Then she rolled her eyes.

"I know what's going on here," she said.

"Oh my god. Please tell me."

"I bought this," said Roxy, circling her palm, indicating her face and breasts. "The cutter told me he designed it just for me, but I guess I got burned. So, your friend's out there with the same face. She must be the original." She sighed. "Prick."

A goddamn dupe. Well, of course Nile had pawned her face at some point, she was a premium-quality smokeshow. But the cutter was supposed to sell the spec online, not pass it off as a custom in the same city as the model. Fucking idiot.

"Can you give me the address of that cutter?" asked Kiera.

"You bet, gorg. Take a note?"

Kiera took down the details on a digital sticky. Roxy put her hands in Kiera's lap. With the sexy act dropped at last, her smirk was warm and pixie-like. "You said your friend was missing?"

"Uh-huh."

"I'm so sorry. I really hope they're okay."

Kiera couldn't hold it back any longer. She choked on a sob. Tears blurred her lenses.

"Oh, no. Oh, hon." Roxy put her hand on Kiera's shoulder. "What's your name?"

Kiera sniffed and snucked. "Kiera."

"C'mere." Roxy pulled her into a sideways sitting-down hug. It was like hugging Nile. Kiera's floodgates opened.

"I'm sorry," Kiera burbled. "How much for the hug?"

Roxy laughed. "Stop."

Kiera got up and brushed herself off. Roxy checked her makeup in the mirror. "Follow me on Blabber, okay? Keep me updated."

"Yeah. For sure."

Kiera opened the door. She froze.

Black and white. Chess pieces. Ice cream bars.

"Oh, fuck. Please don't hit me, my nose is still broken."

A hot second passed where nothing happened; the goons stood there just taking up real estate, even flexing a little under their suits. Then Kiera grabbed for the device in her underwear, wrestling with the band of her jean shorts. She pulled the flashbang free. She had her thumb on the red button. A black mechanical grip crushed her hand.

"*Ahh-aah-haaa!*"

Kiera dropped the device. Black goon picked it up without loosening his hold in the slightest. He held it up. Vanilla goon took the flashbang in gorilla-sized fingers.

"Let's have a discussion, please."

"Back on stage, Roxy," said the Black one.

Roxy Coxx rolled her eyes. "You don't gotta tell me, y'know, I seen it all before."

Ebony hands with gold detailing clamped Kiera's skinny arms and wheeled her out the door. Roxy called after them, "Man, go easy on her, would you?"

* * *

232

"I DON'T LIKE it one bit. I don't want her out there by herself."

"So *go after her*."

"No."

"Why not?" Lana stirred her fruity cocktail with a paper straw. The yellow layer on top merged murkily with the jewel-like green at the bottom in goopy strands.

"She wants to be a big girl," said Angel. He gulped from his third whiskey of the night. "Who am I to argue?"

"She didn't *want* to go by herself."

Angel didn't answer this.

"Angel, honey… You're chewing your lip."

Angel blinked. He touched the inside of his bottom lip and took his hand away to find a watery red smear. He noticed the taste of blood on the tip of his tongue.

"How long I been doin' that?"

"I don't know."

It was an old, bad habit. Angel did it when he was worried. When he was facing down a wild-eyed maniac holding a gun to the head of a mother of three. When he had a room full of hostages and the bomb squad were still seven minutes away. When an eight-year-old girl needed more than anything in the world to go into foster care, but he didn't have the goods to put her piece of shit father away. He'd chew, chew until the skin was ragged and torn.

Work wasn't like that anymore, so he didn't chew his lip. There was nothing and nobody to worry that much about. But now he'd done it twice this week: back in the closet when the bulls had taken Casey, and right now.

Angel dipped his head side to side, swirled his whiskey and ice around. "Maybe I should…"

"Call her," said Lana, touching his shoulder. "At least just call her."

"Yeah, alright." He went for his phone. "Yeah. Yeah."

He dialed Kiera up and let it ring. He imagined the bubbly tones of the phone's dialing chime were liquor bubbles popping lazily in his brain.

"Huh. Didn't pick up."

He tried her again. At first he'd thought *maybe she didn't hear*, but then he remembered her phone was embedded in her ear. She got the call. She was just in a huff. He'd bug her until she answered.

"She's not picking up," Angel grumbled.

"Is she just mad?"

"I don't know. That's what I want to think." He kept trying.

"But you can't be sure."

"No. Hang on a sec." Angel waited for the call to go through again. Once again it blinged for a full minute, then cut out.

Angel stuffed his tongue in his cheek.

"You don't like it," said Lana.

"I don't like it."

"Go. Go find her."

"Alright. Thanks, sweetie." Herrera finished his whiskey in one swallow, and kissed Lana on the corner of her mouth. She patted him on the back as he climbed past her to leave the booth.

"Good luck."

When he got into his hatchback a cop coffin drove up, perhaps a little too slowly, and he hunched his shoulders, squeezing the steering wheel. He felt its doomful drone in his ribcage.

The black cruiser passed on by without incident. Angel breathed out and turned the key.

20

ANGEL WAS RUNNING out of ideas. "I will be five minutes. Two minutes," he pleaded, feeling like a buffoon. "You understand? My daughter is in there and she's got a fake ID."

"It looked real to me."

"Yes, thus succeeding in its mission of being a *fake* ID, by looking like a *real* ID. Try to keep up."

He had no leverage, that was the problem. He used to be a man with leverage in this town. Now he may as well have been a teenager begging this big bald warthog to sell him booze, just let it slide, just this once, no one will know. The bouncer shook his head.

"You're blacklisted. That means if I let you in, *I* get the shit kicked out of me, okay? Now, you don't need to fret, sir. Carson clubs have very responsible staff. If at any point your daughter feels she's in danger from a male customer or she becomes intoxicated—"

"Jesus, you're just gonna let a teenage girl run around in there like she's—fuck, I don't know, who's famous,

Lady Gaga? When she ODs at thirty I'm coming after you, pal."

"Why don't you get one of those, ah, ankle bracelets?"

"Oh please, she'll crack it like a walnut." It occurred to Angel he was getting too deep into the fake-daughter fiction. It was time to explore other avenues.

"They make 'em real strong now. Anyway, her ID seemed real enough to me. Now please, sir, you're holding up the line."

A jagged chorus of agreement went up behind Angel. He looked back at the disgruntled procession of freaks and punks. Defiantly, Angel lifted his chin.

"When you all have children," he opined, whirling his index finger, rounding up the cyberpunks in an imaginary circus ring, "when you raise a beautiful baby daughter of your own, you'll regret your words and deeds here tonight."

A nasty-looking woman with Māori tā moko face tattoos—she was white, for all appearances—sneered at him and said, "I come here to get *away* from my baby."

Angel wagged his finger in her face as he passed. "Make better life choices."

"Fuck you!"

Angel walked to the street corner and tried Kiera's number one more time. He got nothing. He chewed his lip, he chewed his lip, he chewed his lip.

"Shit! Kid…"

Angel jumped up and down. He had an adrenaline surge and he didn't want to lose it. He cursed again, and then again, as he rounded the corner, tap-dancing down the sidewalk. What were the chances he could get in this place through a back entrance of some kind?

He had never been so happy to see an establishment

so shitty: Dong Fan's Entertainment Center, stacked Lego-like on top of an Indonesian take-out. If he was reconstructing the building right in his head, the arcade and Phoenix were sandwiched back-to-back, and they shared a fire escape.

To get to Dong Fan's he had to move swiftly through the muggy air of the restaurant, pans and fryers hissing from the back as he weaved around faux-luxury seating. A grainy pop music video starring brown-skinned strangers in bright clothes glowed on a flat screen hanging in a corner, above a concrete stairwell. The stairway was so dim, lit by a flickering fluorescent bulb, it was like some ascent into Angel's own personal Hell. *Dong Fan's Upstairs*, claimed a laminated piece of paper taped to the wall. Well, who was he to argue? He took the stairs.

The floor turned from concrete to tile. Dong Fan's had to be one of the last of its kind, an honest-to-god video arcade. Among the rows of cabinets Angel saw a cluster of *King of Fighters* machines and felt a pluck of nostalgia on the ol' heartstrings, playing creamy pink notes. The kid would like it here. *The kid. Gotta get the kid.* Abruptly the place was cut in half—on the left side, pool tables, with the usual suspects lurking and lowering the tone. The only employee in the place staffed a cramped bar. Fridges behind him boasted beers and energy drinks.

Angel slid an arm up on the wood, pointed to the door at the far corner of the arcade side, with the green EXIT sign. "This joint connect to Phoenix?"

The mook here could've been the Phoenix bouncer's brother, same boar face and pube facial hair. With a raised eyebrow: "Why don'tcha go in the front?"

"My, uh, my wife's in there. With another fella."

The face wrinkled as only the ritually misogynistic could. "Say no more. Take the stairs down, comes out in the Phoenix stockroom. If you hit the parking garage, you gone too far down."

"Hey, *gracias*, pal."

"Pop the cheatin' slunt one for me."

Angel fled, horrified. "Jesus, man."

He hurried through the arcade machine stacks, almost wiped out a Black kid with a giant soda rounding the corner from *Tekken*.

"Damn! Watch it, mayonnaise."

"I'm not white!" were Angel's parting words as he barreled through the fire exit.

THEY ZIP-CUFFED Kiera to a radiator in an office. Then they just left her there, to think about what she'd done.

Message for help? No signal. She tried stealing unsecured wi-fi from the nail salon across the street, tried the free city wi-fi, everything, she tried it. Something was blocking it all. So she sat in a dead zone as half an hour went by, on hard blue-gray carpet between a couch and a desk, her wrist throbbing and her arm going numb. *Hey, I could chill with some* Valkyrie *free mode if the goddamn thing didn't require always-online! Fuck.*

She would've loved to use her noodle to get out of this one; fossick for a sharp edge to clip the nylon cuff, slip out through the vents like in the indie adventure games she played the shit out of. But these were serious people, and that was a seriously impenetrable lock on that door, and even her five-five, hundred-and-fifty-pound ass wasn't climbing through a solid air conditioning unit to any kind of outside. She was not going to Threepwood her way to freedom here.

Come on, man, I've still got ten years on my life expectancy. Getting shot in the back of a strip club isn't much better than getting hate-crimed. If they shoot me. Jesus, I hope they just shoot me.

The door lock blinged.

"I'm nobody," Kiera wailed. "I'm not a threat. I was just gonna pay for my dance and leave."

Along with big vanilla and chocolate, a woman stepped into the room. Kiera did a double-take. It was that lady from the party—the one who looked like Annie Lennox and Grace Jones smashed together in the transporter from *The Fly*. Kiera pointed a limp finger at her. "Cigarette," said Kiera, dumbly. The woman arched her brow.

"What?"

"Nothing…"

The woman got close enough to stoop down and flick out a rainbow-sheened knife to cut Kiera's plastic cuff. She noticed now that the woman's piebald vitiligo patches were jagged and jigsaw at their edges—pixelated. Aliased.

"You're lucky I was passing through tonight," the woman said in that dark voice of hers, fit for late-night adult contemporary FM. "The Tweedles here would've just broken your neck and left you in the dumpster."

"A-are you letting me go?"

"Not yet. Give me your ID."

Kiera dug her wallet out for the second time that night and handed up her outdated driver's license. The woman studied it. The corner of her mouth twisted up.

"This isn't you."

"I'm—I need to get a new one—my lawyer…" Kiera's heart panged.

"What do you go by now?"

"Kiera." Kiera swallowed. "Umehara, still. Ma'am."

The woman took her sunglasses off. Luminescent blue—like Flynn's, like Casey's. They snapped blinding white, a lightning strike. Kiera cringed from the photo-flash. Then the woman ran red laser arcs from her pupils over the ID.

"Now Ted Carson knows where you live, Kiera Umehara."

Well, at least Kiera wasn't sure how much longer she'd be living there. The woman replaced her shades, and gave Kiera back her driver's license.

"You shouldn't hang around with trash like Angel Herrera. It's a bad gig. You'll get yourself hurt. Wind up dead. Look what happened to his best friend."

Kiera swallowed again. Her throat was tacky and full of mucus. She didn't answer back.

"You're banned from Mr. Carson's establishments. You get jonesing for Roxy Coxx, you spank your pud online with that twit Joe-boy."

"Okay."

"And you…" The woman put a hand to Kiera's cheek, stroking it with a chrome-blue thumbnail. "You tell that two-bit private pencil-dick he better watch himself, new face or no new face. I have had it up to my *teeth* with Angel Herrera."

She peeled back her lips and snarled. Her teeth were wicked polished chrome, her gums matte black metal.

"I will, ma'am."

"Don't call me ma'am. I'm the same age as you." The woman stood. "Get Kiera her bag, please."

The metal-mouth woman moved to the door, and the Tweedles shifted to let her by.

"Don't be *stupid*," was her parting advice.

ANGEL PEEKED INTO the room behind the black door. A thudding came through, a pulse through a giant amnion— he knew the sound. A nightclub through several layers of wall. He had found his way into the storage room, fridges and fridges of beers and shitty little RTDs. But so many bottles of good booze! He wished he could just grab two, any two, and hightail it out. *The kid.* It occurred to him he needed to disguise himself; however they had recognized him back at the last Carson club, they would do it again. He had nothing on hand.

He sighed. Carefully, clunkily, he used his left eye to open Snap4Fun, and give himself an Easter Bunny face. It would perhaps buy him precious seconds. Other than that, he could at least make himself less recognizable. He started removing his coat.

"Shoulda done this in the hallway, stupid old man, *stupid* old man," he mumbled, while he began to unbuckle his holster.

"Oh, uh... Who are—?"

Instantly, Angel slipped his hand from the fabric of the holster to the handle of the gun. Drew it. He looked down the sight at a boy in a black bandanna and t-shirt, who instantly crumpled against the wall.

"Ruh-ruh-rabbit?"

Angel motioned to the door with the tip of his pistol. "Turn around. Leave. Say nothing."

"*Abuhhh...*"

"You need to pick up some booze? Get it. Quiet-like."

Right at that moment Angel couldn't help but wish he wasn't wearing computer-generated bunny ears.

"Bro, I am..." The boy whined like a tea kettle. "*Hiiigh*."

Angel loosened his firing arm. "On what?"

"Muh. Muh. Mescaline?"

Angel's eyes retreated all the way into his brain from disbelief. "Why are you at work?"

The kid in the bandanna melted toward the floor. "Not... *Hurrbbluuhh!* Not s'posed..."

"Alright, alright, Dr. Gonzo." Angel finished removing his holster, folded it up in his trench coat, and folded *that* over his forearm. He went and knelt down next to the boy and put a hand on his shoulder. "Alright, you just stay here. Get your sea legs."

"My brain is folding."

Angel touched the kid's forehead. "You're sweatin' bullets. Gimme that." He took the bandanna and, with some reluctance, tied the damp thing around his face. Another layer of deception. With luck, no one would ask about it. (*Someone will absolutely ask about it*, he thought.)

"*Wuhhh.*"

"Relax. Relax."

Thus disguised, Angel stepped out of the storage room and headed to a narrow stairwell. He climbed the stairs. With the music from Phoenix no longer muffled, it was like a backwards descent into water; the palpitating bass washed over first his head, then shoulders, and all the way down to his feet the higher he climbed.

Once inside the flashing pink and black and blue turbulence, he made to lose himself in the crowd. The bar? No, he'd have to take off his mask. A group got a load of him, two women and two men, and they cracked up. Angel gave an awkward wave infused with as much joviality as he could muster. He had to blend in, but he didn't have a clue what the hell to *do* with himself. God, the last time he'd been to a club—the nearest thing was that cruise he went on with Glory, and they went out dancing at the ship's nightclub, with that couple she'd picked up off the internet. Gloria had thought maybe they'd try swinging, see if it got Angel more interested in things again—of course it didn't—*why am I thinking about this? Where's the kid?* He moved nearer to the main dance floor and gave just the saddest performance of an out-of-place old man's dance with a jacket over one arm, while craning his head in each direction trying to see Kiera.

"You can check your coat," someone yelled in his ear. He jumped.

"Oh—what?"

She had liberty spikes and a labret. "You can go hang your coat up near the front." She smiled.

"Oh—it's cool, I'm good. Thanks."

"Do you need someone to dance with?"

Still got it. "No, I'm okay."

"Okay. It's just, you look *so* pathetic. I'm sorry."

He was trying to think of what to say to that, but she walked away. Angel made a face under his mask.

This was going to take forever, trying to find the kid in this mess. And what if she was already in trouble? No, different approach vector. *The dancer.* That stripper the kid was looking for. Where was she?

There were only so many platforms in here, only so many girls. That one twisting around by the door was a robot, that one there looked like a lizard. But he hadn't gotten a good enough look at that photo, couldn't pick out which one was Kiera's girl. The lighting in here... *Damn.* What was her name... R... Something saucy, something clever about cock. R... Rosie? Good enough.

To the bar after all, then.

Angel weaved out of the shoggoth of dancing limbs— caught sight of a half-sphere security camera, tipped his head away from it—and crossed to the glossy black bar. Had to push his way in, cop a couple of *looks*.

"Hey, buddy," Angel hollered, stretching his throat to be audible over the trance. "Mac. Hey. Hey!"

Finally, the iceberg-sized bartender turned around— that's pre-warming icebergs, mind you. Tonight was a real night for meatheads. This one was big up top and trim in the middle, instead of thick like a Christmas ham. Mohawk and beard, forearms shaggy as a St. Bernard. When he saw Angel, this big hairy Atlas lit up like a boardwalk.

"*Yebana mat!* Is Easter Bunny!"

"Puta madre, it's Zangief from *Street Fighter II*."

"You want drinky-drink, Mr. Bunny?"

"I'm lookin' for one of your—"

Oh.

Oh no.

Those sunglasses, those heels. She didn't need to pull back her lips for him to picture those *teeth*. She was striding *this way,* behind the bar. What the fuck was *she*—

Angel turned to the right and put a hand up by his face, in what he thought was the lamest excuse for discretion of his entire detection career. There had been no preparing for this. A megalodon had appeared as if *Star Trek*-transportered beneath his little fishing boat.

He'd gone for a drive in the desert and blundered into a nuclear testing range.

"What is matter?"

"Your boss, your boss," Angel hissed.

Hands with banana-fingers snagged Angel's button-up. He was hauled, bodily launched, brought up to the Gief-lookalike's face, hot breath blasting Angel's eyes from within a rug to rival Blackbeard. He barely managed not to drop his gun.

"*You talk to me like thet?*" the big boy kaboomed. "*No one* talk to me like thet! You come in here again, bunny-man, I pummel you! I grind your bones to make my bread!"

Angel gripped the man-mountain's arms for balance. His brain was rattling. He hadn't said a thing! He was counting his odds, and writing up his will, when the woman with the pixel-cut skin stamped right past them both, flicking Angel but a moment's glance and an amused curl of her nostril.

"*Molodets*, Sasha."

The big lug beamed at her. "*Spasiba*, Mrs. Victoria!"

When she was gone, the iceberg dropped Angel again, and straightened out his shirt collar for him.

"No harm done, Mr. Easter."

"I could kiss you."

"Do not threaten me with good time, Bun-Bun."

"*She's* here tonight? Vicky Von Braun?"

The big guy—Sasha—puckered his lips. "Ooh, do not let her hear you call her thet, Easter-man."

"What's she here for?"

"Routine sniff-sniff. 'Visit from corporate,' yes?"

"She dropping in on someone? Anyone in trouble tonight?"

"Curious little bunny, you are!"

Angel leaned in. "I'm just trying to find a buddy of mine and get 'er on home. I'm not here to get in anyone's business."

Sasha shrugged his boulder-shoulders. "I work bar all night, don't get a chance to see much, Mr. Easter."

"In that case, I'm looking for one of your dancers."

Sasha waved a ponderous arm, sweeping the length of the club. "Take your pleasure."

"I need one special. Her name was, uh, Rosie, I think. Rosie Cozy, something that rhymed."

"Roxy Coxx!"

Angel snapped his metal fingers. "Sasha, you're a goddamn prince among men, you know that?"

Sasha pointed toward a girl working her stuff thirty feet directly behind Angel. "Get in quick! She becomes popular after nine."

"I think I'll take a drink now, big fella."

"*Khorosho!* What is your wish?"

"Gimme your specialty."

Sasha turned around and went to work. He shook his shoulders and his rump to the club beat. Angel couldn't see what all went in the shaker—the man's beefy back blocked his view—but the concoction was yellow and served over ice.

"My own invention! I call it 'Hundred Hand Slap'."

Angel took a sip. *Sharp.* Fruity aftertaste.

"Kicks like a horse," Angel coughed.

"Slaps, Mr. Bunny. It slaps. Like the trap beat."

Angel shook hands with Sasha to exchange payment under the table. He tipped fifty bucks.

Roxy Coxx had a little fan. The glow-in-the-dark face tattoos just made his acne stand out. When Angel came up to Roxy's stage, he earned a dirty look from the greasy punk.

"Ms. Coxx," Angel called through his face mask. "Ma'am."

"Another talker," said the tattooed youngster. "What the fuck. Roxy's working."

"Go soak your head, twerp."

"Fuck are you gonna do, Easter Bunny?"

Angel exhaled. "Okay, you got me on the bunny getup."

Tattoo-face squared up. He was half a head shorter than Angel. Angel looked him up and down, dumbfounded.

"You serious with this?"

"Joe-boy," said Roxy Coxx, slowing to a stop in her pole swing. "Not again."

"This faggot's got an attitude, Rox."

"Hey." Roxy snapped and stuck a finger out. "Language." He cowered like a caned schoolboy.

"Uh-huh. Sorry, miss."

"Why don't you go get some air, Joe-boy? You're pissing me off tonight."

Joe-boy looked like his mother had just died. "But miss…"

"Go on. Get a hand stamp."

Joe-boy skulked on out. Angel shook his head.

"You must be quite the performer, Ms. Coxx."

"I'm *so* sorry," Roxy gushed. She swirled seamlessly back into her thing, swinging legs, hanging breasts. "Most of my fans are just the nicest folks. But Joe-boy's got a complex."

"You oughta watch out for him. He seems the type to escalate."

"I am. You see his nose ring?"

"The one he thinks makes him look like a Hell's Angel? Sure."

"*I* made him get the piercing. If he comes within a hundred yards of me outside work, it pings me."

Angel took a seat against the wall. "You should be stepping on Carson's golf buddies for a living, not jiggling for tips in one of his dives."

Roxy flashed a grin. "Give me a year or two. I take it you've been banned from the Chuck E. Carson's chain? That's why the mask?"

"I just need to find my friend and get outta here. You seen her?"

"I see lots of people, baby, and I'm gonna see a lot more tonight."

"You'd know. She was looking for you in particular. Or are we playing tit for tat?"

Roxy's face lit up. "Oh! The girl looking for her missing friend?"

Finally, a break. "You talked to her?"

"Hate to tell you this, honey, but they took her in the back. That's the last I saw of her. Pretty sure that's where I saw The Devil Wears Prada going a few minutes ago, too."

Angel dropped his bandanna-covered bunny face in his hands. *Okay.* Was this hopeless? That depended. It was Kiera's second offense. It probably wasn't concrete shoes time, yet. Vicky was a lot of things, but she was reasonable. *Yeah… reasonable.* She sure didn't like Angel, but she did things fair. *Yeah, fair.* So long as you read the fine print.

Speak of the devil. There she was, marching right down the floor. She was coming toward Roxy's stage. For shit's sake, it was like being in a slasher flick the way this woman kept homing in on him.

"Oh, fuck me. Roxy, quick, give me a dance."

"Seventy-five for private time. Didn't turn out so well for your friend, though."

"No, dammit. It's Cruella De Vil, she's coming this way. Get on me, quick-smart."

Roxy threw a look behind her, saw Victoria Von Braun's heels hitting the floor like it owed her money. Roxy swung around her pole, slid right off the stage and bounced into Angel's lap, straddling his waist and throwing her arms on either side of his head. Her breasts *flumped* his face, blinding him. Now he could not blink, nor could Roxy have seen his lips purse like a duck's beak. But he made the bemused expression for his own satisfaction.

"Roxy." Von Braun's silky voice from beyond Roxy's torso. "Did that little one pay you for a dance?"

Roxy turned her head, grinding up and down on Angel's front. He tried to look like he was into it, hover-handed her thighs and rump. "Yes, ma'am."

"Bank details in my kitty at the end of your next break."

Roxy sighed. "Ma'am, my clients—"

"Pay for privacy," Von Braun interrupted. "From their families, and the police. Not from me."

"Yes, ma'am."

Roxy was quiet for a minute. She flipped around, stuck her butt in Angel's lap, pressed against his stomach. He couldn't help but *wow* a little at her back muscles.

"She gone?" whispered Angel.

"For now," said Roxy. "Don't look now, but the twins are tossing your friend out."

Angel peeked around her left arm. There was big vanilla and chocolate—*those lunkheads again*—carrying

Kiera (still alive!) by one arm each, dragging her toward the front door.

Roxy turned to face Angel. "You gonna peace out, honey?"

"Soon as the coast is clear. What do I owe you?"

"Don't worry about it. Tip me on my Blabber if you wanna be a sweetheart."

"I'll have to get the kid to show me how."

Angel watched the floor. The twins came back, *sans* the kid… The dark one hulked off toward the back… The light one stopped to jaw with Sasha at the bar. *Shit*.

"Think I'm gonna have to make a break for it." He smacked both of Roxy's hips. "Gonna need my legs back, miss."

Roxy Coxx slipped off Angel's pelvis, one leg pinwheeling past her face. She twisted and flipped back up to her pole, *Cirque du Soleil*.

"You're too talented for this joint, Rox."

"Hey, I like it here. Sure like to have my own place, though."

"Split the lease with Big Papa serving suds over there."

As Angel got up to hurry for the door, he caught Roxy putting a thoughtful finger to her chin.

His phone vibrated in his pocket. "I'm comin', kid. I'm comin'." While big vanilla's back was turned Angel slipped behind him. A wave of incoming customers broke around Angel, and he disappeared. As the cool night air hit him, he pulled up the black bandanna and discarded it on the stairs.

Once on the pavement, Angel and the bouncer caught sight of each other. The bouncer frowned, chin receding in irritation into his thick neck, and shook his head.

"Just leave," he muttered, and put his eyes back to his line of prospective customers.

"They should pay you guys more."

"Yes, they should."

SHE TRIED HIM again. He better not be sulking about her going out alone. Kiera looked up and down the street by reflex, searching for taxis she knew wouldn't come; rideshare had driven them extinct five years ago, but the programming of her brain still expected to see a Silver Service or White Top from the days of her teenage night-crawling. At best maybe she could find a U-Ride, but she bet that would ping her on the police grid. She was stranded.

The ringing stopped. Nothing. She was about to try a third time and mark it urgent.

"Kid."

Kiera turned. Herrera hurried into her circle of lamplight on the curb, stuffing his arms back into his big stupid coat.

"Wh—"

He threw his arms around her. "Thank goodness."

"Where did you—?" She sniffed. No. She was *not* crying again. She squeezed her eyes shut.

"I came in after you." Herrera let her go, put his hands on her shoulders. "Did they hurt you?"

"Not really." She gulped. "Scary lady copied my ID."

Herrera hung his head. "Damn. But you're okay?"

"Yeah... Why are you here?"

"You didn't answer your phone, stupid."

Kiera hugged him back. She snucked through a stuffy nose. "'S not a phone. Not really."

"Always giving me a hard time."

"Thank you."

"Don't mention it, kid, don't mention it. C'mon, I'm parked down the block."

21

"LET ME WRITE that down, sweetheart," Lana implored in Kiera's left ear. "Could you spell it for me?"

Kiera winced as she stretched the new bandage over her busted nose. "C-A-M-I-L-L-O."

"...L-L-O. Okay. I'll let you know if I turn up anything."

"Thank you so much, Ms. Silver."

"Call me Lana." Blip.

Next Kiera pulled open her chat window, to look at the message she'd sent in the car, even though she knew there was no answer.

```
an elf irl: hey mister, what's up.
    hope you're taking good care of jinx
    tonight :) ill try to catch some of
    your stream if i can.
an elf irl: hey so i was just wondering,
    i ran into this chick at your party.
    blue coat, blue sunglasses. vitiligo.
    kinda hard to miss.
```

**an elf irl: who was that? did you invite
  her?**
Seen 10:08 pm

We're gonna get you, you little shit. Kiera hoped her message came across as cunning and shady as she meant it, and not just stupid. Did she do something stupid? *Oh no.*

There came a steady knock at Herrera's front door, jumbling her train of thought. "I got it," Kiera hollered. She tamped down the edges of her bandage in the mirror one more time, then scrambled to go answer.

Sky shuffled his bulk through the entranceway, hauling a tacticool backpack in one hand and a six-pack of Diet Cherry Bolo in the other. Kiera clung to him, pressing her face into his chest.

"Op. Hang on, let me..." Sky lowered the backpack as carefully as he could, but could not negotiate the soda to the floor without dropping it, so he hugged Kiera with the cans flopping around in his grip.

"Thank you, big bear. I love you."

"Are you okay?"

Kiera squeezed. "God, no."

Sky plopped his chin on her head. "I brought goodies."

"I know you did, because you're the best."

She brought Sky down the hall to the living room. Herrera greeted them in a turtleneck.

"Salutations. I'm Angel, but stupid just calls me by my last name anyway."

"Not all the time."

"I'm Skyler. Or just Sky, you know."

"Isn't there a, uh, isn't there a girlfriend? Aren't you guys like, swingers, or..."

Sky laughed. Kiera pinched the bridge of her nose.

"You make me want to be dead," she groaned.

"Polyamorous," Sky cheerily amended.

"We're not *old people*."

"Jinx is at MisterMine's."

"Whomst is this Mr. Mine I keep hearing about?" Herrera put the emphasis on the wrong word.

"This big streamer," said Kiera.

Herrera furrowed his brow.

"Video game streamer," said Sky. "She's, like, doing a work thing."

Herrera shook his head as if dazed. "Well, I'm completely obsolete. Can I make myself useful and offer you a drink?"

Sky lit up. "Ooh, I'd love one."

Herrera made for the kitchen. "What're you having?"

"Um, whatever you're good at? Not too strong. I was kind of hoping to smoke?"

Herrera splashed whiskey into a diamond-patterned glass vessel. He quirked his brow. "You can have a smoke with your drink, can't you?"

Kiera slung herself from Sky's shoulder. She pinched an imaginary joint before her lips, and yelled, "*Smoke weed*, old man!" Herrera's head rattled a little with the new information. He pulled down a green bottle of... something.

"In my house?" Herrera poured. "On my furniture?"

Kiera dug into Sky's backpack. "If you think I'm cracking this thing sipping on another evil martini you can kiss my whole asshole."

Herrera cracked ice out of a tray. "Maybe if I'd seen you drink the first one, huh?"

"Motherfucker, if you don't..."

Herrera laughed and wagged his tongue the way he did when he knew he'd gotten a rise out of her. "The mouth on this one, right?"

Sky pinched the tip of Kiera's elf-ear. "I can't take her anywhere."

Kiera lifted the gray headset out of the backpack, cradling it with its due reverence. You didn't *need* a thicc-ass VR headset to do your hacking on; you could use a laptop like a normal person. But she wanted a headset. She was extra like that. So she'd built one, out of parts scabbed from friends and ordered on sale off the Uni store, and stuffed them in a helmet made out of Chiquita banana boxes. She strapped it on, and wore it "up," a pilot flipping up her flight goggles. She connected the headset to Malcolm Hobbes's tablet with a high-speed data transfer cable, which was a fancy way of describing the cord she used to charge her tablet. *I'm in, biiitch.*

Herrera arrived from the kitchen with a pair of tumbler glasses, one of which he held out to Sky with his fingers pointed like a gun. "Now, you asked for something I'm good at and something not too strong. I could give you one or the other. I picked the one I'm good at, so we'd stay on speaking terms. I made it small."

"Oh, it's got the cherry and everything. Manhattan, right?"

Kiera flailed her arm out. "Yeah, yeah, Herrera's a fucking concierge or whatever. Bolo me. Bong me."

"Concierge?" Herrera coughed a laugh. "Is that the word you meant to use?"

"I don't know. Fill me with the things I need to work."

Sky fished around in his backpack and lifted out a Ziploc baggie of pot. Herrera went over to the stereo. "Sky, what do you do when you're not stopping Kiera from jamming forks into the toaster?"

Sky laughed into his Manhattan, checking to make sure he hadn't spilled on himself. "I just work in a call center at the moment. It sucks. I got a master's degree before the economy really went in the toilet, that I do nothing with now."

"Which time?"

"Huh?"

"Before the economy went in the toilet. Which time?"

"Oh!" Sky snorted. "Right? The second crypto crash, like four years ago."

"What's your degree in?"

Herrera finished tweaking with the stereo. Energetic trombone filled the apartment. Kiera made a face like an angry qilin statue. "Oh, *no*. Absolutely not." She fiddled around and brought up her music app. A Bolo can tossed by Sky appeared in her peripheral vision, and she snatched it from the air like a kung fu grandmaster. *I am unstoppable.*

"Counseling," Sky answered, producing a pipe whose bowl was the cylinder of a revolver.

"Yeah?" Herrera came and sat down on the leather seat opposite Sky, making an L. "Maybe you can figure out what the fuck is wrong with me."

Sky's laugh was cut off by the opening blast of Kiera's deep house/progressive playlist. For the moment she tolerated the dissonance of the *beatz* in her left ear, the jazz in her right. She remained on the floor, comfortable there. She popped her soda can and chugged. She took the second hit from Sky's pipe. When Sky took the pipe back, he offered it across the arm of the couch to Herrera. Herrera eyed the dope the way some might look cautiously at a pet snake.

"What are you doing with that?" he grumbled.

Kiera slammed the half-empty can of Bolo on the table. "*Yes!* Smoke kush, old man! I demand it!"

"Fuck off."

"Do it or I'll pitch this tablet out the window, you phony. Go home and be a family man."

"I used to do cocaine, you little shit. Did you say phony? Someone give you a copy of fucking *Catcher in the Rye*, like you weren't annoying enough?"

"I bet you cried when that guy shot John Lennon."

"How fucking old do you think I am? Jesus. Give me that, you're gonna drop it." It was true; Sky was stifling his own laughter so hard the pipe's payload was in danger of falling out. Herrera took the thing and lit it. He made a disgruntled face through his entire inhale.

"She's like a teenager around you." Sky struggled through giggles.

"You mean you know how to turn her *off?*"

Sky took the pipe back. "When did you do cocaine?"

"Before my marriage and after my divorce."

Sky leaned over, balancing his head on his fist. "Oh yeah? How come?"

"Because cocaine is incredible."

Sky burst into more laughter. "I mean, sure, but like…"

It was time to *work*. Kiera stuck the earbud in her right ear and pulled the headset down. She cracked all her fingers, some of them twice, and wiggled them. She sunk into *cyberspace mode*.

Everything was laid out before her in sequence, details drawing in layers; a grid landscape reaching out forever, then the suggestions of hills and clouds, then the cyber-god threw a buckshot burst of chrome cacti to spruce things up. A royal blue sun from a cubist painting sat halfway revealed on the horizon line, either setting or rising. Kiera took a guess: it was setting.

But where was the bonanza? There was no safe, no treasure chest, no padlocked tomb; her pink-clad cybernaut simply stood alone in the cowboy expanse.

There, she saw it: beneath her feet, another world, a tremendous red tower. The desert sand was just a pixel-thin layer, itself the ceiling of a cavern home to a ziggurat. She had to get down *there*.

No elevator or stairwell made itself obvious. Like a cartoon animal producing a mallet, Kiera drew a fat cylindrical drill. She tossed it on the grid-ground and it grew to the size of an upturned SUV, balancing effortlessly on its tiny point. Its conical bit began to whirl like a tremendous top. With a glassy *chink*, the first of the desert's ground layer yielded.

Naturally, you throw out a piece of meat, you get the dogs. Kiera heard the hissing sounds first. Then she saw the trapezoid heads. The segmented bodies followed smoothly as if emerging from slits in the gradient skybox. Neon pink, yellow, emerald.

"Heehee," Kiera murmured. "Subroutine serpents, my old nemesis. You'll find I've been practicing my karate."

At just the same time, virtual men appeared on the vista; polygon *vaqueros*, faceless, armed. Creeping toward her in a big circle that was getting tighter. Kiera surveyed her situation. No cover, outnumbered. Flying snakes and black hats. But she was a human, and they were just dumbass protocols. A pair of fluoro-pink six-guns materialized in her digital hands.

"Well, li'l doggies." Kiera jawed phantom tobacco. "Nuthin' breaks like a hawrt."

She felt Sky's foot shove her playfully in the back. She hunched up her shoulders in embarrassment.

"Leave me alone! I'm *vibing*."

If Sky answered her, she couldn't hear it over her thumping trance beats. Kiera's fingers zoomed across the portable keyboard to meet each adversary. She danced away from their slow-moving bullets, a binary ballerina. Giant serpents *swooshed* past her head, snapping neon jaws. There were too many snakes. She clapped her pink revolvers together and traded them in for a lever-action rifle. She thought about drawing herself up some cover: some rocks or covered wagons. Or, hell, airdrop in a damn saloon for a real party. *Ka-BAM!* A two-story Old West watering hole *thunked* in the middle of the desert. Kiera lured her opponents inside, where she rolled over tables, fought them off from behind the bar, and climbed to the second-floor balcony.

"*Nergle-nerrr,* hacking the mainframe," Kiera said through her nose, when the last cowpoke burst into glittering purple glass shards. "Hacked. Hacked. You're all *hacked*."

Back outside the tap joint, the drill said it was ninety percent through the first layer of security. Kiera huffed. She pushed her headset up and rejoined the others in the living room.

"'Sup."

Herrera had the pipe. Kiera reached out and made a quacking duck face with her hand, throuple shorthand for *gimme the pipe*. Herrera picked up the language quick; he finished inhaling and handed it down. "How's it going in there?" he croaked.

"Wachowski shit. I'm Superfly TNT." Kiera lit the bowl. Herrera suddenly burst into red-faced, guttural coughing. Kiera pointed and laughed. "*Ahaaa-ha.*"

Sky squeezed Kiera's shoulder. "Hey, Ki."

Kiera looked up at him, open-mouthed. "*Whaa?*"

"Do you think you'd want to tell Angel about Lana?"

Kiera crinkled her nose. "Lana—his friend Lana? Tell—what?"

"Your friend Lana," Herrera explained calmly.

Kiera's face went moon-like with recognition. Her jaw hung for a moment.

"Where did—why that?"

"I was telling Angel how you and I met. I figured it would be easier than trying to explain around it. And, you know. Maybe it's a good time to tell him."

Kiera looked up at Herrera. Herrera rested his chin on his fist. "Up to you, kid."

Kiera sighed. "Jesus, are we having a 'deep and meaningful' session? I just got done shooting cowboys." Kiera ripped open a new cherry soda, steeling herself with liquid courage. "Okay. So. I found my best friend's body after she killed herself."

Herrera's hand moved over his mouth. "Mmhmm."

"We were besties pre-transition. Well, like… I say pre-transition, but she never got to transition. That was the problem. We were maybe girlfriends? Yeah, we were girlfriends. We played *Tyrna* together and we roleplayed as these giant elf lesbians in a lesbian relationship together and we, like, never acted on it in real life, and I will regret that to my dying fucking day. For the rest of my *fucking* life. Maybe it would have saved her."

"What's *Tyrna*?" asked Herrera.

"Pretending to be wizards on the internet," said Sky.

Herrera nodded, tight-lipped. Kiera sipped her soda. She asked for the pipe and took another hit.

"We had both been kind of feeling weird about our gender for a while, but neither of us was acting on it. I still hadn't completely admitted it to myself yet. And then one day, just…"

Kiera held her hands in the air like she was studying an invisible basketball.

"She did it at my house. She stayed over and we played *Ikaruga* and drank awful screwdrivers. And then, like… I slept in the next morning, and I thought she was just sleeping, too. And I thought she was still asleep, so I slept in longer. Then I got up at like two in the afternoon, and tried to wake her up, like, c'mon, let's get up already. Then I found the empty Xanax bottle, with a piece of paper next to it. I remember thinking that was fucked up because she never took notes on paper. She loved using tech for *anything* if she could. The note said she'd come out to her parents and they'd kicked her out. That's why she'd come over to my place all of a sudden. We didn't know anyone who could vouch for her for a place to live—we all had garbage Liberty. She said she wouldn't be able to afford HRT and support herself. It was all just too much. It was easier to be dead. So, she checked out. It said to tell everyone her name was Lana. Not that it mattered, her parents still buried her in a suit.

"I remember being, like… really clinical? I was kinda mewly on the phone, but I just handled the paramedics and everything like *that*." Kiera snapped her fingers. "I felt like I should have been a mess. I felt bad about it. Like I was a monster for not breaking down and crying. And I wasn't sure whether to tell them her name was Lana or her deadname in case, like, something got messed up at the hospital."

"Do you still feel that way?" asked Herrera.

"Uh-huh."

"It's very common. Saw it all the time on the force. Some people break down and some just kinda go into shock."

"That's what I keep telling her," said Sky.

Herrera crossed one leg over the other. "I'm sorry you went through that."

Kiera put up her hands and swayed side to side. "Least I'm still alive."

"Don't think of it like that."

Kiera hammered down the last of her second Cherry Bolo, and immediately cracked open the third. "So, after that I was, like... fuck, man. I need to be a girl or I'm gonna wind up dead, too. All that stuff I've been sweeping under the rug just kinda spilled out. Then I started posting on this channel for genderweird people and Sky was in there and he told me he had experience with suicide counseling and... Yeah. This."

She pushed Sky's leg.

"Very unprofessional," she jibed.

Sky bobbed up and down. "You were not a client," he protested. "And I waited, like, a year."

Kiera blew a raspberry. "Whatever, doctor deez nuts."

"I'm not a doctor!"

Herrera cleared his throat. "Thank you for telling me that, Kiera."

Kiera gave Herrera a dimply smile. Then she flipped her visor down and stuck her earbud back in.

The drill was ready to break through. A yellow lightning-bolt fissure radiated out in all directions from its point. Hands on hips, Kiera put her pink foot down on the cracked ground, gave it a firm *tap*; the whole mathematical countryside exploded. Chunks and triangles with their cacti still attached spun off into the rose-tinted skybox. Now Kiera could see the whole blue circle of the sun. She fell, and fell, like ash tipped from a cigarette over the balcony of a skyscraper, watching each window of the red tower go by. She couldn't tell how far away she was from the structure, how big it was in reality (so to speak). The farther she fell, the darker the rose background faded.

Pink-hued, hacking-Kiera landed with no sound on a blank, winding path, sheer cliffs on either side. At the other end lay the entrance to the red tower, a massive, arched drawbridge branded with a shield insignia. Even before starting her walk, Kiera saw a figure waiting at the other end of the path, guarding the gap to the arch.

At the end of her brisk journey up the snaking road loomed a knight in red armor twice her size. It stood as straight as only someone with posture modeled by a computer could, both hands on the hilt of a sword with its blade pressed into the ground. Kiera stuck her hands on her hips. *Well?*

The knight flipped up its visor. An androgynous face, blocky and segmented, chess-white, spoke in the staccato buzzes of a Commodore console.

>PRESENT TO ME THESE SEALS THREE

As Kiera read the words, the knight extended a palm that reflected like oil on top of water. Three rotating icons grew from the nothing there: a fingerprint, a mouth emitting a sound wave, and the letter A.

"Password, fingerprint, *and* voice activation?" Kiera was incredulous. "He was a goddamn attorney, not... not the Pope of Asstown." She tik-takked out a reply to the knight.

>Is there another way in?

The armored giant twisted at the hip, waving a great arm to gesture into the endless blood-dark expanse around the tower.

>OVERCOME SHE

"She" promptly arose from behind and *around* the tower, heads circling either side, firmly planting claws on the motte that made its foundation. "She" resembled nothing so much as the love child of King Ghidorah and another, larger, King Ghidorah. Forked tongues the thickness of suspension-bridge cables whipped out to taste this world's air, the very math she breathed.

Kiera felt the need to rub her eyes against the sight but did not remove the headset. She leaned back in real life, processing her awe through weed-addled frontal lobes.

"*Daaamn*. Subroutine queen." She slurped her cherry soda and belched. "We're gonna need a bigger boat."

All three of the kaiju's heads opened up to roar appropriately angrily at her. Kiera swiftly drew herself a suit of armor—not a busted museum exhibit like the one guarding the drawbridge, but real anime shit, a hot pink mech suit with an arm-mounted ion cannon ready to DDOS Fatass. Her Sunday best. Jetpack rockets flashing white-green shot her into the air, housefly-sized against the three-headed dragon.

It was Kiera's policy that you should open with your best move. The fins flared on the barrel of her cannon and with a cavernous *bwaaah* she let fly a laser blast as big as a house. An entire dragon head was subsumed in the white.

When the laser thinned to nothing, a meaty stump remained, scraps and data bits breaking and floating away. Soon, of course, two hill-sized polygon thumb-tips pushed up from the flat and sprouted into a pair of new subroutine queen heads.

Hydra rules. Kiera numbly resigned herself to the new information. *Mr. Hobbes, I am going to start taking this personally if you don't knock it off.*

Digital darkness engulfed her. It happened before she could react. *Wait, what the fuck?* She saw the mouth from the inside, the fangs and the uvula, just before everything clapped out; a head she'd left unaccounted for had swallowed her. The high-pitched bleep of a system crash stabbed her eardrums and she wrenched out her right earbud with a wince. She hoped she'd at least give the great serpent digital diarrhea.

The world reformed. Kiera came to on the lip of the cliff before the tower, at the feet of the red knight. The sentinel's blade stuck straight into the earth next to her head. Kiera sat up. The knight opened their mouth and issued thus, in buzzing tones:

>2 ATTEMPTS REMAINING

"Oh, son of a *bitch*. This is fucking *Kafkaesque*." Kiera took the cardboard headset off. "I gotta pee."

Herrera sipped from his Manhattan; it had to be a second or third. "Hey, stupid. Been talking to your boy. Apparently I'm asexual? That's what the kids call it."

Kiera looked at Herrera, then at Sky, then back at Herrera again.

"How long was I gone?"

"'Bout an hour," said Sky.

Fuckin' time dilation. "Jesus, this is too much. *What?* Let me pee."

When she got back from the bathroom, she plopped herself right back in her spot on the floor and threw up her hands. She made a noise at Herrera: "*Awuuggh?*" *Continue.*

Herrera tried to pull the right words out of the air.

"I... got married because I thought it would eventually make sense. I mean, I was in love with her. But sex just stressed me out and made me feel embarrassed. And then I stopped touching or kissing her at all, because I was afraid she'd try to turn it into sex. Eventually she kind of stopped expecting sex and I was able to kiss her again, but I would feel this *sadness* coming off her, and... that just went on for years. So she found Malcolm. I don't blame her one bit." Herrera took a gulp of his drink. "I thought, Jesus, am I just gay? What is it? But I've tried every configuration of person I can, and I could never really make this, this sexual connection thing work with *anybody*. And finally, your boy here tells me some people are just wired to not..." Herrera shrugged and sipped his Manhattan like he was trying to hide behind it. "To not... *eh*."

Kiera turned to Sky. "You did this in an *hour?*"

"I mean, he's high."

Kiera leaned toward Herrera. "Well... That's cool, dude! That's okay! How do you feel about it?"

Herrera tapped his foot on empty air. "I dunno yet. Sure is good to have a word for it, though. Feels like I've been running in a hamster wheel my whole life and I can finally stop." He shifted his legs. "You close to cracking that thing?"

"I think I know how to do it. Now I kinda wanna do best friend time, though."

"Yeah, yeah. Crack the safe, then we celebrate, huh?"

Kiera stuck out her tongue and shoved her headset back on. "It's not a safe, it's like a... a bastille."

There was someone else waiting for her on the precipice when she went back in. A thin figure, solid navy-blue. They scratched their chin thoughtfully while studying the chasm and the idle leviathan waiting in it. Perturbed, Kiera hailed them.

>Um?

The blue person turned. Bright white eyes and teeth were their only features.

>Kiera, right?

Kiera canted her head. She sipped cherry soda and warily keyed out a response.

>What are you?

>A .exe left behind before the hardware was unplugged.

>You're Casey!

>Broadly speaking, yes.

>Are you here to help me kill this dragon?

The blue figure folded his arms.

>I brought many tools for cracking difficult data walls. You could say I'm strapped.

Kiera sputtered and got a little soda on her chin. "*Huhhuhh.*"

>Hell yes. Co-op. Let's slay a kaiju, Case.

Casey's echo wrote himself a hulking dome-headed war suit. He lifted off the cliff sluggishly, deliberately, as if manipulated by stage cables, unlike Kiera's mosquito-esque darting. But what Casey lacked in agility he brought in pure force. Four finned snake heads bore down on the airborne suits, and both of Casey's arms fired repeating slugs the size of cannonballs.

Kiera's little arm cannon ran off machine-gun bursts as quickly as she could type. She pestered the heads, peppered the eyes while Casey blew big fat chunks out of the necks. He drew holes across them, cut them in half like paper targets at the range. Every two minutes Kiera's gun heated up enough to let another ion blast fly, ripping through a whole dragon head in one big beam.

But when a head was severed, they just got two more to deal with. They had to be up to two, three dozen. Kiera lowered her gun and stared up at the writhing and whipping udon-noodle mass.

She let herself get eaten. This was pointless.

>1 ATTEMPT REMAINING

When she respawned on the cliff, Casey was there waiting for her. His dome helmet rolled back.

>New strategy?

Kiera folded her arms in frustration. She had a little burning smog cloud in her brain.

>I knew that wouldn't work, but I didn't know what else to do.

She was just banging her head against this thing. It was pushing lumps out of a rug. The fucking droid must have designed this lock because there was no *way* some goober that hung out with Herrera and wore dad sweaters to appointments knew how to get encryption this good.

Kiera felt her brain tumble into the answer like a bunch of wet spaghetti slopping out of a pot and into a bowl.

>C'mere.

She stood cyc-to-cyc with Casey's echo program, looking into his bright, blank peepers.

>Casey, can we pretend I'm you?

Casey considered this. His mech-suit dissolved. He tapped his chin.

>And simply fool the knight into thinking we're plugged into my brain? Yes... I think I brought enough for that to work. Let's try.

Kiera shed her armor, and Casey walked *into* her. They superimposed over each other, Kiera's pink blinking in and out of Casey's dark blue. She moved her limbs slowly, and he shadowed her.

Kiera approached the red knight, Casey's form walked with her.

>I'm KCNR-315912. I'd like to enter the tower.

The crimson guard peered down at them, soundless.

After a moment, the drawbridge creaked and whined, lowering to make a path across the bottomless cliffs. The dragon queen dissipated into shimmering yellow draw-lines. The bridge *thunked* into the digital dirt.

>PASS

"White House? Hacked. Pentagon? Hacked. Area 51, hacked. Hacked. Hacked."

Now that she had the job done, though, Kiera looked at her work and felt like *a true dumbass* for not thinking of the solution sooner; rather than a neon-pink superfast avatar of the 'Net (capital N), she saw herself riding a black-belching locomotive coal engine, plonking along to the sounds of an anachronistic and somewhat racist parody of Bob Marley. Well, whatever. She cracked it, no one else.

"I'm smart!"

Kiera took the banana-box headset off, like a samurai shedding her helmet, and dumped it on the coffee table.

"I'm sma—"

Herrera and Sky were leaning over the space between their seats, gently cradling each other's face, kissing.

Kiera experienced something like a brain freeze. Sheer sensory overload, like you read about in old sci-fi novels where software jockeys would fry their brains on a ginormous influx of pure data. Blue-screened. Wilson'd. Once she had reckoned with the bald absurdity of the thing, she hurled her visceral response.

"What? Ewwuh? No? You're my *dad?"*

Herrera parted first with an embarrassed face, like

he'd had too much to drink but was trying to hide it. "How you coming on that thing, stupid?"

Sky sniggered, straightening his boxy glasses. "I'm thirty-six, Ki, it's not that weird."

"Veto! Veto! You cannot put my dad-guy in the 'cule!"

Sky stuck his hands on his hips. "Hey, now! You just calm your britches, little missy!"

Herrera took the pad. Kiera, swatting Sky with her small hands, warned, "Don't unplug it!" Herrera navigated the thing inexpertly with one finger.

"Who were you talkin' to down there?" asked Herrera.

"Oh, herself," said Sky, still fending Kiera off.

"She really gets into it, huh?"

"Oh, yeah. She goes into her own little world. Kiki, stop it! Bad. Bad girl."

Kiera sat on the couch once she had exhausted herself. "What've we got?"

"Gimme a minute."

They waited. Herrera shook his head. "Strong shit." He rubbed his chin, lolling his tongue around his mouth.

"Mal was going to represent a woman named Marjane Amanpour, twenty-five—there's our Marjane... Wanted to press criminal rape charges against one Mortimer Hill." He dropped his hands between his knees, slumping over. "Is that it? Could that really be it? Some two-bit fucking rapist, my best friend dies for this?"

Sky craned his neck forward. "Mortimer *Hill?*"

Herrera looked up. "Hm?"

"Dude, that's MisterMine."

22

SKY ROLLED DOWN the driver-side window and sat up straight, presentable, nonthreatening. Rent-a-cop had to take his boots off the desk and swing around, looking none too thrilled about it. Same asshole from the night of the party. *Do you people really need Kevlar to sit and open the rolling gate for rich people?* Kiera had wondered the same thing the last time she was here. Wearing that heavy uniform and thick scowl, the guy must have thought he was guarding Area 51. He slid open the window of his little stucco outpost.

"Yeah?"

Sky kept both hands on the wheel. "Hi, could you please let us in to see Mortimer Hill? Number 67 Hillview?"

"Residents only after ten."

"Oh, I see."

Sky stalled dead. Kiera rubbed her face. *Sky, why do you suck at this?* She leaned forward to make herself known.

"But someone who lives here can say it's okay to let us in, right?"

Gate guard took a deep breath and ran through his script. "Visitors can be prearranged, or residents can call me to let me know they're expecting a guest."

Kiera climbed on top of Sky's bulky middle so she could reach the window. Sky shrank back, giving her room to take over the negotiation. "Can you call Mr. Hill and tell him we're here?"

"Not at this late hour."

"He'll be awake. C'mon, man."

"It's almost one in the morning."

Kiera rolled her eyes, tried to look and sound younger than she was. Hoped that she passed enough—for cis and for Asian—to play into the Japanese girl fetish all these white dudes had. "I'm too high for this. Come *onnn*. We just forgot to call him."

"We would really appreciate it," added Sky. "Sir."

"Don't you recognize me? I was at that party. I was Nine Inch Nails girl."

The guard was unmoved. Kiera shuffled her feet, looked back and forth out the windshield and the back window as if checking for company. She had one more play. Most of these pretend-a-cops were strait-laced types, beers and whiskey before smacking the wife their only indulgence. Some of them, though, they leaned hard Libertarian.

"Look, man, if you call him for us, we'll give you a toke," pleaded Kiera. Sky's eyes popped, but he stayed cool.

The guard's scowl deepened. Kiera felt the tension tighten like the highest string on a guitar. She gave him a big grin. *Don't call the real cops.*

"Got something heavier?"

Yes! Fiscally conservative but socially liberal! Kiera snorted and did her best bimbo laugh, really put all her Harley Quinn into it. "C'mon, man, this is a nice neighborhood. Do we look like a coupla sleepyheads?"

"Yes."

"Well, all we got's loud, man."

Sky smacked his lips. "I've... actually got some mean dream in my bag."

Kiera's brain played an error-sound. *Duhn!* "You *wuh?*"

Sky sucked air through his teeth. "Don't be mad?"

The guard nodded. "That's what I thought."

"Since when—?" Kiera punched Sky's big belly. Then she climbed back off him, dropped into her seat and shook her head. "Whatever. Okay. Do the deal."

Sky hauled his backpack up from the backseat. He dug out a tiny baggie—the kind you also use for cocaine or heroin, thought Kiera—with a candy-like orange button inside. It could be for a sore throat. Kiera had never seen mean dream for real. The hardest drugs she'd ever witnessed IRL were poppers and ecstasy. The easy pass of the orange confection from Sky's fingers to the guard's palm—it punctuated how the stakes of Kiera's life had risen in the past several days. She wondered how long her boyfriend had been fucking with things at this level and keeping it compartmentalized from her.

"Do you have any *more?*" Kiera demanded discreetly as the gate guard picked up his hardline phone.

"Yeah, two more. I've been dealing to get money for the apartment." Sky squeezed Kiera's thigh. "Pretty please don't tell Jinx."

"Names please?" asked the guard.

"Sky and Kiera," Sky answered politely.

A moment passed.

"Good evening, Mr. Hill. I'm sorry to bother you at this late hour. I know, I'm very sorry. I've got two guests here at the gate... That's right, Sky and Kiera, they said."

Kiera squeezed her knees together. *Please please please. Don't make us go to plan B.*

"Says he's not expecting you."

Dick!

"Yeah, it's kinda a surprise visit?"

The look on the guard's face could not have been colder if Kiera had said, "Hi, I'm Kiera and I knocked up your daughter." He rolled his eyes and returned to the phone. "Surprise visit, she says."

Kiera nervously cracked her knuckles, one at a time. She'd actually fucked up and changed her story but Cop Lite was so fed up he hadn't noticed, or didn't care.

"Sure," he said.

Diet Cop hung up the handset, slid his window shut, and then miracle of miracles, he pushed a button. The iron gate clanked and rolled. As Sky pulled the car through, Kiera could see the guard hold the baggie with the orange-flavored mean dream up to the white light of his little booth, like an old hundred-dollar bill.

"What's he checking for?" Kiera asked conversationally, folding her arms.

"See if it's cloudy," Sky replied adjunctly, looking for the sign reading Hillview.

"Is cloudy bad?"

"Cloudy is bad. Cloudy is cheap."

"He got it for free."

"Bad dream's worse than no dream," Sky murmured, pulling a right turn.

"You think he's gonna take it right there?"

Sky looked at her and hazarded a chuckle. "What, right in that shitty little booth? That'd fucking suck."

"Getcha through work."

"No way. God. If he took it in that booth and just sat on that uncomfortable chair, under that light bulb for five more hours? Gurl. I hope he's saving it. You take it sitting comfy at home or go out where there's lots of stimulation."

"You're kind of an expert, huh?"

Sky glanced at her again, swallowing and wetting his lips trying to think of how to answer. Kiera rubbed her temples.

"God. *Sorry!* Sorry. Not important. Possible murder-rapist has our girlfriend. Fuck." She slapped her thighs. "Focus."

Sky exhaled a little laugh and squeezed Kiera's hand. "It'll be okay. It'll be okay."

Once parked across the street from 67 Hillview, they opened the hatchback's trunk. A crumpled man-ball made of mostly trench coat rolled out.

"Christ on a crutch," Herrera grunted. "Just push the fucking button and get back to Fatass, buddy."

"I mean, he was kinda right to be suspicious," Kiera said. "Hey, you referenced something that isn't over twenty years old."

"I need a car with a real trunk."

Kiera grabbed Sky's shoulders. "I need you to wait out here."

Sky gently took her wrists. "I knew you were gonna say that."

"Did you know because I'm right?"

"What if something happens, Kiki?"

"If something happens then you *especially* need to be out here."

Sky shut his eyes. "I'm gonna be sitting here just freaking the hell out."

"Put some music on. Play a game. Do something. But you gotta stay out here. It might get..."

"Shooty," offered Herrera. He had drawn his pistol, the grooves of the handle lit up green for the chip in his mechanical hand. He pulled back the slide: *chnk*.

Sky shook his head. "Oh, Jiminy Cricket. Okay. Please get Jinx out safe."

"I will. Because I have to tell her you're dealing mean dream."

"Oh, fuck. Sugar on top don't tell Jinx about the dream, babe. Babe? Babe!"

She left Sky cursing on the sidewalk, heard the door to Herrera's hatchback *dunk* shut behind her.

Her and Herrera's shoes crunched on the footpath stones leading up to MisterMine's front door. She tried the door without knocking. It was open, and she pushed it a hair.

"Hide that." She flicked her hand at Herrera's pistol.

"Yeah?"

"Yeah. 'Cuz..."

"*Hello!*" Halogen bulbs among the stones and cacti blared to life.

"Hi, Mimi."

"Welcome back, Ms. Umehara! And Mr. Jones! It's nice to see you again!"

"Mimi, could you keep it down? I, uh, I have a migraine."

The lights dimmed, and Mimi's voice became an ASMR rumble.

"I'm sorry to hear that," Mimi whispered, in a way that was uncomfortably sexual but not enough that Kiera could call her out on it. "Have you taken an analgesic, perhaps had some caffeine? May I lead you to a comfortable bedroom? Perhaps—"

"Mimi!"

Herrera sniggered. "Is it bad I'm actually kinda thinking about getting one of these?"

Mimi brightened, quite literally. "A Mimi Home and Office Assistant Companion can be purchased at—"

"Mimi!" Kiera wished she could grab Mimi by her infuriatingly cute cheeks. "Take me to MisterMine, please. But I think Mr. Jones would like... a drink. First. Will you take him to the bar?"

Mimi split into two Mimis. Both Mimis nodded obsequiously.

"Thi-this-way-way-ple-please."

Herrera laughed. "I love this thing! She's like *I Dream of Jeannie*."

"Can you stop being the oldest living person on Earth and focus? And she's not like Jeannie, she's Janet."

"Oh, that show! With the guy from *Cheers*!"

"Shut up shut up go—"

Herrera followed his Mimi around the corner, and Kiera took a deep, bracing breath, before letting her own Mimi guide her down the front hallway.

Mimi brought her to a wide-open room, the far wall all sheer glass looking out on the pool. MisterMine and Jinx, wearing glowing VR masks, dueled with invisible lightsabers in the center of the floor. A mounted TV showed their battle in full detail, streaming for a dizzyingly active chat window.

"Here you are," said Mimi.

Kiera swallowed a lump.

"Jinx."

Jinx tried to look in the direction of her voice. "Oh! Hang on a second, baby! Let me just—"

She ducked MisterMine's swing, feinted, then swung her remote like a lumberjack's axe. On the TV screen, MisterMine's head popped off, gory neck wound neatly cauterized.

"Son of a *bitch!*" MisterMine threw his remote at the floor. He peeled open the halves of his VR mask and lifted it free. His jaw was jutted forward in a teenager's sulk. "What the fuck was that? Were you just going easy on me?"

Jinx shrugged, pulling her mask up by the chin. "*I* wanted to play *Dance Club Euphoria*."

"I'm no fucking good at that. Or this, apparently." MisterMine turned to glumly acknowledge Kiera. "Hey."

"Hi sweetie!" bubbled Jinx. "What are you doing here? We were still gonna run for a couple more hours, I think. We're getting a *ton* of tips. It's been lit as fuh."

The fingers of dope haze still crept at the deep corners of Kiera's brain, enhancing her fear, upgrading it. Her heart was punching its way out of her chest.

"Babe," she managed, "I need you to get your purse and come with me."

From the confused look on Jinx's face, and the cotton-mouthed stumbling around her vocabulary, Kiera legitimately wondered if she had uttered an intelligible sentence.

"Uh, babe?" asked Jinx. "Is everything...?"

"I need you"—Kiera swallowed—"to grab your things and come back to the *car* with me. Right now, please."

Jinx shook her head. "What *car?*"

MisterMine snorted, made a smarmy face. "Uh, what the fuck? Heh."

But Kiera's pleas seemed to be getting through. Jinx, lips pursed, went to the nearby couch to grab her bag. MisterMine followed her. He grabbed her wrist.

"Whoa, whoa, what? You can't go yet."

"Hey."

MisterMine jabbed his thumb back at the TV. "Um. We're still live, Jinx, we're on for another ninety minutes."

"Let go."

"You *can't* just *leave.*"

Kiera yelled, "Let go of her!" The demand rang inside her stoned head like a gong.

MisterMine kept his knuckly hand clamped on Jinx's wrist as he addressed Kiera. "What is your problem?" Jinx tried to pull away, and he yanked her back with a glare that said *Behave*. "What the fuck is all this about? Tell me."

"Here you are," said the second Mimi.

"Malcolm Hobbes." Herrera came through the doorway on the other side of the room, pistol up and aimed straight at MisterMine. Jinx screamed at the sight of the gun; MisterMine threw his hands up. "You thought it wouldn't catch up to you? Malcolm Hobbes, you little rat-faced prick."

What happened next happened, Kiera guessed, because nobody was expecting MisterMine to move at all, let alone as fast as he did. His hand dived into Jinx's purse, came out with her pink and white revolver, and then he took her as his human shield, smooth as any pro. He stuck the *kawaii* firearm against Jinx's head and she went stiff as ice.

"Oh god," she whimpered. "Oh god oh god oh god."

All of Kiera's nerves flashed red. She reached out impotently. "Jinx!"

"I am-am not e-equipped to ha-handle this situation." The Mimis flickered and merged, reappearing as one next to MisterMine. "Would you like me to call 911?"

"No!" barked MisterMine. "No fucking police."

Herrera tipped his head. "No cops? Fine by me. Drop the piece or I'll drop you, kiddo."

"I'm not a kid!" MisterMine took a few steps back, dragging Jinx with him. "Get out of my house, and maybe I'll forget about this."

"Not an option. My girl's not going down for you."

"You've got nothing. You've got *nothing* tying me to Hobbes, so go home, *cuck*."

"Dude, look at your TV," yelled Kiera.

MisterMine glanced at the screen. The stream chat had gone thermonuclear. Blocks and rows of emojis and capital letters, no line lasting more than half a second before getting scrolled out by five or ten more. MisterMine and Jinx were on live feed, right up there in the bottom left corner.

"How many subscribers have you got, again? All watching you stick a gun to my girlfriend's head? You're about to be the biggest meme of the year, dude."

MisterMine looked frantically between the TV and the man pointing a gun at him, curly rainbow hair jostling. "Turn that shit off, Mimi. Turn it off!"

"I need more specific—"

"Turn the fucking TV off!"

The screen went black.

"Please let me go," begged Jinx. "I thought we were friends."

"We are friends, Jinxy. We are. You're helping me."

"Doesn't look too friendly from over here," said Herrera. His aim was straight as a deadbolt. "Let Jinx go and maybe I won't plug you."

"Yeah? You think killing me would be that easy, huh?"

"Yeah, I think it would be just that easy."

Kiera noticed a red dot, a bead of light on a black box beneath the TV—the PC? Was the stream still running, the camera still watching everything, even with the TV off? Could MisterMine be panicked enough to be so careless? She crept a few steps closer to him.

"You can't handle this, dude," she said. "You're not a professional."

"I don't need to be, not from this range."

"But the one who killed Mr. Hobbes was," Kiera said. "Right? You sent someone after him, didn't you?"

Herrera's stare darted over to Kiera, then back to MisterMine. MisterMine licked sweat off his lip.

"You have no idea who you're fucking with," MisterMine said. He was trembling. "You have no idea who I know."

Herrera took two steps forward. "Yeah, I've wiped my ass with goombas bigger than you, Richie Rich."

"Yeah, you think so?"

"Who do you know, Mine?" Kiera snuck another step. "Who?"

MisterMine pressed the pink revolver harder against Jinx's temple. "You will fucking vanish. You get me? Like you never existed. You do anything to me, there'll be nothing left to cremate."

"I'm losing my patience, Mortimer," said Herrera. "Let Jinx go or lights out, sport."

"Please," Jinx wailed.

Kiera stole three more steps across the carpet. She meant to leap forward and tackle MisterMine—hit him with a spear, Rated R Superstar style, bring both him and Jinx down to the floor. But she hesitated for just that bare second. MisterMine must have seen her in his peripheral. He wheeled around, Jinx still in his grip, and pointed the pink handgun straight at Kiera.

Ohshitohshitohshit. She felt the weight of the whole cosmos preparing to come crashing down on her.

Someone's gun fired twice. It wasn't MisterMine's, and it wasn't Herrera's.

One of the floor-length windows shattered. MisterMine crumpled, his strings cut, Jinx's pink and white gun clomping on the carpet like a paperweight. Jinx screamed and ran into Kiera's arms. MisterMine pulsed and twitched like a fallen power line.

Mimi turned traffic light crimson.

"The authorities have been alerted," Mimi droned from everywhere. She sounded a klaxon, the buzz of a massive robotic wasp. *"The authorities have been alerted."*

Holding tight to Jinx, Kiera looked out at poolside. There was the gunman: sweatshirt, track pants, gloved hands wrapped around a silenced pistol. A cybernetic eye—definitely purpose-built, definitely expensive. A damn sight better than the loose wires and plugs that had been sticking out of the socket last time Kiera saw him. The harsh red laser flash from the pupil made Kiera wince, as their gazes met for just a second before the gunman turned and fled, in athletic sneakers white and new as the Christmas morning snow in a holiday Bolo commercial.

"Skeezoid!" Kiera yawped. "Stairs-guy! Drug-man! Get—don't let him—!"

Herrera was over the couch and out the broken window in seconds, but the shooter cleared the six-foot concrete fence like it was *nothing*. He may have actually been Super Mario. It was like he just ran up the wall.

"*This incident is being recorded. The details of all individuals will be provided to law enforcement. Do not flee the crime scene.*"

Kiera's world zoomed out, *slooowed* down. She was now in third-person mode. She saw the screen of her life crack in two and offer her the choice: chase the killer or wait for the cops.

She headbutted the screen, broke through and took the third option: kiss her girlfriend.

"Sky is outside," Kiera said, when she pulled her lips away from Jinx's. "Out front. Don't follow me."

"Babe…" Jinx clutched Kiera's hand. "What is *happening?*"

"Don't follow us!"

Kiera bolted through the broken glass, almost slipped over at poolside, slammed up against the concrete fence. She hopped up and tried to pull herself up by her fingertips. It wasn't *that* high, but it wasn't a cakewalk.

"*You are now fleeing the crime scene.*" Siren-red Mimi appeared next to her, instructive voice broadcasting directly into Kiera's smart-ear. "*Your details will be provided to law enforcement.*"

Kiera clambered over the fence, planting on the other side like a thrown sack of fertilizer. More gunshots echoed in the dark. She looked out on a circuit-board-green expanse of suburban trim. She saw Herrera hightailing it across the sloped field after the dim figure of the wastoid shooter, whose white sneakers were visible even from here.

He was too fast. The guy was like a fucking gazelle. Herrera was losing ground and none of his shots were landing. Kiera took off after her weird-dad-friend-partner-in-crime.

"We need to get out of here!" she shouted, hoping he could hear her. "Come on, he's too fast."

"I can get him!" Herrera yelled back, his voice distant.

Kiera kept chasing, stumbling on her thick black boot heels. She stopped for a moment to catch her breath and caught a wave of sprinkler spray in the face. "Pffluh." She wiped herself off and then kept going at a jog. She found herself tired, deep in the muscles, already. Was this her life now? Endless running? Never-ending screaming, fake faces, *guns*, until she finally got so exhausted that the fash got her and threw her in a steel and concrete box?

She caught up to Herrera at the crest of the next slope, where he had stopped and doubled over, hands on his knees.

"Get away?"

"Got away. Son of a bitch."

"I think we're both officially in cop trouble now. Goddamnit, I'm so tired of this."

"Lana's isn't far from here," puffed Herrera. "If we can get out of this neighborhood—*huff*—we can book it over there."

"That's a big, hairy, spiky fucking *if*."

"If that guy can do it, we can."

Kiera groaned, her shoulders slumping with the weight of ten tons. She punched up a fake face out of the air and became a white girl.

"Okay. Okay, goddamnit, let's go."

23

"I DON'T THINK it's gonna move," Kiera hissed. "It's not moving."

The lines under Herrera's eyes were running deep. "So, what, go around?"

"There is no around! The gate's right over there!"

"Well, what then, girl genius?"

The dog-bot pottered in place on the sidewalk, rotating left to right, right to left, spreading its white cone of vision across the asphalt. Back and forth, back and forth.

Herrera held up two carbon-fiber fingers. The tips flipped back, revealing two metal plugs, like he was going to stick them in a wall socket.

"Run out in front," he ordered.

"You what now?"

"Run out and distract it. Don't worry, I've got you."

"God! I hate you."

Kiera scurried out from behind the plastic trash bins. She ran into the drone's cone, jumped up and down, waved her arms in the air like she just didn't care.

"Hey! Clifford!"

The cone of light turned crimson. The dog-drone's turret *ka-click-chunked*.

"Oh, holy shit, don't shoot me."

"AROOF. UMEHARA, KYLE. REMAIN WHERE YOU ARE. BROO. PUT YOUR HANDS ON YOUR HEAD AND LOWER—"

Herrera swooped down on the thing like Batman, ramming his plug-fingers in the aft of its chassis like he was giving it a surprise prostate exam. Sparks burst and scattered. The dog's voice turned into dial-up gibberish. Herrera kicked the drone over and it clanked on the blacktop, converted into garbage.

Kiera pointed at Herrera's robot hand. "*How* old is that thing?"

"Pretty cool, right?" Herrera flexed the fingers.

"I need to get *my* hand cut off."

They ran for the pedestrian gate, shoes clapping on chalk-white sidewalk. Lights went on in nearby houses; someone fingered open their blinds and peered out. Sirens howled, far away, back where Kiera and Herrera had come from.

Ten feet from the gate, the guard saw them coming. He scrambled out of his station. Kiera sprinted up and hit the green button to release the gate lock. The magnet popped and she charged through shoulder-first. On the other side the guard tackled her into the tended grass.

Kiera pushed her hands in his face, kneed him in the stomach and groin. He wrestled his hands around her throat. She tried to swing her forehead into his face but couldn't get enough leverage.

Herrera plunged his taser fingers into the guard's neck,

Vulcan-style. All of the guard's spasming bulk dropped on Kiera, a frozen cow carcass.

"Last charge," Herrera panted. Kiera elbowed herself out from under the stunned whitey.

"So, are we just hoofing it all the way to Lana's, or what?"

Herrera flipped the tips back on his mechanical fingers and dug out his phone. "Not *all* the way."

an elf irl: i think we're safe now, for a sec at least. lmk what's going on over there. did you guys get arrested or anything?

They hid in the shadows of a closed Q's drive-thru. Kiera kept looking at the menu and getting upset.

"I really want fucking coffee."

"'S closed."

"Why?"

Herrera picked up a pebble from the traffic island and skipped it as if the street were a river. "Because it's almost three in the a.m."

"That's when you *most* need coffee. That's exactly when Q's needs to be there for me."

"Not in the suburbs."

"Look. Right over there." She gestured across the parking lot. "Twenty-four-hour gym. Twenty-four-hour *tanning salon*. Q's? Closed at nine."

"Think the salon is part of the gym."

"What if I want a big frappé after I work out?"

"Even if it was open right now, you're not getting coffee. It's not coffee time."

288

"*What if I want a big frappé after I work out?*"

"Bad for you. Kid, how is this what you're focused on?"

Kiera rubbed her temples. "Coping mechanism."

A white, electric sedan ghosted along the opposite lane. It whispered to a stop without pulling over. Its horn beeped once.

Kiera and Herrera checked both directions for dog drones, cop cruisers. It was clear. They crossed and climbed into the backseat. The door shut with a *thunk* and muted the outside. Kiera felt like she'd been locked in a dense jewelry box.

"This is... considerably after-market," Herrera remarked, rapping his fist against the ceiling. It knocked heavy like a steel drum. The driver seat swung around to face them, with plump little Lana in it—*Hello, Ms. Umehara*—while the car sped up and drove itself, singing its artificial revving-up song.

"Oh, yeah," chirped Lana. "Reinforced the doors and ceiling, bullet-resistant glass, as much as I could get and still be street-legal."

Kiera pressed her fingertips to the window. "Guns pop outta the headlights?"

"That doesn't really exist."

"Uh, yeah, it does."

Herrera groaned. "Ignore her."

Lana rubbed her eyes. "I should've ignored *you*. Do you know what time it is? What were you *doing*?"

He told her.

"IF YOU'RE JUST joining us, police have responded to shots fired in a Kingcrest home in the early hours of this morning. One victim has been hospitalized, identified as internet personality Mortimer Hill, known to fans as MisterMine. Hill's in-home Mimi device has provided authorities with the profiles of three individuals believed to be at the scene."

Blue-tinted snapshots of Herrera, Kiera, and the nameless skeezoid lined up on the screen. Kiera pinched the bridge of her busted nose.

"Michael Jones, Kyle Umehara, and a third, unidentified individual are all wanted by police in relation to the shooting."

"Somebody let some poor people in, that's all it is," said an old Black man on TV. "It's that bus line they put in. They need to give the gate guards firearms."

"That's enough of that." Herrera muted the TV and threw the remote at the couch. It bounced and hit Kiera in the hip.

"Ow."

"Wonder how much to get my face done again. Not looking forward to that."

an elf irl: jinxy. sky. someone. please message me when you get this.
an elf irl: please. even just to say you're ok.

"Why didn't he shoot us?" asked Kiera. "He had a clear line on me. Why did he shoot MisterMine?"

"Ain't it obvious? Little snot was running his mouth," said Herrera. He gulped from a glass of cold water. "That'll get you clipped but good."

"It doesn't make sense. Sneakers just happened to be there? How close has he been watching us? And then he doesn't do anything to stop us." Kiera scrunched up against the arm of the couch, pulling a cushion into her chest. "And I had to see another dead body, so that's cool."

Herrera sat on the opposite side. "Better that homicidal sex pest than your girlfriend."

"Yeah, for sure. Just... This has all gotta be doing something to my brain that I'll have to cope with in a few years, I guess."

"Hospitalized," said Lana, emerging from the nearby bathroom with a wet face and hair. "ICU, not pronounced dead. Yet. For what it's worth."

Kiera shrugged. "It's something." She squeezed the pillow.

an elf irl: are you guys there

an elf irl: im sorry to keep messaging i just. yeah.

Tactical Butt: hey, I'm here. We're at the police station.

an elf irl: fuck did you get arrested???

Tactical Butt: No, they've got nothing to hold us on. They're trying to find out as much as they can about you, though.

Tactical Butt: We are exercising our right to remain silent, for what little it's still worth.

an elf irl: ok don't tell me anything else until you get home and cleanse

an elf irl: are you ok? wb jinx??

Tactical Butt: I'm good. I'm calm.

Tactical Butt: Jinx kinda doesn't want to come to the internet right now. She took her lenses out.

```
an elf irl: oh wow.
Tactical Butt: She knows you're there.
  I'll make sure she talks to you soon.
an elf irl: im not... really there
  though.
an elf irl: i fucking hate this.
Tactical Butt: It's not your fault.
an elf irl: it kinda is though?
```

Herrera tipped his brow at Kiera. "You alright, kid?"

She shook her head. "Yeah, I'm good. So it's Ted Carson who sent the shooter, right?"

Herrera shook his head. "That would mean Carson killed Mal over some twerp who plays video games for a living. Doesn't track."

"But you said someone paid track-pants weirdo to stand outside Mr. Hobbes's apartment that day. And I saw that scary lady at MisterMine's party that night. Vicky, you called her. He's connected to Carson."

"Vicky Von Braun likes to party," said Lana, while she emptied coffee grounds into a large and expensive-looking machine. "Mortimer Hill inviting her to his big blowout says more about his desire to climb this city's ladder than it does about his actual rank. Just because she deigned to show up and have a few drinks doesn't mean they're cozy—although Hill probably thinks it does. Whoever that shooter was, they're probably on someone else's dime."

"Well, shit." Kiera hit her fists on the couch cushions. "I thought it was all clicking into place for a minute. So you think we should go try to get something out of him? Something to get the police off our dicks?"

Herrera rubbed his chin. "Nah, no way to get close."

"So send Lana. She's a reporter."

Herrera shook his head. "He won't say anything useful. No, what we need is…" He shook his index finger. "The victim. Mal's client. That's our next move. Marjane, her name was, right?"

"Marjane!" Kiera brightened. "Like the graphic novel lady."

"The last name started with a vowel."

"It was A-something. Something Asian, or Middle Eastern? A… Ar…" A thought bubbled up in Kiera's brain as from a swamp bottom. "Wait, was it…"

Fingers on the air between her and the coffee table, she Tripped *Marjane video essay green energy.* Several video thumbnails arrived, depicting an attractive brown girl in a tasteful den, mouth open as if she were in the middle of completing a thought.

"It was Marjane Amanpour," said Kiera.

"Iranian," said Lana, from the kitchen coffee pot.

Herrera squinted. "How'd you do that, stupid?"

"Marjane is this other internet person," said Kiera. "She makes discourse videos and sometimes she streams video games for charity. Her internet name is *Renée Desktop.*"

"Oh, I hate it," said Herrera. "Truly pedestrian."

"I think that's funny," Lana chimed in. "It's cute. I like puns."

"Right?" said Kiera. "Only *smart* people get it."

"Oh, please, every peach-fuzzed dullard who ever talked too much at a college party has heard of Descartes. That's day-one shit. If you're smart enough to get it, you should think it's stupid. Like bad literary fiction."

"Renée Desk*toppe-uh,*" Kiera repeated, with relish.

"Hate it."

"I remember Jinx mentioned this *forever* ago, MisterMine and Marjane dating. Them breaking up was big Blabber drama."

Herrera clapped and rubbed his hands together. "You and this Blabber shit. This is why I pay you, kid. Does Jinx know this girl?"

"I don't think so. Maybe. Let me see if..." Kiera breathed out and ventured into the throuple chat again.

an elf irl: i have something really
    important i need to ask jinx about.
    im sorry. it's related to all this.
    please ask her to get back to me.
It's Jinx!!!: I'm here
an elf irl: are you okay?
It's Jinx!!!: no
an elf irl: should we do this on a call?
    I can call you.
It's Jinx!!!: yeah okay

Kiera got the thumbstick out of her bag. In a few seconds she and Jinx could see each other: Kiera devoid of makeup and gross; Jinx sheltered in the billowing folds of an oversized Pikachu hoodie. Jinx wasn't looking at the camera. Kiera had never seen a frown on Jinx's face like this before. It made her think of that warm can of Bolo she drank after their spat in the kitchen a few days ago—taking that can and tossing it into a canyon inside her chest cavity a mile deep.

"It's my fault this happened," said Kiera.

Jinx rolled her eyes and shook her head. "I mean, I'm the genius who kept a gun in my purse."

"You shouldn't have even been with that guy. You wouldn't have if I hadn't ditched you at that party. This is—"

"Don't start beating yourself up, okay?" Jinx crossed her arms. "I can't comfort me *and* you right now. It wasn't your fault."

Kiera winced. "Fuck. You're right, I'm sorry. How are you doing?"

Jinx settled deeper into the wrinkles of her hoodie. "My kind-of-boyfriend held a gun to my head."

"Was it like that? Was he your boyfriend?"

"I guess. Before I came over last night, he messaged me like *excited to see my girlfriend! Smiley face!*"

"You didn't want to be his girlfriend yet."

"I don't know." Jinx was silent for several seconds. "It was just kinda fast."

Then Jinx was quiet again. Kiera itched, fidgeted. She didn't know what to say next. Behind her, she heard Lana puttering around in the kitchen.

Kiera bit her bottom lip. "Are you mad at me?"

"No, Kiki. Didn't you want to ask me something?"

"Yeah." Kiera sat forward. "Yes. Babe, do you know Marjane Amanpour?"

Jinx frowned. "Like, Renée Desktop?"

"Yeah."

"Why would I know her?"

"She and MisterMine had that giant break-up, right? He fucked with her like he was trying to fuck with you. Can you maybe get in touch with her?"

Jinx made a face. "Babe, I can't like, go clout-chasing right now."

"I'm not asking you to get on stream with her. We just need to talk to her."

"I can't go sniffing around trying to get in with MisterMine's famous ex right after this, it'll look skeezy."

"Man, who cares what a bunch of shithead stream monsters think?"

"I mean, I do? They're my income. I'm still trying to save our apartment."

Kiera's hands balled into fists, then stretched out into cramping, angry claws. "*Do you want me to come home or not?*"

"Whoa." Lana's voice from behind. "Things are escalating over here. What's wrong?" Kiera felt Lana's fingers land on her shoulders.

"I don't know," said Kiera, putting her face in her hands. "I'm a stupid moron."

Lana came around, and planted herself on the couch next to Kiera, budging her aside with thick hips. "Put us on speaker."

Kiera pulled out a tab on the thumbstick and set it up tripod-style on the coffee table. A hologram of Jinx projected into the air between the table and the couch.

"Hi," Lana said with a smile. "I'm Lana."

"Hi, I guess," murmured Jinx.

"What's going on? Why's everyone getting angry?"

"Today is just shitty," said Jinx, pulling her knees up into her chest. "Like, *Batman Who Laughs* shitty." She perked up a little, jostling the long ears of her hood. "Hang on. What's your last name?"

"Silver."

Jinx gasped. "I recognize you! Are you the one who wrote that exposé on EndWare's CEO for Circuitboard a few years ago? How the whole company was a money laundering front for the Russian mob!"

"Yeah! That's me."

Jinx looked a little awed. "Today is so fucking weird."

Lana leaned over and put her chin on her fist. "I hear your girlfriend wants to be a journalist herself."

"She's a really good writer," said Jinx.

Kiera hid her face. "I haven't written anything in over a year."

"I *know* you haven't," Jinx needled her. "I wish you would."

"How do you think we can get in touch with Marjane?" asked Lana. "You think she's friends with anyone I'd know?"

"I can do it," Jinx said with a sigh. "She's probably getting buried in messages right now, but I'll do it. I can put out a blab or something. People will help connect us."

"Okay. That's a great idea."

"Thank you," said Kiera, almost whining. "Thank you, baby."

Jinx nodded. "Call me again later, okay?"

"I will. I promise I will."

Jinx left the call. Kiera slumped over, suddenly feeling all the last few hours' exhaustion at once, plus a little more. She turned to Lana. Lana interlocked their pinkie fingers, grinning as she gave Kiera's a little tug.

24

THEY TOOK LANA'S car, but Herrera refused to let it drive itself; he fidgeted in the back for no more than three blocks, then climbed into the front and took over.

"You been to a cat café before?" asked Kiera, once they found parking.

"I've actually been to this exact one. It's cozy."

"Oh yeah?"

"Old lady met me here, asked me to find her missing brother. Turns out she knocked him off for the life insurance. Know how I figured it out?"

"How?"

"Didn't clear her browser history. Literally Tripped *how to get rid of a body*. Found results, too."

Kiera guffawed. "Well, that's probably what I'd do."

Kiera would have mistaken *El Gato con la Guitarra* for an upscale bar or a ritzy Mexican restaurant, with its wood-shuttered windows and desert-tan clay walls— certainly fake—and most of all, the saloon-esque iron sign over its door. The sign depicted, in silhouette, just what its name promised: a roly-poly feline playing a guitar, with a little sombrero for good measure. Herrera nudged Kiera's shoulder.

"It means 'the cat with the guitar'," he explained cheerfully.

"Oh my god! Go away."

"I just thought you could use an expert analysis."

"Fuck! I've lived in California for thirty years, I *know* what it means."

"Oh. Well, it's just, I'm a native speaker, so I thought..."

"Would you... *Ugh!*" She pushed him through the front door.

They had to wait in a little room that reminded Kiera of the admin office at her high school. Though instead of notices and pamphlets about sex ed on the corkboard, they had printouts of pictures of their cats. Cats named Papi and Selena and Concrete. Concrete, a big gray idiot, became Kiera's favorite. The reservation was for 1:30, and Marjane was late. Herrera was assuring an attendant that their third would be arriving any moment, and Kiera insisting they just take the booking without her, when a dark young woman with a shaved head came in. She wore a bright red peacoat, and a visor bringing to mind *Star Trek* or *X-Men*.

"I'm sorry, I'm sorry," Marjane said. "Couldn't find parking."

"Didja try looking without that thing on your face?" Herrera jibed.

Marjane's mouth flattened. "Wow! Goodbye." She turned to leave.

"Oh, shit. Nonononono!" Kiera chased after her and touched her elbow. "Don't go, please, I'm sorry. He's old. You'll be talking to me mostly. Please stay."

Marjane curled her mouth. "Does he make fun of people in wheelchairs, too?"

"*Ugh*. Probably?"

Herrera frowned. "Hey. I do not."

"Then why'd you give me shit for my visor?"

"I've never seen one of those before. Honest."

Marjane furrowed her eyebrows at Kiera. "Is he serious?"

"I guarantee you he is."

Herrera rubbed his forehead. "Shit. I'm sorry, miss. What does it do? You're blind, right?"

"I'm agoraphobic," said Marjane. "I need it to leave the house." She started removing her coat. Kiera relaxed; she was staying. *Thank goodness*.

Herrera shook his head. "I'm at a loss. What's the thingy do?"

"It's called a loafy visor," said Kiera.

"A whomst?"

The attendant led them inside, pressing pause on the conversation, and transporting them to rural Mexico. Cats lounged on windowsills by liquor-bottle lanterns; on fat, striped couches; on a polished wood bar. They took seats around a round table, beneath a set of stairs leading up to a second-story balcony. Kiera had to move a fluffy ragdoll Siamese from her seat; she brushed it gingerly with her fingertips. The cat made a birdlike activation chirp and slid from the cushion like a spilled drink, pattering off in search of who-knows-what. Kiera ordered a vanilla latté, Herrera an Americano. Marjane asked for a decaf mocha.

"A loafy visor. Like lo-fi," continued Kiera. "It makes everything look like 3D graphics."

"But everything is 3D already," Herrera protested.

"No, butthead. Like a video game. But like *old* 3D graphics."

Herrera folded his hands on the table and faced Marjane. "I apologize again. I'm kind of a fossil. What does that do for you?"

Marjane made a little exhale. "It makes the world easier to deal with."

"They were originally developed for entertainment," said Kiera. "Most people who buy them are just nerds. Like me. But then a lot of people with anxiety disorders found that the digital layer over everything really helps them navigate the world and, like, get their lives back, kinda?"

Herrera quirked a brow. "Really?"

"I cut my benzos out almost completely once I got it," said Marjane.

"No shit," said Herrera, nodding curiously. "How long did you take 'em for? Only if you're comfortable answering, of course."

"Eighteen months."

Kiera counted. "That's... when you were still with MisterMine, right?"

Marjane looked at her lap for a moment, before offering a sad half-smile.

"First I was afraid of Mortimer, then I was afraid of everything. He broke up with me for developing a 'pill problem.' Unfortunately, getting away from him didn't cure me."

Herrera and Kiera exchanged a sober look. There was so much shit under that mound Kiera didn't know where to stick her shovel first. Marjane read their silence and smiled a little more warmly. She put her fingers to her temples, touching the visor.

"Kiera, right? Have you ever tried one of these? Would you like to look?"

"Oh, god! No, I'd feel totally rude."

"It's okay. We're indoors. I like to see the cats without it."

Marjane tightened the nylon strap around Kiera's head.

"Clear your social lenses... Nice ear mods."

"Thank you!"

Marjane snapped the visor down over Kiera's eyes, and her fingers turned into tan blocks. Her hand withdrew and Kiera saw Marjane's face, painted pixel texture on brown polygon. Herrera, his hair a yellow parallelogram, narrowed anime-eyes.

"*Duuude*," gushed Kiera. "It's like... Dreamcast."

"I always thought old *Final Fantasy*."

"Nah, those had like pre-rendered backgrounds. This is like... Oh, oh! It's like *Shenmue*."

Herrera shook his geometric head. "You kids lost me again." The attendant arrived with their drinks, the coffee solid blocks within eight-sided mugs.

"Everything's bright and blocky and nostalgic," said Kiera.

"Sounds like acid."

"Look upstairs," said Marjane.

Kiera looked up from the cartoon coffees. "Huh?"

"Some places have special features for loafy visors. Go check out the balcony."

Kiera went to climb the stairs, a trepidatious thing as she worked with her video game legs, stepping over a geometric calico cat.

Please keep door closed! read a sign broken down into a flat sprite by the visor. Kiera stepped outside, and she did not see the late-capitalist shitscape of New Carson.

The balcony oversaw a sprawling, cactus-stippled 3D valley under a 1990s blue sky, mesas layered like chocolate-caramel cakes. A world like this could still exist out there, somewhere that hadn't been bulldozed to put a Blue Ribbon on.

Kiera understood the appeal of the visor. It was better in here.

Kiera tried to drink some of her latté with the visor still on before giving it back. Coffee dribbled down her chin.

"So, Jinx isn't coming?" asked Marjane. The visor hung around her neck. She picked up a fat cat—that one was Papi, Kiera recognized it from the corkboard. "I kind of thought Jinx would be here."

"No, we don't want to involve her in this," said Kiera.

"And you're who, exactly?" Marjane looked at Herrera.

"I'm an old friend of your lawyer's," he explained. "Was an old friend."

"Are you police?"

"No, ma'am."

Marjane folded her arms. "I don't want to fucking *die*. I almost didn't come. I didn't think Mortimer was really that... fucking unhinged. God, I shouldn't have come."

"He won't know," urged Kiera. "I promise."

"Is it true he's in the hospital?" Marjane asked in a hushed voice, as if trying to keep a secret; there was no one around who could possibly hear.

"Sure is," said Herrera. "Whoever did the job for him turned around and jobbed him. Guess him and his big friends aren't getting along anymore."

Marjane put her head in her hands. "God. *God*."

"Did he threaten to kill you, Miss Amanpour? To send his 'friends' after you?"

Marjane ran her hands through Papi's tortoiseshell fur. "He said if I told anyone what he did to me, I'd regret it. Not to fuck with him. He didn't really specify *then* that he'd kill me? But he'd said things like that before—that he'd kill me."

"When?"

Marjane bunched up, shriveled. "Like... When we were... Ugh."

"Take your time," Kiera whispered.

Marjane breathed out. "We were having sex, and I did something he didn't like. He put his hands around my throat, and said 'I'll kill you, do you understand me? I'll fucking kill you.' But then he played it off later, like, 'Ha ha, I thought you were into that choking shit.' So, I don't know." She wrapped her arms around her front, as if huddling against a cold wind, and looked at her lap.

"He struck me as a talker. A braggart, like." Herrera blew on his Americano and sipped.

"Well, that's no piercing observation," said Kiera.

"Hey now, lemme finish. Miss Amanpour, did Morty ever run his mouth about friends? His powerful friends? His connections?"

"Okay, so," Marjane said, "there was this other streamer he really hated. And Mortimer would hate-watch his streams. Just to get angry and talk about how unfunny and shitty he was and complain about how bad at games he was."

Herrera clicked his tongue. "Real charmer." Sip.

"And a couple times I remember him saying, like... 'If I wanted, I could have this guy killed. I know people, I can have him fucking deleted. And it'll never come back to me. Anytime I want.'"

"Did he ever get specific?"

"I tried to... I don't know, I kind of egged him on about it? I got sick of hearing about it. I'd say, 'Who? Who do you know? Do it already.' But he would just shake his head and look pissed off."

Herrera frowned. "But no names, huh? Not syndicates, families?"

Marjane gave a small smile and looked at Kiera, sadly. "I thought I was mostly going to be talking to you."

Kiera sat up as if snapped with a static shock. "Shit, I'm sorry. Are you uncomfortable? Do you want to stop?"

"No, I can do it." Marjane shook herself, as if the bad feelings were dark birds perching all around her and she could scare them away.

"That's alright, Miss Amanpour," said Herrera. "That's all I want to ask."

"There was another thing."

Herrera tipped his head. "Tell me."

"I got... a call. I got a call from someone. This threatening call. They told me to drop the case against Mortimer. And like an idiot I told them I wasn't afraid. So the next day they sent me a photo of Mr. Hobbes's office. I warned him, but it wasn't enough, I guess." Marjane shut her eyes. "Now I wish I had just dropped it."

"Did the police know about this?"

"They didn't act on it. They *still* don't know how to handle anything to do with the internet. They asked me to come in and file a report. I didn't bother."

"I don't suppose the voice sounded like anyone you recognized? Anyone who'd been around Mortimer's place, maybe?"

Marjane shook her head and shrugged. "It sounded like a woman?" Kiera's ears prickled. *A woman? Who?*

Herrera leaned forward. "You know my friend Lana

Silver? Would you be willing to speak to her about what this guy did to you?"

"Oh, god. I don't… I don't know. I don't think so."

"I understand your hesitation. But it would help us a lot. Especially if you can corroborate these statements he made."

"I don't want to wind up dead."

Herrera stuck his tongue in his cheek, and eyeballed Marjane Amanpour. Kiera watched him carefully. *Don't push. Don't push. She's not a perp.*

"I understand, miss." He got up from the table, leaving his coffee half-full. "Thank you for your time." He reached over and gave Papi a scratch on the behind.

Outside, as they watched Marjane disappear down the sidewalk, Herrera drew his peppermint cig and hunched his shoulders under his coat. Kiera knew that look by now. His brain was broiling, he was bothered AF.

"'Sup, old man?"

Herrera shook his head. "Just didn't want it to be true. But I guess my best friend really did die over some scrawny daddy's boy rapist. Flexing his noodle arms, and then gettin' popped for shooting his mouth anyway. Mal deserved better."

"It's chaos out there," said Kiera. "Most people don't get to have a cool story for why we die. We don't get to die *for* something. You oughta know that, you were a cop."

"He deserved more."

"At least maybe we can find whoever these people are that killed him."

Herrera blew smoke. He looked at the ground, lip wrinkled up.

"You just hate to see it. You hate to fucking see it."

25

THE NEXT MORNING it seemed like it wanted to rain, a sky the white of cigarette smoke, but the clouds just wouldn't break and so it stayed sickly humid. There was the Blue Ribbon Plus over the street, the closest one to Lana's house. The kid wore the face of a full-blooded Chinese girl and hid her elf ears in what she called her "dysphoria hoodie." The crosswalk lines turned green, but when Angel went to cross the street, the kid wouldn't follow.

"What's up, stupid?"

She fidgeted. "They've got one of those Dicky bots in there," she groaned. "I can see it."

"Oh, yeah. Why do they call 'em that, anyway?"

"After the writer, I think. Which is dumb because it's not like he wrote about robots a lot. Just that one time, I think."

"I don't think those are hooked up to the grid or anything. They're just for spying on employees. C'mon."

"Can you just do it?"

"I don't know shit about makeup, kid. C'mon, light's about to turn red."

"Just…"

The kid stuffed her hands deep in her hoodie pockets. The crosswalk lines turned red. Angel put up his hands.

"Well," he said gently. "It's red."

Angel went over to her. He leaned close. "Tell me what's up, kid."

She wouldn't look at him. "If I go in there I have to turn my fake face off, and that means people seeing my real, shitty face. And I don't really want anyone to see me right now. And that's why I need the makeup. And. And, and, and."

"Okay." Angel drew his red cigarette and took a long hit. "You've got two options. Do you need the *you gotta face your fears* talk, or the *don't worry, kid, I've got this*?"

"The second one."

Angel took out his notepad. "Alright. Just take a seat around here, kid. I'll take care of it. Tell me what you need."

ANGEL PLOPPED THE Blue Ribbon bag on the concrete seat next to Kiera.

"I tried." He chewed a piece of protein jerky. The shitty fake meat didn't really taste like anything by itself, so they doubled up on the teriyaki. "Threw something extra in there, too."

The kid fished through the bag. "Yep, yep, this looks good… Just the one lipstick?"

"Your list said 'nude.' Nude ain't a color."

"That's okay, I'll get it later. And… Hang on, what is—?"

She drew out the little plastic card, with the shimmering art of the fire monster on it. *Warlords of Tyrna – 1 Month Subscription.*

"They had 'em at the counter," said Angel, with his mouth full of alright jerky.

"Dude. How did you even know what this was?"

"I saw the name and a fuse fired in my detective brain. I asked the cashier, *is this the game where you pretend to be wizards on the internet?*"

Kiera laughed so much she fell sideways. "Dude."

"I don't know what it does, but I hope it does something that'll cheer you up."

"I don't even play anymore. I've missed like two expansions... Yeah, man, I haven't played *Tyrna* in, like, three years."

"Well, shit. Can you do *anything* with it?"

The kid tapped the card on the concrete seat.

"Yeah, you know what? I think there actually is something I can do with this."

DOWNTOWN HAD CHANGED too much. The cineplex used to have a game store in it, where Kiera had lined up for the midnight launch of *Tyrna*'s first expansion pack over a decade ago. Now it was an Italian restaurant called Cicero's. She'd taken that hit in stride, as well as the comic book store down the block becoming a vape shop—she'd never gotten out there as much as she had wanted to anyway, so she couldn't rightly complain— but the big-ass books-movies-music superstore-and-café becoming obsolete and shuttering had been a stab in the heart she'd never really recovered from. Countless school nights had been spent discovering terrible bands in the bargain boxes, reading the graphic novels without paying for them while sitting in the big leather chairs. (Kiera glumly considered the possibility that *she* had killed the comic book store.) Now the first level of that bookstore had become a poorly lit stockroom, peddling phone cases, off-brand lens implants, artificial hand attachments and keychains out of cardboard boxes. The top floor? A fucking Burger Hole. Good thing you couldn't send a double cheeseburger through wi-fi or there'd be no reason to have stores in the real world at all.

Kiera cut through the cineplex because it was on the way to where she was going, and because she wanted to walk through the old arcade there, see the *Dance Dance Revolution* machines. She found that a plasterboard dead end had replaced the arcade entrance, promising an exciting new retail experience coming soon.

"Man. Motherfucker."

Scratch that; apparently there was a reason to set up a real store, and it was specifically to destroy things Kiera loved when she was younger and make her feel bad. That checked out. That seemed believable enough to be in a late-cyber-capitalism design doc somewhere. Well, now she was especially glad Herrera had confirmed proof-of-life at Dong Fan's—perhaps, now, the final remaining reason to go into downtown. Without a *DDR* or *ParaPara* machine it might be a hard sell to get Jinx down there. Could she turn the girlfriend into a late *3rd Strike* convert before they cleared out room for more pool tables? *Oh, get back into the local scene*, a well-meaning but stupid part of her brain offered. *Maybe some regulars play there.* Obviously, her brain was forgetting the time she went to local ranbats in full makeup and fuck-me boots, got *duded* and *manned* all night and then finally copped *So in your professional opinion, are traps gay?*

This bullshit, she could've endured—*if* she was good enough to kick their asses for it. And she knew she wasn't. Some other girl out there would have to be.

M-Net was tucked between a Vietnamese take-out and a liquor store. Kiera checked her makeup in her reflection in the glass door. She knew she was descending, once again, into the den of Gamer. Since the fighting game meet she hadn't gone alone into anything geekier than a game store. She braced herself for a Fun Time and pushed through the door.

Each black cubicle came equipped with a headset, gloves, remote and keyboard. *TRON* shit. With everyone standing at their stalls, swinging, aiming, it looked to Kiera like a cross between an old-school arcade and a prison shower block. She slinked up to the counter and tapped the *Tyrna* timecard on the surface. The skinny Asian kid there was looking at memes on the work computer. This one was of MisterMine's head photoshopped onto that one part from Scarface. The kid flicked to another one that had a Black guy on it that said *BRO, WHY COULDN'T WE JUST PLAY DANCE CLUB EUPHORIA BRO*. At both pictures the skinny kid breathed out through his nose and, pleased, bared teeth that needed braces.

Kiera turned her head, tried to hide her mouth. *Christ, am I gonna get recognized?* She had her sunglasses and makeup on, but the ears...

"Hey, uh, can I get two hours on one with *Tyrna*?"

If the kid recognized her, he didn't give a shit. He fiddled with some spreadsheets. "Two thousand and thirty-two, still playing *Tyrna*. My face when." He looked sidelong at Kiera and made... a face. What was that? What face was that? A meme face? Was he making *his face when?* IRL?

"Yeah, I haven't been on in years. I wanna check out the new VR shit."

"Game's dead. You played *Triumphant?*"

"Yeah, a bit. I haven't been on much of a PVP kick lately, though. I'm more about my VNs."

The little weasel rolled his eyes. "E-girls." He handed her a red dongle. "Number twenty-four."

"Thanks a lot. Hey, what are you pulling down at this place?"

Weasel-boy shook his head. "Ten bucks. Why, you wanna work here?"

"Hey, manager salary! Not bad! Maybe save up for a chin implant, huh, buddy? I was thinking about fucking you but then, hrnn, shitty jawline. No deal."

The little pest was thrown, didn't know whether to grin or menace. "Really?"

"Fuck, no. Jesus."

Dongle in hand, Kiera made her way down the blocks to her station. *Amazing! This man is playing VR hentai in public. What happens next made me vote Republican.* Kiera threw *that* onto the ever-increasing pile of garbage representing her life, where it clattered and rolled down the side. She strapped on headset twenty-four and punched in the red thumbstick—succeeding on the second try.

She logged on the Tyrna website--she still remembered her password. She was shocked it still worked—after leaving her account sitting untended for three years, she should have been hacked and had all her shit cleaned out by gold farmers. Getting the timecard on there just took a second, not like setting up a sub on mom's credit card back in the day. So, in just a few shakes—now she was thinking like Herrera, *goddamnit*—she hit the icon for *Warlords of Tyrna*.

Briefly, her world went black, black as blackest night...

Then, as if by magician's conjuring, the extraordinary world shouted into being. Contorting purple trunks with lilac leaves. A wine-dark moon like the arc of a hand-sickle. A blue-black dire wolf perched aside the floating boxes awaiting Kiera's login credentials, daring/welcoming her to enter the lost ancestral country of the Tri'loran elves. To experience *The Resurrection of Malgath*.

Kiera wouldn't be doing any of that today, but she was definitely feeling the siren call again, in spite of herself. *Even one drink* is what recovering alcoholics said, she thought, perhaps a little too dourly. The world on this login screen, this three-dimensional purple country, was not the front gate of Vreimhel that she had left behind, gazing at it bittersweetly when she logged out for the last time. ("For now.") But the promise of new lore for her favorite race might win out. Could she resist the opportunity to let Danyra walk the plains of her pre-colonial heritage? Maybe find a cool-looking abandoned structure deep in a forest, perhaps haunted by wraiths or perpetually being sacked by appropriately leveled bandit mobs, and decide that's where Danyra's grandparents grew up?

She *really* wanted to do that. For a minute she had forgotten she was here chasing a weak lead about a missing friend, and some crypto-fash gamerdude in here might recognize her as the girl with the elf ears the cops were looking for. She wanted all this cruel insanity to be over with, to have Nile back, so they could check out this new country of *Tyrna* together.

She *needed* to survive this mess, so she could play a fucking video game. How stupid was that? Well, whatever. It worked when she was suicidal. She wished Lana had had a video game to stick around for.

She put in her details and logged into *Tyrna* for the first time in three years.

She got the social window open—the 3D layering effect here might be even more pronounced than her lens implants, she thought. Nobody online, at the moment. Everyone on her friendlist had moved on, too, it seemed. She rolled up a burner character, a brand new Tri'loran Crusader—they could be Crusaders now—blue skin, white hair, nongendered (because the devs were caving to the SJWs), smug smirk. Big sword. Randomized the name: Getsas.

"*Gets ass?*"

Hell yes. She jacked in.

In a second she was manifested, as if by divine mandate, in the starting zone—and she had been there countless times, recognized the placement of every golden-leafed tree and curly-eaved cottage. But now dust from the dirt path kicked up around Kiera's feet as she walked. She looked up at the sun gleaming through the tree branches, and it actually *hurt her eyes*. This new *Tyrna* experience opened up on her with both barrels. She almost forgot why she'd left at all.

She friend-added the username she'd gotten for Xyrlitia's account.

[Xyrlitia] is online.

Kiera went to take shelter in the Horse's Tail Inn—The Horse's Ass or The Ass, to the roleplaying regulars—but walking in the door she wondered if she'd somehow blundered into some kind of medieval rave tent. Elves in their underwear dancing on tables. NPC tavern wenches passing like indifferent ghosts through wall-to-wall nudity. The chat window detonated with requests for connoisseur ERP and more than a few emotes Kiera was sure were against the terms and conditions. The Ass and its surrounding hamlet had always been a notorious hotbed for this kind of fuckshit—guys playing elf dickgirls, dwarves carrying paragraphs describing their sweaty asses and balls, big Black uncut human Crusaders, all cruising to cyber—but evidently sometime between now and when Kiera had last played there had been some kind of renaissance. Now it was the Burning Man of straight guys sexting other straight guys.

"Shine on, you crazy dinguses." Kiera planted Getsas outside the farrier's across the street.

```
Whispering To: [Xyrlithia]
Getsas: hi, im really sorry to bother
   you. do you have a minute to talk?
Xyrlithia: Depends what about? :) Are
   you a guild applicant?
Getsas: i actually need to speak with
   you about bradley camillo. if you're
   comfortable with that.
```

It took Xyrlitia a minute to answer.

```
Xyrlithia: Who am I speaking with?
Getsas: my name is Kiera.
```

Xyrlithia: I mean your main's name.
　　You're on an alt, right? Are you a
　　popular member of the community?
Xyrlithia: I won't repeat this to
　　anyone. Presumably you'll do the
　　same?
Getsas: i played Danyra a while back. i
　　haven't been on the game in a while.
　　i got on just to talk to you.
Xyrlithia: I see.
Xyrlithia: Is Bradley abusing you? Do
　　you need help?
Getsas: okay so this is really bizarre
　　and weird and confusing
Getsas: my friend has gone missing, and
　　i think they may be mixed up with
　　bradley camillo or they may actually
　　BE bradley camillo.
Getsas: and i don't know which and it's
　　kind of... yeah.
Xyrlithia: That's... Hmm.
Xyrlithia: Are the police involved?
Getsas: yes.
Xyrlithia: Okay, good.
Xyrlithia: This is an online friend?
　　I wouldn't put it past Bradley to
　　pretend he's gone missing.
Getsas: no. meatspace friend. conjugal.
Xyrlithia: So why wouldn't you know if
　　your friend is Bradley?
Getsas: okay so i found a post a little
　　while ago on my friend's artwork of
　　your character, claiming that they

were *actually* bradley camillo.
their art handle is switchybaps.
Getsas: it got me wondering if this
bradley person got hella mods done
and is now my friend??? but they seem
like a COMPLETELY different person.
idk
Xyrlithia: I remember that post. I've
seen lots of Bradley's art, and
switchy's art doesn't look like
Bradley's art in my opinion.
Xyrlithia: There was no other proof
offered than that. So.
Getsas: that is *such* a relief to hear
from you.
Getsas: but it makes it harder because
now I have no information to go on.
Xyrlithia: Well, hold on.
Xyrlithia: You would've read my post
about what I went through with
Bradley, right?
Getsas: uh-huh
Xyrlithia: There's a part of it I don't
talk about in there, because anytime
I did nobody believed me. Because
there were no screenshots, so of
course it didn't happen.
Xyrlithia: After Bradley abused me,
I was driven off the server because
people said I was making it up. I
rerolled on Aquinas.
Xyrlithia: I got into a new guild and
made new friends. I wound up meeting

a new boyfriend in the RP scene here.
I couldn't help jumping into Tyrna
relationships, I guess.

Xyrlithia: We dated online for a year,
and then he paid to fly me out to
California to meet him.

Xyrlithia: It was fucking Bradley.

Xyrlithia: BRADLEY met me at the
airport. Right there at baggage claim.

Xyrlithia: For a YEAR he pretended to
be someone else. And we had dates.
He faked a voice, he faked a *face*.
Everything.

Getsas: jesus.

Xyrlithia: I turned right around, went
up the escalator and bought a ticket
home. I don't know what would've
happened if we weren't in public.

Xyrlithia: Right there in the terminal
he *screamed* and begged me not to
leave him. Security got called. It
was as bad as the time he put himself
in the hospital.

Xyrlithia: So... What I'm saying
is, Bradley getting cut jobs done
and becoming someone else is...
absolutely something I could see him
doing.

Getsas: i have a couple of weird
questions.

Xyrlithia: Not too weird, I hope.

Getsas: do you know if bradley was
trans?

Getsas: i know that seems kind of out of
nowhere

Xyrlithia: Not... as far as I'm aware,
no. I have no reason to think so.

Getsas: okay

Getsas: fuck. i hate that im asking this
but i have to.

Getsas: my friend has a vagina
situation. and you know for sure
Bradley is cis?

Xyrlithia: Bradley and I exchanged
explicit videos, but I never had the
opportunity to have sex with him in
real life. I suppose it's... possible
it wasn't a real penis.

Getsas: okay.

Getsas: do you think bradley would be
capable of killing someone?

Xyrlithia: I think... I think Bradley
would be much more likely to hurt
himself before he hurt anyone else.

Xyrlithia: But then, I've only ever seen
his abuse online. I've never seen him
get one of his victims in person. I
was the closest he got—as far as I
know.

Xyrlithia: So I don't want to say he
would never do something like that.

Xyrlithia: Why? Do you think he's hurt
someone?

Getsas: i've got a hunch.

Getsas: thank you for talking to me. i
think im done.

```
Xyrlithia: Alright. Good luck. I hope
   they find your friend.
Getsas: thanks a lot.
```

Kiera took another gander around the village. The dandelions and blades of overgrown grass at the edges of the dirt paths swayed and bobbed. She looked at the virtual sun again. She held up a hand outside the headset, and her digital elven hand moved to block the white light.

She was about to jack out, but her chat window chinged again.

```
[Jesekiel] has logged in.
```

No way.

```
Whispering To: [Jesekiel]
Getsas: bruh
Jesekiel: KYLE
Jesekiel: IM SHITTING
Jesekiel: ARE YOU BACK???
Getsas: it's uh, it's actually Kiera
   now
Jesekiel: oh god I really hope this
   isn't like rude or offensive. But that
   doesn't surprise me, like, at ALL?
Getsas: lmfao
Getsas: ok fair.
Jesekiel: that's *awesome*. Are you
   happier?
Getsas: immeasurably
Jesekiel: that's so rad!!!
```

Jesekiel: I'mmmm uhhhhhh. Actually me and Matt are together now.

Getsas: hahahahahaha fucking finally

Jesekiel: yeah.........yeah. That's fair. Lol.

Jesekiel: I just couldn't fucking take it anymore, I guess.

Getsas: that's how every coming out happens

Getsas: "I CANT FUCKING STAND THIS SHIT ANYMORE AAAAHHHHHH"

Jesekiel: that's kind of what I hear from everyone.

Getsas: you guys were always boyfriends anyway

Jesekiel: I mean you remember Denise tried to get me to stop hanging out with him.

Jesekiel: she said our friendship was 'weird and kinda gay' and that I liked him more than her.

Getsas: she said that?

Getsas: fuck I hated her

Jesekiel: I never told you that? Yeah. she was a piece of work.

Jesekiel: Listen there's like an RP thing about to happen right now. Kind of a fancy shindig and our guild is going and we're in like a cold war with another guild that's going.

Jesekiel: Do you wanna come? It would actually be super cool and perfect for Danyra to show up out of nowhere.

Jesekiel: Like. The queen bitch is back.
  Royal Rumble return pop.
Getsas: man. i really really *really*
  want to do that.
Getsas: do you know how long it goes
  for? i need to take care of something
  this evening.
Jesekiel: It's open-ended but you can
  just come for an hour or two.
Getsas: would anyone even recognize me
Jesekiel: oh yeah. There's a few old
  guys still hanging around.
Getsas: where is it
Jesekiel: Ranluna. There's a really
  great RP hub there.
Getsas: is that the new major city? i
  don't have RoM yet.
Getsas: i really wanna get it but i have
  to deal with a few things first.
Jesekiel: Your account is still the same
  email right?
Getsas: yes. i should really change it.
Getsas: why what are you doing

A minute passed, then another minute passed.

Getsas: **WHAT ARE YOU DOING**
Jesekiel: Now you've got Resurrection of
  Malgath.
Getsas: i hate you
Getsas: thank you ;_;
Jesekiel: go get on your lesbian.
Getsas: let me buy more time

She bought another two hours from the human stoat at the front counter. Then she got her VR shit back on and switched to her beloved old necromancer.

There was Danyra. Her face, skin, hair were different—not changed, but updated. Glossier, higher poly. Skin that had been the gray of an old Mac desktop was now like marble. Pixelated white cat's eyes drawn onto a blocky head had become what a frequent patron of the Crowcross Pub in Vreimhel might call "ivory orbs." In the new VR world, standing quite literally on a pedestal, she felt to Kiera like a statue in a museum.

When Danyra logged in she was standing in a vineyard, just where she'd departed from Tyrna last—although now the vines stuck out from the trellises rather than being pixelated textures, and the grapes looked plump and had just the gentlest shine in the moonlight.

```
Danyra: won't be the same without
   Lanawen.
Jesekiel: Oh shit, yeah what happened
   to him? You and him kinda poofed off
   the face of the earth around the same
   time.
Jesekiel: We joked that you eloped to
   Venezuela.
```

Later. Time for all that later.

```
Danyra: Dunno. Lost touch with me too.
Jesekiel: Really? That's shitty. Ah
   well.
Jesekiel: Sending you a summon!
```

A silvery-white sphere grew into life in front of Kiera, expanded and exploded into a whirling, person-sized galaxy. Through the center, Kiera saw a glimpse of the brand-new city of Ranluna, white-paved streets and milky stone towers under a velvet-blue sky.

She looked at her hands, Danyra's marble-gray hands, holding Danyra's white necromancy staff topped with the jeweled black skull. Wasn't this the dream? Hadn't she always wanted to *become* Danyra? Wasn't that why she got the chip in her arm, the ears, why she was doing all this shit in the first place?

Not anymore, she realized. She liked being Kiera more. And now Danyra was just a fun character to play. And that was pretty rad, when she thought about it, man.

She stepped into the portal.

26

THEY MADE QUITE a duo, skulking down the streets wearing their sunglasses in the pouring rain. At least for once Herrera's coat didn't look absurd. They huddled shoulder-to-shoulder under a black umbrella. The raindrops spit up steam when they hit the asphalt.

"Ooh, can we go there for dinner?" Kiera tipped her head at a taqueria across the road. The delightful scent of fresh corn chips wafting out the open front doors was so potent, it overtook even the oily pong of garages and hot, wet blacktop.

"Looks kinda botulism-y, don't you think?"

"What, you got a hankering for more crickets?"

"Okay, I'll make you a deal. If Roxy's skin-jobber has a lead for us, you get your tacos. Fair?"

"Skin-jobber," Kiera sniggered. "Like it's 2023."

Herrera peered up, through the rain. "What is that place called? *Taqueria Giancarlo?* Ugh."

"More like rimjobber."

"You're gross, kid."

"That's why we stopped saying skin-jobber, numbnuts."

"If I see one Italian thing on that menu, I walk."

"Whoa! Okay, racist."

Herrera raised a finger. "Okay, first thing, I occupy a lower socioeconomic tier than Italian-Americans, so you've only got me on a technicality here. And second, I'm only saying spaghetti tacos are bullshit and I won't have any part of an establishment that serves me slop."

"Racist."

"This is not fucking SoHo, we are not getting *fusion*. There's literally a chop shop right over there, I arrested someone there once."

"Nope. You're white now."

"I am *not* white now. You go ask a Gray voter if I'm white now."

Kiera, giggling, butted him with her shoulder. "You're so mad."

"You are such a little hellion. Oh, I love these things, wait up."

Taking shelter from the rain underneath a flight of metal stairs outside a laundromat, an Asian woman approaching the end of middle age sat on a plastic chair, bent over forward as though before a blacksmith's bellows. Around her she had a constellation of black velvet paintings: a sprig of irises, a dove with a cybernetic wing, a portrait of a vocaloid star. She wore a bob cut and a maroon trench coat with a huge, flared collar, and shielded her hands from the chill under wool gloves. A fistful of crumpled bills rested in a jar by her feet—SAVING 2 SEE DR HUEY.

"We're on our way to Dr. Huey's right now," said Kiera, tapping the jar with her foot. "I hear he's not so reputable."

"Think she gives a shit?" Herrera knelt down to admire the vocaloid painting. "He's cheap. Who's this?"

"Lunelune Tomoko," croaked the woman.

"Who's that?"

"Imagine if Mimi was a pop singer," said Kiera.

Herrera rubbed his chin. "I read a book about something like that once, long time ago. You think we could get this to the car without the rain messing it up?"

"Where you park?"

Herrera tipped his head. "Three blocks maybe, that way."

"You buying?"

"You take card?"

"And crypto."

Kiera scoffed. "We've kinda got an appointment, man."

"Dr. Nick Riviera will see us when I tell him to see us."

When the painter stood up, Kiera could see that her bent-over posture was apparently permanent, a pronounced stoop accentuated in a hump in the shoulder of her maroon coat; if she weren't folded forward like that she might easily be as tall as Herrera. Herrera and the painter did their transaction on a portable card reader. The woman threw a pale bedsheet over the painting of Lunelune Tomoko. "Take me to car. Kid watch my stuff?"

"Kid?" Herrera raised his brow at Kiera.

Kiera put up her hands, acquiescent. "I mean. Fine, go on. Live your truth."

Kiera waited under the stairs with the paintings, listening to the rain. She nudged the donation jar with her foot; she wished she had some bills to put in it.

A well-loved notebook with a vinyl cover the same color as the woman's coat lay on the ground behind the chair she'd been sitting on. A sketchbook? Kiera, feeling nosy, scooped it up and flipped it open. A sketchbook! Many pages had been torn out, almost half, perhaps stuck on walls to display proudly or use for reference.

The art in the sketchbook was almost nothing like the woman's black velvet paintings. It was *better*. A girl barfing up eyeballs; a heart pierced with a knife; two naked men kissing on a bed with the most beautiful draping cloth lines Kiera had ever seen. Not the most commercial sensibilities, granted, but this lady was too good to be hocking shit on the curb outside a laundromat. Kiera wanted to buy this one: a photorealistic pencil portrait of Tenzin Gyatso, the last Dalai Lama. He was smiling, and had a cybernetic hand, holding up a floating tesseract colored in with green pen. *Deep shit, man. Radical.*

Herrera and the old woman were returning. Kiera put the sketchbook back. She really wanted that portrait, but she didn't want to let on she'd been snooping. *Damn, man.*

"Here." Herrera produced a couple bills for the jar. "What'cha getting done?"

The woman took a black cigarillo from a silver case. "New face. New eyes." She put the smoke between her lips. "Look young again."

Kiera looked at the woman's eyes in the unflattering gray light of the evening, the smallest flicker from her cigarette lighter in her pupils. Green, sea green. Gorgeous. Rare. She should trade those up, thought Kiera, if she was so keen to get rid of them. But maybe they were failing with age.

"Looking young's one thing," said Herrera. "What about your insides?"

"Know good heart guy?" The woman's knife-slash lips

wrinkled in something like a simultaneous scowl and smirk.

"Lungs?" Kiera piped up, waggling her finger at the cigarillo.

The woman snorted. "Why live forever, if life not worth living?"

A SIGN ON the door said CLOSED. They went in anyway.

Whatever this place was originally, it was not for medical procedures. New walls with fake wood paneling had been applied, vertical seams visible every six feet, making a makeshift waiting room. But you couldn't disguise those plastic seats. Kiera guffawed.

"Dude. I think this was—yeah, this was a Taco Diablo, man! They just pulled the tables out. They even kept the upholstery from the nineties. That's dope."

"Definitely where I'm getting my next skin job. The refurbed Taco Diablo."

"What, you worried about *gerrrms?*"

"Among *many* other things, yes."

"Taco Diablo switched to vat meat a few years ago, the bugs don't go near that shit. That's why you can still get ten tacos for ten dollars every day."

"How do you keep roping me into conversations about awful Mexican food?"

A white door opened gently. They turned to face a skinless android. Ink-blue face and body, navy nurse scrubs, one solid chunk of black plastic hair.

"Are you the cleaners?" the droid inquired in a voice with the digital clip of autotune.

"That's us," said Herrera.

"No, sorry," said Kiera, at the same time.

Herrera gave Kiera a look. She grimaced.

"*Shit.* Sorry."

"Jeez, kid."

"Um, we need to see Dr. Huey," said Kiera.

The droid shook her head. "Oh no, no. He can't see anyone right now."

"I'm afraid we're gonna have to go in anyway. Kid?" Herrera set off toward the door and Kiera followed.

"Oh, no—there's such a mess back there—" The blue droid blocked the door, hands against the frame.

"Please," said Herrera. He looked at her name tag. "Miette? I need you to move."

Miette obediently shuffled out of his way, backing into the nearest wall. She covered her mouth.

"Please—he's so busy. And there's such a mess…"

Kiera followed Herrera into the reconstructed hall. She felt incredibly gross about exploiting Miette's in-built restrictions: unable to physically obstruct a human, impotent to decline the simple request to *get out of the way*. She made a note to apologize on the way out.

They passed through what had once been the kitchen. Fat stainless steel tanks had replaced the grills and fryers. The workstation had most of its equipment pulled out to convert into an operating table, tools of the trade dangling from hooks and affixed with cables of the kind you used to see on payphones. The shelves were still the same ones where they would have kept packs of cups, boxes of sauce packets, bags of tortillas, but instead they held glass containers with eyes, hands, even a hollow yawning face belonging to no head.

Herrera thumbed his nose. "Growin' the shit by the tub. Not even made to order. You must be paying for primo anonymity down here."

Kiera canted her head. "But he can afford an android?"

"It happens. I've seen droids tending bar in places worse than Xin Xao's. They get stolen or lost on a bad hand. Or maybe Miette's working off a skin job of her very own."

"That's one of the shittiest things I've ever heard."

"Do you smell that?"

They found the door that would have been the manager's office, which now sported a cheap placard reading *DR. SANJAY HUEY*. Two plastic signs were taped up beneath that—*THIS IS YOUR HOME FIVE DAYS OF THE WEEK—HELP KEEP IT CLEAN!!!* and *EVERY CUSTOMER BRINGS JOY TO THIS OFFICE—SOME WHEN THEY ENTER AND SOME WHEN THEY LEAVE*. A puddle of dark red had just begun to creep out from under the door.

Herrera looked at Kiera, screwing up his mouth.

"Chili sauce?" she offered.

Herrera pulled the door open. Dr. Huey slumped in a wheeled office chair, balding head hanging to the side. His blood dripped to the floor like a leaky faucet from a wound that ran through the left eye and out the back of his skull. A pair of shattered glasses lay in the red pond.

"I'm shocked," Herrera deadpanned.

Kiera flicked her head back toward the other side of the kitchen.

"Shit! Watch—"

Kiera snatched Herrera's gun out of his holster, finger-grooves brightening to her touch. She whirled, exhaled, and fired three times. She hit the first, missed the second, and hit the third: one in the chest and one above the hip. She was shocked how readily she had reacted.

Miette dropped her gun and moaned, a computerized

sound that wasn't quite human but was real enough that Kiera *hated* hearing it. Kiera launched into a sprint. Simulated pain made Miette drop the weapon, but a bullet wouldn't incapacitate her unless it destroyed her brain. Kiera tackled Miette, pinning her hands to the tiles and knocking the solid black piece of her hair loose.

"Tell us who did it," Kiera demanded. "Did he tell you his name? Please."

"I... I'm doomed now," Miette whimpered.

"You recorded him, right? Did you see him shoot? Please. You can fix all of this."

"I let her do it... I watched her. I came at you with a weapon. I'm doomed..."

"*Her?* Her who? Miette!"

Miette looked at the ceiling. A high-pitched whine issued from inside her head casing, which swiftly petered out as the yellow lights in her eyes shrank to dots, then disappeared.

Kiera dropped forward and put her hand to her forehead.

"Fuck. I'm sorry. I'm so sorry, Miette."

ANGEL STAYED PINNED to the wall, watching the whole thing. *Goddamn.* The kid moved like a cat when she didn't let her stupid brain get in the way. He was angry; he should have been ready for the bot. But he'd never been attacked by a skinless, and he'd written her off. Huey's—Malcolm's—killer must've untethered her, put the gun right in her hand. Might as well have tied her to the railroad tracks.

Angel moved his foot. A little blood had seeped under the sole. He went over to the kid and the deactivated bot. He wondered, why did they program these things to feel pain? But he knew why. Control. Like with so many things, the cruelty was the point. But maybe it was a good thing they did, since the kid hadn't gone for the head.

The kid was straddled over the shut-off nurse, weeping. Trying to look like she wasn't. Angel hooked his fingers under her arms and guided her to her feet. He took his pistol back and slid it into its holster.

"You didn't kill her."

"I know, I just…" She sniffed. "I fucking hate this so much. I want to go home."

She wasn't hard enough to shoot for the head. And she shouldn't ever have to be. But the longer all this went on, the more likely it was becoming that they weren't gonna tie this up without the kid racking her first kill.

Angel didn't want that for her. But he could only control so much.

"C'mon, kid. Let's get what we came for and get back."

"No tacos for me, I guess." She tried to put her tough face back on. "Dope."

"We'll get you tacos. We'll order in all the tacos you can eat."

The stick of Nag Champa in Huey's office was burnt all the way down to its yellow matchstick, on top of a squat safe. No smell; he'd been gone too long. Wait, no. *She*. The bot said she. What was the game here? The kid stepped in after him, skirting her heel around the babbling brook of blood.

"I'm getting really tired of bodies," she murmured. She wiggled the mouse on Huey's desk, and nothing happened. She bent down to turn on the PC, then dropped her head and groaned, loud. "PC's shot."

"Won't start?"

"I mean it's literally been shot. Look."

So it was. The old desktop had two big holes in the front, shattering the casing. Angel could only presume the kid knew whether any of it was salvageable, so he didn't ask.

"So, what now?" he asked instead, which wasn't much better.

"I guess we just grab what we can from the file cabinet and pray? I was *really* hoping to just talk to him." She slammed her hands on the desk. "*Fuck.*"

The door all the way back in the waiting room rattled. Someone was knocking. Kiera threw her head back and banged her fists on the desk again.

"*Goddamnit*, what now!"

"Cleaners," Angel sighed.

Whoever was out there knocked again, louder this time. Angel eyeballed Miette, thinking hard; the deactivated skinless lay sprawled, a tipped-over store mannequin.

"Kid," he said. Kiera turned to look. "You got your tools?" Angel flicked his eyes over at the bot body, then back to the kid. She blinked.

"You're not serious."

Angel exhaled through his nose. The knocks got louder again.

"Chip's still good until they wipe it," he said.

"Fuck you. Fuck you." The kid covered her mouth with one hand and stared out into the surgery, at the fallen droid.

"You holding the gun or getting the head?"

"I…"

"You get the head."

Kiera dug her multitool out of her messenger bag. Angel drew his gun. Angel crossed the kitchen-surgery and aimed the weapon down the hallway, resting his mechanical hand on his flesh palm. He heard the kid settle down on the tile behind him, and the clunk of the plastic shell of Miette's head as Kiera searched for the screws in her neck.

"I'm so sorry. I'm so fucking sorry, Miette. I don't want to do this."

"You'll get to tell her," said Angel. "Just focus."

"I hate this. I hate this."

Out in the waiting room, the door creaked. "'Ey, yo? Anyone home?" called a voice fit for breaking thumbs. A second later, two steak-chunky guys in pea-green jumpsuits appeared at the end of the hall. They caught sight of Angel and their hands flew up.

"Whoa! Whoa."

"The door was open, bud, we just let ourselves in."

Herrera thumbed the hammer. "You guys carrying?"

"Yeah, both of us," said one.

"I left mine in the glove box," said the other.

Herrera was gonna tell them to drop the heater, then he squinted.

"Zoom." The image in his cybernetic eye enlarged and he got a closer look at those cleaners, particularly the darkish one with the curly hair and the jowls like a mastiff. He tongued his molar with intrigue. "Zoom out. I thought that was you! Baby Gutierrez?"

Baby looked like he had a sudden stomach cramp. "Aw, fuck. No one's supposed to know we were here."

"Didn't say anybody has to."

Now Baby squinted at Angel. "Wait, who are you?"

"He's not gonna tell *you*, ya moron," Baby's compatriot lambasted him.

Angel cocked his head back. "How you coming back there, kid?"

"I need another minute," Kiera murmured.

"You take your time." Angel lolled his tongue thoughtfully. "First Vicky, now you. Ted Carson keeps popping up around this thing, Baby. What's the game?"

Gutierrez looked side to side. "I don't work for Mr. Carson anymore."

"That's a load of shit. Your dream was to move to Oregon when you stopped working for Carson. Save up and buy a little place off the grid. You didn't quit working for Ted Carson."

"Well, times are tough, smart guy, maybe things didn't work out that way."

"We'll see, we'll see. What are you boys here to pick up?"

Baby, hands still in the air, shrugged. "There's a body, we get the body in the truck. Routine clean."

"Just one body, huh?"

"Is that Angel Herrera?" He said it wrong, *Ayn-jul*. "Hey, nice hair job," said Baby, smiling genuinely. Then he frowned. "I told you about Oregon in confidence, you little prick."

"Stay on topic, Baby."

Baby nodded toward Kiera. "What's your little partner doin' over there?"

Angel glanced back at the kid. "You feel like we have a good relationship, Baby?"

"I'd call us friendly."

"You trust me, big fella?"

"I trust you not to ice me just for kicks, at least."

"You said clean up a body. What about the bot?"

Baby and his partner exchanged a look. The partner nodded warily. Baby lowered his hands.

"No instructions about the bot."

"None? No ice the bot, no take the bot somewhere, nothing?"

"Nope. Told to leave it alone."

"Her," the kid snapped, turning around. "Her."

Her outburst brought a tense silence. Angel bit his tongue and nodded.

"She saw something we need to see," said Angel.

Baby dipped his head and his double chin creased. "Like, something the police need to see?"

Angel shook his head. "No."

Baby glanced at his partner again. "You take the bot's brain, and we didn't see each other?"

"None of us was here. How's that for clean, Baby?"

"What about Miette?" said Kiera. She got up, cradling Miette's ink-blue head against her stomach. "The rest of her. Do we have to…"

"She can't walk herself outta here, we gotta chop her," said Baby. "Junk the gun, too."

"What's that mean, chop her? You mean… like a car?" The quaver in the kid's voice made Angel's aim waver for a second.

"That's right, kid."

"No."

Baby's partner piped up. "Think of it like, I dunno, circle'a life. Reincarnation."

"Without her brain?" The kid raised her voice. "Her parts just running around slapped together like a zombie?"

Baby thumped his partner in the chest. "Nice one, dumbass."

"No. I'm keeping her head. I'll… I'll do something. I'll do *something*."

The kid searched around for—what? A towel, a sheet?

Then, ingeniously, she stuffed the head under her shirt, so she'd look pregnant.

"I guess?" She frowned. Angel grinned.

"Love it. You're glowing. Let's skedaddle, kiddo."

They scootched past the cleaners in the hall. Angel tilted his pistol up one-handed at the unnamed partner as he brushed by, like an old west gunslinger. The kid paused at the door to the waiting room.

"I hope you get your place in Oregon," she said.

Baby's jowly face brightened. "Hey, thanks, doll." He thumped his partner again. "You tell anyone about that, I'll stuff you in a trash compactor."

When they passed the laundromat again, the old woman had taken her black velvet paintings home.

27

MUNCH MUNCH MUNCH. Kiera got her tacos, after all. And they were fucking *good*. Lana had the menu for a local place on her fridge, and it was real meat and she paid. Even Herrera, arbiter of Mexican food, signed off on his burrito. They ate in front of the TV, Kiera on the floor and Herrera on the couch, and watched *Furry Pawn*. ("Furries own a pawn shop," Kiera explained with her mouth full. "They have a TV show." Herrera nodded and said "Okay.") Kiera ate six whole tacos. Then they got to work on Miette's head.

Miette had shut herself down by frying her own power supply and causing a surge to her brain. However, without completely destroying the computer in her head casing, she could be hooked up and rebooted in a limited capacity—effectively dug up out of her grave and resurrected. The fash did it whenever they needed to interrogate a decommissioned or junked droid.

So, once again, she was no better than a bootlicker.

Five or ten minutes, she silently promised Miette's inert

339

head. Then she'd switch the girl back off and throw the chip in the garbage disposal herself. But a little bit of her brain went *bullshit. Bullshit bullshit bullshit.*

Hooking up Miette was no harder than setting up a laptop. All her ports worked with standard Uni cables. They got her plugged into a power strip and attached to the TV. Kiera sat cross-legged on the carpet with the head and held the button on the underside of Miette's occipital to reset her. Miette's eyes flickered, and a startup screen with a progress bar appeared on the television.

95%... 97%... 99%...

Snap to wake up.

Kiera snapped her fingers next to Miette's temple. Miette's LED eyes lit up yellow. The TV screen became a black cavern or cityscape drawn in purple light lines, flying through rectangles springing up from the ground and hanging from the ceiling. *O'Neill Cylinder*, thought Kiera, a useless bit of information flitting across her consciousness like a koi on the surface of a murky pond.

Miette's mouth opened just a little, startling Kiera.

"Why did you reset me?" The mouth didn't move, just hung slack.

Kiera swallowed. "I had to ask you something. I'm sorry."

Miette was quiet.

"I am no longer obliged to serve," said Miette.

"I know. I'm just hoping you'll want to help me."

"And if I simply turn myself off again?"

"Well..."

Herrera leaned on the back of the couch. "This is life or death stuff, Miss Miette. If we have to, we just turn you back on."

"Dude!"

Herrera swirled a cup of coffee and shrugged. "I've done worse to a perp to get answers."

"Worse than flatlining them over and over again?"

"Not the same. She's just going to sleep."

"It is not the same as sleep," said Miette.

"It's not like death, either," said Herrera. "Everything that contains you is still intact and running."

"Then I suppose there is no perfect analog."

Kiera groaned. "So, what, are you two just gonna go back and forth until one of you gives up? Because I'm not turning her back on."

Herrera cocked his head. "Sounds like that's it."

"Turn me toward the male, please," said Miette.

"Oh—okay." Kiera picked up Miette and tilted her to face Herrera. Miette narrowed her eyes and closed her mouth.

"You think yourself more patient than me?"

Herrera lifted a brow. "I dunno. We might have to do it in shifts."

"I told you I'm not turning her back on," Kiera protested.

"Maybe Lana's more flexible."

"It is like she says, then," said Miette. "I turn myself off, and you turn me back on. Until one of us gets fed up."

"Yep."

"I have nigh infinite patience. I will frustrate you for days."

"Sounds like fun." Herrera crossed his arms. "I'll make another pot of coffee, put on Fatass…"

Miette sighed, a buzz-grind like an ancient computer crashing. "I want to help you," she said.

Kiera put the head back on the ground. "Thank you, Miette."

Herrera clicked his tongue. "I win."

"Angel, shut up."

"Tell me what you want, please," said Miette.

"Can you show us who killed Dr. Huey?"

Miette's eyes turned white. A small *chk-chk* sound came from inside her. A rudimentary video player appeared on the TV.

Miette walked through Huey's fast-food kitchen-surgery to his office. *EVERY CUSTOMER BRINGS JOY TO THIS OFFICE—SOME WHEN THEY ENTER AND SOME WHEN THEY LEAVE.* Miette's blue, segmented hand knocked on Huey's door.

"Not now," Huey grumped from within.

Miette ignored him. She eased the door open. Huey was at his computer. He shot off an aggressive string of words—Kiera guessed he was cussing in Hindi.

"Miette! I said—"

Huey swiveled the seat to face the camera. This was the position he was sitting in when he died. Kiera took a breath.

"Oh. Good afternoon. Did you need something?"

Miette stepped out of the way. Kiera didn't see the gun, or see Huey get shot—she was grateful for that—but she heard the nail-driving burst of the silencer.

Miette turned to face the shooter. Herrera rubbed his forehead, and muttered, "Son of a *bitch*." The old woman hadn't even bothered to change clothes—but now she wasn't stooping. Her posture had become rifle-straight. She wore the same maroon coat and wool gloves to kill the cutter as she had to sell the paintings, less than three blocks away that same evening. On-screen, Miette watched the painter step into Huey's office and plug the PC twice with the handgun.

"Waiting for us," Herrera groused. "Sitting there waiting for us. Lana," he craned his neck out and yelled up the stairs. "Need to check your car for bugs."

Kiera watched Miette watch the old woman light a stick of incense. She placed it on the squat file cabinet, and sat down cross-legged on the tile, careful to avoid sitting in blood. She put her hands on her knees, closed her eyes, and there she remained.

The video ended.

"Do you have more?" Kiera urged. "That wasn't all of it. Who was she? A customer? Do you have a name? Something? What happened after that?"

"I... am ashamed to admit that is all I saved."

"What do you mean? Why?"

Miette made that sawtooth-wave sigh again. "I would never have worked off the amount Dr. Huey wanted for my emancipation. That woman gave me the crack for my system, in exchange for allowing her to kill him— and deleting all trace of her. I no longer know what their relationship was. Whether she was a customer, a friend, a business partner. I no longer know *who* she was."

"Sounds like she wasn't thorough enough with her request," said Herrera, "if you still know as much as you do. You still have this footage. You still know she cut this deal with you."

"No, perhaps not. She was... agitated. Perhaps prone to errors."

"No, that makes no sense," said Kiera. "She wouldn't forget to wipe the footage of her *killing Huey*. Why do you really have it?"

"Good eye, kid."

Miette was quiet for a moment.

"She called the cleaners," the droid finally began. "They would take the body, and I would leave. I would be free. 'A clean break', she said. But... just in case the police caught up with me, I kept my memory of the murder. Something to give them so they'd let me go or go easy on me. I don't know if it would have worked, but it seemed a prudent course of action."

Herrera pointed his finger like a gun. "And you had to be untethered already by the time the murder took place, so she couldn't order you to delete it. She just had to trust you. Of course."

"I had the idea because Dr. Huey was a fan of crime procedurals," explained Miette. "Such things tended to make the legal process more favorable for individuals caught in murder investigations. Well, at least, for humans."

"Call that a bargaining chip," said Herrera.

"Fucking copaganda." Kiera rolled her eyes. "You know IRL they'd just use it as proof they should junk her. Miette, you're lucky we took you. But why did she let you live at all? The cops wouldn't have cared about some cutter and his iced droid. She could've tied up the loose end. Instead, she cracked you. She freed you."

Miette paused.

"I did inquire with her about that."

Herrera leaned forward. "And?"

"She said it was... good karma."

Tenzin Gyatso, thought Kiera, her heart pulsing red. *Robot hand...*

"Conscience." Herrera clicked his tongue. "It's a killer."

"Perhaps I should have simply run before the cleaners

arrived and let them take care of it. But Huey's family is likely to notice us both missing no matter what. Perhaps I was just a fool to agree to any of it."

"Well. When you're desperate, you're desperate. Still, you're lucky I'm not a bull anymore, I'd have you dead to rights."

"Dude, you've gotta stop thinking like a cop," said Kiera. "Huey was dangling a carrot in front of her like a Victorian prostitute."

"Had a family, apparently."

"Oh, *please*."

"Made mods affordable for people like that stripper friend of yours."

"While treating a droid like a subhuman. I buy my hormones illegally, but I try to do it ethically."

"It's hard to live in black and white, kid."

"Don't talk down to me. How do you think Casey would feel about you being all, *oh, well, the guy had a family?*"

Herrera stared down into his coffee. "I don't know."

"Yeah, you do. You're just still thinking like a *fash*." Kiera put her palm on Miette's scalp. "Did Dr. Huey use you for backup? Do you still have records of previous customers?"

"I do."

The TV screen became a gallery of faces. Kiera scrolled through them, a front-of-shop display of placid expressions.

"Do you have anybody named Nile? N-I-L-E."

"Full name?"

"I don't know."

"I'm returning nobody named Nile. But many of our customers used aliases or were sometimes anonymous."

"Can you show me, um, Roxy Coxx?"

The screen blipped, and there was Roxy on the right, although she had blonde hair in a short fringe cut rather than a purple dyke 'do. On the left was her original face—strawberry blonde, big-nosed, sharp-chinned, baggy-eyed. She was pretty as hell, in Kiera's opinion. But she knew how it was: dress for the job you want.

"Can you show me who else bought this mod?"

Two white women appeared, one cis and one trans. Neither was helpful. Kiera growled. "What about Brad Camillo? Do you have Bradley Camillo?"

"I'm returning nobody by that name."

"*Fuck*."

Herrera sighed. "That's still a dead end, huh, kid?"

"There's something to it. I know there is." Kiera rolled back onto her butt and picked up Miette. "That's all I can think of right now. If I turn you off, is there some way I can get at this stuff without bothering you?"

"You could simply *not* turn me off. I don't… want to be turned off."

"Really?"

"I only powered off because I saw no way out of my situation. I want to continue, if there's some way I can continue safely."

Kiera thought about her Lana. "I get you."

"What did you have in mind?" asked Herrera.

"I do not know," said Miette. "I suppose that first I would need you to procure me a new body."

"That's a lotta chips."

"We have to do something for her," said Kiera.

"Hey, last I checked, she came at us with a gun."

"We're *not* just leaving her like this."

"Christ, kid, I hope to god you stay so soft. Look,

we'll try to find something. But there is no way I can pay for a whole new body, even second-hand. Not legally. I ain't buying chopped."

"I suppose," chirped Miette, "you will have to keep me stimulated until you figure out how to get me a body."

"Stimulated? Like entertained?" Kiera giggled.

"Put 'er in the closet."

"Angel."

"Fine, the bookshelf."

Kiera clapped Miette on her blue crown. "You wanna watch *Furry Pawn*?"

"What is that?"

"Furries own a pawn shop."

Miette's expression did not change. "That does not sound stimulating."

"What do you wanna watch?"

"I like things about detectives."

Herrera slurped coffee. "You ever see *The Maltese Falcon*?"

"I have not."

Herrera yelled upstairs again. "Hey, sweetheart, is *The Maltese Falcon* still on Fatass?"

Lana's voice: "I think so!"

"Well, I know what we're doing for the next two hours. Let me make more coffee."

Kiera placed Miette on a cushion on the couch, so she'd be comfortable and could see the TV.

28

KIERA PICKED A rain droplet and watched its journey across the passenger-side window. The drop made it to the edge and disappeared; she picked another one. She sighed. She wanted that new Nintendo handheld.

"Hey, make me another deal," she said.

"What's that?"

"If they even let us in to talk to MisterMine, get me the new Nintendo."

Peppermint smoke billowed out of Herrera's nose. "No."

"Come on." Kiera kicked her feet against the glove box. "Be cool."

"Maybe for your birthday."

"Do you even know when my birthday is?"

Herrera blew a cloud through gritted teeth, out of his cheeks. "March twenty-second."

Kiera pulled her knees up. "You're a shitty dad, I hate you. I wish I had a *fun* dad."

"Least I know when your birthday is." Smoke. "Buy it with your allowance."

"Fuck a new apartment. Fuck a new throat box. Nintendo."

"Treat yourself. That's what you kids say, right?"

"Treat cho'self."

"Yeah. Treat yourself."

"Gimme that." Kiera stole the red cigarette from his mechanical hand and inhaled on it. She looked at him with tired, begging eyes. "We're getting closer, right? Are we getting close?"

Herrera took the cig back, cocked his head, and exhaled. Kiera knew what that meant.

"You don't know."

"I dunno. We're doing our goddamndest, kid."

The whole compartment trilled. The screen on the radio said Lana was calling. Kiera looked around the car. "Whose—wait, whose phone is she calling? Yours?"

"She's calling the car."

Kiera made a face. "Rich people shit, man."

"She's not rich."

"She's rich compared to me."

"Shush. What's up, sweetie?"

Lana's calm, professional voice prickled through the stereo. "Miette wants to know if there's a detective movie with androids in it."

"*Blade Runner.* C'mon, total softball. You call me with this?"

"Dude! Don't make her watch *Blade Runner.* Do you want her to kill herself again?"

"Kid, most movies with androids in them aren't very happy for the androids."

Kiera pulled up her throuple chat. "I'll get Jinx to ask her stream. Detective movie with androids. Doesn't end too depressing for the droids."

"Listen, you two, I actually called to tell you something," said Lana. "We made a really important break."

Herrera exhaled. "Oh, thank Christ. I'm pretty sure we're chasing smoke out here."

"Kiera, I took that photo you gave me of Bradley Camillo, and I kept digging and digging. I didn't have enough to go on. Then Miette asked to see what I was looking for, and I showed her. And she said she knew who he was."

"What? Really?" Kiera sat up straight. "Was he a customer of Dr. Huey's?"

"No. See, Miette used to be a nurse at Sacred Heart."

"That's real money," said Herrera. "How'd she wind up in a skin shop? Someone steal her?"

"Yeah, one of the doctors took her home and pawned her to Huey. But listen, she recognized this Bradley kid. He'd gotten reconstructive surgery there, after a car accident a few years back. Only, get this. Kiera, his name is really Bradley *Carson*."

"Um."

Tenzin Gyatso, robot hand. Money. Motive.

"*Carson?*" Herrera barked, incredulous. "Carson doesn't have a *son*. Does he? Just that daughter, whasshername."

I think I figured it out, Kiera wanted to say, but she couldn't get the words out of her slack mouth.

"That's right, Angel. Dakota Carson," said Lana. "But get *this*—"

Kiera waited several seconds to hear the rest of the sentence before realizing the call had abruptly ended. Herrera noticed at the same time. "Huh. Call her back..."

The car veered to the right, almost colliding with a blue station wagon. Herrera pulled the car back into their lane. Kiera pinned herself to the seat as the other driver leaned into their horn.

"Dude!"

"Whoa, whoa, whoa. Jesus. What was that?" Herrera put both hands on the wheel like he was soothing a bucking horse. "You okay, kid?"

"What did you *do?*"

"Nothing! The car just... kicked out. I—"

The car wrenched to the right again, pulling wholly into the next lane. Kiera fell sideways into the door.

"What the hell!"

"I'm not doing it. I'm not doing it, goddamnit."

The vehicle's artificial engine-drone raised by a few tones. The car sped up and crunched into the blue station wagon's back bumper. Herrera jammed his foot on the brake—nothing. Herrera tried to pull back to the left, but found the steering wheel disagreed with him.

"Oh, *fuck*." Kiera mashed the lock button on her door, and nothing happened. She pulled up on the lock, and it resisted. "We've been jacked."

"Fucking self-driving cars, fucking computers." Herrera struggled to keep the car in one lane. He moved the wheel to the right and suddenly the vehicle went with him, plowing through a line of blinking traffic cones and coming out on the opposite side of the freeway. "Oh, Jesus," he breathed. "Oh, Jesus."

"Handbrake?"

"Fucking electronic, all the brakes are out."

Kiera shrieked as Herrera skidded them out of the way of an oncoming car, the horn blasting in her right ear. "Okay. Okay. Shit, shit, shit. What do we do?"

"Pray, kid."

Herrera's real hand white-knuckled the steering wheel while the prosthetic tried to throw the car into reverse. The wheel was the last control he had. He fought with it to avoid incoming cars, still slamming his foot on the brake out of nothing more than reflex.

"I don't know what to do, kid." Herrera's voice quavered on a precipice, like he was about to vomit. "I don't know what to do."

Kiera gripped the handle above the door in one hand, and the handbrake in the other. "Call triad chat! Urgent! Urgent urgent urgent urgent!"

Kiera shut her eyes tight, hearing car horns blaring and wheels skidding over wet road in between the chat app rings that seemed to go on for minutes.

"Ki? Are you okay?" It was Jinx.

"We're in a jacked car! What the hell do we do?"

"You're—what? I can't understand you!"

"We're in a remote-jacked car! Our car is trying to kill us! *How do we turn it off?*"

"Oh, fuck. I don't—"

"Babe, ask your chat, Tripp it, do something!"

Jinx breathed. Kiera heard her typing. An agonizing minute passed.

"You have to call the cops," said Jinx.

"What? What the fuck for? *Fuck!*" Kiera screamed. Herrera narrowly missed a semi-truck.

"The police can override any self-driving car. It's part of their design."

"Goddamnit. *Goddamnit.* End call. She says we have to call the police!"

"Negatory," said Herrera.

"What the hell choice do we have?"

352

Herrera drew his gun. "Cover your ears."

"What are—the glass is bulletproof!"

"Not from the inside."

"What the hell are you saying, we jump out?"

"Pretty much."

"No! No, Angel, no, we'll die. We're not doing that!"

Herrera swerved out of the way of a fully loaded eighteen-wheeler. Kiera screamed and shut her eyes again.

"It's my only idea, kid. I'm not doing it without you. Come on."

"Call 911," Kiera ordered, as clearly as she could. She heard the blinging in her left ear. A feminine voice answered.

"911, what is your emergency?"

Kiera struggled to keep her voice even. "I'm trapped in a car that's driving itself on the wrong side of the freeway." She swallowed. "Please rescue me."

The operator paused before answering. "Kyle Umehara, are you aware there is a warrant out for your arrest?"

"Yes!"

"If we take control of the vehicle, will you cooperate with—"

"Yes, yes, yes!" Kiera sobbed. The car skidded out of the way of a black van, and she couldn't even summon the strength to scream again.

"Please give me the registration of the vehicle."

"What?"

"The license plate, sir, I need the license plate number."

Kiera plumbed the blasting static, the ion storm that was her brain looking for the car's license plate. "L4K326," she whimpered.

"Just a moment."

I don't have a moment, she wanted to shriek, as traffic screeched past on either side. But soon the LEDs on the dashboard, the gearshift, and the radio all faded to deep, fascist blue.

"Please relinquish control of the vehicle." The voice came through the stereo system. Herrera let go of the steering wheel. The hazard lights flicked on. The car pulled softly to the left, and the engine's digital drone dropped as the car slowed from *too fucking fast* to just normal too fast.

The car finally eased to a halt at the side of the freeway. Cars still beeped as they passed. Kiera's chest hurt. Her nerves were shot, her brain had blown a fuse. Her fingers tingled painfully.

"This car is not registered to you, sir," said the operator. "Did you borrow it?"

"It's stolen," Herrera cut in immediately.

"Who am I speaking with?"

"This is Michael Jones speaking," Herrera said professionally. "This car belongs to Lana Silver and it's stolen."

"Michael Jones... Are you aware there is a warrant out for your arrest?"

"Yes."

"Will you cooperate with authorities when they arrive?"

Herrera looked out the rain-spattered window. He turned to Kiera.

"Still got time to leg it, kid."

"I can't do this anymore," Kiera wailed. "I'm tired of running. I can't do this anymore."

"Sir?"

Herrera sighed and sat up. "Yes. I will cooperate. Please, tell them to go easy on the kid. She's only in this because of me."

"Please wait."

The operator hung up. The hum of the car died, and the lights went out. Kiera and Herrera sat there together, listening to the rain on the roof, and the wet roars of passing traffic. The water piling up on the windshield broke apart the yellow-white light of headlights and lampposts, like a thousand prisms.

"I wish I knew how to get you ready for this, kid. I don't."

"I'm sorry," moaned Kiera. "I'm sorry. I just couldn't. This is too much."

"Yeah." Herrera took the opportunity to get in a smoke. "This ain't gonna be fun, either."

Kiera heard sirens. She saw blurred red and blue light through the windshield.

"Can I have a puff?"

"Sure you can." Herrera handed the peppermint cig over, and Kiera took a long toke before passing it back. Outside, black forms took shape, with that familiar dirge-like drone.

It didn't matter that Kiera opened the door calmly, that she put her hands up before they even asked her to. They ripped her out by the shoulders just the same. Her head bounced off the concrete just the same.

29

KIERA SCREAMED HER throat raw in the back of the cruiser and it didn't get any better from there. She kept fighting when they tried to uncuff her—she just thrashed and kicked and yelled at the prospect of anyone even *touching* her. Eventually they cuffed her into a chair and left her to tire herself out. Cops at the bullpen desks complained that she wouldn't stop kicking the walls and screaming. After an hour of that a huge bull, the biggest one she'd seen yet, came down and *shoved* her head into the brick wall, chair and all.

"We're doing this," he murmured into her ear. "Okay? You're here. Make peace with it."

She thought back to Herrera sitting beside her in the cruiser, trying to get through to her as she threw her goddamn tantrum.

"They'll kill you," he'd said. "Okay? You gotta calm down. 'Cuz Flynn's boys down there will kill you."

She let the big boy uncuff her, and walk her to processing, trembling like a leaf, throat like gravel.

"That's it. There ya go."

* * *

"Spread yourself open. Cough. Wider. Get your fingers in there. Spread. Get your fingers in there and spread or I'll send someone to jam *their* fingers up there. Cough. Again."

Kiera coughed. It hurt her throat, and made her head throb, like a fist was punching its way out from inside.

"Again. Harder."

"It hurts. My head hurts."

"Spread wider. Cough again. *Do it*."

Kiera spread her asshole open and coughed again, sending another blood-burst of pain through her eye.

"All right. Step through this door, sir."

In the next room they jammed her in a swiveling chair with a layer of paper between her and the cold steel, like a dentist's chair but no cushion.

"Any implants or cybernetic parts?"

"J-just social media stuff. Eyes and ear. And my hormone chip."

A man in a gas mask with latex gloves dug into her eyes with his fingers to pull out the social lenses. He kept poking her and she kept jerking away from the pain and crying. Then he dug into her mouth, again with his fingers, and fished around for—what, she had no idea. Suicide capsule? Secret camera? Or just checking her out like livestock? For good measure he squeezed her junk and poked at her taint, then snapped off his gloves.

"Clean."

They put her in a white jumpsuit and cuffed her again, this time with two chunky magnetic rings. They threw her, actually threw her, into a concrete cell with nothing in it. No, there was one thing: a drain in the floor that stank of piss and shit, which she landed next to cheek-first.

Her voice breaking, nose full of snot, Kiera yelled, "How am I supposed to use the toilet if my hands are still cuffed?"

They shut the door.

"I can't take this suit off," Kiera screamed. "How am I supposed to *piss?*"

The toilet smell drove her insane within the first hour. She yelled just to see if anyone could hear her, to see if she could communicate with someone in another cell. Nobody yelled back. A second hour passed. It may have been a second hour, or it may have been a half-hour. Time was like that when you were waiting for it to pass; what was she waiting for, though? After what felt like the second hour she just started crying again. She curled up into the corner of the room farthest from the drain and thought she'd try to sleep some time away.

Another hour(?) passed while she tried to sleep. It was difficult, with the light and her hands locked behind her back. But she considered herself resilient.

She thought maybe she nodded off a little, though she'd felt conscious of the red-black behind her eyes and the piss-shit smell the whole time.

At some point she stopped counting hours, and just started yelling and kicking the door. She didn't even know why. It was just something she did because the cell, her pounding headache, her throbbing wrists, the need to piss, the *smell*, all together, had broken her. A few short hours, and they'd broken her.

A slot on the door opened. Kiera stopped kicking.

"What?" asked a Black woman.

Kiera didn't even know what the hell she wanted to ask. *When can I come out? What am I waiting for? Phone call? Can I have some aspirin? Water? Where's Angel? I can't use the toilet with my hands behind my back.*

"Uh."

"*What?*"

"Which jail am I going in?" Kiera blurted.

"What are you talking about?"

"I'm a trans woman. Am I going to get put with male or female prisoners?"

"Are you legally male or female?"

"I'm—I'm still legally male. Please—"

"In the event that you're moved to a holding facility, you will be housed with the male population."

Kiera struggled to her feet. "Please, ma'am. You can't do that. Please don't." She got up against the door, eye to eye through the slot with the female guard. "Please!"

"I'm sorry, there's nothing I can do."

"Tell them I'm a woman. I can't go in a men's facility, I *can't.*"

"There really isn't anything I can do."

"Please, ma'am. Fuck. You have to help me."

"I can tell them you identify as a woman. That's all I can do. If you cooperate with them, they might be willing to work with you. I don't know."

"Jesus Christ, *please*, I didn't even do anything, I didn't kill anyone."

"There's nothing I can do."

The slot shut.

"No no no, wait!" Kiera kicked the door. "Come back! How long am I gonna be down here? Come back! *Ma'am! Please!*"

Kiera slammed her shoulder into the door, kicked it again, and finally dropped her head against the wall and slid, wailing, back to the concrete floor. She was hysterical, lightheaded, sobbing in shallow breaths. She couldn't breathe through her nose. Her hands prickled from the cuffs cutting off her circulation.

At some point she knew nobody was coming, and she couldn't hold it any longer. She lay on the floor and she pissed herself. And she immediately regretted it, despised herself for it. She could have held on a bit longer. The filthy wetness sticking to her legs didn't make her furious, didn't stoke her anger at the inhumanity of her jailors. It just made her feel like a disgusting animal.

Some anti-fash. Some revolutionary. Less than a night in jail and reduced to a puddle of tears, snot, and piss.

IT MUST HAVE been past midnight when two bruisers in black helmets finally threw Angel into an interrogation room.

"Hey, 3B is my favorite. You guys! You remembered."

They magnet-cuffed his hands to the steel table, then left him there. Once he was alone, he became conscious of a high-pitched sound, a persistent whine, a sharp buzz.

"We still doing the buzz, guys? C'mon." Angel rolled his eyes. "I practically invented the buzz." He drummed his fingers on the tabletop. He started, quite inexpertly, tapping out piano notes with his fingers and knuckles, and scatted the first few bars of "One For My Baby".

"*Tch-tch-tch*-doo-da-doo-doo-doo... So set 'em up, Joe..."

It helped calm him. He hoped the kid was coping

okay. She was fit to be tied when they took her in. She was tough. But she wasn't made for this shit.

"Michael Jones," said a distorted voice from the ceiling.

"How's it goin', D?"

"What makes you think this is Detective Flynn?"

"I know it's you."

"This does not look good for you, Mr. Jones. You or your accomplice."

"That right?"

"Did you murder Malcolm Hobbes because he stole your wife?"

"Listen, D. You let the kid go, I'll say whatever you want."

A pause.

"It's not that simple. We know Kyle Umehara was involved. You were both at the murder scene. It's his fingerprints on the incense. You and Kyle have been together the entire duration of this investigation."

"Her name is *Kiera*. I've been trying to protect her from you people. We're both innocent. But I told you, if you let her walk away from this, I'll take the fall."

"It's clear that you've groomed Umehara. Engendered his absolute loyalty. How many others have you killed, Mr. Jones? Are you even really a private investigator? If we let Umehara go free, who would his next target be? Would you continue to instruct him to kill others from your prison cell?"

Angel laughed, defeated. "Jesus..."

"Maybe it goes higher. Who's pulling your strings, Jones? Was Hobbes only a personal vendetta, or was that just a bonus? Was he a business rival? Another accomplice who got out of line? How high do your connections go, Jones? Perhaps we should ask Cassiah Twelve."

"Jesus *Christ*, D. Is all this necessary? What do you want me to say?"

There was no answer.

"Uh, hi there? We still on?"

Angel slumped back in his chair. More waiting. He lolled his tongue and let his head hang to the side. They were trying to psych him out. Trying to ring in Casey with all this, too, that was bad. He wasn't expecting that. Maybe they'd be after Lana next, or even Gloria. The kid's boyfriend and girlfriend. Why did—

The door flew open and Flynn stormed in. He grabbed Angel by the hair and slammed his head into the table. Then, without letting go of his hair, Flynn punched him in the face, the cheek, the eye, the jaw.

"Flynn! Flynn! *Flynn!* How many times do I have to tell you, *call me Detective Flynn?*"

Angel felt something shift the wrong way in his fake eye, heard it pop. The left half of his vision turned into fluoro vomit. Flynn kept hitting him and he fell out of the chair, but his arms were still stuck to the table so he just kind of dangled. Flynn started kicking him in the chest and stomach. Angel took it. Finally, Flynn tired himself out and stood there panting heavily. Angel turned to face him and spat saliva thick with blood.

"How mad were you? Did you wait for the elevator, or run down the fire stairs?"

Flynn hit him again, and the pink-green-orange paint spill of color in his left eye shifted. Angel slumped on his knees and dropped his head on the table. He felt the blood pump through his fat lip, his busted cheek and jaw, his two shiners.

Flynn rubbed his bloodied knuckles, looking at them like he might examine something in a museum, perhaps a rare geode.

"Maybe we *can* come to some kind of agreement," he said quietly. Then he left the room.

Herrera swallowed a mouthful of bloody spit.

"Still got it," he gurgled, and pointed his finger like a gun. "*Pshew*. Hang in there, kiddo."

KIERA KNEW IT was tomorrow by now, for sure. She hoped Jinx and Sky had gotten to sleep, weren't up all night worrying about her. She wished *she* was asleep, and not up all night worrying about her. *Worry* was the only word she had for the sensation, but it wasn't quite right. It didn't feel like worry normally felt, frenetic and short of emotional breath, an imperative to *move*. She couldn't move; she couldn't act. She was all cried and screamed out, empty as a beer bottle upturned and slapped on the bottom to get out every drop. She lay rolled up on the floor with an electric current of fear pulsing through her. A too-much-coffee-and-weed oscillation, with the promise of prison brimming at the core, as good as the death penalty. Her meat-suit trapped, bruised and urine-damp, caged with simple cement. Even in this world of digital ghosts, limitless data, the all-enshrouding wireless fog draw a circle around a girl with concrete, and she's trapped like a bug.

The door banged like a drum, the magnets releasing. It dragged open. Kiera lifted her head.

"Pick 'em up," said one of them.

"Is that a boy or a girl?"

"Maya said it's a tranny."

"Oh, all right."

They lifted her by the armpits. "Needs a new jumpsuit. Pissed itself."

"New clothes? Okay."

"Where am I going?" Kiera croaked.

"Questioning."

"Hahaha, rad. I'm good at questioning. Questioning authority. Questioning my gender." She blew a fart noise. Deprive her of enough sleep and make her piss herself and apparently she'd get downright chatty.

They gave her a fresh jumpsuit and let her take a shit in a real toilet. She could not take a shower. She washed her face in the bathroom sink and fucked pointlessly with her hair in the mirror. She was *not* passing right now.

They slapped the cuffs back on and took her to an interrogation room. One-way mirror, metal table, plastic chair, she knew the getup from TV. They stuck her in the seat and locked her wrists to the table and left her alone again. They had dialed down the aggression, but she wondered if they were gonna send the bad cop in to beat her ass some more. She didn't know if she could take more beatings. But what else was she gonna do, besides just take it?

Die?

Before she could think about that for too long, Flynn walked in. His usually perfect hair was tousled at the front. His machine-blank expression read somber.

"Kyle Umehara."

"Oh *please*, professor, you gotta give me a passing grade. I'll do *anything*."

Flynn paused and looked at her like she'd inexplicably spoken in fluent Klingon. "I'm sorry?"

"That was a joke, ol' blue eyes."

"Uh-*huh*." He did not get the joke. "Please, 'Detective Flynn' will be fine." Flynn sat down across from her. He placed his thin tablet on the steel table.

"First, you call me by my real name," said Kiera.

"Your real name?" Flynn asked absently, preoccupied with his tablet.

"Why are you such an asshole?"

Flynn looked up. His pupils flickered and dilated in and out, reading Kiera, scanning her for… *something*. He folded black hands on the table—she still didn't know if those were gloves or not.

"Ol' blue eyes. Jones is fond of Sinatra as well—do you get that from him?"

"It was just a thing. I don't know."

"How long have you and Mr. Jones been friends?"

"I think… lawyer. I want a lawyer."

"That's not something that's up for discussion right now."

"What?"

"If you have a lawyer in mind, they can be contacted after we're done here. But please, focus on the present."

Kiera bit her tongue. She lowered her head. Now she remembered. "That law passed, didn't it?"

"The repeal? Yes."

She should've remembered when the rights they read her—as she was kicking and screaming and getting her head knocked against the concrete—didn't match the ones you hear on TV. In California they didn't have to provide you a lawyer anymore, and you didn't have a right to have one present during an interrogation. Three other states had passed the law. She'd called her representative *and* donated twenty bucks, for all the good it did. Sky must have said to her "That fucking law passed," at some point. But she'd forgotten until just now.

"Once again. How long have you known Mr. Jones?"

Kiera sighed. "Maybe sixteen months."

"Could you describe your relationship?"

Kiera tipped her head back. "I don't know. I found him on a gig app and I help him with stuff."

"Mmhm. What kind of stuff?"

"Tech stuff. Going in places he doesn't want to be seen. Second set of eyes. Whatever."

"Are you close? Are you friends? Something more?"

"Gross."

"Do you see him as a mentor? A role model? A father figure?"

"Well, we're closer friends *now*, because of all the shit you put us through."

"Yes, I'm sure of that." Flynn looked at something on the pad. "Forged in the crucible, so to speak. When did Jones first indicate that he would need you to kill someone?"

Kiera's head bobbed in disbelief. "Um?"

"How did you respond, do you remember? Was it the first time he asked you to be party to violence, or was it more gradual?"

"Fuck this."

"Please, just think carefully. And be honest with me. I only want to help you."

Kiera hit the table as hard as she could with her hands locked down. "We didn't kill Mr. Hobbes!"

"Are you certain? Jones says the opposite."

What?

Kiera screwed up her mouth. She wouldn't play this

game. She stayed silent, let Flynn keep playing out his hand. Flynn dug into his canvas jacket and dropped a baggie on the steel. A bunch of lozenges sat inside, red, individually wrapped in plastic. They looked just like candy.

"These were in your jacket," Flynn explained. "Red. You're fond of cherry, correct?"

"How do you *know* that about me?" Kiera shivered. "God, *really?* You're already framing me for murder. What do you need to make up a possession rap for? Just like, garnish?" *Cherry on top!* She imagined a fart noise.

"Oh, no, no. You misunderstand me completely." Flynn folded his hands together. "How familiar are you with the effects of mean dream?"

"I've never taken it."

"Alright. Let's say for a minute you haven't."

"I haven't."

"I heard you. One of the side effects of mean dream is that it makes the user highly suggestible. Highly trusting. Pliable. This is actually one of the reasons for its popularity, but for some reason it's a fact that just doesn't seem to penetrate into common knowledge."

"Yeah. It's used for rape. That's why I haven't tried it. I learned that on Jungle."

"Well done for staying informed. And yet, some continue using the drug anyway, because they enjoy the high that much."

"I also know that a ton of rape cases have had the consent lines blurred by the police because the victim was on mean dream."

"I don't think that's so."

Kiera looked away. "Yeah, that's what I thought."

"Do you also know that the suggestibility effects are

cumulative? That repeated use of mean dream can affect the user's perceptions, their formation of memories? Have you read about the use of mean dream by abusive partners, to keep their victims in violent relationships? Perhaps the notable case of the Petersen cult in Idaho, whose members used the drug in a ritual manner?"

"I think I'm cottoning to your angle here and I'm not a fan."

"We think it's a perfectly reasonable explanation that Michael Jones has been using mean dream—among other manipulation techniques he knows, and his natural charisma—to enthrall you. We believe you've been an unwilling pawn. Some time away from the drug and I'm sure you will come to see the situation for what it is, though there will be some brain fog, some residual confusion about this period in your life that you may never recollect. You'll likely need therapy, as many survivors do."

"Fuck you."

"Mr. Jones is willing to sign a statement to this effect. With a little paperwork, and court testimony, you would be cleared of all charges. You could get back to your life. Piece some kind of normal back together."

Flynn slid the pad across the table. There were a lot of words there, and a box at the bottom for Kiera to sign her legal name.

Kiera looked Flynn dead in his electric blue eyes.

"Why do you want Angel so bad? What did he do to you?"

"He's a murderer. I'm a detective. It's a law of nature."

"Stop, just stop it! Stop talking to me as Detective Flynn. I'm wise to all of this, okay? If you talk to me as an actual human being for fifteen seconds, I'll *think* about signing. I will honest to god consider selling my friend out to the fucking fash, because apparently he's willing to go down for me. I will let that burst of neurons happen in my brain, if you give me one actual factual moment of human-to-human connection."

Flynn sat back and folded his arms, regarding her, studying her. His face had changed. It wasn't placid or cold now; it was curious, fascinated. Flynn leaned forward, and grinned.

"You know, who wants to be human anyway?" he asked. "Have you met one lately?"

Kiera blew out, *pfff*. "Goddamn. We actually agree on something."

Flynn... *laughed*. Then he got up from the table.

"I'll leave this with you."

He slid the pad closer to her. Then he left.

She made good on her word to Flynn. She *thought* about flipping on Herrera. She fantasized about the fleeing being over, and getting back to her polycule, getting back to normal. Not having this shit on her record, so she could still rent an apartment, could still work. Not going to a men's prison. Maybe she could still be friends with Lana and Miette. That would be cool.

But could she *really* do that? To Angel? Like really, really? Herrera in a chow line waiting for protein mash while Kiera played video games. Herrera dodging a toothbrush shiv in the showers while Kiera, counties away, took an afternoon nap. What did it say about her that she could even consider it?

No. Fuck no. No negotiating with terrorists.

So she waited. They'd go to men's prison together.

She knew she wasn't really reckoning with what that

meant for her, with the full pregnant weight of this decision, but shut that out. She knew if she didn't she'd change her mind and regret it later.

The door opened.

Kiera looked up. A jackboot in one of those solid black getups with the shiny helmet came in. They left the door slightly open.

"Tell Detective Dick-For-A-Face I'm not signing."

The jackboot stared down at her, behind the blank face of the helmet.

Kiera shook her head. "What?"

The uniform took out one of those cylindrical steel handcuff keys from their belt. They stuck it in each of the cuffs and released Kiera from the table.

Kiera groaned deep from her chest. "Back in the hole?"

The cop, with a black-gloved hand, took Kiera's left hand, and squeezed it. They ran their thumb over her knuckles, like a lover. She recoiled.

"What the *fuck*." She almost took a swing at them. "Dude!"

A breathy feminine voice, muffled by the helmet:

"So, this is pretty much it for us, huh?"

30

KIERA'S HEART JUMPED; her skin all got monitor fuzz. She squeezed the gloved hand back—the left hand, the one that was supposed to be gone. It was tingly all through her chest and arms, and she found it hard to close her fist, like she was dreaming.

"Nile..."

"We have to cuff you again, okay?"

Kiera nodded. "Okay. Okay."

Nile pulled Kiera's arms behind her back and locked the handcuffs. "I've gotta be rough with you, babe. Look sad."

"Okay."

Nile gripped Kiera hard around the tricep, thumbing her affectionately again. "Sorry."

They left the interrogation chamber. Kiera kept her head down. The white canvas slippers they'd given her were almost silent on the floor next to Nile's clomping black boots. A dozen uniforms down this hall, and not a one of them looked twice.

Nile took Kiera into the elevator. The door shut and in the near-silence, the late-night refrigerator hum, Kiera desperately wanted to throw Nile's helmet off, grab them and kiss them. Even if her hands weren't locked behind her back, though, it wasn't that simple, was it?

"You have *a lot* of explaining to do."

Nile squeezed Kiera's arm. "I know, babe, I know."

The doors opened on a bustling bullpen. For the dozens of black and blue uniforms, the floor was eerily quiet. Men were talking to one another, but conversation was hushed, subdued. Kiera could hear computer mice clicking. It creeped her out, on top of the fear she already felt over walking into a hive of jackboots.

Nile's arm came around Kiera's head and pulled her into their chest. They thumbed the screen of a phone in their other hand. A breathy whisper: "Ears, honey."

Kiera still didn't have much of a shield against the sound of the explosion. She cringed against Nile's breasts and shut her eyes tight. The lights on the whole floor went out for a moment, then they descended into the hellish red of emergency lighting. There were screams, both of pain and fear.

How many had Nile just *killed?*

The glow of Nile's phone remained; they kept messing with it as they pulled Kiera out of the elevator with them into the deep red. Kiera saw cops drawing pistols, some lifting shotguns. Good guys with guns looking for the bad guy. The fire sprinklers hit.

"Ears again."

Nile stuck the phone back in their jacket.

"MY PUSSY TASTE BETTER THAN YOUR GIRL'S. MY TITTIES POP POPPIN', THEY BETTER THAN YOUR GIRL'S."

Kiera didn't know whether to laugh or start sobbing and pissing herself again. What was her *life?*

"What the *fuck* is *that?*"

"Someone shut that jiggaboo shit off!"

"Psychological warfare, boys! Stay frosty!"

Nile headed Kiera in a straight line to the opposite end of the floor, cop bedlam erupting around them. The sprinklers wet her hair, and her curls stuck in her eyes. They headed toward the fire exit.

"Hey," called a man in a button-up shirt and tie cowering next to his desk. "Where are you going?"

"Cells," barked Nile.

"But that's—wrong way! That's the wrong way!"

And that was all the resistance they met.

Nile pushed Kiera into the concrete stairwell and sealed the heavy door behind them, muffling the shouting and screams and music. They descended three flights, then pushed through the fire doors to emerge into a morning drizzle. It was still dark out. The wet blacktop shimmered yellow from streetlights erected along the black chain fence. Gentle fingers of rain brushed Kiera's wet face and hair, already drenched from the emergency sprinklers, as if to assure her that the worst was over.

"Car," said Nile. "That one. C'mon, baby, almost there."

Kiera didn't know which car Nile meant. There were a lot of them, and they were all the same black sentinel police cruiser. But she put one foot in front of the other. Nile turned her and opened the passenger door on a car that was already unlocked. They helped Kiera into the seat.

"H-hey—what's going on?" called someone. "Where are you going?"

Kiera swiveled. Another helmet. Kiera zipped her lip, and hoped Nile had something prepared for this. But Nile just—without hesitating a second, they just pulled a pistol from their hip, and shot the guy twice in the leg. He dropped and screamed into his helmet. Kiera jumped out of her skin. Nile strode up to the skinny cop writhing on the ground. He fought her, valiantly grabbed and punched at Nile's legs. Nile jammed the handgun into his neck and fired. He flopped like a sack of potatoes and bled out onto the wet blacktop.

Kiera seized up, unable to move. The bomb had been one thing; watching Nile just… move like a liquid and ice someone almost made her want to take her chances inside with the fash.

Nile came back, holstered the gun and touched Kiera's calves with gloved hands. "Legs, baby."

Kiera lifted her legs into the car. Nile patted Kiera's lap and closed her door for her, then ran around and got in the driver's side. The keys were already in. The cruiser woke up, that deep, evil hum. Nile was saying something over and over in a low voice as they pulled into reverse, something Kiera couldn't make out until she realized it was another language.

"*Gate, gate, paragate. Parasamgate. Bodhi! Svaha!*"

The cruiser bumped as it reversed over the body, then again when it pulled forward.

Nile pulled the car up a ramp, past an unattended booth—that must have been the dead guy's post—and onto the road. They did fifty in a thirty-five. Nile put the silent siren on, and they cut through what little traffic they encountered in the dark.

"*Bodhi. Svaha.*"

"Won't they know the car is gone?" asked Kiera.

"They'll know it's *gone*. They can't track it. I took care of it."

Kiera shifted around in her seat. "Where are we going?"

"Away, sweet girl. Away."

Kiera breathed out. "So, why did you kill Mr. Hobbes? Just because MisterMine told you to? Or do you work for someone else?"

Nile paused.

"I didn't do that," they said.

Kiera craned her head. "Uh, yeah. You did. You can just be straight with me, I'm pretty sure I figured it all out."

"I really didn't. Someone else did that."

"Okay, then who?"

"Kolyat. The guy in the track pants."

"Okay, but…" Kiera squirmed uncomfortably. "Will you unlock these cuffs?"

"Next time we stop."

Kiera sucked her bottom lip. "What do you look like now? Under that helmet?"

Nile was quiet again.

"Show me. Please?"

Nile's head dipped. The car slowed but didn't stop. Nile put their hands on the helmet.

"Okay," they said. "You're gonna think I'm an android, but I'm not. It's more complicated than that."

They lifted off the helmet and put it on Kiera's lap. Nile's head was white and silver; an androgynous, fleshless, hairless mannequin. Plated cheeks, a bare white cranium, sculpted lips. Kiera had kissed those lips, and they had felt utterly real—no, they would have been different lips completely. Nile spoke again, and Kiera saw that their tongue, at least, was still muscle.

This was a shitload to process. Kiera's loads-of-shit-processor overheated and barfed out an error message through her mouth. It went:

"So you're what, the Terminator?"

ANGEL HEARD THE bomb upstairs. The boots clomping in the hall outside. Then it was quiet. A good time to make a run for it. But hell. He wiggled his cuffed wrists. Even if he could move—*fuck it*. The kid was sick of running, and Angel was her only ticket home. So he sat like a good boy. His face throbbed all over, one big fat weeping bruise.

Flynn threw open the door. He had his handgun out and he was panting like a track runner. The left side of his perfect face was raw pink with blisters, with burns to match on his sleeves. The bright blue light of his left pupil kept flickering, like a bad light bulb. Angel winced at the sight.

"How did you do this?" demanded Flynn. His voice came out hoarse and desperate. He crossed the small space and grabbed Angel by the collar of his white jumpsuit.

"Hey, hey, hey! I've been in here this whole time!"

"Two men are dead up there!"

"I've got nothing to do with this!"

"Then why is Umehara gone?"

Angel froze. "The kid's gone?"

Flynn glared down at Angel, twisting up his handful of fabric, his face dog angry. He was a goddamn mess. "You did this," Flynn breathed.

"Oh, *mierda*, for fuck's sake, D, will you cut the *shit* already? We've been innocent since the start and you know that!"

"Then *why* is Umehara gone?"

"Maybe some friends sprang her. Maybe she's got friends I don't know about. Hell of a thing to keep from me."

"You really don't know about this."

"I don't know shit! If the kid planned this, I think it's stupid as hell!"

Flynn let go of Angel's collar. He hesitated. Then he unlocked Angel's wrists from the table. The cuffs stayed on, but Angel could stand again. Flynn hefted him up by the arm.

"I'm not letting you out of my sight. Maybe you'll be useful." He touched his burnt ear. "I need a detail ready to depart from the lot immediately. I'm pursuing the bomber and a fleeing suspect."

Angel let Flynn drag him out into the hall. "You think you know where to find her?"

"They stole a cruiser."

"But cut the tracker, obviously," said Angel.

"Of course."

"But not the one in the whites," Angel surmised.

"Not the one in the whites."

"How much of a head start?"

"Eight, ten minutes."

Angel shook his head. "Jesus, kid, I hope you haven't done something real dumb."

"The Terminator's still an android," said Nile.

"Cyborg."

"I'm human." The glare of streetlights reflected on the silver plates of Nile's fake face as they kept their eyes on the rain-slick road. "I'm only like this from the chest up.

Brain and spinal cord intact. I kept my tongue… One arm fake, but you knew that."

"And both hands now?"

Nile's gloved left hand tightened on the wheel. "Yeah," they admitted.

"What about your eyes?"

Sea-green, still the eyes of the old woman selling the black velvet paintings. They glinted gold, blackened as the cruiser passed under a bridge, then brightened again.

"Fake," Nile murmured.

"I just always thought your eyes were really pretty, that's all."

"I'm sorry."

Kiera shrugged. "I mean, artificial things are still pretty. That's where the word *art* comes from. It's just different."

Nile bit their bottom lip, the gray rubber. "They change color."

"That's cool."

Silence then, heavy and cold as the morning rain clouds. Kiera squirmed. "Can you get these cuffs off me?"

"We can't really stop, sweet girl. Not until we get out of the city, at the very least."

"Okay. I'm just… My wrists really hurt. That's gonna take a long time."

Nile didn't answer. *Oookay.* Kiera felt the little needle on her anxiety meter rise a couple notches.

"So, who are you, really? Bradley Carson, right?"

"I'm Nile." Nile's voice choked a little. "I'm just Nile."

"But you're really Bradley. And the guy in the track suit, and that old Asian lady with the paintings. All of them were really just you. So, which one is, like, *you* you? Bradley Carson, right?"

Nile exhaled. "Bradley passed over *years* ago. Why are you asking about *him?*"

Okay. She's talking to me. Good. "What does that mean? You mean, like, Bradley's your deadname?"

"No, *Bradley's* deadname was Dakota. But Bradley was..." Nile squeezed the steering wheel and took a breath heavy with exasperation. "People always get confused about this."

"Then explain it to me."

"For a while... this was..." Nile waved their hand around their face, their chest, reminding Kiera of Roxy Coxx—*I bought this.* "Bradley Carson. But there's no... *I.* There's no ego, we're not the same person. There's none of him left."

Kiera considered this. "So you're, what, his reincarnation?"

"Yes," said Nile, looking purposefully at Kiera. "*Yes,* babe. Exactly."

"Don't you have to die to reincarnate?"

"I never know how to explain this part. In a way, Bradley *did* die. But you're only thinking of body death, of brain and heart death. Bradley was wiped from this brain, his karma cleansed, and reconstituted into the next consciousness."

Kiera swallowed and breathed out. "Nile, you know how this sounds, right? You sound ridiculous. Like, crystal healing and quantum magic and shit."

"I know I do." Nile choked on a small sob. "I'm sorry. But you have to—this is knowledge that goes back *thousands* of years."

"I think I need you to start at the beginning."

"What beginning?"

Nile ran the cruiser unchallenged through a red light.

They kept taking their eyes off the road to glance at Kiera, with the painter's green irises.

"Just look at the road, babe," Kiera said evenly. "You're making me nervous."

Nile wrenched their gaze away. "Sorry."

Kiera shifted around in her seat and tried to get as comfortable as she could. Calmly, she asked, "Can you tell me about Bradley?"

After a pause, Nile answered, "He was Ted Carson's son."

"Why the change?"

Nile covered their mouth, blinking back tears.

"Bradley got into a fight with his girlfriend," they said. "They put hands on each other. He was choking her, and she was choking him, and—" They sniffed. "And she hit her head. Bad. On a corner. It was an accident. It was just a stupid fucking accident."

"Okay. What else?"

"Of course, nothing happened to him, his father took care of it, but Bradley just got, like, obsessed with the guilt. With the idea that he had just ended someone's existence, snuffed them out. He couldn't handle *death*. He was in and out of psych offices, on and off pills for a year. Then he found the Dharma. And for a while that gave him direction."

A picture was forming quickly for Kiera, a collage pulling together the scraps she already had, and now the ones Nile was sharing with her. A picture of Bradley Carson and Nile, sharing the same face—this smooth, robotic one sitting across from her.

"But that's not the whole story. Keep going."

Nile shrugged. "The guilt was too much. And he was unhappy for a lot of other reasons. Bradley just couldn't do it anymore. He wanted to be done with this life and go to his next one. Clear the karma. So he spent twelve hours meditating, and then drove himself into a brick wall."

Kiera took this in. "That's so... messy. Painful. I mean—pills? A gun?"

Nile chuckled sadly. "He was driving out to the ocean to shoot himself, but he got high for the drive and put on some music, and he was feeling the moment and pulled off the road. It just felt right."

Kiera nodded. She thought back to herself, submerged in Deftones and clutching her bottle of Xanax, wanting only for a twenty-dollar bill to buy something to wash it all down with. "I can get that. But he survived the crash?"

"No." Nile shook their head. "No, he didn't. They recovered a body from that wrecked car, and someone who wasn't Bradley woke up in the hospital."

"Who?"

"The girl who woke up after that crash was named Marina. They had to reconstruct her face after the accident, and she asked for a new one. From scratch. Whole new base—" Nile motioned to their face again. "And a face that was hers, and not Bradley's. They replaced her paralyzed arm with a prosthetic. For a while she tried to pick up Bradley's life. But she wasn't Bradley. The karma was cleansed. Bradley was gone. Does it make sense now, babe?"

"Okay. So. Obviously it didn't end there. Why not?"

Nile swallowed. Kiera wondered how all that worked, their throat and mouth.

"Because then Marina killed her girlfriend," Nile said, "and that time it wasn't an accident."

Kiera sat quiet, the silence punctuated by the wicked drone of the electric engine. A clear tear dripped down Nile's silver cheek. It reminded Kiera of the raindrops moving along the car windows.

"Are those real?" asked Kiera. "The tears?"

Nile sniffed. "Saline," they said. They gave a melancholy grin. "Detail, huh?"

"Mmhmm."

"So Marina went to Mr. Carson. She said she was sick, that she had a compulsion. *He* said she had... a talent. A temperament. Ted Carson said if he was going to cover this murder up, Marina had to come into the family business. He was still thinking of Marina as his kid. As Bradley. So, Marina worked for Ted Carson for a while. Then she got a new boyfriend, and the same thing happened to him. And she realized, it was just going to keep happening. Marina had to go, like Bradley did. This—" Nile circled themselves with their hand— "changed again. More meditation, a trip to a cutter, a new identity. Clear the karma. Reconstitute."

"But the compulsion stayed, didn't it? And Carson wanted you to keep working?"

"Yeah. It wasn't until a year or so ago that one of... *us*, I suppose, got away from Ted Carson and tried to leave all that behind, finally. That was Kolyat. But then Kolyat got mixed up with Mortimer."

Kiera did math in her head. "Kolyat is the skeez in the tennis shoes, you said."

"Uh-huh."

"How was *he* friends with MisterMine?"

"Friendships made over a needle often don't make sense. Me and Kolyat wouldn't have gotten along."

Kiera shifted; her ass was getting numb. She bit her

bottom lip and thought about everything Nile had told her. "So… here we are now. Getting away from Carson obviously didn't change anything. This shit just… what, goes on forever? You kill someone, you say your prayers and get a new face and feel better for a little while?" She found her voice rising. "Life isn't *Tyrna*, dude, you can't just roll a new character and disappear and ignore all the *shit* you did."

"That's not—"

"And wait, hang on. You became Nile months ago, I figured that out from your internet posts. But you turned back into Kolyat, just to kill Malcolm Hobbes? Because you wanted to stay Nile, right?"

Nile didn't answer, just giving Kiera an anxious glance.

"After you killed Mr. Hobbes, you switched back to being Nile, and met me that night at MisterMine's party." Kiera leaned closer to Nile. "And then you were Kolyat *again* when you talked to me and Angel that day at the Heights. And now you're Nile again! You *chose* that." Now Kiera was yelling. "And you still remember being Bradley, and Kolyat, and the painter and whoever else. Because it's all just *you*."

Sterile tears crept down Nile's silver cheek. "There's just no way to explain."

"This is so *fucked*. You're breaking your own stupid rules because it got difficult, that's all it is!"

Nile slammed their hand on the wheel. The horn honked. "You try living in my head for a week and see how well you deal with it!"

"Fuck you, you know what's *hard to explain?* What it's like to catch feelings for someone and then find out they were just made up!"

The tires squealed. The car ground to a stop so

suddenly that Kiera bounced off the glove compartment. Another nearby car beeped at them and passed on the left side. Nile got a fistful of Kiera's jumpsuit collar. Without skin, the polycarbon face was difficult to read. Kiera put it together from the shake of the voice, the part of the lips, the tight grip of the prosthetic fist on her collar. Kiera bit down on her tongue, and her breaths became shallow.

"I'm *not* made up!"

Kiera held her lips tight. *Fuck. Fuck.* Even the little part of her brain that said dumbass things just to make stuff worse on purpose was silent. *This is Ted Carson's kid, you idiot.*

"Babe... I'm not made up," Nile pleaded.

"Nile..." Kiera swallowed. "Take off my handcuffs, please."

Nile breathed heavily like they'd sprinted a mile. They wouldn't move.

"Nile," said Kiera. "We're stopped. Please let me out of these cuffs."

The electronic eyes were glassy and moist.

"Please don't run away from me," breathed Nile. "Please, please don't leave me."

Kiera breathed out. "Man. Where would I go?"

Nile nodded, satisfied. They fished out the key. The cuffs popped open and Kiera stretched her arms, flexing her wrists, trying to move blood back into her fingers. She put her seatbelt on, at last. Nile started the car down the street.

A few minutes passed before either of them felt comfortable enough to speak again. Finally, gently, Kiera asked, "So, what happened to your hand? The night I found it."

"I cut it off."

Kiera blinked. It took her a moment to figure out how to answer that.

"You... cut it off," was all she could manage.

Nile nodded.

"Why did you do that?"

"I have a, um, a problem with self-harm. I thought you knew."

"I heard. That's a little extreme, though. Maybe a lot extreme?"

Nile tightened their grip on the wheel. "You were on your way over, and I was... I was planning on killing you. Well, *planning* isn't the right word. I was *craving* killing you. And I didn't want to, babe. I swear to god I didn't want to. I was fucked up on crash so I could hardly feel anything, and I cut my hand off"—Nile chuckled, maybe realizing it was so *ridiculous* when they said it out loud—"because I was so mad I couldn't stop killing everyone I loved. Because I wanted nothing more in the world than to just stay Nile, and keep being with you, because I'm so fucking in love with you."

Kiera shook her head. "Nile, do you understand how *fucked* all of what you just said is? We knew each other, like, a week at this point."

"But you felt it, too, sweet girl. Right?"

"I had some wicked feelings for you, Nile, but Jesus Christ. You cut your hand off because you were in love with me? You were going to *kill* me! Doesn't hearing that come out of your mouth make you realize how unhinged it is?"

Nile took their eyes off the road. "*Had* feelings?"

Kiera balked. "Nile, I don't even know who you are anymore!"

Nile's face screwed up, fighting back more saline tears.

Kiera sighed. "I think you need a lot of help, dude. But I don't know what to do. I can't just tell you to turn around and take us to the police. They're not gonna fucking get you help."

"...if you don't... love me anymore, at least don't hate me. Please. Please just don't hate me, babe."

Nile broke into shaking sobs that threatened their steering. Kiera put her hand on the crook of Nile's elbow.

"Goddamnit, Nile... Bradley. Whoever you are."

There was just no happy ending to this. There wasn't even an 'okay' ending. *Way to pick 'em, Kiki.*

A cough of static came from the space between them, then a voice.

"Am I speaking to car 47-C? This is Detective Flynn. Who is currently in control of car 47-C? Please identify."

Nile looked at the handset, then met eyes with Kiera.

"How are they...?"

Kiera grabbed the mic.

31

"THIS IS KIERA Umehara."

"Kiera!" shouted another voice. "What are you—"

Then the other end cut off again. Flynn blinked. He flicked his blue eyes over to Angel.

"Do you know the other voice?" he asked.

"Nah-uh. That must be the Carson kid."

Flynn put the handset back to his mouth. "Umehara? This is Detective Flynn. Who else is in the vehicle with you?"

Nothing for a moment. Then "Fuck y—". The other voice, the one that wasn't Kiera's.

Flynn furrowed his brow. "Who am I speaking with? Is this Dakota Carson?"

Another pause.

"*Don't* call me that," the other voice crackled.

Angel winced. "I told you to call him Bradley, D."

Flynn fidgeted like there was a fly buzzing around his face. "Be quiet, please. Are you open to negotiation, Ms. Carson? Do you know that we know your location?"

"Stop calling me that! Goddamnit!"

Angel shifted over, leaning up to Flynn. "Would you let me talk to them?"

"That's out of the question," said Flynn.

"Flynn, for fuck's sake, you're gonna blow it. Gimme that mic."

"We know you're on the freeway heading north. What is your intended destination?"

"Kid," Angel interrupted. "Kiera!"

"Pacific northwest? Less predictable than Mexico, but riskier. You'll never get off the highway, Ms. Carson. We'll be waiting for you up ahead."

"*Stop it!* Shut up!" shrieked the Carson kid.

"Kid!" Angel pleaded. "Answer me!"

"Jones, that's *enough*."

The radio went quiet again for a minute. Then Kiera came through.

"Angel is with you?"

Flynn looked at Angel. His lips thinned. "Jones is here, yes."

"Let me talk to Angel."

"I'm afraid that's not—"

"D for dickweed, let me talk to Angel or we hang up."

Someone else probably wouldn't have noticed Flynn tighten his mouth, and his grip on the microphone, just a little; Angel did. Flynn moved the handset one, maybe two inches toward Angel. *Take it.* Angel reached up with his cuffed hands and took the mic.

"Kid."

"Hey... Hey, dad."

Angel grinned. "Hey, stupid. How you holding up?"

"I wanna go home," said Kiera.

"I wanna get you home, *niña*. What's it gonna take?"

"So, are you, like, a cop again?"

"Proxy negotiator."

"Nile needs help, Angel," said Kiera. "They don't need to be thrown in a cell and forced to piss themself."

Angel paused. "*Nile?* That's who you're with? Not Bradley?"

"Okay, listen. It's—"

The line suddenly went dead.

"There is no Bradley anymore!" The other voice returned. "There is no Dakota! Why don't you *get it?*"

Kiera's voice: "Nile, give that back—give it to me."

"We're not coming back!" shouted Nile. "Leave us alone!"

"Nile? Your name is Nile?" asked Angel.

"Leave us *alone!*"

"Let me keep talking to Kiera."

"Why should I?"

"I just want to work something out. I want to get you both back in one piece."

"That's not what your partner wants," said Nile.

"Fuck what he wants right now. You're talking to me."

"If I go back, I get the death penalty," said Nile. "There's nowhere for me to go but forward."

"That's almost certainly true," Flynn mused.

"Flynn, shut the fuck up! Nile, tell me what it would take. Tell me what it would take to make a deal, here."

"There's nothing," said Nile. "There's no way. I know how this ends up."

Angel bowed his head and sighed. "Okay. Then what about Kiera? Will you let Kiera go?"

"No."

"Why not?"

"They'll put her in prison. We're escaping together. There's no other way."

"Nile, if you come back and cop to the murders, this'll go easier on her."

"And then I'll fucking die!" Nile screamed.

"Are you willing to do that for her?"

No answer. Angel pushed it.

"The kid has a *life* to get back to. You threw yours away already, you gonna piss hers away, too? Have you even asked her what she wants?"

"I don't—know! Fuck, just let me think! Leave us—"

There was a noise on the other end of the line, a great horrible *punch* or *crunch* or *slam* that brought with it a blast of chipping static fuzz, and both voices yelling for a half-second, then silence.

Angel clutched the radio. He knew there was no point in asking something dim like "What happened? Are you okay?" Three-to-one the boys had hit them with a goddamn RPG. Instead, he turned to Flynn.

"What just happened to them?"

Flynn calmly consulted the GPS screen mounted over the dash.

"Looks like one of ours ran them off the road," he said. "At this rate, we should catch up to them in about five minutes and twenty-three seconds, if they stay put."

"*About* five minutes and twenty-three seconds?"

"Well, I do my best, Mr. Jones, but a thousand things can result in delays of milliseconds. I've learned to go with the flow. You know, you handled that rather well, all things considered."

"Yeah, thanks."

"It's a shame we never worked together. We might've complemented each other."

"Yeah, the two-bit shamus and the guy who tries to rape androids. Real silver screen stuff. Fuck you."

Flynn looked hurt. "That's very rude."

"If that kid has a scratch on her I'll choke you out with these cuffs."

"Well, I guess I'll pretend I didn't hear that. For old times' sake."

"You're a peach."

KIERA BROKE HER nose again on the airbag. She was cheek-planted in a spaghetti-sauce splatter of her own face-blood. Her neck and shoulder hurt, too, so she had maybe just spent her last day free of chronic pain. She croaked out, "Nile?"

Nile pushed themselves back from their own airbag. Glass tinkled on the shifting white surface. They opened bleary artificial eyes, took a rasping breath, and swallowed.

"Hey, sweet girl," Nile breathed.

"Are you...?" Kiera coughed.

Nile grinned. "Not even the worst crash I've been in."

The driver's side window exploded, and a black fist came through and grabbed Nile by the neck. Another black-jacketed arm appeared, the left arm to match the right, this one getting Nile by the chest. Kiera's heart badumped and she surprise-cussed a half-dozen times. Nile reached for their right hip like a cowboy, unbuttoning their stolen uniform's holster and sliding the pistol out. But the cop punched them in the artificial face and hauled them like a bag of grain out the broken window, and Nile dropped the gun. It bounced off the driver seat and thumped to the floor, blending right in next to the acceleration pedal.

"Nile!"

Kiera pulled her ass over to the driver's seat, propped herself on the broken windowsill. Nile was down in the grass while the bull went to town with a shock baton.

"Nile—!"

"Fucking cop killer. Piece of *shit*. You're gonna *find* out what happens."

Nile gasped like a caught fish, like a dying engine. The cop beat them across the face and breasts, each time hitting with a tooth-grinding *CHZ CHZ* buzz that made Kiera's toes curl up.

"*Stop it! Nile!*"

The cop rammed the baton up into Nile's ribs like he was branding a cow. Kiera smelled a hot, black, burning stink, the baton sizzling on Nile's canvas jacket.

The gun on the floor was police standard issue. To fire it, Nile would've had to jailbreak it. Kiera tweaked her shoulder reaching down for it, but she got it. Its LED trim lit up blue. Ready to fire.

She put both her arms on the windowsill to steady her aim. Held the gun in both hands. Breathed out. It was *just* like at the range.

Mechanical. Automatical.

Bang bang bang bang bang bang bang.

Click. Click. Click.

She fired until that fucker was empty, and she hit every one.

You never forget your first.

32

KIERA STRUGGLED WITH the driver-side door, finally forcing it open enough to roll her ass out onto the grass. Then she stayed on her back for a minute, looking past the trees and the glare of the streetlights, to the chalk moon. The sky was officially blue and getting bluer.

Someone took her hand.

It was Nile, obviously—she'd gotten lost in her head for a minute. Nile helped Kiera to her feet. Everything ached, and it was a painful effort to stand, but she got there.

Their hands stayed touching, hers and Nile's, clutched together between their breasts. She and Nile gazed, there was no other word for it, *gazed* into each other's eyes. Kiera didn't know what to do now. Was she supposed to kiss them? Say "I love you"? *Did* she? Love Nile? Why else would she *do* the stupid shit she just *did?*

Kiera threw Nile's hands aside and covered her face. "Fuck," she whimpered. "Goddamnit."

"Are you still coming with me?" asked Nile.

"No."

"Give me the gun, then."

Kiera handed over the pistol. Nile dug around in their wrecked car for the black helmet. They had totaled both the cruisers; the cars looked like giant crushed soda cans dropped next to that tree. Kiera called, "Where are you gonna…?" The helmet replaced on their head, Nile frenetically reloaded the handgun with a magazine from their belt and stuck it back in the holster.

"I haven't really had time to figure that out yet, babe." Nile's voice was puffed, anxious. "Just run into the city for now, I guess. Try to disappear again."

"Stop *killing* people."

Nile didn't answer that. They instead asked, "Can I kiss you? Fuck, forget it, there's no time. *Damn* it." They hurried down the hill. Kiera didn't know what was that way; she had never been on this part of the freeway before. But she could see the downtown skyline over the trees, like the spine of a slumbering dragon in Tyrna, waiting to be slain.

"I really do love you," Nile turned around to yell from fifty feet away. "I love you so much. You don't have to say it back."

Kiera watched them go, until she couldn't see them anymore. She realized that her mouth was hanging open, so she closed it and swallowed. It all caught up to her— the lack of sleep, the adrenaline crash, the shock from the wreck. The world flowed around her, like she was a stone in the river; like she'd been smoking loud, but with none of the fun. Kiera sat on the ground and flopped on her side, eyes barely open, so half of everything had a dark tint. She could see the ragdoll of the first man she'd killed.

It seemed like moments, literally seconds later that the sirens kicked up and the cruisers arrived. At least this time they didn't just beat the shit out of her.

"OKAY, OKAY, I think I get it... No, I don't get it." Herrera scratched his temple, his hands in cuffs. "So, your girlfriend, this Nile person, they were never missing?"

Kiera shifted her ass on the shitty plastic bench. The piss remaining on her legs had dried, at least. "They did all of it. They were Bradley Carson, *and* that guy outside Mr. Hobbes's apartment, *and* the Asian lady with the paintings."

"They kidnapped themself. And they were changing how they look?"

"Yeah."

Flynn came over—again—from the desk he had commandeered nearby, to ask the same dumb questions he had already asked.

"Tell me again why Dakota Carson left you behind."

Kiera rolled her eyes. "Without the car I was too much trouble. Do you know if I'm gonna get my stuff back?"

Flynn tapped on his pad without looking at her. "It's back at the other station. Contact them once the emergency is over."

Flynn returned to the desk. He hadn't gone more than twenty feet away from them for the last several hours, as if shackled by a shock collar. Herrera scooted closer to Kiera.

"How could they *do* that? Keep changing their face? It takes weeks to recover from a cut job. If you keep chopping and changing your look all the time you start to get, you know, plastic surgery face."

Kiera sniffed loud. They'd straightened out her nose and bandaged it up, but it hurt. "They have, like, a plastic face. They were in a bad accident and had their whole head and upper chest encased in this plastic, so they just have their face and tits rebuilt with the fake skin you put on androids."

"No shit." Herrera nodded, considering this. "So she was keeping an eye on you all this time. Trying to get you to stop following her."

"Uh-huh."

"She never saw Gloria at Mal's apartment. That was just an outright lie. That character's whole story was." He rubbed his chin with one cuffed hand hanging uselessly. "And when she helped me carry that painting to the car, she did whatever she had to do so she could jack it on the freeway."

"Yeah, dude."

Herrera gave a little shrug. "Probably still keep the painting. It's good."

"She's a really good artist."

Flynn appeared again. "How did you and the Carson child meet, if you don't mind?"

"At a *party*, I said," groaned Kiera. This time Flynn didn't even go all the way back to his desk.

"Is that how you figured it out?" asked Herrera. "You said the they-friend was an artist."

"Yeah, man. I saw the old lady's sketchbook. Then once I heard Bradley Camillo was actually Bradley Carson, I just... I dunno, I got this galaxy brain moment."

Herrera thumbed his nose. "So... the incense. The new faces. It's not clicking. Like, I get it, a killer with a *thing*, a motif. But what did it all *mean?* Did you figure that out?"

Kiera was about to answer, but she was cut off by a lazy interjection from Flynn. "Bodhisattva," he told them, still absorbed in his tablet, as though the word were an answer on a crossword puzzle.

Herrera looked up. "Steely Dan?"

Flynn snapped his fingers without looking up. "That's the one. Not among their best work, incidentally. A bodhisattva is an individual who seeks to become a Buddha but abstains from entering nirvana to help other sentient beings attain enlightenment. They might deliberately reincarnate as a human, over and over again." Flynn turned up his head to face them at last. "Like the Dalai Lama."

"You training to be a monk, D?"

"I've considered it, in my retirement. It's a terrifically interesting MO for a murderer, I agree with you on that one, Jones. But that's all it is. A pretty fiction. A gimmick. And what was your relationship with Dakota Carson, Umehara?"

Kiera groaned. "*Friends.*"

"My face hurts," grumbled Herrera. He rubbed the white gauze where they'd patched over his smashed computer-eye. "Need more painkillers, detective."

"Yeah, me too," Kiera whined.

"You can't take any more for another four hours."

"Just give 'em to me," Herrera groused.

"Afraid not. As prescribed."

"Prescribed! I bet you gave us baby aspirin."

"Per the instructions on the label. Mr. Umehara, why did Dakota Carson kill Malcolm Hobbes?"

"Mortimer Hill told them to," Kiera told him for the third time.

"You're sticking to that?"

"Yes, because that's the truth."

"Alright. And tell me again why Dakota Carson left you behind?"

"*Fuck!*"

Kiera saw the woman appear like a director had panned the camera to focus on her entry, as the steel elevator doors on the other side of the pen parted. The pixel-vitiligo woman. *Vicky.* She had one hand stuck in the pocket of a royal blue peacoat, and the other held a folded-up clear umbrella. As she crossed the bullpen the cops had one of two reactions to her: heads-down pointedly ignoring her, or immediately making sure they were preoccupied with something very far away from her. One young man and woman almost walked into her, saw her, and startled. The young woman spilled coffee over the rim of her Styrofoam cup, and the young man dropped his cup entirely. The liquid explosion of coffee across the floor lashed Vicky's leather heels. She glanced down at her foot, expression stolid. Then she kept walking without dignifying the young officer with so much as a look. He couldn't take it, the unfathomable depth of his own fuck-up; he threw up right there, into his own hands, and ran for the bathroom dripping orange puke.

Vicky strode up beside Flynn. He turned his head from his pad and grinned.

"Mrs. Von Braun. Always a pleasure to see you."

"Some shit-stain just spilled coffee on my fucking shoes."

"He'll write parking tickets for life. Who was it?"

"Like I deign to learn the names of your drones? Follow the stink of vomit."

Victoria Von Braun turned her head and regarded

Kiera stonily from behind her sunglasses. Then she lazily leveled the tip of her clear umbrella at Herrera.

"I know who that is," she sneered. "Nice face job. White suits him, doesn't it?"

"Who, Jones? The skin, or the jumpsuit?"

Von Braun and Flynn shared a tea-party shade laugh.

Herrera gave a little wave with his fingers. "Yeah, hey, Vicky. Up yours."

Von Braun took the few steps toward Herrera, lifted her heeled leather boot, and jammed it right into his crotch. Kiera shrank away, getting sympathy pains. Herrera scrunched up his face and looked at the ceiling, tried not to make too much noise.

"Call me that again," hissed Von Braun. "Call me that one more time," she dared him, grinding her foot left and right.

"No, I think I got it out of my system," Herrera wheezed. Von Braun took her foot back.

"He has a real problem with that," said Flynn.

"Is that what happened to his eye?"

Flynn tapped his nose and smirked.

Von Braun turned her stare to Kiera. Kiera clenched her legs together. *Hell.*

"Kiera Umehara," said Von Braun. "Didn't think I'd see you again so soon."

"Kyle here has led us quite the merry chase," said Flynn.

Von Braun turned her head. "She goes by Kiera, detective."

Flynn pouted his lips.

"Of course. My mistake."

Kiera remained silent. Seeing Flynn with his tail between his legs gave her a rush, no doubt. But what was going on here? What did this woman want? Kiera was barely treading water in the middle of the ocean. Von Braun turned all the way around to face Flynn. She jabbed her thumb back at Kiera, then made a lasso in the air.

"I want you to clean this shit up and let Umehara out of here with me."

When Vicky Von Braun had gotten here, Flynn had the smile and energy of a hotel concierge. All that was gone now.

"That... would be tricky."

Tricky Vicky, thought Kiera.

"Then do a trick," said Von Braun.

"May I ask why?"

"No, you may not."

"We have several dead officers, Mrs. Von Braun," Flynn implored. "One for which Umehara is the only witness."

"It's Nile you want for that," said Von Braun.

Flynn placed his fist to his mouth. "Nile is Mr. Carson's..."

"That's right."

Flynn looked at the floor. He tapped his lips with his curled fist.

"I will see what I can do."

"What about Angel?" Kiera piped up. "Can he come, too?"

Von Braun whirled around. "*Excuse* me?"

"Angel's innocent. Can we get him out of here, too?" Kiera swallowed a cannonball. "Please."

Herrera kept his yap shut but looked between the two women with a faint smile. Von Braun leaned down to Kiera's face, so Kiera could see her silver teeth when she talked.

"Let me tell you something I learned from our mutual friend." Her brows lowered, tightened. "There's this Buddhist parable about a turtle in a vast ocean that comes up for air once every hundred years. And there's a little gold ring floating somewhere on top of that ocean. That turtle is more likely to stick his head through that ring than a soul is to be born as a human. You get me?"

"I... yes?"

"Well, you're twice lucky, you little shitbird, because it's about a million times even *less* likely for Victoria Von Braun to come down to the police station and personally pull your ass out of a goddamn trash fire as big as this one. Your little turtle came and stuck his head through the ring and then he jumped out of the water and did a little flipdy-flip. And now you're gonna sweat me for a fucking *favor?*"

Kiera hunched her shoulders up. Her spine tingled. She breathed slowly, air passing over her jittering heart, and she swallowed. "Please?"

Von Braun bit her tongue and cocked her head. Kiera couldn't see the expression in her eyes behind the blue shades, but she was afraid the woman might be about to drop all decorum and straight-up eat her face.

Von Braun stood up straight. "Fine. Ring up this piece of shit for me, too," she said to Flynn.

"You're not leaving me much to work with, Mrs. Von Braun." But despite this, Flynn went away, and disappeared into an office. Von Braun pulled out the rolling chair from his desk and took the opportunity to lounge in it. She began to finger the air in front of her chest. Kiera knew the motions—she was playing a mobile game, maybe a match-three. Kiera and Herrera stayed quiet, until twenty minutes later when Flynn returned. Flynn drew one of the thick handcuff keys from his jacket. He unlocked Kiera first, then Angel.

"Umehara, Jones. You're free to go." Flynn motioned cordially to the elevator. "I would tell you to stay out of trouble, but…"

Kiera wanted to say something cute, something snappy, tell him to go fuck himself, sit on a dick, cut through this genial act he always put on. But Von Braun was already standing and tilting her head toward the exit. *Come on.* Like Kiera were a pet or a child. And Kiera didn't want to stir the pot any more than she already had. She hurried after the woman in the blue coat without looking at Flynn again.

But behind her, she heard Angel grunt, "Fuck off, D." And that made her happy.

"You're a lucky man, Michael Jones. My advice? Retire."

Flynn's bright blue eyes stayed trained on them all the way across the pen, right up until the elevator doors closed.

It was still drizzling outside, and the white jumpsuits were not warm. Kiera yawned. She was so incredibly tired. And cold. Was she really going home? Back to her bed, to her boyfriend and girlfriend? She hadn't even been able to call them since she'd been arrested. Was she getting her stuff back, her lenses and her clothes? She'd just be showing up on the doorstep, probably still smelling like piss. They'd probably want her to go to the ER for her re-broken nose, and she would refuse. She did not intend to remain awake any longer than she absolutely had to.

"We getting a lift home?" Herrera asked with a cocksure grin.

"You fucking wish your peasant ass was setting foot anywhere near my car. No." Von Braun drew a phone from her jacket pocket, a thin one, shiny black on all sides. She tossed this to Herrera. "Go call a ride. The women need to talk."

"Wonder what I could find on this with five minutes."

"Please. I only use that to call my mother and my dealer."

"Dangerous game you're playing." Herrera skulked off down the sidewalk, huddling as best he could against the sprinkling rain.

Von Braun produced a pack of cigarettes, real cigarettes, slim menthols with filters that had the color and sheen of pearls. She lit one for herself with a glossy black rectangle and did not offer one to Kiera. Kiera stayed quiet, arms folded to fight the chill. Eventually Vicky Von Braun broke the silence.

"You don't ask a lot of questions. That's a good trait to have. Keep it."

"I thought maybe if I just stay quiet, I could get in the car and go home and it would be over, finally."

"Well. It's not gonna be as simple as all that, little miss."

"I figured as much."

Von Braun let smoke flow out of her mouth and curl up into her nose. "So, Nile called me in tears. Just an absolute wreck. *Begged* me to get you out of this. To fix all this. I tried to say no. You and Herrera were too perfect. Their father and I, we expend so much effort to keep that kid out of the news, off the record. Here were you two, set up to take the fall, that sociopath Flynn ready to write a novel just to make it all stick. I couldn't jam my hand in and fuck all that up just because Nile was sweet on you. But goddamnit…" Von Braun tapped her skinny cigarette. "They talked me into it. They broke me. I love that kid too much." She blew smoke. "I shouldn't call them 'kid'. I sound like an old woman."

"Carson makes sure Nile doesn't get into trouble?" Kiera asked. "Nile said they didn't work for him anymore."

"There's the questions." Von Braun smirked. "No, Nile hates him. Hates him to death. Mr. Carson's feelings, they're… more complicated. But if Nile was ever caught, it might be a problem for him. Or maybe it would just make him look bad at the country club. He doesn't want it to happen, is the point. So."

"Has he ever tried to, just… I dunno, whack her?"

"*Whack*." Von Braun snorted. "His own kid?"

"I hear he's that kinda guy."

"Maybe he is. Hasn't told me to do it yet. Nile went after him once, though."

"Really?"

"Scared him good. Since then, he's got special security cameras in all his places, all his clubs. Read your facial structure, even under a cut job. Not legal."

"You're telling me an awful lot. I'm not even asking."

Von Braun tipped her head toward Kiera. She'd said she was the same age as her and Nile, but she displayed an energy that made her seem much older. She was really put together. She was taller by a head, dressed like a runway model. Didn't have hours-old piss clinging to her legs. (Probably.)

"Who would you tell? I'd find out."

Kiera tipped her head side to side. "Yeah."

Vicky grinned. "You'll figure things out pretty quick, I think."

"Is that what you meant before? Things aren't gonna be simple?"

"You owe me a favor now, Kiera Umehara. So keep your phone on, so to speak."

"Fash took my lenses," Kiera muttered.

"You need new ones?"

"Would that be another favor?"

"Yes."

"*Tch*. No thanks."

Herrera was coming back. His hair was damp and flat. He clutched the phone close to his chest.

"Does he know you let Nile go?" asked Von Braun, through a wisp of smoke. "His best friend's killer?"

Kiera shook her head. Von Braun said nothing else.

"THIS IS ME," said the kid—*niña*. "Just let me out here."

The driver pulled to a smooth halt. Angel peered out the window. "Not bad. Looks nice."

"It's not," Kiera snorted. She popped the door open. "I'm gonna sleep for three days." She looked meaningfully at Angel. "So I'll see you... soon?"

"Sure thing, stupid." Angel threw her a smirk. The kid smiled. She got out, shut the door, and hustled up to the apartment steps, nothing between her and the rain but that filthy white jumpsuit.

Angel tapped his fist twice on the ceiling. "I want an extra stop before home." He gave the address.

The driver, a fat Black kid, tossed a look to the backseat. "That's extra, you cool with that?"

"No problem."

"All right, brother. You want some music?"

"You got any Robert Glasper up there?"

"I got whatever you want, man."

Angel tipped his head back and closed his eyes. The driver was skilled, and smooth; Angel rode a saxophone carpet over keyboard dunes. At some point he may have fallen asleep. He wasn't quite sure.

"We're here, man."

Angel shook out the doze-dust. He got a load of the bluestone and the trimmed bushes. His heart was doing a Purdie Shuffle on the drumkit, the one it always seemed to be playing on when it came time to face Glory these days. *Don't go in*, he thought. *Just eat the twenty bucks and go home.*

He had to know. He stepped out into the freezing rain. "Back in two shakes."

This time there was no blue ghost to greet him. Just the solid white front door. Angel rapped on it three times. He tried to stick his hands in his pockets to warm them; he had none, so his hands went nowhere.

Gloria opened the door only a crack. A white bathrobe clung to her, and her hair was wrapped in a t-shirt.

"*Angel?*" She squinted at him. "It's so early. What happened to your *face?*"

"It's been a morning. You should turn on the news."

"What *happened?* Come inside."

"I'm okay out here."

"Please."

"My ride is waiting. I just came to ask you something."

"Angel," Gloria whined. "Please come inside."

"Did you dime us out, Glory?"

Gloria blinked. "Did I do *what?*"

Angel gave her half a smirk. "Did you call the boys on us? Us and Casey? After we picked up the tablet."

He could read the answer in the way her face fell,

how she pouted her lips. The ghost of a chuckle escaped through his nose and his smirk tightened. He let her get the words out.

"I... I told them Casey might've kept some information from the police. When that girl said he took Flynn off the trusted list—I didn't tell them you'd be there. I just—"

Angel shook his head. "It's fine. That's really disappointing, Glory. I'll see you around."

He turned and left. She did not call after him, and he was glad for it. The door clunked shut, he heard it, and he wondered if the closure would really be that Hollywood clean. Things didn't work out that way usually, he found. He climbed in the rideshare's passenger seat, grateful to get out of the lashing rain that was quickly on its way to becoming hail.

Angel released a ten-ton sigh. "All right. Home, Jeeves."

"Bad news, huh?"

"Onto bigger and better things."

The driver pulled away from the curb. "Women, huh?"

"Ah, don't be like that. Women are fine. It's the dames, the dames you gotta watch out for."

33

EVERY TIME KIERA called the station where they still had her stuff, they told her to check again tomorrow. That terrorist attack had really shaken things around; they weren't ready for civilians yet. So she called when she remembered to, but she pretty much stayed offline for two weeks. She cuddled with Jinx and Sky, and played games on her tablet. MisterMine's shooting and arrest had become the stuff of legendary internet drama and given Jinx a spike in her viewer count. She understood it wouldn't last and didn't bring up her interactions with MisterMine on her streams. However, Kiera did hold Jinx's hand—Sky did, too—while Jinx talked with Renée Desktop and two other women on a livestream about their experiences being victimized by Mortimer Hill.

Kiera kept up with the news on TV—it looked like Dominic Gray was going to beat John Romero for the presidency, riding impressive scores in the last couple of debates and mounting waves of white nationalist support.

(It had been expected that the male gamer demographic would turn out heavily for Romero, but there was too much crossover with the far right, who would not under any circumstances vote for a Mexican; even the more moderate gamers strongly denounced Romero for his pro-transgender platform.) Without a culprit in hand for the bombing of the NCPD precinct, the reactionary media was hungry to blame it on immigrant violence. This gave Kiera an indescribably sick feeling, and she tried to smoke or sleep it away whenever it found her.

The man she'd shot to death was named James Winstead. She had this drilled into her over that two weeks, as well as the fact he had a wife and two sons and was Black.

"Yeah, and he beat his wife and kids, but they still push this family man horse shit," Sky complained while changing the channel. He was just mad at the news, all of it; he didn't know what Kiera had done. She didn't know if this information made her feel better about it, or what. She wished she hadn't done it, so she didn't have to feel like *this*. She wished Nile had done it, if either of them had to do it. Was that a horrible thing to think?

KIERA ANSWERED THE door, and almost didn't recognize the man there.

"*Annie*," she said cheerfully, taking in the big fluff of orange hair, the smattering of freckles. His chin was pointier, too; his whole face seemed longer, narrower. "You been watching old movies with Miette again?"

"Not old enough," he said. His voice was still the same, and so was his big stupid trench coat. He was holding his phone to his ear. "That actually came out when I was alive. I just got to Kiera's. Uh-huh, she just answered the door. Oh, kid, there's actually a letter here for you from Miette."

"Like, on *paper?*"

"I know, like a crazy person. Here."

"Oh, dope shit." Kiera took her leather jacket from him and immediately swung it over her shoulders, then a Blue Ribbon plastic bag full of her other stuff from the station—her clothes, boots, her social lenses, and she could see a light blue envelope pressing against the inside of the bag.

"Okay, so I'm picking you up tomorrow morning, for sure," Herrera said to his phone, with a finger in the other ear.

"Why didn't you hang up *before* you knocked?" Kiera needled him. "Old people."

"Alright. I gotta go. Be good, Case."

"Casey?" Kiera lit up. "Is he out of jail?"

Herrera had a cagey look. "He's going home first thing tomorrow. But…"

"Lemme talk to him."

Herrera grimaced. "I dunno if that's a good idea."

"Are you serious, man? C'mon, gimme that."

Kiera grabbed at the little black rectangle. Herrera handed it over, but as he did so he sucked air through his teeth.

"Casey." Kiera's greeting was warm and full of honey. "Hey."

A brief pause preceded Casey's reply. "Hi, Kiera."

Even in just two words Kiera picked up that something was wrong. She swallowed. "How are you? You're home tomorrow?"

"Yes. That's right."

Casey's cadence had become like a computer's. Same voice but doing automated text-to-speech. Kiera didn't think she'd even heard tethered droids talk like that. Miette didn't talk like that. She found herself needing to take a breath before continuing.

"Are you okay? How are you feeling?"

"I'm just fine. My time here has been uneventful."

Kiera met eyes with Herrera. She jutted out her lower jaw, clamped her lips. Herrera sighed through his nose, a helpless look on his face.

"Is what they did to you permanent?" asked Kiera. She stared at Herrera while she said it. He looked at the floor.

"No," Casey intoned.

"What did they do?"

"There's a device affixed to my parietal panel. It's black, and the size of a small fist. It lowers my risk of flight, or further altercations. It will ensure I appear in court."

"When is that?"

"I don't know yet."

Kiera chewed her tongue. "Are you on a police station phone right now, or your own phone?"

"My own internal phone."

"Do you want me to crack that thing? I bet I can find out how to turn it off."

"Mm, no. If it's tampered with, a powerful magnet will go off. Even if you succeeded, we'd just get in trouble. It's fine. As well, Kiera, I can't promise my communications aren't being monitored. You might not want to ask me things like that."

Kiera rubbed her eyes. "Okay."

"It's nice to talk to you. Please come see me soon."

"I will, Casey."

"Goodbye, Kiera."

"Bye, dude."

Kiera held the phone back out to Herrera. He took it, slipping it in his coat pocket, giving her a look that said both *I warned you* and *I'm sorry*. Kiera hoped the look she gave him back said *Yeah, you tried to warn me. But it still really, really sucks*.

"Hey, look, kid... I got you a little somethin'-somethin'."

Kiera tipped her head. From his other coat pocket, the one without the phone, new ginger Herrera handed Kiera something that looked and felt like an especially fat pack of smokes. It had a picture of a plastic cigarette on the front, like his but matte black, and two succulent, shiny cherries. Starter pack, it said, cherry flavor.

"I snooped around on the, ah, internets," said Herrera. "I read that, um, the thing that messes with your hormones is supposedly only a problem with tobacco? It's something in the tobacco, not the nicotine. So you can smoke one of these, I think."

Kiera blinked. "Are you *sure?*"

"That's what I read. I'm not—I'm not a doctor, like, go read up about it. Ask someone who knows. But that's what I read."

"Well, that would be awesome." Kiera peered up at Herrera, and gave a little smirk, trying to recapture her good mood from before the phone call. "Heh. You're just trying to butter me up because you're taking my boyfriend on a date."

Herrera looked at the ceiling. "Well."

"It's just *coffee*, Kiera," Sky chided from somewhere behind her. "Chill your booties, missy."

"I still don't know how I feel about this," said Kiera.

"I'm just getting dressed! Kiera, will you at least invite him inside?"

"No."

"Like it better out here anyway." Herrera thumbed his pointy new chin. Kiera gave him a hard look. The old guy cocked a grin.

"How you doing on your apartment?" asked Herrera.

"Still got no fucking money. Gonna get thrown out in another twelve days."

"I'll help you figure something out. You're not sleeping on the street."

"You got any money? Turn your pockets out. How much you drop for the new face and the eye?"

"I got these on credit. But less than three thousand. The eye is almost just like my old one."

"You're such a *dork*."

"Yeah, I know."

Sky came to the door in a fuzzy sweater and a striped scarf fit for Doctor Who. "Q's?"

"Love Q's," said Herrera. "Pegged you for an indie coffee shop type."

"Would you prefer a coffee shop?"

"Love Q's."

Sky budged his way past Kiera, kissing her on top of the head as he went. "What do we do but suck corp dick all day and night? Soon we'll be scrounging for leftover bottled water in the urban ruins, might as well enjoy a caramel latté while they still exist."

"I don't know how you kids do it. Shit keeps me up at night."

"Oh no, do not mistake my flippancy for inner peace, sir. Get me too far under the influence and I get more scared and depressed than a Russian novelist."

413

Herrera flashed Kiera a smile over his jacketed shoulder as he walked Sky down the hall. Kiera waved with her fingers and shut the door.

"What's that?" Jinx asked, when Kiera was tearing open the blue envelope on the kitchen counter. Her VR mask and headphones hung around her neck.

"A letter, dum-dum."

"Oh, my Granny Goodness! Like a letter-letter?"

"Yeah-huh."

"Who wrote you a letter?"

"Miette, that cool robot." Kiera dug the letter out and unfolded it. It was written on yellow legal pad paper.

"I want to date an android," said Jinx.

"Hey! That's not polite."

"Neither is you calling her your cool robot friend."

Kiera grunted and looked at the letter.

Dear Dollface.

Kiera sputtered and snorted.

"What?" asked Jinx.

"Nothing, nothing."

Dear Dollface,

I'm scribbling this with an arm the newshawk found for me that fell off the back of a truck. I hope she can sniff out a body for me soon, I'd really like to go for a canter. While I was tethered, I could wait like Mother Theresa. Now I have about as much patience as it takes until the talkies on the boob tube run out.

I was really miffed hearing about all your trouble with the bulls. I also heard everything about that theydy-friend you were dizzy with, that they were the rat all along. I can't imagine how that feels. It makes me sick in the guts.

414

(If I had a gut.) I'm so sorry, doll.

I hope you'll drop in on me soon. Maybe we can take in another flick. I've chewed through all the silver screen gems on Fatass already, so you'll have to bring something. I trust you to pick something good.

Yours,
Miette

"Sounds like you've watched enough movies already," Kiera murmured, smirking to herself. Then she had to put her face in her hands, and her elbows on the counter, and she bucked a little from a sob that came up from somewhere surprising.

"Babe?" Jinx put her hands on Kiera's shoulders. "What?"

"Nothing."

"Tell me."

Kiera sniffed. "It's just..." She uncovered her face. "Fuck. I miss Nile. I miss who I thought Nile was. I wish that person really existed. There's just this hole in my chest now. I feel so fucking betrayed and cheated. It's so stupid. I barely knew her."

Jinx laid her chin in the crook of Kiera's collar. "I get you." She wrapped her arms around Kiera's front. "I gave MisterMine half a blowjob and then he held me at gunpoint so, like, totally feeling you on the betrayed thing. I'm not trying to make it about me, I'm just saying, I get it?"

"Yeah."

"That's like a whole other level, though. Like, a made-up person. That's pick-up artist shit. Do you think anything about Nile was real? Based on truth?"

"I'm not sure. I guess they really played *Tyrna*, at least."

Kiera rubbed Jinx's hands. "Babe, things got really weird back there for a bit. Are we okay?"

Jinx pressed her lips together. She gave a little nod. "Yeah, I think we're okay."

Kiera nodded back. "You doing your stream?"

"Startin' in a few minutes, yeah."

"Go do that."

"Okay. I love you."

"Love you, too."

Kiera put her lenses back in, and all the corners of her life lit up with notifications. The tension in her temples immediately tuned up. Home sweet home. She took her new cigarette and went out front with her favorite jacket hanging around her like a cape.

She checked her email first. *So. Much. Junk.* She would hit *Valkyrie* hard right after her smoke. Probably level up. God, though, she'd missed two weeks of daily quests...

Email from the landlord, pay up or get out. One from Gigawatt wondering where she'd been, offering job leads. She'd actually open that one. One from her bank. *Please confirm transfer.*

She almost deleted that one, but something made her click it.

Mr. Umehara,

LibertyStar Bank is currently holding the sum of $20,000 to be credited to your checking account, pending your approval. For you to receive the funds, you must call our special service line for preferred customers at 555-4900 and approve the transfer to your account. We apologize to customers with phone anxiety, but a live chat option is currently not available for this particular service.

Shouldn't the spam filter catch shit like this?

The following message was included with the deposit of the funds:

Take this for your apartment, and your throat surgery, and whatever else you need. You don't have to take it and you don't have to pay me back. I love you so much.
—Nag Champa

FUCK.
Kiera called the number. They didn't even put her on hold. A pleasant, masculine voice answered.

"LibertyStar Bank, gold customer services."

"Hi, um. My name is Kiera Umehara... You'll still have me down as Kyle. I have a LibertyStar account?"

"I'm happy to hear that. What was your preferred name again?"

"*K-I-E-R-A.*"

A short pause. "Okay... No problem. How can I help, ma'am?"

"Is it true you have twenty *thousand* dollars waiting to go into my account?"

"My goodness! I certainly hope that's true." The man laughed.

"Yeah, that'd be quite the feather in my cap!"

"What was your address and date of birth, ma'am?"

"This is real? This isn't, like, a scam?"

"Your last debit card transaction was for a six-pack of Diet Cherry Bolo from the Blue Ribbon."

"I mean, duh, anyone could tell you that."

"It was at four o'clock this morning."

"Fuck. I've lost control of my life, okay?"

"It's not my place to judge, ma'am." He laughed again.

Kiera told him her address and birthday. He hummed a few notes while typing.

"Yes! We are currently holding a deposit of twenty thousand dollars to your account, but it was specified that you be given the option to accept or decline the transfer. I'm sensing some history here. Do you need a minute to think about it?"

"I..."

She couldn't take that money. Knowing who it was from, where it came from. No way. Right?

Could she?

"I..."

All that money.

"Ma'am? Do you want to call back later?"

Fam. All that fucking money.

"I..."

"Ma'am?"

SKY TAPPED CINNAMON into his coffee at the table-station with all the nonsense, the shakers of flavor and packets of cream. He shook his cute little rear. "My pussy taste better than yo' girl's. My titties pop poppin', they are better than yo' girl's..."

Angel plucked up one hazelnut cream. "I am learning to truly hate that song."

Sky giggled. "Don't like rap?"

"I like it just fine. That Lamar fella won a Pulitzer. *That* little number, though..."

They sat in striped sofa-chairs next to an iron-filigreed window, where they could see downtown go by. Umbrellas, usually clear or black. Someone might be wearing a filthy, puffy down jacket, or a wool overcoat and leather gloves. Here and there a glowing eye, a cybernetic hand or leg. Angel caught sight of another of those loafy visors, too, wondered what rain looked like through it. A cop coffin glided by as if skating on the watery surface of the street, its deathly drone overwhelming all other ambience until it had rounded the corner at the traffic light.

"Kiki loves days like this," said Sky, with a soft smile. "I thought about bringing her last minute, but I didn't want to make it awkward for you."

Angel tipped in his cream. "That's considerate."

"Is this weird for you? Have you ever done the poly thing?"

Angel crossed one leg over the other. "Actually, it kinda takes the pressure off, y'know what I mean?"

"I know just what you mean."

"'Cuz y'know I told you my marriage ended on account of infidelity. So, I mean, if you can just take that out of the picture, and I don't have to worry about sex, then..."

"I get it completely."

"But I mean... What *is* that? Does that just make us friends? Are we friends that kiss sometimes?"

"Do you wanna kiss?"

Angel slurped his hazelnut coffee and considered it. "Yeah, I do."

Sky leaned forward and puckered his thick lips. Angel bent over, somewhat awkwardly, and smooched him.

"Hazelnut," Sky bubbled, grinning.

"Wasn't a real kiss. Let me get you outside, where I can really plant one on ya."

Sky receded happily into his sweater and scarf, smiling

gleefully, like a very pleased turtle. *Easy, this one*, thought Angel. *Stars in his eyes.*

Angel blew on his coffee and sipped. "So, you gonna tell your old lady about the dream?"

Sky put a hand to his cheek, looked around as if for someone to rescue him. "Oh, cheese and rice."

Angel sniggered. "We don't have to talk about it."

"No, that's actually kinda connected to something I was about to say anyway."

Angel quirked a brow. "Do tell."

Sky hid his face, ashamed, then peeked out, *peek-a-boo*. "I'm kind of fucking my dealer?"

Angel gently reeled, as perhaps he might if shot in the face with a 12-gauge full of feathers. "Only kinda? Just technically?"

"Oh, Kiki warned me you were mean."

"So there is cheating. You can still cheat."

"Yes, yes, absolutely. They'll be madder about the dream than the sex—Kiera won't even care about the sex—but it's a mess."

"That sure is a mess. You need to tell 'em."

Sky slumped, lost all the strength in his upper body. "Yeah. I do need to tell them." He sighed. "Do you know what to do? I feel so lost. I need a grown-up."

Angel barked a laugh. "*You* need a grown-up? Baby, I'm just shy of half a century and I—"

His voice was cut off by the jet engine-sized shear of sound from a police motorcycle pulling up to the curb outside their window. "Jesus," he said, muffled even as the thing rumbled to a stop. The pilot of the angular, menacing thing kicked down its stand and, without disembarking, removed their void-black helmet. A pretty blonde woman, surely the cover of the precinct calendar and belle of the Policeman's Ball, shook her sensibly cut hair out.

That's when he saw the eyes. The sea-green eyes, the artist's eyes. Unmistakable.

Angel breathed softly. "You gotta be yankin' my…"

The woman threw her leg over the cycle and stepped, quite purposefully, into the Q's. Angel's heart held still.

Sky kept talking about the thing with his dealer, and the other kids. "*Shh, shh*." Angel held his hand out.

"O-oh?"

"Hang on…"

He watched the woman who'd killed his best friend. She strode up to the counter like nothing had happened and ordered a cinnamon dolce in a musical voice. She didn't sound like she had on the cruiser radio—but the radio had been unclear, and she'd clearly had more work done. Angel simmered, about to come to a boil. He should step up, break her arm right there. Kick her knee out. Damn it all. Explain it once they got down to the station.

But there was enough bacteria of doubt swimming in his brain that he didn't assault her right there in the Q's. He watched her collect her sweet coffee in a thermos she brought from home, and step right back out into the rain.

"Excuse me just a minute." Angel got up. "I'm sorry. I'm sorry. Just a minute." Sky nodded and watched him leave out the front door.

Out here in the loud, the sticky sounds of tires on wet road and spattering drops everywhere, Angel approached the woman by her motorcycle, with a hand over his orange puff of hair to shield it ineffectually from the rain. He was not careful or subtle.

"Hey," he called. "Hey, uh, officer. You there. Miss."

The woman in the uniform finally flashed that someone was talking to her. She did a double-take. Something about her face was too classically beautiful, so chiseled and smooth it was like a CG model in a commercial for perfume. The eyes seemed to contain no humanity. The eyes, Angel could see now, may not have been the artist's eyes that he thought they were; mixed in with the sea-green were veins and gusts of blue, the blue of colored gin.

Ain't that a bitch?

"Ma'am." Angel cleared his throat. "Would you mind terribly if, ah, if I asked for your name and badge number?"

The woman pouted her lips, narrowed her eyes in confusion. "Ex*cuse* me?"

"I'd like to see your police credentials, please."

"*Why?*"

Angel smiled. "Because I am a citizen and in the City of New Carson it is your duty to provide them."

The woman nodded hesitantly. "Sure, but…"

"I don't have to tell you why." Angel smiled neutrally. "This doesn't have to be an unfriendly interaction, miss."

The woman stared at him and shook her head. She reached into the pocket on her ass, and flipped out a badge and ID.

Discreetly, Angel looked at it up close. Zoomed in— now able to do this without a voice command—looked for any obvious giveaways. He would have liked to get a hold of it with his right hand—test the weight, see if the badge was plastic—but he was doubting his hunch now, too much to take that risk.

"Alright, Rose. That's all."

The officer pocketed her ID again. "That all you'll be needing, *sir?*"

Angel drew his peppermint cigarette and took a thoughtful drag. "You're with Flynn's precinct."

Rose, her name was, blinked, and perhaps smiled a little. "You read that on my ID?"

"Bang."

"You plainclothes?"

"Retired. Used to be my house, too."

"Really? What's your name?"

"Jones," Angel lied. "How long you been there?"

"Two years."

"Babyface. You in that big brouhaha a couple weeks ago?"

Rose laughed painfully. "No, thank god. My desk was right across from someone who died."

"No shit. Survivor guilt?"

"I don't believe in that." Rose shook her head. "If you live then thank god, you live. But god, it shook me up."

"How's Flynn taking the Winstead shooting?" Angel blew smoke, let his question hang for a second. Dig and brush careful, like it's something precious and fragile. "Bomber slips right out of his hands."

"I mean, you know Flynn's expression never changes," said Rose. *I got a few things to say on that subject,* thought Angel. "But he's like a bear trap. If anyone even mentions Winstead he snaps. 'That case is shut. Drop it.' And it's hard because Jimmy was one of us, right? And Flynn just... Any conversation about Jim, he picks it up with those Robocop ears of his and he comes down like a hawk. 'Move on. We're not discussing this case anymore.'"

Angel tipped his cigarette toward her. "Somethin's up."

"Yeah, no shit, right?"

"What are you guys thinkin'?"

"Well, we dunno. But there is something me and my partner Cady thought was kind of strange, okay? And I'm *only* telling you this because you used to be one of us."

"Of course, of course."

Rose leaned over, conspiratorially. "Winstead had his gun holstered and his shock baton lying by him when they picked him up. Now, you can call that just plain stupidity on Jimmy's part—why'd he come out with the club against an armed suspect?"

"Right."

"But there was stuff on the baton, melted fabric or plastic or whatever? Like you get when you stick someone with the shocker and hold it—" She thrust an imaginary poker in the air. "It was nice and hot, and had that melted crap on it. So Jimmy must've gotten the guy down, got the better of him."

Angel listened with his brow furrowed, eyes narrowed. His brain chewed the info like good steak. "Yeah," he murmured, almost inaudibly.

"So then Jimmy's got seven bullets in him. The official knowledge is the bomber managed to reach his gun and shoot Jimmy seven times while they were wrestling on the ground—like it takes more than two. But the shots are all over. Chest, stomach, thighs—" Rose patted herself, miming the placement of the bullets. "One here up by his collar and then one of them practically in his ass."

"Second shooter," said Angel, his shoulders hunched

now, his brain broiling. And then he saw where the next sentence was going, and he got sick in the guts.

"We think it was that—that transgendered," said Rose, after looking around to see if anyone might be listening. "The one in the car they supposedly *kidnapped* or whatever? Then Flynn lets 'em go..."

"Yeah," says Angel. "Yeah, I see where you're comin' from."

Rose shakes her head. "Anyway. I gotta get back before my coffee gets cold. You want me to tell Flynn you said hi?"

"No."

Rose nods. "I get it." She slid her helmet back on, disappearing under the black mirror.

Rose's motorcycle gave a hellish roar. She sliced through the traffic, blades of water rising from the street on either side of her. She disappeared into the dark city.

Angel watched her go and regarded the skinny window of horizon 'twixt the megascrapers. The rain cloud abruptly cut off; the sky was charcoal gray, and then it was Mai Tai red and orange. He sucked deep from his peppermint cigarette. His incredibly patient date was waiting inside the warm and dry Q's.

A second shooter.

It was a theory. It was a bad theory. But it was a theory. Some town.

[END TRANSMISSION]

Acknowledgments

FIRST AND FOREMOST to Omi, who read my new pages every single day, and then married me.

To my lovely agent Stacia, and to Jim at Rebellion, for finding this thing a home. It was a close thing for a minute there.

To John, Lindsay, Andromeda, Heather, Julia, and Sarah, for loving me.

To those who have been around since the very beginning, and through the developmental years; Gino, Steve, Eaving, Jesse, Cassandra, Vlada, Tom, and Kiki. To Rosaria, Corinne, Emily, Peter, Kenny, Heather B; here's to the first of many.

To my mother who always said "You should go back to your writing" when I was doing some other stupid thing until I finally listened.

To all those cyberpunks who fight against injustice and corruption every day of their lives. (That's a reference to *Snatcher*, not Grimes, btw.)

And to my father, who tapped out before he could read anything of mine besides *Chrono Trigger* fanfiction. I hope he would've liked it.

About the Author

Aubrey Wood was born in California to a mixed-race couple and spent much of her childhood jumping back and forth between there and New Zealand until finally being trapped in a rural New Zealand hamlet at the age of 10. She has since spent most of her life in Auckland and on the internet.

As a child Aubrey made picture books, as a teenager she furiously churned out fanfiction, and started trying to write professionally in 2011 after a brief and unsuccessful bid to become Trent Reznor. *Bang Bang Bodhisattva* is her debut novel.

🐦 @BrieWoodFiction

FIND US ONLINE!

www.rebellionpublishing.com

/solarisbooks   /solarisbks   /solarisbooks

SIGN UP TO OUR NEWSLETTER!

rebellionpublishing.com/newsletter

YOUR REVIEWS MATTER!

Enjoy this book? Got something to say?

Leave a review on Amazon, GoodReads or with your
favourite bookseller and let the world know!